Andrew Greig was born in Bannockburn and now lives mostly in Orkney and the Lothians. His first novel, *Electric Brae*, was shortlisted for the McVitie's Prize. Recognised as among the leading Scottish poets of his generation, he has also climbed on a number of Himalayan expeditions.

Praise for *The Return of John Macnab*:

'Greig's novel does not depend on the original, save for inspiration, and stakes out, as it were, its own ground. He introduces a female character, Kirsty Fowler, a sometime journalist with attitude for whom the word 'feisty' should have been coined, and proposes a thrills-and-spills idea Buchan would never have considered: entry to the Balmoral estates when the 'Illustrious Personage' is in residence . . . Greig achieves most of what he sets out to do, and does so with the kind of panache Buchan himself had. No previous knowledge of its predecessor is required, though it would help. You could read it in an afternoon and the conclusion – "nothing so clean-cut as an ending" – is happy' Ian Bell, *Scotsman*

'Buchan's legions of admirers need not fear. Greig has achieved the impossible: he has written a Scottish novel, very much set in the here and now, which somehow remains true to the spirit and feel of the original . . . He knows and evokes the Scottish highland landscape (his novel is set in the Grampians, whereas the original was further north and west) in all its infuriating grandeur . . . the tone of the book – despite the sex – is curiously chaste and nostalgic; it is in that sense truly Buchanesque' Harry Reid, Glasgow *Herald*

Also by Andrew Greig

Novels

Electric Brae

Poetry

Men on Ice
Surviving Passages
A Flame in your Heart (with Kathleen Jamie)
The Order of the Day
Western Swing

Mountaineering

Summit Fever
Kingdoms of Experience

THE RETURN OF JOHN MACNAB

Andrew Greig

First published in 1996
by HEADLINE BOOK PUBLISHING

First published in paperback in 1996
by HEADLINE BOOK PUBLISHING

A HEADLINE REVIEW paperback

10 9 8 7 6 5 4 3 2

ISBN 0 7472 5353 6

Typeset by CBS, Felixstowe, Suffolk

Printed and bound in Great Britain by
Cox & Wyman Ltd, Reading, Berks

HEADLINE BOOK PUBLISHING
A division of Hodder Headline PLC
338 Euston Road
London NW1 3BH

This one is for the usual suspects, with love and thanks.

You know who you are.

The lines on p.146 are from Norman MacCaig's poem 'Recipe', with many thanks for his permission and for elucidating the finer points of the Spey Cast. As for the rest, the excerpt says it all.

TO WHOM IT CONCERNS!

You are hereby informed that, for reasons too numerous to mention but which include an excess of rain, midgies, boredom, absentee landowners and the Criminal Justice Act, the undersigned intends to take a salmon or a brace of grouse or a deer, from the estates of Mavor, Inchallian and Balmoral respectively. This will be done by fair means during the last three weeks in August.

In addition, a wager is proposed with the owners of these estates. The game will be taken and returned to you. The loser will pay £5,000 to the charity of his/her choice, and in addition undertake to vote for the political party of the winner's choice in the next general election, which cannot come soon enough in the undersigned's opinion.

For any further information, consult *John Macnab* by John Buchan. Please signal your acceptance of this wager in the letters page of *The Scotsman*, or be damned for a faint-heart sheltering behind your money and the law.

Sincerely,

J. Macnab

John Macnab

1

Begin the afternoon in August when an old blue Ford Escort quietly enters a small Highland town. Now beyond the last ghillie's binoculars, it turns left at the barber's and tackle shop, left again, and parks round the back of the Atholl Hotel. The driver checks the mirror for passers-by, then sits for a moment listening to the radiator grumble.

He gets out of the car. At this point in his life he would have turned forty. Most likely he was wearing black – dark jeans, black jacket, some worn old favourite shirt.

He looks up at the hills that circle the town, sees the upper slopes are purple with heather and reminds himself he mustn't say so. Certain things about his country invite clichés. Certain things about his country are true.

Nevertheless, Neil Lindores nearly smiles as he takes out a suitcase and backpack. He leans protectively over the boot, then lifts out a bulky rod case which he holds on to while locking up. The sun's full on his face. The lines around his eyes won't go away – though lately he sleeps better – nor will the first grey streaks through the dark hair he cuts shorter as he gets older.

His movements are purposeful but still an imaginative person watching from the window of the near-empty hotel bar might think he'd once been in a bad accident, or been ill, and is now recovered but bears a trace of that shock inside.

Apart from that blend of energy and injury which only an extremely alert observer might guess at, and the oddly bulky rod case, there's nothing remarkable about him, and as he picks up his baggage and heads for the back door of the hotel, anyone watching would likely have already turned away and gone back to their pint and newspaper and laptop.

He checks in with the barmaid-receptionist. Her name's Shonagh, though he doesn't know that yet. How long is he staying? Maybe a few days, maybe longer, he's not sure – that all right? No problem at all. He'll be up for the hillwalking? Ah, yes. She glances at his rod case. If he needs information about permits for Mavor, just come and ask.

Permits? He hesitates. Yes, if the weather's poor he'll maybe do some fishing.

His long mouth twitches slightly as he writes *N. McGillivray* in the register, then asks after the glassy-eyed stag's head above Reception. That's Mr MacPherson. The poor beast looks shocked, indignant, resigned, his mouth locked open in soundless protest.

'Hi, Archie.'

'How did you know he's called Archie?'

He smiles and she thinks he looks quite different then.

'It seemed a fair bet.'

Neil strokes the worn rust-coloured muzzle for luck, then quickly shoulders the rod case before Shonagh can, picks up his bags and hurries upstairs holding his room key like it's the key to the kingdom.

Shonagh puts away the register and goes back through to the lounge bar and its single occupant sitting by the window.

'Stranger in town?'

Shonagh nods.

'Name's McGillivray. Looks a Gael but talks Central Belt. Seems all right.'

'And he's maybe here for the hillwalking. Or maybe the fishing. I heard.' She stretches and sighs. 'Another man who can't make up his mind. Check this out.'

Shonagh puts her hand on Kirsty's shoulder and looks at the laptop's screen: this week's 'Fiona's Diary'. Just the usual tittle-tattle, Kirsty says defensively. Nothing ever happens round here. Three hillwalkers pulled off the Mavor estate by Lachie and the boys turned out to have nothing to do with the so-called John Macnab. But the estate intends to prosecute them anyway for Aggravated Trespass. She has views about that dubious piece of lawmaking but there's no way old Dorward will let her air them, so she's restricted herself to a couple of wisecracks.

'When you first turned up here, *m'eudail*, I'd a notion you needed the quiet life for a while.'

'So did I, damn it.'

Kirsty folds up the laptop and drains her pint. She glances up at the half-page circled in red and pinned above the bar. The biggest news for years and already it's turning yellow at the edges.

'And you might as well close the book on that one, Shonagh.'

'So it's a hoax?'

'It's a load of bollocks, that's what it is. Somebody had a good idea one wet weekend then chickened out.' Standing at the bar she glares at the empty glass in her right hand, then flips it over her shoulder. Without looking she catches it behind her back in her other hand. Thumps the glass on the counter. 'I'll away and file my column at the office. Catch you at the dance, lover.'

'Hey, Kirsty—!'

She stops at the door.

'Yes?'

'You must have broken a few empty glasses practising.'

She laughs.

'Na. Spilt a few full ones but.'

In the dim lobby Kirsty nips under the reception counter and opens the register. *N. McGillivray*. She frowns, unable to place what's bothering her. On her way out she pats Mr MacPherson. Hang around here too long, my friend, you get stuffed.

Alone in the bar, Shonagh shakes her head. That Kirsty. She picks up the glass and turns it in her hand, tosses it up a little. Then a bit higher.

She catches the glass with both hands and swirls it out. She leans on the cash register and watches the water seep from the draining board. She's feeling quite gruntled. The sky looks good for the weekend, and the dance tonight has possibilities, and though she always said second sight was a lot of haivers, she would later admit she knew something had already begun.

* * *

Neil locked his door, sighted along the rod case then put it carefully in the wardrobe along with a small heavy box. He piled a couple of blankets on top, unpacked his clothes, laid the maps out on the bed. He put his paperback *John Macnab* on the bedside table, the Munro book next to the maps. He checked the time, then moved the only chair so he had a clear view down on to the street, sat down and swung his legs up on to the window-sill. He pulled out a small notebook from his jacket and with a pencil added a few further notes, most of them ending in question marks.

When he'd finished he stared into space for a while, turning the gold ring on his finger. If asked, he'd have admitted the way he felt was honest enough but the way he lived was no longer truthful. He nodded to himself, then with some difficulty eased the ring off and placed it gently on the bedside table.

He went back to the window and looked out over the little town. He thought of a piece of doggerel his uncle once wrote. *How ill advised I was and rash / To start upon this foolish dash.*

Even in Kirkintilloch the sun was shining as Murray Hamilton eased the screws off the front licence plate on his old Kawasaki. His eleven-year-old sat on the steps of the council house with her guitar, hesitating between one chord and the next. His boy Jamie was kicking a football against the lean-to.

'So,' Tricia said, 'is this the end of a glittering political career?'

He took the new plate from her and squinted into the light. Five years on the Council till he'd resigned, a thousand committee meetings, ten thousand doorsteps – and what had changed?

'Time to try anither way, Trish.'

The thread caught in the bolt and he began to tighten.

'You'll not be much of a dad in jail.'

He put down the spanner.

'I'll stop right now if you want me tae.'

Behind them Eve at last found the new chord and strummed it cautiously.

'I just said be careful. And don't get hurt.'

'Right, darlin.'

Tricia began loosening the rear plate. She glanced at her husband's bowed head and for the first time saw that his tight red-gold hair was starting to thin around the crown, and the edge of his beard was touched with grey like the first touch of frost. Still, she grinned as she put the screws down carefully beside her. Might as well be a bit daft before we're all past it.

In the office of what we'll agree to call the *Deeside Courier*, Kirsty scratched away at a peeling wainscot panel as old Dorward checked through the printout of 'Fiona's Diary'. At the same time, with much twiddling of his glasses and apologetic coughing, he informed her that he was soon taking retirement on his doctor's advice. His nephew Alec would take over the paper.

'I don't think you two get on so well?'

'Not since he pushed his luck at the Highland Show and got a swift smack in the kisser, no.'

Old Wormwood coughed and suggested she should maybe start looking elsewhere. Admittedly young Eck was morally and intellectually challenged, but he was family and an undisturbed retirement was called for. She should try a few features for the nationals, and he'd keep his ears open. Something would come up.

Kirsty shrugged and got her nail under a particularly satisfying strip. No problem, Mr D.

She'd find a job somewhere, he assured her. She was quite good at this, whatever she'd done before.

That was almost a question. She chose to let it go by and die among the other bugs entangled in the cobweb over the door. Old Wormwood coughed and continued.

'Even if your heart's not entirely in it.'

She perched on the side of his desk and grinned at him.

'My heart went out to lunch some years ago and hasn't been seen since. I expect it's sunning itself on a beach somewhere.'

Dorward looked at her over his half-moons. He was deeply fond of Kirsty and just as glad she wasn't the daughter he'd never had. He sighed and made another couple of cuts to Fiona's deathless prose, then handed it back.

'I've cut yon wisecrack about the Criminal Justice Act. This isn't the *West Highland Free Press*. The rest's fine. Cheeky, but fine.'

She nodded and took back her copy.

'I'll finish this off at home.'

'A right pity John Macnab didn't show up. We could have done with some shenanigans round here – grand for circulation.'

She paused for a moment at the door.

'Does the name McGillivray mean anything to you, Mr Dorward?'

He thought about it, shook his head.

'What should it mean?'

'Something. Anything. Wouldn't it be nice if once in a while something, anything, meant something?'

He nodded sympathetically.

'I find a large whisky helps, Kirsty.'

'It will. Bye . . .'

He watched her go and heard her bounding whistling down the stairs, and then the office seemed a little dimmer and he felt a little older. He sighed and went back to his editorial on the abiding problem of drink in Highland life.

In a garage on the outskirts of Fort William, a man in battered fatigues and a streaked Barbour jacket finally laid down his spray gun, stepped back and checked out his van. It had taken three coats of black to obscure Sutherland's Mountain Highs and the phone number. Pity, but it had to be done. Now to paint out the windows.

The mobile phone on the front seat beeped. He grabbed it but the caller wasn't the one he'd been trying not to wait for. He listened and nodded.

'Eighteen hundred hours then, matey. And max operational security, right? See you . . .'

He probably hummed the theme from *Danger Man* as he went back to work.

Behind the bar someone had pinned up a familiar newspaper cutting. TO WHOM IT CONCERNS . . . The name *Mavor* was underlined in red. It struck Neil that the Macnab Challenge read as though written by committee. As in a way it had been.

He sipped his pint, rolled a cigarette and looked round the big empty lounge bar. Faded tartan carpet, the fifties wood-veneer panelling, scuffed linoleum dance floor, the plywood stage.

Seventies pastel plastic lampshades. Another stag's head, absurd and so familiar, its stilled cry something else about his country that was true. Coal-effect gas fire in one corner, a real log fire burning low at the far end of the bar near the windows.

The room looked like it had seen some good nights. He glanced at his watch. He'd thought at least one of them would be on time. He wandered over to the window, picked up a copy of the local paper left lying on the table there. He sat down and flicked through it. Seemed like nothing much was happening. Three letters about John Macnab, two for, one against.

He lit the cigarette and played a few minor chords on the table. The barmaid was reading a book at the far end of the counter, and something about her short curly hair and solid shoulders was vaguely familiar. But he couldn't place it, so he opened the map and the Munro book and settled down to study them both, to envisage for the hundredth time the lie of the land. No matter how closely you read the contours and rehearse your plans, the reality on the ground is always different. Always. He thought he accepted that.

Heading up the gradients towards the Spittal of Glenshee, the bike was losing power. Murray Hamilton changed down but something wasn't right. He pulled in at the side of the road. Gasket shot, Scotland's oil sprayed to the winds.

He sighed and set off towards the call-box a mile or so up the road, sweating inside his leathers in the heat of the afternoon. Occasionally drivers slowed, then something about this small, stocky, bearded figure made them drive on.

He pushed in the coins.

'Alasdair? A wee change in plans. Bike's knackered.'

'No problem, old sport. I'm on my way. Plan F.'

'Whit's Plan F?'

Alasdair's sigh swooshed down the phone.

'Plan F is you're F'd and I bail you out as usual. Don't move.'

'Finished with my paper, mister?'

Neil looked up, covering the map with his elbow. Youngish woman. Tall. Then the colour clash resolved into a bright orange jacket and a spray of ginger hair. She put one foot up on the window-seat.

'You'll be up for the hillwalking?'

The hair pulled back loosely from her wide forehead wasn't ginger but some kind of burnt autumn.

'Oh, uh – maybe. Here's your paper,' he added lamely.

She nodded, more to herself than to him. The colour of beech leaves at the very end of autumn, he thought. A kind of burning red-brown. And crinkly, the kind that can never quite be controlled.

'Not exactly the best time of year for it.'

'The midgies? Ach, they're usually not bad on the tops.'

She was silent for a moment. Her eyes were watchful, wide-set under that flare of hair.

'I was thinking of the stalking restrictions,' she said. 'What with the Criminal Justice Act and all. Unless you want the gamies chasing you.'

He laughed and looked away, pulling on his cigarette.

'Sounds a bit wild for me.'

'Really?' she said. 'You look game enough to me.'

It was his turn to stare and hers to look away with maybe a faint flush under that freckled skin.

'I just came over for my paper,' she said, 'but I'll join you if you want.'

He sighed and folded up the map and a vision of stalking two ghillies across a bealach in the moonlight. She came back with a whisky and stood with her back to the window.

'Our Mavor estate here will throw you off even on a Sunday. Don't you think that's wrong?'

He took his time.

'Yes,' he said. 'But it doesn't concern me. I can maybe do a bit of rock climbing.'

'Not maybe fishing? Or even real salmon fishing?'

He stared at her. He could do without this. Strong straight nose, high inquiring eyebrows. A mouth ready to laugh or scorn. The cool eyes belonged to someone else altogether.

'I was looking out the window and saw your case of rods,' she said. 'Sorry, we're kind of nosy round here.'

'No, really? I'd be after trout,' he continued after a pause. 'But why don't you sit down and continue this interrogation in comfort?'

They discussed rods and casts and flies, and established each knew a little about it but were mostly bluffing. Was he waiting for anyone? No, but it was possible he might run into a pal or two. What did she do round here? She did this and that, mostly this, she said, and ordered another whisky. Would he have another pint while waiting for his pals?

He would. But he wasn't particularly expecting anyone. Cheers.

What did he think about this John Macnab lark? What John Macnab lark? She pointed to the newspaper.

> ESTATE OWNERS STILL ON ALERT. No comment from Palace. SECRETARY OF STATE CONDEMNS POACHING WAGER. SNP DIVIDED. HOAX? See Editorial and Letters inside.

Oh, that Macnab. He'd seen the Challenge pinned above the bar. She said it read like it was written by committee.

He looked at her while she tucked her hair behind her ears again. He murmured it seemed all right to him. She shook her head and the first few strands escaped and fell over the collar of the orange jacket. Cobbled together, she insisted. Didn't he find that instructive?

He shrugged, said it sounded like a silly-season story and probably wouldn't come to anything. She agreed Mr Macnab was leaving it a bit late.

Neil nodded and lifted his pint. And inquired whether she thought the salmon was possible.

She agreed that maybe it was. But anyway not many folk round here gave Mr Macnab much of a chance. Now one of the local lads could maybe pull off the salmon at least. It was not entirely unknown round these parts.

Neil rolled another cigarette and said he was sure it wasn't. Where did they go if the poaching mood took them? Up above where the wee river joins the Alt na Harrie, she said vaguely. But she knew for a fact that Mr Aziz who owned the estate had hired extra men, including most of the local wide-boys. Without inside knowledge this Macnab had little chance. They'd even opened a book on it. He could get good odds.

What odds?

Ten to one against pulling off Mavor.

Ah. Like he said, he wasn't really a betting person. But were most people for or against this Macnab?

She hesitated. Divided, she said. A lot were for, even some of the Tories. But he had to remember that people made their living from the estates one way or another and they knew what they were paid to do and who paid them. Even if one or two had done the odd spot of poaching in the past, that wouldn't stop them going all out to catch another poacher. It was almost a matter of honour. And then there was the bonus. What bonus?

Five hundred quid for whoever catches him.

Neil said he'd put a fiver on Macnab pulling off his first objective.

She laughed. Good on him. She'd already put on a fiver herself. Just following the healthy Scottish instinct to back a loser.

He glanced at her then.

'You don't sound Scottish.'

'Army childhood,' she said briefly. 'The Rhine, Cyprus, the Rock.' She looked away through her glass. 'From nowhere, really. Hey, Shonagh – come and take this sucker's bet and add it to the book? Just write your name here.'

As he wrote out his name and an address there was a bang on the window. He looked and saw Murray and Alasdair grinning and waving in the street outside.

Idiots. They might as well have run up a flag. He quickly excused himself, picked up his map and book and went to head them off.

She looked closely at the entry in the betting book before handing it back to Shonagh.

'That one seemed able to resist your charms, Kirsty. It's extraordinary.'

'It's unprecedented, that's what it is.' She looked thoughtfully out of the window. 'Maybe Mr Maybe has something else on his mind.'

'You're supposed to arrive separately,' Neil hissed as they shook hands. 'What kept you?'

'Transport logistical problems, old sport,' Alasdair said.

'Aye – ma bike's fucked.'

The back door opened and beech leaves in autumn came out whistling.

'So you've found each other then,' she said. 'Hi guys. See you around, Neil.'

'Aye, cheerio.'

She stopped and turned after a couple of strides.

'I do hope we haven't thrown away our money,' she said.

And she strode out of the car park, long-legged in blue jeans, hands in the pockets of the orange jacket, the bush of autumnal hair bouncing jauntily along behind her. She was still whistling something, a tune Neil couldn't quite place.

'You haven't been wasting your time,' Alasdair said. 'Who's she?'

Neil shrugged.

'Miss Colour Clash of the year? She just descended on me with a lot of questions. I gave nothing away.'

Murray looked round uneasily.

'Let's stop standing around like stookies and get aff the street.'

They hurried towards Alasdair's van. It was late afternoon and the sun was melting over the sandstone of that Highland town.

'You're the folkie, Murray,' Neil said. 'Remind me what "Annie Laurie" sounds like.'

'Afore my time, pal.'

Neil and Murray climbed into the back among the piles of gear.

'Where to, youth?'

'Operational HQ, matey. Pete's place.'

'Is Pete discreet?' Neil asked, leaning back on the defunct Kawasaki.

'Na. But he's in Tibet . . .'

The van pulled out and headed north.

This is the bird that was winged but flew on. This is the fish that was seen in the sky. This is the stag that was shot but not wounded. This is the story that cannot be told.

Save what can be saved, then resume. As Neil used to say.

2

Some details glow, some turn to ash. That Ford Escort was certainly bog-standard, blue and heavily rusted along the sills, but Neil could as well have been carrying a green tweed jacket that August afternoon as wearing a black one. And surely Kirsty was drinking whisky not beer – she only did that over-the-shoulder trick with a shot glass. And perhaps Neil exaggerated her hair, though she'd have wanted people to know the colour was natural and the orange jacket in the best possible taste.

But about her age that day we can be precise: it was her thirtieth birthday, though not even Shonagh knew that.

Kirsty Fowler drove up the hill road in the old green Wolseley that was the second-last item she kept from her former life. Up on the brae where her rented cottage looked over the village (principal occupations: tourism, forestry, sport and rumour masquerading as news), the summer breeze was strong enough to clear away the midgies. She had no excuses left.

She stood by the car for a moment in the late afternoon sun, smelling the sharp resin of the pine trees around the cottage, and a faint peppery sweetness in the wind off the hills. For a moment she was walking up the High Street past the Heart of Midlothian, turning to the law courts with the smell of the breweries drifting up from Fountainbridge . . . She shook her head, walked quickly across the yard and pushed open the ill-fitting door.

Charlie lolloped through to greet her. She passed a hand over his shaggy but loyal head, then stooped to pick up the cards lying on the mat. Two of them. She checked the postmarks, then dropped the birthday cards unopened on the kitchen table. Deal with that later.

She went through to the bedroom and picked her copy of *John Macnab* from the shelf. She flicked through the pages, whistling a tune that seemed to have got stuck in her head. No luck. She put the book back next to the other Buchans. Another might-have-been.

She changed from working clothes into old cords and the faded Black Watch shirt while Charlie whined at the door. She glanced out at the pile of logs Hamish and Gerry had delivered off the back of a Forestry Commission pick-up, sighed and picked up the axe. She'd read somewhere that if you force yourself to smile, a smiley mood will follow. It was not entirely untrue. She opened the door and Charlie bounded into the yard, barking joyfully. She followed, determinedly singing, 'It's a ha-ha-happy day' under her breath.

She selected a fat log, set it upright on the chopping block, steadied herself – the two whiskies with cool and distant Mr Maybe had left her light-headed. She swung the axe out wide, right hand up near the axe-head, looped it over her shoulder ('Let the weight do the work,' Lachie had told her, 'just relax'). With a slight pause at the top of the swing, she drove the axe down, sliding her right hand into her left. The blade chonked clean through and split off a segment. The log toppled off the block. She bent over, set it up again, brought the axe up and out and down again.

Only steady concentration without hurry or expectation could do this job well. She'd learned that much living here. Only solid work and hard play could stop you thinking about the things you didn't want to think about.

It's a ha-ha-happy day. The blade swung, the sun shone yellow-white on the newly-split logs that would do her till winter if she stayed that long.

'Come on down, space cadet!'

Neil came out of his dwam as Alasdair brushed by with another box of provisions, mostly bottles and cans. Already Murray had the bike out round the back of the cottage out of sight of the road, and was working away on it, silent and methodical.

Neil grinned to himself as his friend – the kind you've known so long you can't remember why you are friends or even if you are – paused to push up the sleeves of his pullover. It was his reflex whenever he got down to things, a reassertion that he at least was a working man. And within minutes the sleeves would slip down his muscular forearms. Neil watched him and decided to see Murray's life as the battle of the sleeve. He never really wins and he never gives up and he needs something to kick against.

Neil followed Alasdair into the kitchen and looked round at the piles of clothes and rod and ropes, packs and sleeping bags, telescopes and radios and climbing gear. For a moment he saw Helen shake her head then turn away to hide her smile, and then he couldn't see her.

'So when do we start, Al?'

Alasdair put a bottle of whisky on the table, then pulled a shotgun from a pack. He wiped the barrel on his sleeve then sighted along it. He passed it to Neil and grinned.

'We just have, old sport. Call in the red dwarf.'

Kirsty paused and straightened her back, and rubbed her rising blister. This country-girl shit was ruining her hands. She'd be stiff tomorrow, but she wasn't totally unfit, not at all.

After a certain age a girl had to look after herself. In nearly two years here she'd given up the fags and switched from urban gin to rural whisky. She'd learned how to do a lot of things well enough, from loading sheep on to a Land Rover to holding her own at drunken ceilidhs. She could be a passable local journalist. Under Lachie's instruction she could now keep the wood-burning stove going all night, adapt her voice to the country and western that was the folk music of these parts, play competitive pool without being an embarrassment, and flick a reasonable cast. And in return she'd taught young Lachie a thing or two.

The shirt clung to her back. Tom's shirt. The only thing she'd kept of him.

She unbuttoned the cuffs and folded them back up her arms. After all, a shirt is only a shirt. And she liked her sweating self. This sweat, at least, was honest.

She looked round the yard. The leaky cottage that was home for now, the village below, the Atholl where the action would be that night, the sun splintering through the trees. And the old green Wolseley, the love of her life along with Charlie.

The shirt was Tom's, but the neat way she'd folded back the sleeves, that efficient final tuck, that was her father. Everything else was hers.

The sweat was cooling down her back and the sun was getting low. She freed the axe from the block and went back to work. After the first flush only stubbornness gets you through to the end, and she was very stubborn.

* * *

Murray put down fresh mugs of coffee on the table among the maps and took out one of his rare thin cigars.

'See the ghillies on the hills as we drove in?' The others nodded. 'Thicker than cowpats in July.'

'That woman in the bar told me they've taken on extra local laddoes.' Neil leaned over the map with a pencil in his hand. 'The Alt na Harrie, right?'

Murray nodded.

'Mid Pool, halfway up the gorge.' He pushed his sleeves up and frowned. 'Got the bum's rush frae there once, years back. Politics apart, I've a wee score tae settle.'

Alasdair's knee was jumping as though receiving impulses the rest of him was deaf to, as he looked up from his notebook.

'Sod the politics, matey. This is a ploy for the sake of it.'

Murray jabbed his forefinger at him.

'This is about land access, land use and land ownership. The fuckin Criminal Justice – right?'

Neil sighed and broke in.

'They've opened a book on John Macnab. They're giving ten to one against us pulling off the first hit.'

Murray exhaled and nodded sombrely.

'Sounds about right.'

'Excellent!' Neil and Murray looked at each other. 'There'd be no point if it was easy,' Alasdair continued. 'But it'll go, I tell you.'

'Aye, aa the way tae the jail.'

Alasdair drew a line across his notebook.

'Time for some scran – I'm cooking.'

Neil looked up from the waters of the Alt na Harrie and the hillside he'd recced two months back.

'In that case, I'm off to the chippie.'

He got a quick grin from Murray before Alasdair picked up another can of lager and headed for the kitchen.

'It'll go, squaddies,' he insisted. 'We've three months' planning behind us. We're in place, we're fit, between us we've got the skills.' He paused at the door and put the can to his lips. 'Train hard, fight easy.'

'Montgomery?' Neil inquired.

Alasdair shook his head.

'SAS. Now let's see if it's true . . .'

Humming 'Summer Holiday' very badly, he began to rummage among the provisions.

* * *

It was dusk and getting cool when she split the last log. She whistled on Charlie and he came bounding through the trees, arfing through his straggly beard. She bent wearily and began stacking the logs inside the porch. She could've left them scattered in the yard but her father's voice commanded her to see the job through, and whatever her feelings about that man, something in her obeyed.

She stacked the last log, opened the door then hesitated. She went back and picked up the axe she'd left lying on the ground. She hefted it in her raw hands, thinking of young Lachie and of the man who had commanded a regiment and still tried to command her, though there'd been no contact between them for two years. Who still demanded impossible standards.

She swung the axe out and up and over, bedded the blade deep in the chopping block. She pushed grimy hands through her damp hair, picked up an armful of logs and went in, kicking the door shut behind her.

Now in Pete's place with the remains of Alasdair's Bully Beef Surprise cleared away, Alasdair and Murray were arguing again while Neil sat back, trying to place that tune. It reminded him of rain, falling leaves, and a bridge somewhere.

Three months of frantic planning, arranging free time, acquiring gear, disagreeing over the Challenge letter Neil drafted and redrafted to include their different points of view, to get them this far. This was the first time they'd sat down together since the wet chalet holiday when three bored, restless, bickering friends first passed time with a fantasy of resurrecting a legendary poaching wager.

Neil looked into his cooling coffee. The fact is that though no one's actually said it, now they've arrived with the van, Murray's broken-down bike and the astonishing collection of equipment Alasdair rounded up, they feel stupid. Outside in the dusk are the real Cairngorms, not the ones on the map, not the ones they've been effortlessly mastering in their heads over the last months.

Real hills, real ghillies, real policemen. On the road to Aviemore they saw the extra activity everywhere, the signs barring access, the gamekeepers with walkie-talkies and the occasional shotgun, hard-looking blokes in Land Rovers with binocs, even a couple of police on motor bikes.

They don't have plans, they have fantasies. There must be more to life than this. Once there had been.

Alasdair glanced across and saw Neil was gone again. He nudged Murray and the two of them started clearing the table.

Alasdair had been through this before. The early stages of a big Himalayan or Alpine trip. You turn up at the mountain and the mountain's too big and your very cold feet are stuck to the ground.

Only one thing for it. He set up more coffee and a quick dram for the troops.

The important thing is not to stop. Otherwise you find yourself in a chair unable to get up. You might find yourself held down by a hundred little threads your life has spun.

So Kirsty made herself rise from the armchair where she'd slumped. Across the window she pinned up the blanket that served as a curtain. Moving easily in the near-dark she found the matches, turned the brass tap and lit the fragile mantle above the sink. It hesitated, flared yellow then bloomed to hissing magnolia.

She filled Charlie's bowl and watched for a moment as he went to it like a wagging Hoover. She shivered, feeling the damp shirt cold on her back. She filled up the stove, spun open the vent, slid back the damper, heard the draught take.

She unscrewed the funnel from the oil lamp, put it on the table beside the two cards. She carefully filled the lamp then lit the wick and watched it flicker without direction or purpose. She clicked on the glass funnel. The flame rose and filled out the hanging mantle. It still seemed odd that anything so frail as a cotton mantle could glow so brightly and not be consumed.

Those cards. One was her sister's writing, large and careful and painstaking with the dots above the i circled. Looking more closely at the envelope she saw that the circles were in fact heart-shaped. Oh my God, she thought. And the woman's thirty-five, big house in Barnton, stuffed-shirt advocate husband Fergus doubtless having an affair. Emma and Jennifer at Mary Eskine's. Sheila had done everything right and the funny thing was her father, their father, had no time for her. 'Girl's plain damn lazy,' he'd say in that hoarse bark. 'Spineless. No guts.'

She opened the card, read the few lines, took in the overt plea and the hidden one. She put the cheque under the clock. She'd decide later what to do with that.

Her mother's card from London. Looping writing, exaggerated verticals and quivering, uncertain horizontals. Possibly sober, hard to say these days. Bent over the table, she felt the familiar tightness in her throat. She opened the card, thinking she should never have given them the address. Still, at least they'd kept their word and not given it to Dad or anyone else.

Or maybe they had and he'd still not written.

Enough. She skimmed through the card, left the letter till later. It would be the usual lamentations, reproaches, if onlys and why nots; the bright resolutions, vague mention of her latest companion, a quick stab at her ex-husband, and towards the end a vodka-inspired blend of bright tomorrows and tragic yesterdays or sometimes the other way round.

She put the Jenners' tokens under the clock, picked up the lamp and went through to bath and change for Saturday night at the Atholl and the Canoe Club dance.

As she dried, Kirsty checked herself out in the steamed-over mirror. Not a bad body, a bit on the full side but long and strong, and some people had liked it. On the whole, she liked it too. Breasts would drop in time but not yet, not yet. Silly old tart, she muttered to Charlie on the bed. His tail thumped, the perfect yes-man.

She wiped the mirror, pulled back her crinkly hair and looked closer. So this is what being thirty looks like. The country-girl bit didn't do much for the complexion either. A few fine lines round the eyes, the first permanent crease at the corner of the mouth. Character lines, right? I don't feel old, I just feel . . .

Might as well celebrate. Have a good time, give a good time. In his gawky way, Lachie was so appreciative. Funny how a man so good with his hands on machinery and sheep and fences, and so delicate with a rod, could be that awkward and unsure in bed. It was touching, she found. Bonnie . . .

Then she had it. 'Annie Laurie'! Not the tune itself, but the title. And then she knew where she'd seen the name McGillivray before.

She knelt on the bed and reached for the book next to *John Macnab.*

Yes. Yes, yes, yes!

Ah Charlie, she was wasting sweet pearls on the desert swine as she began to dress and make up and twist up her hair to become the person she needed to be for the night ahead.

Alasdair drained his dram and looked at his troops. Time to get them moving before morale slumped further.

He got to his feet. Murray would be dropped off at his anonymous B & B, then Neil at the edge of town to walk back to his hotel. They'd rendezvous for a summit conference later tonight.

Where? Neil's room at the hotel. There was some sort of dance on, so no one would notice them. Up the back stairs – they shouldn't be seen together in case someone had done their homework and guessed they must be three. Twenty-one hundred hours – A-OK, chaps?

Hit the road before it runs away.

3

Kirsty went bumpity-bump down the old dirt road on her bike, free-wheeling towards the lights in the strath below. Her lamp juddered off into the trees, hit white sparks on a weasel's eyes, made deep shadows that exaggerated the dangers of the road ahead. Trying to hold down her skirt with one hand while steering with the other, then realizing that was silly, no one was watching and who cares anyway? Both hands on the bars now, she let go her brakes.

She sang 'Some Enchanted Evening' as she bounced downhill. Cool summer night on her face and about her the murk of the spruce plantation that spread like a prickly rash up the hillside. She was fizzing inside, a bottle of champagne shaken to the point where she had to burst over someone.

Shonagh. She ought to get a second opinion. She could be wrong. It could be just a tiny coincidence. She wrestled the bike down the track, twisting and turning, bumping in and out of the ruts, just in control. Sure, tiny as my backside.

She turned on to the main road with just a glance, came flying into town under the lights, still singing like a linty. Someone whistled. She glanced, gave him the fingers, then saw it was Jamie the Post and changed it to a wave. Friends were allowed to whistle.

'Hey, Jim boy!'

'You got the twa cards for your friend?'

'Uh . . . yes!'

'Strip a willow wi me later?'

'In my dreams!'

She pulled down her skirt and biked on, swung hard left into the car park behind the Atholl, braked and pulled off a skid-turn stop she hadn't tried since she was twelve and broke her nose showing off once too often.

She glanced at the blue Ford Escort as she went in. Wonder

where you are, Mr McGillivray. She stood for a moment in the dim lobby. The noise from the big bar was deafening already. Through the half-open door past Reception she saw Shonagh hurrying along the bar, shouting and pointing, taking orders. No point trying to talk to her now.

She stood for a moment, undecided. In front of her was the board where the room keys hung. She opened the register. Number twelve. The key was on its hook. Well, of course it was. McGillivray who had other things on his mind, Mr Maybe who had stared levelly back at her then gone his way, he was out with his wee friends somewhere.

She glanced through to the bar, then leaned over the counter and lifted the key from its hook. Right then she crossed a line. And once across it, like ducking under a fence into private property, everything felt different and alive. New dangers, new delights. Yes!

She patted Mr MacPherson for luck and hurried up the stairs.

Neil walked towards the Atholl through the end of the gloaming. The hills were black humps against a paler sky and the night air was blowing hills and heather and adventure down into the valley. Somewhere up there was the debatable high ground where landowner and poacher were born to confront each other.

Damned copywriter's rhetoric! Who cares. It felt right and lifted him up. He didn't believe they'd pull off even the first hit, but right now he didn't care. He'd been becalmed, stuck, for a long time. Ever since Helen. Now he felt like a wind-filled sail.

He nipped a rose hanging over a garden wall by the police station. Petals colourless now but cool and silk-soft on his fingers. He stuck it in the buttonhole of his jacket and daundered on. All he had to do was find a way of growing up without giving in.

Kirsty checked the flyleaf of the Munro book. *Not* McGillivray. She glanced out of the window then went straight to the wardrobe. She put aside the little heavy box of ammunition and took out the rod case. Standing at the window, she slid out the big rifle, squeezed the canvas and felt the telescopic sights.

She raised the rifle to her shoulder and felt wonderful.

Neil crossed the car park and went into the hotel. As he entered the lobby he saw the back of someone hurrying through to the bar where all the racket was.

'Hang in there, Archie,' he said, then lifted his warm key from the hook and went up the stairs still humming.

The Atholl bar was bright and crowded and smoky as she pushed in. The few tourists were still in the dining room, everyone else she knew, and most she liked. Hi to Hamish and Gerry and the lads from the Forestry Commission. She waved to the boys in the Smoked Oyster Band. Maybe a song later, Kirsty?

She just smiled, nodded, not wanting to seem too keen. Big hello from Lisa and Janet up from Newcastle for the Nature Conservancy with the ghillies round them already. The young doctor grinned, his fiancée didn't. Don't believe everything you hear round here, girl.

She came up behind Lachlan and pulled on his ponytail. He started, grinned, put his arm round her shoulders as she got her order in with Shonagh. Wide bright brown eyes, not unlike Charlie's, grinning away and woofing in her ear.

'Not needed in Deeside tonight, Lachlan?'

He ducked his head, not sure how much she knew or cared. Nor was she. His foxes' teeth dangled white against his tanned neck.

'You know how it is, Kirsty.'

'Certainly do, Lachie. Certainly do.' She winked at Shonagh. 'Make that a double.'

'Special occasion, *a graidh*?'

'Aren't they all, *m'eudail*?' she replied, poorly mimicking the Lewis lilt. 'Yes, we might be in for an interesting time tonight.'

Lachie nudged her.

'Aye, I've brought my toothbrush.'

She put her hand on his arm.

'Steady, boy. We'll see which way the wind blows. You know how it is.'

Lachie looked at her plaintively.

'But there's nae wind tonight.'

Kirsty grinned and picked up her drinks.

'Then we'll just have to whistle for one.' She pursed her lips and made a piercing whistle above the hubbub. 'Hey, Gerry!'

Gerry looked up from a sweater as hairy as his beard and waved her over. She nodded and set off through the crowd towards his group. Shonagh watched her go then bent over the bar.

'Looks like you're paying for this one, Lachlan. Wouldn't you be better off with that reliable lassie in Deeside?'

Lachlan reached for his wallet.
'Reliable makes me think of washing machines.'

The beer was cold and metallic but the whisky in her other hand was warm, and she felt the flow in her head and the flow going round the room and she was warming to a good time. No need to think of other birthdays, other times, of Tom and the high jinks they'd had before he lost it. Not after her little trip upstairs. If she'd felt like champagne before, this was the raw buzz of cocaine, like in the old days before she stepped up to the mike to do her number.

Another drink, her round. The band opened as always with a bluegrass version of 'Walking the Dog', and as she nodded her head at the bar she was ready to take her life anywhere, no matter how unlikely the harmonies.

Upstairs in room twelve Alasdair spread out the Mavor map on the bed. They'd agreed to start with Mavor because it seemed the most possible of the three hits. At least catching a salmon was soundless. But poaching against local wide-boys? They had to come up with some angle, something to give them an edge.

'Climbing,' Alasdair said. 'That's our secret weapon. You talked about that pool halfway up the falls – show me where it is.'

Murray ran his pencil up the blue line, stopped and circled.

'Right here. Mid Pool. Long time back there used to be some kind of ladder. Dinni think anyone goes there now, it's too difficult.'

'Perfect. See these crags bordering the river? We go up the falls by night. I'll climb the side walls, and you jumar on after me.'

'How do we get into the estate in the first place?' Neil asked. 'We don't even know that they've assumed the Mid Pool is impossible. And what if they're watching it from above?'

'It's overhung from above. I did a quick recce of the whole river when I was guiding near Shelter Stone last month. From above, I reckon all you can see is trees and a wee stretch of water. Look . . .'

They opened their cans of beer and bent over the map. The noise from below came bouncing up through the floor. It sounded like a good time.

'Could do without yon racket,' Neil muttered.

Murray pushed up his sleeves and laughed.

'Mind the time at that ceilidh in Ullapool? Christ, you and Helen were loupin like—'

'I mind it.'

A missed beat, then their heads converged over the map again.

Kirsty spun and birled, set and changed partners, whooped and birled again.

She would bop till she dropped, even to the Smoked Oyster Band's bluegrass version of 'Honky Tonk Women'. She would bawl herself hoarse to 'Your Cheating Heart'. She would smooch happily in the head gamie's huge arms while the band gave their country-soul all to 'The Green Green Grass of Home'.

And why not? She would only come this way once, and she was still nearly young. And something had fallen her way, something too full of possibilities to even think about right now.

And later, when the dance was over and the doors locked and only one light left on in the Atholl bar, she would get up on the little stage and do her party piece, 'A Gal You Don't Meet Every Day'. And much later, when Shonagh murmured in the corner into the lovably neat ear of someone she believed was going to last beyond tonight, and the hard core slumped by overflowing ashtrays, Kirsty went up again, and with a nod to Jimmy on the accordion, very quietly and with a catch in her voice that could have been from drink and other people's cigarettes she whisper-sang, looking at nobody there, 'I Can't Give You Anything But Love', and when she'd finished she left the room hushed for a while.

'Sounds like they're reaching the sentimental stage downstairs.'

Murray nodded, crushed his can and lobbed it into the waste-paper basket.

'And we're going round in circles. There's tae many unknowns here.'

'Have another beer, chum.'

They sat back and opened a can each and were silent for a moment. Neil glanced at Alasdair.

'So, Jane get back from Cham this morning?'

Alasdair studied the far corner of the room.

'No.'

Murray giggled and wiped foam from his beard.

'Tae busy partying wi Jean-Pierre, pal.'

Alasdair glowered at him suspiciously.

'How did you know he's called Jean-Pierre?'
'I dinni.'
Neil looked down to hide a smile as Alasdair scowled. Murray took another deep swallow.
'Aye, it's a problem carrying out a military exercise when you canni even keep track of yer wife.'
'And you could get a fat lip, Trotsky!'
'Not frae you, squaddie.'
'Hey!' Neil spread his arms. 'John Macnab, right?'

Lachie's arm round her waist outside the door.
'Can I come hame wi you the night? Please, eh?'
'Another night. I'm needing my bed.' His mouth opened. '*Alone,*' she added firmly.
Downcast, his hair flopping forward, he really did look like Charlie.
'Och, Kirsty, I'll no stay. I just . . .'
She stood back from him, staggering slightly. The last couple pushed between them with a glance and a joke, heading back to their warm shared bed. The night was mild and still. She could hear the river at the back of the town. She hesitated. He really did look miserable.
'I know, Lachie. I know.' She put her hand to his chest, holding him back. 'But not tonight, right?' He looked down and hunched his hands in his pockets and she felt rotten. 'Look, you really would be better off with that girl in Deeside.'
He stepped back and stared at her.
'What are you doing here, Kirsty? Eh? What for are you here?'
And he kept staring, swaying slightly forward and back, then threw off her hand and walked away.
She shook her head and tried to remember where she'd left her bike.
'All right, *m'eudail*?'
'No. I'm a silly old tart and I hurt nice people.'
Shonagh put an arm round her. For a moment Kirsty let go and leaned into it.
'Shonagh, what am I doing here?'
'Scraping a living like the rest of us. And having fun with the lads and being a silly young tart.'
Kirsty laughed and snivelled and dried her eyes on her sleeve. She sat on the nearest wall. Shonagh sat beside her and put an

arm through hers. Where Kirsty came from women didn't do that. Pity. It felt good.

'Kirsty?'

'Mm?'

'What *are* you doing here?'

The river was clear and loud, carrying everything away.

'Three months,' she said. 'I'll give it another three months. If I still can't answer your question, then I shouldn't be here.'

'Don't run off. Stay. Settle.'

'What, with Lachlan? You must be kidding.'

Shonagh stood up suddenly.

'Come on, I'm freezing my arse off here. I'm meeting someone.'

'Looked more like merging to me. You'll have her ear off.'

'Cheeky beesom. Will you stay at my place or cycle back?'

'I'll ride back. Things to think about.'

Together they found her bike round the back. They said goodnight. Kirsty switched on her lights, pulled her coat round her knees. Shonagh put her hand on the handlebars.

'Lachie's my cousin,' she said. Her voice was not entirely friendly. 'It's all very liberated having fun, and some of the lads need a bit of shaking up, but I'll ask you to have a mind of him.'

Kirsty looked down and nodded several times. Shonagh's hand came off the bars.

'Now off home with you. Phone if you want to get together.'

Here it came again, that feeling of being in the wrong. Not able to pass the most basic requirements of being a human being.

'Thanks,' she said. 'Sorry. I get carried away.'

'Just a word. Pals?'

'Pals.'

'Sure you don't want to stay?'

Kirsty shook her head.

'Don't want to be the gooseberry.'

Shonagh laughed and nodded.

'This could be the biggie.'

'Rather you than me.' Kirsty made a sucked-on-a-lemon face. 'Lurv.'

'Anyway, Pat's a bittie jealous.'

'That's ridiculous! I'm not your type. You told me that.'

Shonagh grinned and hugged her quickly.

'I did, didn't I? Night . . .'

Kirsty watched Shonagh walk away, and saw a shadow detach

itself at the end of the street and link an arm through Shonagh's. Nice pair. Nice, nice, nice.

She slung one leg across the bike. As she did so, she glanced up. The light was still on in room twelve. She saw a shape move across the curtain, and another. And another. All three of them.

She knew what she had to do.

They were all round the map again, Murray kneeling, Neil sprawled on the bed, Alasdair bent over with his pencil. Nine empty cans on the floor. The din from downstairs had finally stopped.

'Can you get your bike fixed for the getaway?' Neil asked.

'Can a Cabinet Minister lie?' Murray retorted.

'And how do you get from the gorge to the road? It'll be daylight by then.'

'So either we use a decoy runner, or—'

There was a thump on the door. Alasdair's pencil went through the map. They looked at each other.

Another knock.

'Don't answer it,' Alasdair whispered. 'Did you lock the door?'

'Sure. Key's on the table.'

More knocking. And this time a muffled voice.

'Room service!'

They looked at each other. Neil shook his head.

'Not me.'

'Room service! Open up, please.'

Neil cracked.

'I didn't order room service,' he called.

As a key scraped in the lock, Murray and Alasdair fought to bundle the map under the bed and Neil was on his feet moving towards the door when it opened.

She was carrying a tray with a bottle of whisky and four glasses. She flipped a familiar book on to the bed and smiled sweetly.

'You are John Macnab,' Kirsty said. 'And I claim my exclusive.'

4

'You're barking up the wrong lamppost there, young 'un.' Alasdair lounged on the bed in what he imagined to be a posture of extreme casualness. 'I wish him luck, but it's nothing to do with us.'

Neil still had one hand up as if to bar entry. 'I might have put a bet on him,' he said, 'but so did you. We're not him.'

'But you could pass round yon bottle,' Murray added. 'Nae hard feelings.'

She hesitated, like the pause of an axe at the top of the backswing.

Her mouth twitched.

'Bollocks,' she said. 'Absolute bollocks. Unless you can explain the contents of that wardrobe.'

Neil lowered his hand, still blinking from something he'd seen flash by him. Murray untangled himself from the map and got to his feet.

'Fair enough, doll,' he said. 'We surrender.'

Alasdair flopped back on the bed and groaned.

'We never got past first basic. How did you twig?'

'I work for the local paper,' she said. 'When the Challenge appeared, I did some research. I guessed I was looking for three, almost certainly men, of a certain age shall we say? Then your preoccupied friend here turned up with the bulkiest rod case I've ever seen and an awful lot of maybes. And if he's N. McGillivray I'll eat my jeans.' She turned to Neil. 'I happen to have read *The Thirty-Nine Steps* too. McGillivray was the bigwig at Scotland Yard, right?'

'"Annie Laurie",' Neil sighed. 'The signal on the bridge.'

'I couldn't resist it, just like you couldn't resist using that name.' She grinned at him. He felt like a seventeen-year-old caught in the act, guilty and giggly at the same time. 'Anyway, when two more of you turned up I was fairly sure. So I, ah, investigated further. Then after the dance I saw your light on, so I thought I'd introduce myself.'

'A journalist,' Neil said. 'That does it.' He waved towards the only chair. 'You might as well sit down since the game's over.'

'I don't think so,' she said.

She put the tray down on the dressing table, then turned back to them with the whisky bottle held protectively across her chest. Annie Laurie? Neil thought. Bloody Annie Oakley more like.

'The game isn't over,' she said. 'It's only just begun and I want in on it. And I mean *in*, not some decorative role. Otherwise you're all over the papers in two days' time.' She paused and spelled it out for the dim. 'I want to join John Macnab.'

Murray kept his head down as he smoothed out the map. Alasdair rubbed his moustache and stared like she'd come in through the bathroom window, not the door. Neil felt something like sherbet up his spine.

'Nae offence, but we ken nothing about you.'

'Look, I've four glasses and a full bottle of whisky here,' she said. 'And I'm offering you a deal.' She was flushed now, speaking fast. 'I've local knowledge. I know the gamies and the ghillies. I can handle the press because you'll need public opinion on your side. You need me.'

'But there are no women in John Macnab,' Alasdair objected.

She put one hand on her hip and dangled the bottle from the other.

'Well, there is now.'

She stood waiting. Murray pushed up his sleeves and nodded slowly.

'Could make sense,' he said. 'I never wanted to copy Buchan. Then again, I dinni like this squeeze.'

She turned her attention on Neil. 'What do you say, Mr McGillivray?'

'I say we're being hijacked and I'd like to know where you're planning to take us.'

Alasdair looked at the back of his hands. Special Forces training didn't cover what to do with pushy women armed with whisky. He looked up.

'You say we need you but I don't think so, old girl. Can you shoot like Neil? He used to split hairs at Bisley.'

Neil coughed.

'East Neuk Rifle Club, actually.'
'Same thing. And he's a kind of writer too.'
She looked at Neil. He shrugged.
'Copywriting,' he said. 'Junk.'
'Can you fish better than Murray?' Alasdair continued. 'I doubt it. Can you lead extreme rock? Stalk? Experienced in low-profile infiltration. Nothing sexist, old sport, but what can you really add?'
She wavered then. The scene wasn't supposed to play like this.
'Take a seat,' Neil said gently. 'He's an unreconstructed sexist swine, but he's got a point. Are you easily blackmailed?'
She stared at him.
'Nobody makes me do anything,' she said.
Neil nodded.
'Good. Then credit us with the same.'
She bowed her head for a moment, then walked over to the window to hide the shake in her right leg. She stared out at the sodium-lit street. I've got to split them up, she thought. Got to offer them something.
'Neil, would you say I can find things out or not?'
'You could winkle a pearl from an oyster and he'd still think he was having a good time.'
She winked at him.
'Right. And unlike you guys, in my position I'm allowed to ask questions. The one person no one suspects of the crime is the person who's reporting it.'
Alasdair eyed the whisky longingly. A bold young woman. Not unlike his dear wife Jane, at present paragliding in the Alps in tandem with that smooth git Jean-Pierre.
'Look, girl,' he began.
'Don't you girl me.'
Alasdair flushed and started tugging the strands of his short moustache. Murray grinned, pushed up his sleeves. Neil leaned back on the door-frame with his arms folded and watched the show. 'I can call my female friends girl, but you can't. I'm sure Neil could explain it to you. So what's it going to be, boys? Do you want this adventure or not?'
'Look, *woman*,' Alasdair began. 'What is your name, anyway?'
'Thought you'd never ask. Kirsty. Pleased to meet you.'
She held out her hand. After a pause, he shook it.
'Alasdair,' he said gruffly. 'Pleased to meet you. The wee one's Murray, the tall one's Neil.'

'Well hi, boys.'

Her bar-room voice. She's taking the piss, Neil thought. She's definitely taking it.

'Hi.'

She reached out and picked up Alasdair's mobile phone.

'Sorry about the blackmail,' she said. 'Let's try it this way. If you really want to know the General's plans, ask the General. Right, Alasdair?'

'Absolutely, old girl,' Alasdair said and picked away at his moustache. 'What are you talking about?'

'I'm going to phone Abdulatif Aziz.' She paused and added with heavy sarcasm, 'Who owns the Mavor estate. He's here for the summer season. I met him once.'

'Will he remember you?' Neil asked.

She smiled, a big, amused smile.

'He'll remember,' she said. 'I'll ask him for an interview and try to find out exactly how he's deployed his men. Would that help?'

The Macnabs looked at each other.

'At this time?' Neil asked.

'He's either up or he's not. Word is he keeps late hours.'

She picked up the phone book and went through to the *en suite* bathroom while the men stared at each other.

'Mr Aziz? It's Kirsty Fowler. Yes, from the *Courier* . . .' She shut the bathroom door.

'Well . . .' Neil said eventually.

'Exactly,' Murray added.

'Gobsmacked, mateys.'

They looked at each other, then at the full bottle of whisky on the dresser.

'It could fit,' Murray said at last. 'Changed days, right? That was then, this is now.'

'Kid's got style,' Alasdair admitted. 'Neil?'

'I think we need her about as much as she needs us.'

'Which is?'

Neil was about to answer that when the bathroom door opened and Kirsty flipped the mobile to Alasdair.

'Tomorrow afternoon. Sympathetic interview, his side of things. I'll use my, ah—'

'Feminine wiles?' Neil suggested.

'Something along those lines. Do you have any problems with that?'

She looked round them all.

'Wile awa,' Murray said. 'You're doing no bad so far.'

'And I've got a notion how to return the salmon according to the original wager. Will that do?'

The men looked at each other. She waited. Neil cleared his throat.

'If you can do all that, you've more than earned a place. We haven't a clue how to deliver the salmon.'

The others nodded.

'Murray?'

'Who am I tae sail agin the wind?'

Alasdair glanced longingly at the bottle, then frowned down at his hands. She broke the seal on the bottle and stood over him.

'Yes, or no?'

He hesitated. It was a decent blend and he had a thirst.

'Make it a large one, old girl.'

'Time for thumbnail sketches and introductions,' Neil said as they stood for the toast. 'Attempting to get over their latest mid-life crisis on a dreich holiday, three gentlemen undertook a wager. But we're not gentlemen.' He looked round them all. It seemed fairly undeniable. 'We are: a vertically challenged Glaswegian radical with two tykes and a mysteriously happy marriage – so you'd be wasting your wiles there, Kirsty. But if you want your house extended, repaired or well and truly plastered, he's your man. Then: one slightly knackered mountain guide with incredibly secret Special Forces connections that everyone knows about, and the butch haircut and moustache of an American gay a few pinnacles short of the full peak.'

Alasdair pulled at his moustache.

'You don't think it suits me?'

'It's charming, youth.'

'Uh, and I'd hoped it was dead macho,' Alasdair grunted. He glanced at Kirsty and she saw his right eyelid flicker and from then on she never quite saw him the same way.

'Last and least,' Neil continued, 'a sad case second-rate copywriter who badly needs a change to – well, he needs a change. Kirsty?'

She sniffed her glass and considered.

'The fourth Macnab just wants to have fun,' she said. 'All-singing, all-dancing, with a spot of poaching on the side.'

She raised her glass.

'Kirsty Fowler,' she said. 'To John Macnab.'
'Neil Lindores. To John Macnab.'
'Murray Hamilton. John Macnab.'
'Alasdair Sutherland. John Macnab.'
They clinked glasses.
'To John Macnab!'
'OK,' Kirsty said. 'Now let's hear your plans . . .'

'Not bad,' she said. 'I've never heard of anyone fishing the Mid Pool on the Alt na Harrie. The ghillies are a bit stretched and they might not have covered the falls.' She looked over the map now spread over the bed, and dug back into her memory. 'Murray, are you sure you can land this salmon?'

He grinned.

'Sure as can be,' he said. 'Nae guarantees when they're not feeding.'

'So how do you get them to take the fly?'

'Irritate them,' he said. 'Tease them till they go for it out of habit.'

'Is that hard?'

'Hard enough. But compared to the way you did for us, it should be a doddle.'

'I'll take that as a compliment. OK, gather round, my children. Stay away from the lower river -' her finger stabbed – 'they're bound to have that sealed tighter than a well-digger's arse.'

An appreciative chuckle from Alasdair. She knows how to play us, Murray thought. Al's in the net already though he doesn't know it. She'll handle Neil differently. She'll give him a lot of line.

'But there's still a pile of water coming down the Alt na Harrie. I don't see how you can force your way up against it to the Mid Pool.'

'That's not our game plan,' Alasdair said quickly. 'The idea is I do a rising traverse up one of the sides. And when I get there, Murray gets hauled up the rope I've fixed.'

'He'll get soaked.'

'He'll probably get half drowned, but he's a tough little bugger, aren't you, sport?'

'Oh aye. Abso-bloody-lutely, old chap.'

'But we need to know if someone standing there, off to the east –' Alasdair pointed '– could see Murray fishing the Mid Pool.'

'Not from above. And not if they were right there, which is the natural lookout for covering the lower river. There's a slight rise up to the gorge. Anyway, the trees block the view.'

'You're sure about that?' Neil asked.

This time she definitely blushed.

'I'm sure,' she said. 'Take it from me. You can't be seen. But,' she went on quickly, 'even if you can somehow climb up the walls and get up to the Mid Pool, if they station keepers at the bottom you'll never get near it.'

'So will they be watching it?' Neil asked, still speculating as to what she'd been doing in that spot and with whom.

'The ghillies are being awful close-mouthed. Under instructions, I guess. Even Lachie – well, they're not saying much. So I've got to find that out from Aziz. Most of the rest you can recce for yourselves.'

Finally Neil yawned and said he was knackered and didn't they have beds to go to?

They agreed on the Game Plan for tomorrow, then Murray said goodnight, Alasdair slipped the bottle under his jacket and followed him down the back stairs. Neil watched Kirsty as she gathered the tray and glasses.

'So how did you know about the rifle?'

'I borrowed your room key and peeked earlier. Sorry about that.'

'That's all right.' Neil handed back her copy of *John Macnab*. 'I peaked years ago.'

'Too soon to be sure about that,' she said.

He nodded, didn't seem very convinced though.

'You're very observant. More like a detective than a journalist. You really are a journalist, aren't you, Kirsty?'

The tray shook slightly and the glasses jittered.

'Oh yes,' she replied. 'Ever so much. Eager cub reporter, that's me. Thirsty Kirsty. Ask anyone.'

He looked at her. She looked steadily back.

'It was a great entrance. Great act. What do you do after the show?'

She laughed quietly, low in her throat. He saw the little muscles move.

'Mostly I go to bed with Charlie and a good book.'

He didn't rise to that, just nodded like he'd expected it.

'Time to make a good exit,' she said. She put her hand briefly on his arm. 'Goodnight, Macnab. See you tomorrow.'

'Aye, if we're spared.'

'Gloomy soul, aren't you?'

He looked hard at her then smiled briefly.

'I know I've got a hot date with oblivion.'

'Well, I've got a hot date with tomorrow,' she said and closed the door, then ran down the stairs to catch the others before they left.

Neil lay in the darkness with the night breeze slowly birling the white curtains through the open window. Big day tomorrow. It was as if they'd finally stepped on to a moving walkway and were being carried away somewhere, much faster than usual.

He wondered where they got off. Three weeks at the most.

It's not a problem to be solved but an adventure to be lived. That's what Helen would say. So live it, you Presbyterian fool. Live it, then let it go, like Kirsty.

And you believe her?

He lay watching the curtains wrap up nothing and unwrap it again.

Murray waved as Alasdair's van sped off up the road. Must get the bike back on the road, he'd a feeling it would be needed.

He stood at the door of his B & B. The moon was up but dimmed by cloud. A poacher's moon. He stood grinning in the darkness, humming 'Bonnie Annie Laurie' as he felt for the key.

By the time Kirsty had biked up the hill road to her cottage to be greeted by a rapturous Charlie, she was nearly sober and wanted to sleep for a thousand years but still reluctant to go to bed and end the day.

She stoked up the stove, thinking about the men who made up John Macnab. Murray a small dark troll. Those extraordinary muscular forearms. Not to be played with, that one. Hard to say what he was really about. Then Alasdair with his military nonsense and clearly a soft touch. Some sort of renegade from the county classes. A player, a bit wild. She could relate to that. And Neil. She smiled, remembering her entrance, their startled, guilty faces. Neil the preoccupied one with the slight dark delay before he responded. He responded to her, then he moved out of range. He'd picked up on the theatre of what she was doing. Nice shoulders too, not that that counted for anything.

As she brushed back that goddamn crinkly uncontrollable hair her father had passed on to her, she thought about her meeting with Abdulatif Aziz tomorrow. How to handle it? How to handle them all?

Brush in hand, she paused and studied her face in the mirror. Nose too long, upper lip too straight and severe – Dad again – lower lip too greedy. Dear old Mum to thank for that. And how to handle the woman that was now one-quarter of John Macnab?

'Silly, silly old tart,' she muttered to Charlie.

She parted the curtains and stood in her pyjamas looking down over the few lights still on in the town, then at the darkness of the Mavor estate beyond it.

She picked up her pillow and hugged it absently for a moment. If she kept her head, she could give them all the run-around. She tossed up the pillow and shouting 'Yes!', punched it clear across the room in her delight.

Alasdair let himself into his mate Pete's empty cottage. He made tea and did his stretching exercises routine, the one that had become essential in the last few years.

He finished up with a quick set of squats and a hundred press-ups.

He sat down breathing heavily and picked up his tea. That Kirsty – lot of fire, lot of spark. Bold as a brass monkey. Bit like his dear wife, only younger.

He thought about life without Jane. If she was at it in Chamonix. If she went off and didn't come back. He allowed himself this for only a few seconds a day. It was staring into the big nothing.

He pulled across a sheet of paper and started planning the logistics of a getaway.

She lit the candle and rolled under the duvet. She listened to the stove creaking and Charlie whiffling as he settled back to sleep. Happy thirtieth birthday, Christine.

She watched the candle flame waver and stretch. What are you up to, woman?

To tell the truth, even just to yourself, you have to first know what the truth is.

Outside in the moonlight, the axe was bedded in the log. She'd done her bit for the day. She'd stacked her pile and had her fun and let out a little emotion with a song, and started something for reasons she didn't understand.

She let the day's events sink through her like water through coffee grounds. Sometimes it kept her awake half the night, sometimes it didn't.

She licked her fingers, then stretched and pinched out the candle flame.

5

It was a clean bright morning and Neil had the windows down and the cassette playing early Springsteen, nostalgia music, as he drove to pick up Murray. He sang along, thumping the wheel, enjoying the music of the past and the curves of the back road through the beech and birch and rowan. The air smelled like white wine ought to taste but doesn't unless you've a lot of money to burn, and he felt fifteen years younger. Tramps like us . . .

He spotted Murray standing at the corner by his B & B with a small pack in his hand, and slowed for him.

Only it's not nostalgia this time, he thought. Maybe my life isn't like an hourglass, more and more run away and less and less to come. I've had the wrong picture stuck in my head these past years, now it's surely time to find another.

'Grand morning, youth!'

Murray, neat and trim and organized as always, already pushing his sleeves up those Popeye forearms, slid into the passenger seat.

'Seen worse, pal.'

'Aye, warm for December.'

Pause.

'Braw!' they said together, and laughed as they accelerated down the road.

Alasdair left the shower, knotted a towel round his waist and stood outside in the sunshine with the mobile in his hand. He looked at all the little scars, the missing tip of his pinkie, the swollen knuckles where arthritis was just beginning to bite.

He could lose her.

She could leave.

She could get work as a nurse anywhere. They had no children. Nothing to keep her.

He stared at the phone in his hand. Too much thinking. He needed to be *doing* again, to push the envelope as the test pilots said, then lick the stamp and post it.

He could understand Jane's need to do the same, to push her limits, and why she'd added paragliding to her skiing. But was that for a new challenge, or because that smoothie Jean-Pierre did both? Before leaving for Cham, she couldn't quite look him in the eyes. Or was he being paranoid? OK, he *was* paranoid about Jane, but he didn't think he'd imagined it . . .

She was bored with him. He'd always said he wasn't very bright. Not educated bright. She and Neil had more in common. Not surprising they used to . . .

Wake up! Concentrate! He badly needed some hard climbing. That at least he could do well. That didn't scare him in the least.

He took a deep breath and jabbed the buttons.

'This is the answerphone of Jane and Alasdair Sutherland. I'm afraid Alasdair is away at the moment and I'm back from Chamonix but I've gone out to see friends.'

Alasdair grimaced and gripped the waist-knot of his towel.

'Perhaps, when you've time, you could phone your husband at Pete's place.'

He switched off the phone and went inside and closed the door.

As they parked the Escort round the back of Pete's cottage, Alasdair jumped down from the black van, rubbing his big hands on his troll trousers.

'I've a surprise for you squaddies.'

Laid out on the kitchen table were three sets of old tweeds: the breeks, the jackets, heavy wool socks, the deerstalkers.

'Thought we might as well do it in good style.'

'I'm no wearing yon,' Murray protested.

'They're practical kit for crawling through heather. You'd rip those lightweight trousers to hell, and denim's useless if we have to lie up through the night. Tweed's good camouflage, too.'

'He might have a point,' Neil said, slipping on the longest jacket. He tried on the deerstalker, pulled it down over his eyes and checked himself in the mirror. 'Theatrical costume for a theatrical event. Shame we don't have a fourth set.'

'They'll only be worn for active service,' Alasdair said, 'so there'll be enough.'

Grumbling something about Sassenach twats, Murray tried on his gear. The trousers came down over his shoes but the hat fitted.

'Hey, stumpy, you'll just have to take them up a bit!'

They stood in complete tweeds and looked at each other. They looked – they felt – quite different. There was a wee pause and the ghost of a different age passed through the little kitchen.

'All right,' Murray said gruffly. 'Likely this was some underpaid ghillie's outfit onyway. I'll only wear it for the hit, mind.'

They changed back into normal gear. Alasdair put three coffees in the microwave and they got down to some late-twentieth-century logistics.

An hour later they emerged. They left Murray with the Kawasaki. Through the mysterious fraternity of bikers, he'd already been able to get spare gaskets and borrow the tools he required. Then Alasdair and Neil got into the bog-standard blue Escort and set off for the south-east boundary of the Mavor estate.

It's unfortunately true – go take a look if you don't believe me – that in the morning light and with dew still on the slopes, the Cairngorms look like beached purple whales. Stranded and ruinous. A beautiful disaster slowly dying under its own weight.

Up on the hillside above her cottage, Kirsty hugged her knees and sighed. Despite having lived here for two years, she wasn't really an outdoors person. For her reality was still bars, clubs, streets, shops, good times. Reality was urban. For her, the hills were just a backdrop. She didn't have a feel for them as part of the action, the way someone like Lachie or the Macnabs did.

Would they accept her? If they didn't, what other game did she have left to play?

She stood up and called on Charlie. No use brooding. Get down to the town and get some work done. First of all check in at the office, finish up there then go and visit a certain posh little restaurant and see a man about a fish. And it would be an idea to drop in at the Atholl for the ghillies' crack before going on to the big house . . .

She set off down, brushing through the coarse grass where dew crushed the sun to tiny shaking rainbows.

They moved low and cautious up through the scattered birch and rowans where the berries were already beginning to glow, eased the last branches aside and crawled to the top of the rise.

'Here?'

Alasdair crawled up beside Neil and raised his head cautiously. From the top of the little knoll they looked down on the single-track road that bounded the Mavor estate.

'Yes. Definitely.'

They took out binoculars and a telescope and started to scan the hillside opposite. Neil checked an empty Land Rover by the dirt road that ran into the estate. Then he found one figure sitting against an old shooting butt, saw the glint of binoculars. Anyone sitting up there could command most of that section of road and hillside, with perhaps a couple of blind spots.

He looked off to the right and found another watcher. Between them they'd the hill covered. Night entry, then. If anyone could get past them at night it would be Al. Getting out by daylight was another matter.

'That one's well positioned,' Alasdair murmured. 'But what's with his ear?'

Neil adjusted the scope and looked again. The first gamie had what looked like a row of teeth hanging from his ear.

'Weird, huh?'

'Dig the ponytail. I'd say he was into Garbage, the Cocteaus and Captain Beefheart.'

'Ghillies ain't what they used to be,' Alasdair sighed.

Neil went back to studying the ground and distance between the two watchers and their Land Rover. Three minutes? Four minutes? If Murray appeared over the rise below the Alt na Harrie, would they run back for the Land Rover or chase after him? He glanced at Al, but he seemed lost in his own thoughts. Earlier he'd asked if he'd heard from Jane yet, but got a suspicious glare. Rights of access, Neil thought. We need privacy but we need access to each other and all.

He scanned the fence carefully, looking for a weak spot. At last he found one. A wee burn coming down . . .

'Try these, youth.'

Alasdair handed him the most powerful binoculars he'd ever used.

'A loan from the TA. Unofficial, of course.'

Now he could pick out the top of the narrow gorge where the Alt na Harrie began to tumble. Impossible to climb up against the force of that water. Climbing the sides was the only way, up to the Mid Pool that Murray remembered. From above it would be screened by trees and an initial overhang. But from below?

'Off to the right, youth,' Alasdair murmured.

He swung the binoculars and found the river where it came into view again. More trees, looked like rowan and small birch.

And further along, where they gave out, he saw two figures approaching each other on the far bank of the Alt na Harrie. The pool that Alasdair proposed to reach by the gorge could only be a hundred yards from the two watchers who were now standing gesticulating.

'This Kirsty woman had better be right about those sight-lines.'

'She seemed very sure.'

Alasdair grinned.

'She did that. What do you think that was about?'

'I don't.'

Neil passed back the binoculars and started to roll a cigarette.

'She's got style, I'll give her that,' Alasdair said.

'She's got an original notion of colour coordination,' Neil conceded.

'And it might help having an insider. The first John Macnab had whatsisname, Fish Benjie.'

'Kirsty will want a bigger role than that. There's enough of her to be Janet Raden too, and still have a lot left over.'

'She sussed you pretty quick, matey.'

'She did that,' Neil conceded.

'Sharp as a needle, I'd say.'

Neil lit up and considered.

'Sure, but can she sew with it?'

There was a silence while Alasdair wrestled with that one.

'You're not talking about her home-making abilities?' he said finally.

'Nope.'

'But you reckon she's OK?'

Neil shrugged.

'She's all right in my book. Wouldn't necessarily trust her but— Hey! At the top of the gorge, among the trees.'

Right enough, just a flicker of movement in the trees where someone was guarding the river from above.

'It's not a problem as long as he stays there, but if there's someone at the bottom of the gorge, we've had it.'

'But otherwise you think it's on?'

'If Murray and me can't get from the road to the bottom of the gorge in the dark without being seen and then climb up the sides to the pool, my name's not John Macnab.'

'But your name's not John Macnab.'

'That's what's worrying me.'

They looked at each other and burst out laughing. This must

be male bonding, Neil thought. I haven't done much of that in a long time. Not any sort of bonding.

He turned over and lay on his back in the soft grass. He felt the sun working into the hollows around his eyes, smelled the day warming up. It was another new morning; she should have been here.

He stretched, and felt something loosening.

Murray washed the grease off his hands and settled down at the kitchen table to make up some casts.

Setting up coffee and putting aside a cigar for later, he pushed up his sleeves and prodded out a selection of flies. He thought about it. August dawn. A floating line, casts of one or two flies. Try a Stoat's Tail as the tail fly, something furry for the bob. A Black Pennel or one of his own flies he'd made the week before.

Right. He pulled out two arm-spans of eight-pound line and snicked it with his Swiss Army.

As he worked the old excitement was there, like a pal too long forgotten. He could feel the pool still and brown in the middle, birling and eddying a bit by the banks, creasing over hidden stones. Pale light off the water, wind gusts darkening the surface as you tried to keek through to what was underneath . . .

He hadn't fished for salmon in too long. There hadn't been the time or money since the kids and the political work. He'd have to adjust his technique, forget the quick strike for trout. He must pause to let the salmon roll over the fly and take it down, remember to tighten the line rather than strike . . .

The admission rippled across his mind that he wanted to do this not just as a small up-yours at the rich bastards who owned what should never be owned, like land and water and people's lives for starters. There was an atom of delight in the thing itself, to be back fishing again, a joy that went back to when he was a wean in Ayr, with his dad, before the family ever moved to the city. Somewhere along the line he'd lost that delight. Busy busy busy, trying to keep the head above water and change the world, even just a wee bittie. Except in moments with the weans, he'd lost the joy.

Trish had surprised him. She'd been all for the ploy from the first. It's time you grew down, Murray. It's time you were a bit daft again.

He held the Stoat's Tail up to the light and threaded it first time. Last time he'd used one of these, a permit hadn't been needed for brown trout. Native species, yes? They'd quietly had that law changed. Just another small, mean nail in a coffin the size of Scotland.

Suddenly he was aching to get out there again and kiss a hidden hook on to a swirling surface. If Al could get him there, he reckoned he could take that salmon. Just a wee blow against everything that was being taken away. It would be, ah man, it would be so fuckin *sweet*.

Late that afternoon Kirsty pulled up her Wolseley next to a rather nice old maroon Jaguar and steadied herself for a moment. There'd been the swift gin and tonic with the restaurateur to seal that arrangement, and a chat with Lachie over a couple of whiskies in the Atholl. She'd got as much about the patrolling of Mavor as she could without rousing suspicion. As she'd left he'd asked to come by tomorrow night for 'a bit word'. She had a good notion what that word would be. And he was right, of course he was.

She re-clasped her hair, smoothed down her kilt and salmon-pink silk shirt, picked up the black jacket and checked herself in the driving mirror. Nothing tarty, he wouldn't go for that, just bright and wide-eyed yet professional.

She looked at the big house. Fine grey granite with a later wing and some late Victorian twiddly bits. It looked in good nick, the gravel was smooth and the new curtains were right. Some nice wood, and wellie boots at the front door and . . .

He was standing in the front door looking at her.

She swallowed and got out of the car, walked over to him and held out her hand.

'Kirsty Fowler,' she said.

For a moment she thought he was going to kiss her hand, but instead he shook it, firmly rather than the gentle pressing Arab greeting.

'I remember,' he said. 'It was last year at the Show, and you were wearing a long green dress that suited you well. Shall we go inside?'

'You left the car back up the road?' Murray asked when they returned to Pete's cottage. 'Nobody saw you two come in here?'

'Yes, and no. Aren't you being a bit paranoid?'

Murray sat back and frowned as he coiled up his casts.

'Dinni think so. A fella came by while you were away. Asked some questions. Said he knew Pete but seemed as familiar with him as I am with the inside of Balmoral. Luck I'd put the tweeds away, and Al's gear was lying about, so I said I was up for some climbing.' He picked up the Swiss Army, ran his thumb along the blade. 'Na, this is for real. They're checking it out everywhere.'

Alasdair nodded.

'Max. op. security from here on in. We meet only when we have to and vary the rendezvous.'

Neil picked up a long dull fly and turned it gently between his fingers.

'Will this bit of fluff take in a salmon? I thought they're supposed to be wise.'

Murray took it from him and dropped it in the box.

'This bit fluff is cried a Stoat's Tail, and salmon – like you and many another – can be taken in by appearances and old habits. So you reckon you can scaff me up to yon pool for first light?'

Alasdair nodded and went over to the cupboard.

'Here's a wet suit,' he said. 'Hope it doesn't interfere with your casting.'

He dumped it on the table.

'Wet suit,' Neil said, and held it up. 'I've heard of safe sex, but this is ridiculous.'

'Best be married and not play around, pal. That's safe, isn't it, Al?'

Alasdair buried his nose in a coffee mug.

'That depends,' he muttered.

Neil scraped back his chair.

'I'll take your bike out, Murray. If we have to fall back on Plan B, I'd better get some practise in.'

He left by the back door and the two sat till the bike engine faded. Murray wound up the last of the casting line.

'So how's Plan A?' he inquired.

Alasdair banged the mug down and stared out of the window.

'Plan A is we look stupid and end up in jail.'

Murray stared at him.

'Take it easy, you big daftie. If you've a problem wi Jane, it's nothing to do with Neil.'

'You think so? They were an item once, before we ever started.'

Murray levelled the little Swiss Army knife at him.

'I know so,' he said. 'Don't even think about it.'

'Yes, but—'

'Talk to yer wife, for God's sake. Now how's about sorting out the gear for this hit?'

Alasdair went over to the cupboard and pulled out two backpacks.

'Bit of a wobbler there, old sport. Sorry about that. Right: face paints, climbing books, helmet, slings, hip flask, harnesses, rope, jumar clamp . . .'

Kirsty backed her car into a little stand of trees, then walked down the road towards the cottage. A mauve-grey mist had settled over the moorland but higher up the sky was a flaming dissolve, and for a moment she was hooked out of herself and had the sense there were no boundaries beyond which she could not pass.

She stopped and stood with the feeling. Now the high ridges were turning flat black, a few yellow lights snapped on in the dark. Like a gig, she thought, when the lights go down and the stage is waiting and your pulse begins to knock. Only this time the point was not to be seen by any audience at all.

The feeling passed and she shrugged and hummed 'Making Whoopee' softly to herself. It had been a very interesting day. She was having fun and would have more, so long as she didn't stop to think about it too deeply.

She paused, seeing again Shonagh's hand coming down on the handlebars. 'I'll ask you to have a mind of him.' Sometimes she was too clever for her own or anyone else's good.

She dropped that thought away quickly like a shirt into the dirty-clothes basket, and walked on towards the cottage. The thin curtains were drawn but the light showed through and silhouetted round the table were three heads. Very clever, lads. Great security.

She tiptoed up to the window and looked through the gap below the curtain. There they were, gathered conspiratorially over a map – Alasdair making military gestures, Murray nodding and flicking his right arm as he demonstrated some fishing technique, and Neil sitting back with his long-fingered hands clasped behind his head, grinning like a dope. Nice to see him smiling.

She pressed her face to the pane. She felt absurdly touched as if they were hers in some way. Wee boys playing a boys' game.

So what did that make her. What *is* a woman's game?

She looked at them again and felt herself excluded. They were men and had known each other for years. She had to find a way to break in.

She rapped on the window and laughed as they started like guilty things, then hurried round the back.

* * *

She flung open the door, took three tripping steps into the room and flung her arms round herself.

'I'm in love!' she said.

'Whit?'

'I'm in love,' she sang.

'Aye, but with what?'

She threw her arms out wide.

'I'm in love with a *wonderful guy*!!'

The three men looked at each other.

'Hold it right there,' Neil said.

He hurried into the bathroom. She held the pose uncertainly with her arms outstretched. He came back with a bottle of shampoo and thrust it into her hand.

'You've got to wash that man . . .' he sang.

'Gonna wash that man!'

'Right out of your hair.'

'Right outa my hair!'

He seized the shampoo arm, clasped his other arm round her waist.

'And send him on *his waay*!!' they sang and chorus-line kicked round the kitchen until Murray and Alasdair rolled their eyes in despair. She came to a halt, her face inches from Neil's as he bent over her gallantly.

'You know, you're all right when you loosen up a bit,' she murmured.

He bared his teeth.

'Go on, I just love it when you patronize me.'

'Quit arsing about, you two!' Murray said.

They let each other go. Kirsty sat down, Neil pulled up a fourth chair and leant negligently over the back of it.

'Some enchanted evening . . .' he began.

Murray shook his head but grinned.

'Are you two bevvied or something?'

Neil looked at Kirsty.

'Not me, laddie,' he said. 'How about you, Kirsty?'

'Nothing a bottle or two of champagne in the big house and a couple of drams at the Atholl wouldn't account for.'

Nevertheless she straightened her jacket and pulled her hair back off her face and tried to look sensible.

'Private Macnab reporting from reconnaissance – sah!' and she threw a ragged salute.

'So how did it go?' Alasdair asked. 'Any good intelligence, old thing?'

'Yes – you need thicker curtains, sweetheart,' she said and ran her hand over his military crew cut.

'Right ho, old bean,' he said, blushing like a schoolboy. 'So what did you learn? What's this Aziz like?'

'Abdulatif? Oh, a bit of a goat, I'd say.'

'An old goat?' Neil asked.

'Not at all. A young goat. With oiled horns and a neat black moustache. Pretty fanciable, actually.'

Neil scowled.

'A flashy wanker.'

'He's got money,' she conceded. 'But he's smart and not all patter. In fact he's quite formidable.'

'You mean he didn't fall for your feminine wiles?'

'Wiles? I used no wiles. Apart from a well-cut shirt and my natural charm.'

'Aye, verra nice too, Kirsty,' Murray said. 'Now stop winding up Neil and tells us how it went.'

She opened her mouth, thought better of it.

'All right,' she said. She leaned back in her chair. 'Pour me a drink and picture it, my friends . . .'

No doubt about it, he was clever and charming and in no way a joke. Neat, slim, wearing casual slacks and shirt, the same height as herself. Spoke very good English – two years at Cambridge – with a hint of a French accent. *Très* sexy. Very black eyes that grew darker still when he talked angrily about this thief Macnab. Why weren't the police doing more? They seemed to treat it as a joke. They said no crime had been committed yet. Probably a hoax, they said. Perhaps it was because he was a foreigner that they wouldn't help him. But hadn't he bought the land? Didn't he offer employment and pay good wages?

What did Kirsty say to that?

She said she'd made inquiries and yes – she touched his arm briefly – he paid good wages. He was considered a good employer. And no, she didn't think the local police were racist, except perhaps about the English. But most of them were Highlanders and there was a long history in Scotland behind attitudes to poaching and land ownership.

When Abdulatif had calmed down and a housekeeper brought in afternoon tea to the study – log fire burning for all that it was

August, the room smelling of wood smoke and beeswax and summer drifting in through the open window – she'd agreed it could be a hoax. Every day that passed without incident in any of the three estates made it more likely. Perhaps this John Macnab had looked at the practical problems and been frightened off. There seemed a lot of extra people guarding the estate.

He scowled and told her how many and how much it was costing him, plus the overtime for the regular staff. Would she print that in her newspaper?

Yes she would. She had come to represent fairly his point of view. She would guarantee him first sight of her interview, with a right to reply. And if he would like to give her some background off the record, that's where it would stay. Everyone in the village was talking about whether the estate could be protected. She'd be fascinated to hear his thinking on that. Didn't he have an army background?

And so she ended up standing at his elbow in front of the big estate map framed on the wall while Abdulatif outlined his strategy. The patrolling of the boundary fence. Men on the hill, here and here and here, especially to the north. Land Rovers at all the entrances, including the dirt roads. Then the guards on the river itself, day and night, covering all the pools his factor thought fishable. All in touch by walkie-talkie. What did she think? Could this impudent rascal succeed against him?

He smiled at her. Lovely white teeth, brother fox. Lean brown arms. He smelt of warm skin with just a hint of cumin. Nice. Sure of himself as a man without being sleazy. Most of the men she met these days were either Neanderthals or in a constant state of apology, but he was neither.

'You're enjoying this, aren't you?' she said.

He put his hands on his hips and looked up at the map then at her.

'Very much, Miss Kirsty. It is good to have an intelligent and attractive woman to talk with. Your upper class are very dull.'

'That's not exactly what I meant. You're enjoying trying to stop this John Macnab.'

He smiled and touched her arm, briefly, as she had his.

'I know what you meant. Yes, I am enjoying it. But also I am angry. I am not accustomed to this lack of respect.'

'Abdulatif, you are sounding very Arab.'

'Miss Kirsty, I *am* very Arab.'

'So I'll tell you this –' she poked him lightly in the chest '– with us a challenge can be a mark of respect. There's no honour in taking on an inferior opponent, is there? I've been in Morocco, and I know it's the same with you.'

God I'm sounding pompous, she thought. But he is a worthy opponent.

He stared at her for what seemed a long time.

'Yes,' he said quietly. 'A worthy opponent. I had not thought of it that way. Thank you, Kirsty.' He paused, then broke away to press a bell.

'And now,' he said, 'we will drink some champagne on the lawn and talk about Scotland and Morocco and men and women.'

'And honour,' she said.

'Of course. You are honourable, aren't you?'

'Of course. In my way. But I'm surprised you drink.'

'At home, never. But here I do as others, except in Ramadan. At home we could not be friends like this.'

He opened the French window for her and they went out to the lawn. He filled the glasses then raised his up and said, 'But I shall win, you know.'

She laughed and held her glass to his.

'To victory, then!'

'To victory!'

Kirsty drained her glass and looked at them all.

'And that's about it,' she concluded. 'It doesn't sound like they're using infrared glasses or night vision enhancers. I've shown you where they've got the river covered. And no mention of anyone at the bottom of the gorge.'

Alasdair filled the glasses again.

'Did you ask him directly about that?'

'I thought it might look odd if I didn't. So I pretended to be stupid and asked him about that section of the river.'

'And?'

'And he laughed and said the factor had assured him no one had fished there since a couple of young guests had abseiled down to a pool and nearly got killed. And with a man watching at the top, abseiling in would be impossible.'

Murray clinked his glass against hers.

'Well done, lass.'

'Thanks, laddie. To victory!'

'To victory!'

When they'd drunk their toasts, she put her glass down and paused a moment.

'There's one other thing I got out of it,' she said. 'An invitation to a dinner party there, the night after tomorrow. Of course, I accepted.'

'You're crazier than paving!'

'What better alibi could I have? You see, I've solved the problem of the return of the fish to the big house.'

She sat back, enjoying the effect.

'It's very simple. Everyone knows that when Abdulatif has a dinner party, he orders the works from the local chi-chi restaurant in town. And this morning I just happened to chat with a local businessman who, shall we say, owes me a couple of favours. You see?'

'I'm beginning to,' Neil said.

'You'd give Rommel a hard time,' Alasdair said. 'Cheers.'

'Mata Hari, Janet Raden, and Fish Benjie rolled into one,' she said modestly. 'Child's play, really.'

Neil got up and went to the cupboard. He emerged with a deerstalker and put it gently on her head.

'I crown you John Macnab.'

She adjusted the angle and checked herself in the mirror.

'The principal boy,' she murmured.

They sat up another hour, getting the last details in line. Tomorrow midnight they'd be going into action. Not one of them didn't feel the quickening pulse and the turning of the stomach, and it went to their heads better than whisky.

Eventually the bottle was removed from Alasdair and he consented to go to bed. Murray sat on the motorbike, waiting for Neil.

'Like a lift back, Neil?' Kirsty asked.

Neil hesitated. Murray clicked the bike into gear.

'I'm offski,' he said.

'Sure, Kirsty.'

Murray drove into the night. And as Alasdair began to draw up his battle plan he winced to hear two ragged voices burlesquing 'Some Enchanted Evening' before the sound of the car faded.

6

So who's this Pete, the climber whose cottage John Macnab used that summer for the Mavor estate? Where is he, so conveniently absent? Will he suddenly return to sink or save them?

Pete will never appear in this account because he spent that summer stuck in a series of fly-blown shacks on the Chinese-Tibetan border waiting for an entry permit that never came. By the time he got home the only signs left of the previous occupants were three empty bottles of whisky and a profusion of tyre tracks round the back. Poor pissed-off Pete, standing in the empty kitchen reading a cryptic scrawl: *Ace action with big fish on Death Wall. Must go AWOL. Cheers youth – A. S.*

Death Wall? Pete wondered. Never heard of that route. Big fish? Obscure even by Al's standards. Still, as the tired Pete (whom you will not meet) sat next to his dusty rucksack waiting for the kettle to boil and the autumn leaves whirled by outside, he had a definite sense of something having gone on in that room. The angle of the four chairs, an indefinable smell, the glasses on the draining board, the squint mirror and a pale green hairslide left on the sideboard: all suggested movement, meetings, hasty partings. Something had been going on and he'd missed it.

Sit next to the ghostly Pete as he moodily drinks his tea, and look at that squint mirror on the wall . . .

'Get outa ma way,' Murray grumbled as Alasdair butted in. 'I'm doing ma make-up.'

Alasdair finished rubbing under his throat and turned away from the mirror.

'Let's have a look at you, wee fella. Did you do behind your ears? Back of the neck? Now close your eyes while I do the lids.'

'Is this strictly necessary, or just part of the games you play with Special Forces?' Murray said as Al carefully blackened his eyelids. 'I feel a right stookie and it doesni match ma tweeds.'

'If you want that big fish, it's necessary. There's ghillies on that hill with better night vision than you'll ever have. Did I tell you about that time I got within touching distance of an alert sentry on an exercise in the open Pentlands?'

'Aye,' Murray grunted. 'Often.'

'It's the little bits that people forget, like the back of the ears. You trust me and do exactly what I say till we get to the pool. Then it's over to you. OK?'

They turned away from the mirror and looked each other over for any places where white skin still showed.

'Aye, OK. But we look bloody ridiculous.'

'It's all ridiculous, don't you know. Life and all that. So let's do it right, eh?'

Murray rubbed in the last of the blacking.

'Let's go.'

Alasdair bent closer to him and sniffed.

'Is that a clean shirt?'

'Of course.'

'Change it. I can smell the washing powder from here. Outside, a good ghillie could sniff you at twenty paces. Trust me.'

Grumbling, Murray changed his shirt and put the tweed jacket back on, picked up his pack in one hand and his short poacher's rod in its canvas in the other.

'Let's go, old sport. The van should be there at twenty-three hundred hours.'

'Otherwise known as eleven at night.'

Still, at the door Murray held out his hand.

'Good luck, ya nutter.'

'Luck shouldn't come into it. Good luck.'

They shook on it, then slipped into the night.

'I'm right sorry, Kirsty. I like you fine, it's jist . . .'

Lachie hesitated at the bedroom door. She lay in the warm crumpled bed that a few had shared but where none had been allowed to stay the night. For the first time she regretted that.

'I know,' she said. 'And I agree.'

He picked up his donkey jacket. Already Charlie was whimpering outside the door.

He quickly leaned over, kissed her once on the lips. He put his hand through her hair, then kissed her cheek. She'd always liked his wide eyes, and the smell of hills about him. He really looked like he was about to greit.

'I'll always . . .' he started. He cleared his throat. 'You'll aye be grand in my book, Kirsty.'

'And you in mine, Lachie. You in mine.'

He left. She lay awhile looking at nothing in particular, wishing she'd never given up smoking.

She got up and made some tea. And when she'd settled back in, avoiding the damp patch and allowing Charlie for once on to the bed, she picked up the map of Mavor and rehearsed the future till it was time to dress and go and do it live.

Neil stopped the van at the top of the hill and switched off the engine and then the lights.

'OK, guys?'

Muffled grunts from the back. In the front passenger seat Kirsty was still bent over with laughter.

'Right, I'll go through this. I start up, lights on, and we go down the hill. When Kirsty calls, you open the rear doors.'

'Won't the interior light go on?' she objected.

'Glad you asked, kid,' Alasdair said. 'I've disconnected the interior and brake lights.'

'Wouldn't we be better to free-wheel down with the engine and headlights off?'

'Dead give-away if anyone sees. We do it the pros' way. Tell her, Neil.'

'Where the road dips round the bend, we're out of sight from the hill. We stop. They jump out. Then a couple of seconds later we reappear like nothing's happened.'

'Sure you and Kirsty can manage the bike?'

'We got it in, we'll get it off.'

'Let's go to work.'

Neil was reaching for the ignition when he saw the headlights coming.

'Get down! Under the blankets!'

'What's up?'

'Car coming. Christ! It's slowing down.'

'Police!' Kirsty hissed.

The car came to a halt, its headlights shining full into the cab. A uniformed man came out slowly and ambled up with a flashlight in his hand.

Kirsty wound down the window and stuck her head out.

'Hello, Jim,' she said. 'They've got you doing nights now?'

'Ah, it's yourself, Kirsty. Aye, the Chief Constable's on our backs with this John Macnab palaver. We're doing random checks.'

'Lots of overtime, Jim.'

'I'd rather be in my bed. And wha's this?'

He shone the light on Neil.

'Hi,' he said. 'I'm a friend of Kirsty's.'

'And can I ask why you're sitting here without lights?'

'Um . . . Well . . .'

Kirsty coughed.

'Neil's a . . . close friend. We came up here to . . . you know, be by ourselves.'

She leaned into Neil and put one arm possessively across his shoulders. The policeman grinned.

'I prefer the comforts of home myself.'

He casually flashed his torch into the back of the van.

'I'm thinking it will rain later, so I wouldn't hang around too long, even with your blankets. You'll let me know if you see anyone you dinna ken on the road.'

'I will that, Jim.'

She snuggled closer to Neil.

'Goodnight then, Kirsty.'

'Goodnight, Jim.'

'Sooner this nonsense is over the better,' he grumbled. 'Lot of fuss about nothing at all . . .'

He switched off the torch and went back to the car. After a long pause he drove away.

Kirsty slowly eased away from Neil.

'Coast's clear. Jesus, my heart rate.'

'Mm. Shall we go now?'

'Give him five minutes in case he comes back. Jim MacIver is a canny man. All right in the back there?'

'Aye. Weel done, cutty sark.'

They sat doing nothing much for a while. Neil checked his watch, Kirsty watched the half-moon coming and going behind the clouds. A fine night for adventuring, she thought. A little stroll on the wild side, for old times' sake.

Car headlights came round the bed. She leaned her head into Neil's neck. Her hair tickled on his face, her breath was warm on the hollow of his neck. The police car hooted once as it swept past.

'Be still my beating heart,' Neil murmured, flicked on the

headlights and they set off down the road.

'Coming up,' Kirsty said.

'Doors open.'

'Right, the burn's twenty yards down on the left. You'll find the bottom two strands have been cut and re-twisted. Then you're on your own.'

'No problem, youth. Just be there if we have to bail out in a hurry.'

'I'll be there.'

Murray and Alasdair crouched in the back with their packs as the van went into the dip.

'Kirsty?'

'Murray, I'll be there. Have fun.'

'For sure.'

'Good hunting.'

Neil quickly hit the brakes, and for a moment they were stationary. The van lurched slightly, then the rear doors closed.

'Follow everything I do, Murray,' they heard Alasdair whisper as half of John Macnab disappeared through the trees and into the night. Neil drove on out of the dip.

'How much chance have they got?' Kirsty asked quietly. With the moon out, it was worryingly light.

He glanced at her.

'I don't know. Al's pretty good at this, even if he might strike you as a bit off-the-wall.'

She nodded.

'I think he's Neanderthal but sweet. He sends himself up, doesn't he?'

'I certainly hope so.' He braked gently for a tight bend coming up. 'We've been friends for yonks. Hard to say why, but we are. Talking of which, hadn't we better get our story straight? The lovers in the moonlight bit?'

'It was the best I could come up with. Do you mind?'

He straightened out of the bend and peered down the next stage of the road. 'Na, it's good cover for when we're seen together. Coming up here . . .'

He pulled into a small lay-by. Working quickly, they opened the van doors and humped out Murray's motor bike. They pushed it up a path through rhododendrons and left it where it couldn't be seen from the road or the estate opposite.

'I can get off here,' Neil said. 'You take the van home and get some sleep.'

She yawned.

'Too excited. I'll wait with you here till it's time.'

She lay back and stretched her long legs up on to the dashboard then reached for the flask.

'Coffee?'

'Ta. Cigarette?'

'No thanks.'

He rolled up, accepted the coffee and lit up. They sat in silence for a while.

'Neil?'

'Yeah?'

'Think I will have that cigarette.'

He rolled another and passed it over.

'Used to,' she said. 'Among other things. Long time ago.'

She lit up. He glanced at her face in the yellow flame of the lighter. Long straight nose and mouth, eyes hidden in shadow. For a moment she seemed someone else and a long way away.

She passed back the lighter and they sat waiting for first light. From time to time they chatted, filled each other in on selected pieces of each other's lives. Mostly they were silent in the not unfriendly dark.

Alasdair slid down into the burn and eased open the cut wires. He slipped under, Murray passed him with both packs, then he reached behind the post and twisted the strands together again. He crouched, shielding a pocket light with his hand and checked his compass bearing.

'Follow me,' he whispered. 'Do everything I do. There's a ghillie a hundred yards on our right, and another further up on the left.'

Murray, and particularly Murray's knees, would remember that night for a long time. After a while he wished he'd brought his daughter's skateboarding pads, because Alasdair seemed ready to crawl every yard of the way if he had to.

They stopped for long periods where Al just lay sniffing and listening and looking, then crawled on up again. At first the ground was damp, soft moorland, then the heather began. It scraped and tickled their faces. They came to a drainage ditch, Al grunted with satisfaction and they crouched and crawled up along it.

The moon was hidden now: all Murray could see was the darker darkness of Sutherland's arse and above that a slight paleness where the skyline began. They were climbing more steeply and finally arrived on some kind of rock outcrop. Al was just wriggling over the top of it when he stopped so suddenly Murray got a boot in the face.

He was about to protest when he saw how still Alasdair was, so he froze likewise with his face pressed to the rock. Somewhere off to the left he heard a scraping sound. Then a small sigh. Ten feet away, the darkness moved. He saw the pale glimmer of hands, then of a face, turning their way.

Then the moon tore itself free from cloud and the rock was flooded with light. It was all Murray could do not to put his hands up in surrender. It was impossible they wouldn't be seen, the man was virtually standing on him. He willed the rock to yield and swallow him up but it didn't. He lay with his heart hammering, saw the moon shadow sweep across the rock towards him.

A crunch, then another. He looked up cautiously and heard rather than saw the man disappear to their right, in the direction of the river. Alasdair slithered swiftly over the top of the outcrop and down into a hollow where Murray joined him.

'I can't believe he didni see us,' he whispered.

'Look behind you, but close one eye first.'

Murray looked. In the distance below were the street lights of the town.

'That's why,' Alasdair said. 'Spoiled his night vision.'

'Did you smell him, eh? Talcum powder?'

'Coal Tar soap,' Alasdair said. 'And he'd had a ciggie. He wouldn't smell anything with that up his nose. These guys just ain't trained.'

Murray found his upper arm and squeezed it through the jacket.

'I take it all back. You're a genius, Mr Sutherland.'

A flash of teeth.

'Everyone's got to be good at something. We can move faster now. That was their first line of defence.'

From then on they moved at a rapid, scuttling crouch. At first it was a relief after the crawling, but soon Murray's upper thighs were burning. Still he followed on, glancing up and understanding that they had to keep below the skyline. When the moon came out, it was time to drop down and check the compass, then wait till it was dark again and push on.

Gradually Murray became aware of a sound like a light breeze through the heather. But there was no breeze to speak of. It was the river. Not just the river, but the unmistakable wallop and grumble and swoosh of many small falls. Then he could smell it. He'd forgotten water had a smell, and then a faint sweetness of trees.

He smiled to himself, wishing Tricia was here to share it all. He hadn't felt so alive for years, nor his senses so alert. It was like being a wean again, so close to the ground and so in touch.

He caught up with Alasdair and tapped him on the shoulder.

'What's wrong?'

'Nothing. Magic, isn't it?'

Alasdair's teeth shone white.

'The world's your playground, matey, if you look at it like that.'

'I dinni.'

'I know. Poor sod that you are . . .'

Finally the ground became bare and there was no cover. Then it dipped sharply on the right and the river was white and loud below them.

'Careful here. I'll go first.'

Alasdair faced in and worked down the slope, grasping clumps of heather and feeling with his feet. Then he was on a ledge of wet rock next to the river rushing by him. He glanced at his watch. Maybe fifty minutes till first light.

Murray was beside him and already pulling off his clothes to change into the wet suit. Then they both buckled on climbing harnesses, tied in to the rope, then looked up ahead.

The gorge proper started in darkness where the side walls rose. The waterfall was a series of drops and pools and swirling channels pouring down out of the night. Somewhere up there was the Mid Pool, the one Murray had been lying on his stomach looking down at years ago when two muscular gamies had manhandled him away.

'Can you manage this, little 'un?' Alasdair said. 'You could get half drowned in there.'

'I'll get there if I have tae grow gills,' he said grimly. 'Just mind ma wife wants tae see me again.'

'Then you're a lucky man.'

So Alasdair set off. He shuffled along the ledges, then they abruptly gave out. There was nothing for it but the left-hand wall. He ran his hands over the rock, not liking it one bit. Wet and slippery, not much off the vertical.

He adjusted his head torch in case he was forced to risk it, gave a tug on the rope to let Murray know he was going up.

Grimacing with distaste, he put a couple of fingers to one ledge and found the beginnings of a hand-jam in a whisper of a crack on the right, and slowly levered himself up into the darkness above the foaming Alt na Harrie.

He did not like this. He definitely did not like it. He couldn't see properly, he couldn't put in belay runners because of Murray, the moisture from the fall cancelled out any adhesion from his rock boots. He'd no protection at all, and if he fell into that river he was in real trouble.

So he tried to stay as little above the river as possible and just traverse, but the logic of the wall kept driving him up and up. The lower sections quickly became overhung, cut out by the force of the water. The top was crumbly and anyway if he stuck his head over there was a real chance of being spotted by anyone waiting at the head of the gorge.

It has to be said that Alasdair Sutherland had unshakeable confidence in his abilities. He had also, for all his careless bravado, a clear grasp of his limits. That was why he had survived several Himalayan trips and more years in Scotland and the Alps than he cared to count, when far too many of his friends were dead. He didn't mind putting on the style for other people – though it never fooled Jane – but he never kidded himself.

Now he was worried. He wasn't a rock specialist. He was good, but nothing on the whiz-kids around these days, though you seldom see their stripy tights on dripping walls in forbidden Highland estates by night.

With one toe in a lay-back crack that was going nowhere fast, he took a chance and switched on his head torch and took a closer look at what was ahead, and then wished he hadn't.

He studied the bulge. It was smooth as glass. No way of getting above it, doubtful if he could down-climb and get past it that way. The good news was a fairly sturdy rowan growing out of a crack at the far side of the bulge. The bad news was that even if he had an ape factor of plus ten, there was no way he could reach it.

He had to do something fairly unorthodox. Something much too unorthodox for him ever to recommend it to his clients. It was too whacky to recommend even to himself. He'd done something like it once before when his life had depended on it. Maybe it did again.

He reached as far up and across as he could, took a nut from his climbing rack and diddled into a niche just above the bulge.

He tested that nut several times, pulling on the sling from different angles.

Then he clipped into the sling and felt secure enough to reach back into his pack and finger out a short length of rope he'd put there just in case.

He passed the rope through the sling, knotted the ends and clipped that to his harness. Then he unclipped the main rope from the sling, and pulled himself some ten feet of slack from the patient Murray paying out the rope worlds away.

This was really crazy.

'You are really crazy,' he muttered.

It was a pity, he thought, that Jane never saw him climbing at the edge. It was the only thing he *was* much good at.

He inched back to his left and up on two horribly chancy moves. Now he was level with, and some six feet to the left of the nut. He fixed the rowan in his torch beam. Nine feet? Ten?

With a wordless shout he let go and pendulumed down and across.

He caught the rowan trunk with his outstretched hand, whapped his other hand round it and hung there a moment. He swung his feet up, hooked them round the tree, used a free hand to wrap a sling round and clipped in. Working on adrenalin, he untied the emergency rope, pulled it through, then set up an abseil and lowered himself over a short overhang to the safety of the ledge he'd spotted.

He stood there for a moment with his head bowed against the damp rock wall. Then he looked up. The sky was getting lighter and there was no time for emotional indulgence.

He undid the abseil, set up a belay, then tugged down the rope to Murray and waited for him to start coming on up the river as best he could.

It took a long time and several sudden worrying jerks on the rope. Finally Murray came crawling out of the near-darkness, poked his head up through a flurry of water and with quivering legs stood just feet below him.

'Hello, Ratty!'

'Go eff yourself, Moley!'

Murray was drenched as an otter, a bad cut above his eye, and the wet suit was ripped across his shoulders. He bent over and vomited water and whatever else was left in his stomach.

'That's the worst of it! We'll press on before it gets light.'

Murray nodded dully.

'You OK?'

More curses called down on Alasdair Sutherland and every bastern Highland river that ever flowed.

'I'll take that as a yes.'

Through more retching, he was told how he could take it.

Undaunted, Alasdair set off along the ledge, moving much more easily now. Finally he got down to boulders at the edge of the current and scrambled his way along and up them. He came at last to a big boss of rock where the river poured in one smooth fall, edged his way up the side grabbing anything that came to hand, and finally pulled himself gasping round the corner and flopped down at the edge of a dark pool. He lowered his face into the water and drank deeply.

They had arrived.

7

The light didn't do anything so dramatic as break that morning. It was more as if somewhere up in the gantry of the hills, a giant hand slowly pushed a lighting rheostat from closed to open. Ten minutes earlier, when Neil had taken up his position on the lookout knoll, the hillside opposite was just a sensed bulk. Then the slope appeared, the road, the fence, a mirk still lingering where the gorge must be.

He heard the day's first woodpigeon in the trees below. The harsh rattle and thrash of a pheasant. He picked out the Land Rover by the dirt-road entrance, looked for the two men but couldn't spot them. He reached for a sandwich and when he looked again there was colour in the grey, dabs of green on the lower slopes, dim purple drifting over the heather on the upper ground. The curved moon was floating into a pale gash in the sky above the hills.

Some enchanted morning . . . It was a rather more sophisticated effect than those he and Kirsty had sat in the van reminiscing about from their musicals days. He smiled to himself, sure that she, like him, would have found the setting moon a little over-the-top.

What had Murray said about catching a salmon? 'Sometimes they go for the fly though they're no hungry, like a memory of when they used tae feed.'

Aye, well. He checked his watch, then switched on the walkie-talkie and pressed the transmit button.

'Fish three to little fish four. Are you receiving me? Come in please.'

'In position, old pike. Staying tuned. Over, out.'

Neil put down the radio. Alasdair had emphasized they had to keep transmission short, to lessen the chance of anyone else cutting in on them. He picked up the binoculars, found the trees at the top of the gorge, then the intervening slope that hid the lower reaches. Sooner or later, one or two men should appear over it. More than two meant trouble.

The radio crackled.

'Fish two to fish three. Come in please. Over.'

Alasdair's voice was half drowned by the rush of water in the background.

'Fish three receiving you. We're in place. Are you? Over.'

'Both in position. Fish one about to commence. No problems. In fact everything's A-OK, old sport. Stay tuned. Out.'

Neil laid the radio beside him in the grass. All he could do for now was wait, licking chill dew from his fingers.

In her car, Kirsty hugged the radio to her chest and pulled the travelling rug up to her chin. Alasdair Sutherland was a lamb in wolf's clothing. And he'd done what he said he could do. Now it was up to Murray. She'd faith in him just from the calm, precise way he'd prepared casts and strapped up his rod. He had these amazing forearms, red-gold-haired and muscled – from serving his time as a cooper, Neil had said. Not a bundle of laughs but solid and sardonic, the kind of person who'd carry through whatever he was up to.

And Neil? Could he deliver? She thought of his face in the green dashboard glow. Dark and bony, the high cheekbones and long mouth – surely a Celt for all his East Coast origins.

He hadn't asked many personal questions and she'd appreciated that. Hadn't volunteered much himself. Despite that they'd been chatting away quite the thing, mostly about music, then he seemed to lose interest and was silent for ages, smoking and leaning against his door of the van and looking out into the night. One moment she'd felt herself reeling him in, nicely in control, and the next he was off the hook and away. Irritating. Up here men tended to slobber over her like Charlie. A few played it cool. Some tried to impress. And one or two simply didn't take to her. But he was none of these. He just smiled a little, glanced away, then returned with a look as thoughtless as afternoon.

She blinked away Lachie closing the door behind him.

And who was this Helen that Murray had let slip? What was it about Jane?

This was not the time or place. She huddled deeper into the travelling rug and bided her time.

* * *

'What d'you want me to do?'

Murray finished towelling his hair dry, then pulled on the deerstalker. It went strangely with the torn wet suit.

'Feed me some chocolate then stay out of ma way.'

Murray crouched at the edge of the pool, not taking his eyes from the water as he swiftly jointed the rod, miraculously still unbroken. He clipped in the reel, pulled the line through.

'Cast box.'

'Cast box, sah.'

Murray hesitated over the different casts, glancing at the pale light, the smooth and ruffled surface of the water.

'Wouldn't this be easier with a spinner?' Alasdair asked.

'Uh-huh. Easier still with a worm. This is ideal for worming.'

'But it wouldn't be good form?'

Murray glanced at him and flickered his first smile for several hours.

''Fraid not. Not good style, pal.'

'That's it, then.'

'Aye.'

(Good style. Good form. Not right. Not on. True poaching, like climbing, is an intricate, artificial game. If you want to get to the top of a hill, why not walk up the easy way? If you want a fish, go to the fish shop.

The game depended on self-imposed rules and restrictions. Exactly what those rules were was argued about frequently and sometimes heatedly, those weeks in August. Each of them had different views on the details, but they all accepted there was a right way and a wrong way and the difference mattered. They could break the law, but they mustn't cheat. That solidarity across differences still warms me as I think on that summer.)

Murray followed his first instinct and tied the single Stoat's Tail cast to his line.

He stood up, feeling cold and stiff and bruised. He surveyed the pool from the little falls that fed it at the top to the lip at the bottom end where the water was smooth before sweeping over the outlet. The water was yellow-brown yet clear, classic Highland river. In the first light a slight haze hung over the pool like it was breathing. There was some turbulence under the surface. He sensed areas where there were rocks, the kind of places where salmon would rest up before pressing on to their spawning grounds.

'Right,' he said. 'Tell you what I'm for. Landing net.'

'Landing net, sah.'

'Extend it and leave it there. The problem's tae keep the fish in the pool.'

'If there are any.'

'If I hook wan and it goes over the edge there,' Murray continued, 'I'll lose it for sure. Weight of the water, right? After the flurry when they're hooked right, they aye turn downstream, and I've very little downstream to play wi.'

'Why not use a stronger line and just heave the bugger in?'

Murray stared at Alasdair like he'd suggested singing 'The Sash' at a Celtic match.

'Don't tell me – not good form?'

'Not good at aa. Anyway, the hook probably wouldni hold.' He dangled his cast in the water, letting the tufts get damp and heavy. 'So I have tae *walk it up*. Soon as I hook it – rod upright, let no line out, be very strong. The reverse of the usual. Before it has time tae think, I strike and walk up along the bank – stay out of my way – to the top end where I've some room to play it. In theory, the salmon follows like a dug on a lead.'

'Does it work?'

Murray grinned at him from under the deerstalker.

'Once in a while. Did you bring the shades?'

'Shades, sah.'

'Put them on and climb a bit up yon tree. I want you for ma eyes. The polarized lenses cut out the water-gliff.'

'There's more than I'd suspected to this lark,' Al said. He reached up and levered himself on to one branch then another. He sat there in tweeds and shades and deerstalker, happily swinging his legs. 'Maybe I'll take it up when I'm knackered and past it.'

'Dinni wait too long then. Right now, ya beauties . . .'

Murray got to work. He set his line flowing with a few wristy flicks, then cast up to the top end of the pool. It looked good to Alasdair but Murray shook his head and went at it again, this time pulling back at the last moment on the line, and the cast kissed the surface then slowly sank a little as it moved down with the current. When the line had drifted to the outflow, Murray retrieved it with another flick, rolled his wrist and spun the line back to the top end.

Up his tree, Alasdair watched enthralled. He respected competence but this was more than competent. He hadn't seen that truncated Spey cast in years. Murray had next to no room behind him, and was flicking the line in and then rolling it back over itself and out again without ever stretching it out behind.

Time and again the fly landed in at the inflow as Murray worked his way along it. Time and again nothing happened. Alasdair began to get restless, then apprehensive. Ten minutes. Twenty minutes. If the ghillie at the top of the gorge decided to take a walk down the far side, they were in the bag.

The sun hit the top of the trees above them as Murray started casting directly across the pool. Then he tried the smooth patch near the outflow. Then back to the top end again.

Alasdair saw a rock move. A reddish rock seemed to waver and stir.

'Murray! There!'

Murray put his finger to his lips then cast where Alasdair seemed to be pointing. Al gestured again, signalling further out and nearer the edge. Cast again, a very short drift, then he retrieved from the edge. Again, slightly further out, letting the current swing it back in—

The line flicked as the salmon turned it over. Murray waited on till he was sure, his wrist flicked back, the line tightened and swung across the water while the rod arced. Alasdair nearly fell out of his tree, but already Murray was moving steadily up the bank, trying to walk the salmon away from the outflow fall, willing it to obey and follow.

And follow it did. Murray got to the top end of the pool and then the struggle began. Time and again the big fish pulled the line out to the edge of the outflow. Each time Murray, using every trick he knew, managed to turn it aside. He managed to retrieve more line, then had to let it go again. He wasn't sure how well the hook was in. He had to fish hard, really give it stick, but if the salmon hit that line too hard it would break for sure. Not a small fish either, and strong. At times the rod was bent like an n.

He must land it quick or lose it. Each time it made a more direct line for the outflow. What was fair means and what was not? He made a decision.

'Al! Landing net – bottom end! Now, you great gowk!'

Alasdair picked his way as near to the edge of the outflow as he could, reached out with the landing net. Not far enough. Murray just managed to turn the fish aside, persuade it away.

Alasdair crouched on the last greasy rock, stuck his foot out and at full stretch wedged it behind a boulder just below the surface. He looked down over the fall, only eight foot maybe but a hell of a tonnage of water.

'Al! Get in there!'

The fish was zigzagging back down. Alasdair clung with one arm to the boulder underwater. With his other he steadied the net then stretched out. He saw the fin, then the angry stretched mouth. Come away, my beauty, come away . . .

Murray gave a last flick, the big fish turned, Alasdair raised the net under it and it was in. Then Alasdair lost his grip and toppled head first into the pool.

'Fish wan tae fish three and four. Are you receivin?'

Kirsty spilt coffee on her car seat. On the knoll, Neil choked on his Twix bar. Murray's voice sounded calm and deadpan.

'Receiving.'

'Receiving.'

'The big fish has landed.'

Kirsty thumped the dashboard. Yes! Neil lay still, letting the feeling run through him from his toes to the roots of his hair as he reached for the radio.

'Yah star! Any problems? Over.'

A long pause then a chuckle.

'Fish two has been for a wee dook. In fact he's drookit. Looks guy queer in shades.' Muffled noises off. A spluttering that may have been 'Who are you calling queer?' Then Murray again. 'We're gonni bail out now. Be there. Out.'

'Beauty, eh?'

Murray held the salmon up by the gills. Not big, but not small either. Maybe ten or eleven pounds. Silver, brown, turning reddish along the back as the spawning season came on. It was cool in his hands, still flexing, a life from a different world.

'Photo opportunity, old chap. Smile, please.' Alasdair clicked the little compact camera. 'Now spread your hand over your face. OK, that's for Kirsty and proof for the press. Let's go.'

The sun was now full up as they repacked the gear. Murray broke down the rod, stripped the reel. Alasdair had been going to change into his own wet suit but there seemed little point now. He set up an abseil point, pulled the rope through and tied the loose ends.

'No point using harnesses. We'll just face out and whazz down with a hand on the rope. This should be a lot easier than coming up.'

'Aye, fine.' Murray wrapped the salmon in a carrier bag and gently slotted it in his pack. 'You first.'

Alasdair lobbed the rope over the outflow and the water carried it away. He grabbed the rope and lowered himself down the side of the rock and away.

Murray took a moment to himself. He looked around the clear brown pool, the rocks circling it, the trees above against a blue morning sky. It had been a good place, and he'd washed away an old grudge there. He smiled to himself, picturing Al in deerstalker and shades, toppling into the pool at his moment of triumph but still having the presence of mind to keep the net raised as he thrashed back to the shore. A good place. He'd carry a bit of it in him always. It didn't make everything right, but it helped.

He shouldered his pack, took the rope in his right hand and set off downriver.

Neil shifted uneasily as the two ghillies appeared out of the heather and converged on the Land Rover. They must be coming to the end of their shift and were waiting for their replacements. That left some of the upper ground clear, but if they stayed by the Land Rover, Plan B was impossible.

He pressed transmit and tried to call up Al. No reply. He hadn't expected one.

He trained his binoculars on the upper slopes and waited. Murray and Alasdair were thrashing their way downriver, jumping down over little waterfalls, getting soaked and not giving a toss. They'd landed the big fish and no one had stopped them.

They came to the end of the first abseil. Murray pulled the rope through while Alasdair set up the second abseil point. No need to talk, they'd done this before in much younger days and the old habits were still there.

Without a word Alasdair set off on the second section. Murray glanced up either side of the gorge. No one there. But the further down they got, the nearer to the two men patrolling the beat where the river curved and slowed.

He pulled the deerstalker more firmly on to his head, took the rope and set off down the falls where the sides of the gorge became narrow and high.

They might have got away with it. With Alasdair's patient

fieldcraft they might have been able to exit the gorge where they had entered it, and then slowly work through the heather, down the small burn and out through the fence where a green Wolseley driving casually by would have stopped for a moment, then driven on. To this day Alasdair insists Plan A was feasible.

Perhaps it was. But a restless ghillie on the lower beat decided to walk on up a little further to have a fly cigarette and see how the salmon were running at the bottom of the gorge. And at that moment Murray and Alasdair had come to the end of their second abseil and reached the point where they'd entered the night before. As Murray pulled in the rope, Alasdair had scrambled up the bank to check the slopes ahead of them, and so came into full view of the nicotine-addicted ghillie.

Alasdair heard a shout, then the whistle. He looked round and saw the man on top of the cliff at the other side, further downstream, maybe a hundred yards. Saw the arms waving, heard another whistle blast. He saw the man hesitate, and, deciding he couldn't down-climb the cliff and cross the river at that point, run off back the way he'd come.

'Murray!'

'Just a minute.'

'Forget the rope,' Alasdair hissed. 'They've seen me. But they haven't seen you, so it's Plan B.'

'Plan B? I hate Plan B.'

'So do I. You know what to do?'

'Yeah. Good luck.'

'See you at Pete's or in the cells. Bye!'

As Murray abandoned the rope and continued hurriedly downstream in the shelter of the gorge, Alasdair pulled himself up on to the skyline and stood there as if hesitating. He waited till the first ghillie joined the second. The second pulled out a walkie-talkie to contact the man at the top of the gorge, then the two of them hurried towards the lower river. Still Alasdair didn't move until he saw them halfway across and committed. Only then did he take out his radio.

'Fish two to fish three and four, we have a problem here. Plan B. Repeat, Plan B. Out.'

Without waiting for a reply he started running diagonally down to the right, aiming for the complex hillocks and beyond them the comparative safety of a Sitka spruce plantation. Below, the two ghillies had crossed the river and had started running to cut him off. Above, to his right, he saw another on the skyline.

'Right, laddoes, let's see how fit you are.'

'Did you get that, fish four?'

'I got it. I hate Plan B.'

'Me too. But it *is* more exciting. Out.'

Neil put the radio in his small pack, tensed for the off and waited. Two minutes later he saw the green Wolseley pass along the road below, heading for the fall-back rendezvous. He waited to see what the two men with the Land Rover would do. Everything depended on this.

One was scanning the upper slopes with binoculars. Neil followed their direction and picked out a tweed blur stumbling across through the heather towards distant trees. Saw the three ghillies converging from above and below.

After a quick consultation the two men by the road piled into the Land Rover. They reversed out on to the road and shot off in the direction of the spruce plantation, without stopping even to shut the gate.

Go. Neil got to his feet and scrambled down the slope, thrashed through the bushes and found the bike. He pushed it to the edge of the road and started up. The bike sounded terribly loud. Come on, Murray, where are you? *Come on.*

And then he saw a black speck coming out of the trees below the gorge, heading for the upper part of the dirt road. Got him in the binocs. Christ, he was still wearing the wet suit. But he had something bouncing in his pack, that's what counted.

Neil revved the bike, turned into the dirt road and tore on up the hill. He skidded and bounced along, torn between watching the road and the figure stumbling his way.

He did a skid turn and faced downhill again.

'Jump on!'

Murray was doubled over coughing. His face was cut and bruised and the suit was gashed, but still the preposterous deerstalker clung to his head. He got on the back of the bike and clung to Neil.

'Go, Johnny, go!'

Neil bounced off back down the road. He heard a whistle, looked round and nearly couped the bike. Two more men were running down towards the fence – one of them had a radio. They'd call up the Land Rover for sure.

He opened the throttle and they roared towards the entrance gate. They beat the men to it by twenty yards, slewed on to the tarmac road and went hell for leather for the rendezvous.

Murray glanced back and saw another Land Rover turn out of another entrance further down the valley. He shouted in Neil's ear. Neil nodded and bent lower over the handlebars.

The road flashed down into a dip, up a hill, beech trees on the left, the beginning of the spruce plantation on the right. He was already braking as they skidded round the bend and saw the stationary Wolseley facing in the opposite direction.

Murray bundled off the back of the bike, lifted the boot of the car and rolled in. Stray fish scales glittered from his palm as he waved then pulled the boot shut. The car moved away, a wave and the flash of a delighted smile, and Kirsty set off the way they'd come as Neil clicked into gear and revved the bike through a shallow ditch and into the trees.

Kirsty acknowledged the approaching Land Rover. It roared past without slowing. She watched it dwindle in her mirror, then saw another coming up behind her. She slowed into a passing-place and waved as it went by with a furious-looking Lachie at the wheel.

She carried on towards the village but for some time found it hard to steer straight for giggling.

8

Kirsty drove for Pete's cottage, taking the road as gently as possible to spare her secret passenger. She drummed the steering wheel and sang out 'Cock-Eyed Optimist' and blessed the bright day she'd stumbled on John Macnab.

She slowed as she approached the cottage and was about to turn off the road when she glimpsed the rear end of a car parked round the back. Then she saw another familiar rear end, Sergeant Jim MacIver peering in a side window. A deviation from Plan B seemed called for.

She straightened the wheel and carried on down the road, wishing Neil were there to roll her another cigarette.

Alasdair shifted fractionally as more pine needles found their way into his crotch. In addition, a few midgies were starting to find his eyebrows interesting. He considered the repellant in his pack, but rejected it in case a sharp-nosed gamie came by.

He heard another car go past on the road. It was maybe only a hundred metres away, but he didn't dare take the chance. Any factor worth his grouse would have left a man there even though the search party had failed to find their quarry in the wood.

He smiled despite his discomfort. All those knackering courses in the Lakes, in the Black Forest, the Borders and Dartmoor had been worth it. His trainers had done their job. He'd bolted into the wood with the ghillies only thirty yards behind, and still lost them. Cut back hard right, into a ditch, lay motionless face down as they thrashed by him. Eighty per cent of invisibility is stillness. Then he'd followed them as they cursed and hacked through the unthinned forest. When they turned round and beat methodically with half a dozen reinforcements, he had climbed the densest nearby tree with as little sound and disturbance as possible, and had the pleasure of hearing them go by below. He listened as one ghillie paused below his tree to inform a new arrival.

'Ach, Simon, yon ither wee fella has got clean awa. They'll baith be in the next county.'

Simon? Since when are ghillies called Simon?

He checked his watch. He'd heard nothing for nearly an hour. They might have given up. Equally they might have surrounded the wood from outside. He could wait till dark, but twelve hours is a long time to hang around in wet tweeds with midgies playing peek-a-boo in your eyebrows.

He squashed a few to discourage the others and decided to think abut it a bit longer.

Trying not to think like a wanted man, Neil walked across the car park of the Atholl Hotel with the radio under his jacket. After leaving the bike and shoulder-bag with the tweeds and helmet in the woods, he'd walked to town as if he'd been out on a morning stroll, not someone who had aided and abetted a criminal offence and had a fine time doing it.

Inside, he patted Mr MacPherson's muzzle, then leaned over the reception desk to unhook his key.

'Hi, Neil!'

It was Kirsty's pal, the barmaid-receptionist. She was standing in the narrow passage between the bar and Reception. She'd never called him by his Christian name before, and the way she was smiling made him uneasy.

'Uh, hi,' he managed and made to go upstairs.

'You're a bit of a dark horse, aren't you?' she said, still smiling in that way.

'Only when the lights are out,' he said and hurried up the stairs.

He slumped on the bed. He needed a bath and a few hours' sleep. Then he saw the note that had been pushed under the door.

Come down to the bar. Follow my lead. Congrats. Love, K.

Follow my lead? He washed his face and hands, quickly brushed any bits of grass and heather from his clothes, combed his hair and checked himself in the mirror as he tried to settle. Think. They'll know you weren't here for breakfast. You got up early and went for a walk and you know absolutely nothing about any big fish. You've never driven a motor bike in your life.

But he'd passed within twenty yards of the two men as he'd shot out through the gate. Still, he'd been in the tweeds and wearing the helmet with the visor down.

He made a face at the shagged-out poacher's assistant in the mirror. This was already more complicated than he'd bargained for. The town was too small, the same people kept cropping up, and they noticed things and made up the rest.

It was on the hour. He turned on the radio and sat for five minutes. Nothing from Alasdair. He switched off, took a deep breath and went downstairs for whatever awaited him there.

'Hiya, babe.' Kirsty squeezed his hand and kissed his cheek. 'Have a good walk?'

'Aye, thanks,' he said. 'It was . . . good.'

A number of people were looking at him, and none too casually. Kirsty's pal with a grin on her face, a couple of lads who had to be gamies, and the policeman from last night – a burly red-faced man with short curly hair, with his hat in one hand and a dram in the other and very sharp blue eyes.

'This is Jim MacIver, Neil,' Kirsty said. 'You remember him from last night?'

'Yes, of course. Hi.'

'Guess what? It seems John Macnab has poached the Mavor estate. Last night!'

'The poacher fella? So it wasn't a hoax.'

Kirsty shook her head. She seemed to be radiating delight and surprise.

'Did he get his grouse, then?' Neil asked.

'It was a salmon,' Jim MacIver said slowly. '*If* he caught it.'

'Naebody's caught a fish there in ten year,' one of the gamies interrupted. Neil knew him now – the ponytail and a row of teeth dangling from his ear, and dark eyes looking hard at him and Kirsty.

'Got away on a motor bike,' the other gamie said. 'Damned eejit nearly ran me down. He wis as close as I am to this bar.'

'That's never very far, Fergie,' the barmaid said.

Fergie acknowledged the laughter with a grin. Neil edged closer to the bar.

'Like a dram, darling?' he asked.

She squeezed his hand. Her fingers were very strong. Maybe he was overplaying.

'No thanks,' she said. 'I've got work to do, what with this Macnab story. It'll be all over the papers tomorrow.'

'So they haven't caught him yet?'

'Not yet,' she said. 'I think he's probably well away now. It seems he must have passed me this morning when I was driving on the back road. I wish I'd had a camera, that would have been an exclusive.'

Neil shrugged.

'Well, good luck to him. I hope he got his fish.'

One or two nods around the bar, a scowl from the black-eyed tooth fairy.

'You look tired, man,' Jim MacIver said affably. 'Like you haven't had any more sleep than myself.'

Neil looked at him, unsure whether to agree or deny it.

He was saved by Kirsty's pal.

'Aye, so would you be tired, Jim, if you'd been with Kirsty half the night!'

Laughter. Kirsty flushed nearly the colour of her hair. MacIver smiled, finished his dram and put his hat back on.

'I would that,' he said. 'Oh, and did you say you saw a bike on the road?'

'Not that I can remember. I was in a bit of a dwam this morning.'

'Och, our Kirsty would set any man dreaming.'

With that, Sergeant MacIver left the bar, followed reluctantly by the two gamies.

'There's your dram,' the barmaid said. 'And when are you moving in?'

'This is Shonagh,' Kirsty said. 'She's as much a friend as she is a blether.'

Neil shook hands with her over the bar.

'Then you must be a very good friend.'

'So where did you find this patter-merchant, Kirsty?'

Kirsty shrugged.

'The Lost and Found column. I type it up myself so I get first pick. Not bad, eh?'

'You've done worse,' Shonagh said. Kirsty looked down and for once had no retort. 'Take no notice of her, Neil. I hope you stay a while and keep her out of mischief.'

'That's not very likely,' Neil said. 'Here's to John Macnab.'

Kirsty stood on his foot.

'See you later, Shonagh. Me and Neil have a few things to do.'

'I bet. See you tonight?'

'No. I'm invited to the Big House. Posh meal.'

'With Aziz? I wouldn't let her go there unescorted, Neil. And he'll be fizzing since this Macnab poaching.'

'I've a feeling Kirsty can look after herself. Anyway, no one seems to know if this Macnab got the salmon, and if I remember right it's still to be delivered.'

'Well done,' she said. 'Sorry I had to drop you in it. Big Jim has sharp eyes and a suspicious mind.' She took his hand as they crossed the road. 'This is a small town.'

She nodded as the police car turned out of a side street, tooted and drove away on the road north.

'I'll try to stay in character, then. I'm the occasional boyfriend up from the south?'

Neil let go her hand as they stopped by her car.

'Something like that. You don't mind, do you? I mean, it's not a problem?' She looked at him across the roof of the car. 'I know sometimes I get . . .' She shrugged. 'Well.'

'I told you, I used to like theatricals. I never had the chance to play the male lead.'

'Me neither. I was always the female lead's best pal, part of the comic sub-plot, or the one whose fall from virtue brings the heroine to her senses.'

'Your place or mine?'

'Mine.' She opened the door. 'We've a few things to untangle before we can go on.'

'Yes.' He looked straight at her and beat a quick shave-and-a-haircut-four-bits rhythm on the car roof. 'Yes, we do that.'

She drove in silence up the hill. They turned a sharp, rutted bend at the top and there was a green-painted cottage with a rusty roof and a dog barking at the door.

'So you never got the main man, then?'

'Not really.' She laughed and shrugged, but not before he'd noted the tightening of her mouth. 'You?'

He paused.

'I auditioned for it once.' He stared out of the window as she came to a halt in the yard. 'I, ah, she . . . This must be Charlie.'

'How d'you know that?'

'Is he not bonnie?'

Once Charlie had finished slobbering and using his tail to sweep the yard, they went inside. Murray wandered out of the bathroom with a towel round his waist and a big grin on his bruised face.

'John Macnab, I presume.'

'Himself.'

He and Neil shook hands gravely. As Murray turned away, Neil put his arm briefly round his shoulders.

'Well done, wee fella. You done great.'

'Och aye, och aye. Thanks for wheechin me awa.'

'Great bike. Now tell us about the fish.'

Murray told him. The uphill crawling through the night, the man in the moonlight. Alasdair's climb. Murray hauled in up the rope like a hooked fish, slipping and choking. The pool at first light. The Stoat's Tail and the Spey casting. The bite and walking the salmon up the pool. Fighting to keep it from the overflow, Al's swoop followed by his plunge into the pool but still with the landing net held high and the thrashing salmon inside.

It was a story they'd replay many times, but at that moment there was a lot left to do and they daren't stop or they'd fall asleep from tiredness after being up all night.

Kirsty left to go down into town to write up the story and see a man about a fish. Neil and Murray agreed Pete's cottage had got too hot and must be evacuated. Murray dressed, and Neil switched on the radio on the hour.

'Fish two to base. Come in please, over.'

Alasdair's voice was quiet and hoarse.

'Base to fish two receiving. Over.'

'Come and net me, chaps . . .'

He gave the time and a map coordinate and signed off. Neil subtracted ten from the northing, added ten to the easting and wrote down the real coordinate, opened out the map and found the spot. A telephone box by a small bridge just north of the forest, with a few trees behind it.

'Let's go, youth.'

Neil drove the black van while Murray lay in the back under the blankets. There was no sign of anyone at Pete's cottage, so they left the van round the back. Neil kept lookout while Murray quickly cleared the place. This was the dangerous phase, and they knew they were pushing their luck. If they were seen now, they had no convincing story.

Murray did a good job considering his exhaustion. He left the place neat and empty save for one unnoticed hair-clasp and a squint mirror. Then he jumped into the back of the van and Neil drove cautiously on to the main road and set off for the rendezvous.

He stopped outside the phone box, got out and looked around. No one there. Four hundred yards down the road, at the edge of the plantation, was a Land Rover. He felt exposed and went into the phone box and picked up the receiver. And suddenly he did want to make a call, to talk to somebody, to babble and share his excitement with someone who knew and understood.

From the corner of his eye he glimpsed a tweed figure emerge quietly from the ditch and disappear round the back of the van. He put down the phone, climbed into the van and drove away.

It was late afternoon before Kirsty returned to her cottage. Her three co-conspirators were lounging in chairs grinning sleepily at each other. The table was littered with empty coffee cups, the only thing keeping them awake.

'I've talked to a few people and filed my story,' she said. 'And I'm working on a bigger one for the nationals. You've no idea what we've started.'

'Bit of a stushie, then?' Murray inquired.

'You could say that. Old Dorward's going crazy with the phone ringing all the time. If Macnab manages to deliver that fish, the hotels and pubs round here are going to do a fair trade in expense-account journalists.'

'About that delivery?' Neil asked.

'It's in hand. I'm going to crash out now. Will you bang on my door in two hours?'

She went into her bedroom and closed the door. The three men sat struggling to stay awake, occasionally cackling with laughter as they replayed another moment of the escapade. They talked in a desultory way about the next hit – the brace of grouse on Inchallian – and pondered a new HQ. Finally Murray and Alasdair fell asleep in their chairs. Only Neil stayed awake, smoking and thinking, with one eye on the yard outside as the evening sun tangled further into the trees.

He chapped on her door and got a grunt in reply. He roused the other two and they moved all the incriminating gear from the van into the lean-to behind the cottage. The black van was much too conspicuous, and sooner or later someone was going to wonder how come Neil was driving both a blue Escort and a black van. And if MacIver saw Alasdair driving it instead of Neil, he was bound to start asking questions.

They were still arguing about what to do with the van when Kirsty walked out of the bedroom. Gone was what Neil had mentally christened the 'Mountain Girl' who padded around in jeans and loose shirt and trainers. Gone too was the competent smart-arse Ace Reporter.

She stood in the doorway in a full-length grey crushed silk

dress. Over her bare shoulders she had a Shetland shawl. The dress was loose yet clung wherever it could, like Al climbing on Death Wall. For once she'd nearly got her hair under control, twisted up on her head and held in a jade comb, though a few red strands were already starting to escape.

She tottered slightly on her heels and winked at Murray. She'd made up to emphasize her full, amused mouth and cool, unsettling eyes. Neil noticed her long earrings were deep green and her nails were varnished the grey on a gull's wing.

It looked like her, but a different her. He wondered how many of her there were.

Alasdair eventually managed to gurgle that she looked A-OK.

'Don't worry, boys,' she said. 'It's only costume for a scene called "The Exclusive Dinner Party" – I could play it in my sleep and will probably have to. Wish me luck, and don't wait up.'

9

Kirsty's evening at the Big House. She claimed later that she remembered only flashes of it, that there were long gaps in between where nothing registered. After all, she protested, she'd had only two hours' kip in the last thirty-six. And then there was the champagne.

Particularly the champagne, according to Neil. He says that when she tiptoed in at first light and tripped over the settee where he was lying, and collapsed with her hair down all over her face and her high heels in one hand and a bunch of roses in the other, she was still flying. Squiffy. Stocious. Steaming.

Not at all, she giggled, and handed him the flowers for the occasional boyfriend. Drink had been taken, yes. But mostly she had been tired, and emotional. It had been a dreamy night, like being in a film, all heightened.

But what about the fish? Aziz? Had they pulled it off?

Alasdair drew back the curtains and let in daylight. She put her hands across her eyes and commanded him to close them again. Then she swigged from a mug of cold coffee, giggled again, looked round at her audience and asked them to picture it all if they would . . .

The gate was closed at the Lodge when she'd arrived. As she stopped the car a man appeared and asked who she was. She gave her name and explained she'd been invited by Mr Aziz. He checked, the gate was unlocked and she was let in, then the gate closed behind her.

Mr Aziz's orders. They were to stop a certain man from delivering a salmon to the house. There were men in the grounds round the house and a thousand pounds for whoever managed to lay hands on him.

She remembers struggling to keep her eyes open as she came up the drive. The sun was low and sparked glints in the house's grey stone. And Abdulatif in the doorway in a lightweight linen suit with his white teeth and black eyes and a slight sense of danger in the way he moved, and she knew she had to pay attention.

Then she was in the sitting room with the oak panelling and a peat fire in the grate. She had a glass in her hand and she was thirsty, so she drank it and he gave her another. Perhaps she imagined a subtle mockery in the moves he made. Like he too was playing a part, the wealthy, cultivated and ever so slightly predatory Arab entertaining a nearly young and nearly impressed journalist. And the way he looked at her, the way he watched her try to move and sit and be at ease in the unfamiliar dress. Trouble was she liked that edge, that intelligence.

'I hear you nearly caught John Macnab this morning,' she said. 'So it wasn't a hoax after all.' She took a deep drink. Nice stuff. 'I should warn you, Abdulatif, I'm here on duty as much as on pleasure.'

'Duty can often be a pleasure. I find this is so with my work in my country.' He topped up her glass and leaned towards her. 'Unlike you Christians, Kirsty, Muslims do not have a problem with pleasure.'

She laughed.

'I'm scarcely a Christian,' she said, though that wasn't entirely true. 'And I certainly don't have a problem with pleasure. And you,' she put her hand on his arm, 'shouldn't be drinking.'

'I have told you, here I behave as you and others do. In my country you would not wear this dress, though it is most fitting on you.' He held up his hand and really, Kirsty thought, he had most beautiful hands. 'No false modesty, please. We believe that beauty and pleasure are gifts given to us as a foretaste of paradise.'

'To pleasure, then.'

He clinked his glass on hers. She remembers that, the *ting*! and different aspects of his face and hers scattered in the crystal.

'To pleasure and beauty, Kirsty.'

'To beauty and pleasure and John Macnab!'

Careful, girl, careful. Think of your father. Beware of your mother.

'I cannot agree with you.' His eyes weren't black at all, just very dark, but his pupils were jet. 'The man is a thief and a trespasser, whatever you say of honour. My ancestors knew what to do with such people.'

'I'll bet they did, Abdulatif. But you'll have to catch him first.'

'We nearly caught him this morning. There were two of them, or maybe three. We have good descriptions and the police are still looking. Perhaps they did not catch a fish, and even if they did, Miss Kirsty, they have yet to deliver it.' He put his fingers lightly on her wrist. 'Believe me, I will have John Macnab yet.'

His fingers tightened for a moment.

Time seemed to fragment a little after that. They were standing at the big estate map as he explained how Macnab must have somehow climbed up the gorge – a rope had been found. The two men had split up and one had vanished in the plantation and the other was carried off by a man on a motor bike that in turn disappeared into thin air. The head keeper thought no fish had been caught but he, Abdulatif, was not sure. This Macnab was clever. What was her opinion?

She had said she knew very little about fishing. When were the other guests arriving?

There were no other guests. The rest of the houseparty had gone to Edinburgh for the weekend. So she had an exclusive. Wasn't that what she wanted?

'Very exclusive,' she giggled and sat down quickly before her legs gave way.

Then they were walking on the lawn in the gathering dark. She was teaching him 'Some Enchanted Evening', and pirouetting round the shrubbery. His hand was through her arm and the grass was damp with dew through her open-toed shoes. They sat in the summerhouse and shared another glass and she thought she could get used to this life.

She was telling him stories about her misadventures and scrapes in Morocco, and he was laughing and being indiscreet about his father and uncle and the King, and inviting her to his summer home on Mount Toubkal, and then somehow they were talking about sex.

Then she was wandering the corridors of the house, doors opening on to room after room. The bedrooms, ten of them. In two, a fire was burning in the grate and the beds were turned down and they looked so inviting. In case she wanted to stay the night. She looked tired, perhaps she wanted to rest awhile?

Not at all, she said, and set off determinedly in the direction of the sitting room, which she reckoned was a few blocks east of here.

And then she was helping him close the sitting-room curtains, and then – though she did not tell the others this, only Jane, much later – she was kissing him or he was kissing her. In any case, kissing was going on and it was really very heady and interesting, though she wasn't too keen on the moustache.

And then there was a knock at the door and Abdulatif said something in Arabic or Berber and she was walking into a small dining room. A glittering table was laid for two, all candles and silver and white. The lads from the restaurant were laying out big covered dishes on two heated trolleys, and a middle-aged Berber woman she'd never seen before and never saw again after that night was pouring wine.

And then there was just her and Abdulatif and she was standing beside him as he lifted the shiny silver covers off one dish after another. Gazpacho. Warm salad. Tiny goujons of sole. Dark roast pheasant stuffed with chestnut and wild mushrooms. Roasted vegetables. Suddenly she felt very hungry. She needed to eat, then she'd be all right.

He lifted the lid off the last big dish and there was a whole uncooked salmon with a fly still in its pouting mouth, and propped against it a white card and on the card, written with a flourish, *With the compliments of John Macnab.*

'So how did he take it?' Neil asked.

'C'mon, Kirsty,' Murray said. 'Dinni hold out on us.'

She lay wilted on the settee with a mug of water in one hand and a coffee in the other. Her eyes were closed. Her head nodded forward and she seemed a sleepy child come home after a party, and Neil had to find something else to look at.

She lifted her head, pushed back her hair and opened her eyes.

For maybe five seconds Abdulatif had stood there. He said something in Arabic. Then he looked at her without expression, and back at the fish.

'Looks like you got more than you ordered,' she said. 'I'm afraid I can't eat raw fish.'

'No,' he said vaguely. 'I suppose not.' He picked up the card and examined it, then put it carefully in his breast pocket.

'So Mr Macnab has won,' he said. 'Perhaps we can eat now. But first I must make two phone calls. Excuse me.'

Her heart rate gradually slowed and her head cleared as they ate the meal. She drank wine and water glass for glass as they ate and talked. She did most of the talking; he seemed to have withdrawn into his own thoughts.

Was he going to pay the wager? Of course, he was a man of

honour. He wrote a cheque out in front of her, put it in an envelope that he slipped into his pocket. Still, he would like to whip the scoundrel.

She put her hand gently on his arm. 'Come on, Abdulatif, you can do better than that.'

He looked at her for a long time, then nodded.

'You are right, Kirsty.' He put his hand over hers. 'I will do better.'

And he almost smiled before changing the subject. They talked the rest of the meal away, and then they were back in the sitting room and there was music and Arabic coffee with cardamom and rosewater, and she kept fading then coming back to herself, and there was more peat on the fire and another glass and the skin on the back of his hands was brown and smooth and sweet as Drambuie, and she asked for another glass of iced water because she hadn't made up her mind yet.

'Mind up about what?' Alasdair asked.

'No wonder you've problems wi Jane,' Murray told him. 'So what happened then?'

There was talk, lots of talk. And laughter. And silences, long silences with his fingers moving between hers as she stared into the fire.

And then they were going upstairs, round and round all the way up on to the flat roof of the tower. It was beautiful up there, all the stars out and the night wind waking her up, and the dark humped hills smelling sweet and an owl calling. And she thought how different it must be to own all this, and she was humming bits from *The King and I*, trying to imagine Abdulatif without any hair and deciding she preferred him as he was but maybe without the moustache.

She leaned on the parapet with his arm loosely round her waist and sighed. Maybe for all the things she wouldn't have and wasn't – quite. Or maybe she was just sleepy. It really was time to go.

But he'd turned towards her and he had something in his hand. An envelope.

'What's this?'

'For you,' he said. 'It contains a cheque and a note for John Macnab. But I think it simplest to give it to you. Don't you think so?'

She stared down at it, then turned to look out over the parapet. He took her by the shoulders and made her turn to face him. For all his slimness he was very strong.

'You must think me very stupid,' he said.

She shook her head.

'No. Not stupid. Not like that.'

'I had a feeling . . . but I didn't listen. Until when you saw the salmon, Kirsty. You were the wrong kind of surprised.'

He clasped the back of her neck and pulled her in. When he kissed her this time he bit her lower lip once, twice. Then he let her go. She stood, hesitating.

'You have had your fun at my expense,' he said. 'And your pleasure. Now it is time for mine.'

She rallied for a moment.

'So don't I get to enjoy it too?'

He ran the back of his hand down her cheek, across her bare shoulder and lightly followed the curve of her dress down over her breast to rest on her waist.

'Your pleasure, Kirsty, shall be my pleasure. I assure you of this.'

'Jesus!' Neil muttered. 'Where does this guy rent his dialogue? So how did you manage to get away?'

She smiled up at them all but said nothing.

'You stayed and slept in the other bedroom?' Alasdair suggested.

'Don't be daft,' Murray said. 'She had a night of passion in the swarthy arms of her fancy man. Didn't you, Kirsty?'

She pushed herself up on to her feet and tried to look regal, mysterious and aloof, which is hard at six in the morning with bare feet and a crumpled dress and your make-up smudged and mind gone on a long vacation.

'I'm off to bed,' she said. 'Please put your flowers in water and don't wake me for a long, long time.'

She swayed cautiously to her room and closed the door.

10

MYSTERY MAN IN SAUCY SALMON SWOOP!
POACHING PRANKSTER SCOOPS THE POOL
IT'S A STEAL!
MADCAP MACNAB MAKES MERRY!

Kirsty laughed and picked up another weekend paper.

'The tabloids have decided we're cheeky but fun.'

'The *Telegraph* has us down as sixties degenerates . . . groovy!' Neil said. 'Pass us another scone, Murray.'

'Missed your chance, pal. Sorry.'

'What do the posh papers say?' Alasdair inquired. He lay full length on Kirsty's couch, stuffing his face with digestive biscuits and warming his feet on her back as she flicked through the pages.

'Al, change your socks or hang your feet out the window. Let's see . . . *Scotland on Sunday* editorial: *Macnab takes one against the head.* They approve the spirit but make law-abiding noises. The inside columns: *John Macnab – anarchist or agitator?*'

Murray threw down his paper.

'Read the high-heid yins press statements? Usual gutless wonders.'

'Give me a McVitie's, Al,' Neil said.

'Bit late for that, old chap,' Alasdair mumbled through the remains of the last one.

'The *Sunday Post* disapproves,' Kirsty noted. 'What a very strange newspaper. *Sunday Express: Secretary of State Hits Out.* "Wanton vandalism and theft . . ." Valuable resources diverted from the fight against crime . . . More police powers, no respect for law today and blah blah blah. Where do they find these people?'

'Here, Murray,' Alasdair said, looking up from the *Glasgow Herald*, 'are you a latter-day Robin Hood or a class-war thug?'

'Awa tae fuck.'

Kirsty looked up from the *Sunday Post*.

'Here, you're not in a Jim Kelman novel now.'

'You wantin tae censor ma language? Language of ma culture and class?'

She stared back at him levelly.

'Bollocks, Murray. You like making love with your wife? Then don't use it to curse with.'

She raised the paper again as Murray muttered something about bourgeois wankers but didn't take it any further. Neil smiled to himself as he pushed down the coffee plunger. It wasn't often Murray was wrong-footed. Neatly skewered, in fact, between his late-conversion feminism and an affirmation of his class as the repository of reality and worth.

He rolled his first cigarette of late Sunday morning, the perfect one, the one he kept smoking for. He poured the coffees and distributed them. Kirsty winked as she took hers and went back to reading and the room was full of sunlight and the day after, of coffee and tobacco and Alasdair's socks and wood smoke from the stove.

Neil watched his cigarette smoke unkink and rise. For a moment, nothing was missing.

'Here's a piece about Macnab as post-modern situationist,' Kirsty noted. 'Not in the *Sunday Post. Fiction into Fact and the Cult of the Derivative.* Fair maks yer heid birl, as Murray would say.'

'Nip,' Murray grunted. 'Nip, no "birl". Now here somebody's done their homework instead of blethering. Remarkable piece of fishing, the writer reckons.' He nodded. 'I wouldni disagree! Drawings of the gorge, photies of the local cop and the ghillies we gave the run-around . . . And a big fish on a dish. And our Mr Aziz.'

'What's he have to say for himself?'

'Landowner's statement and interview. Takes it well, honours the bet, a gentleman and a sportsman . . .'

'I had to lay it on thick,' Kirsty said. 'Egos to smooth, and he did let me take an exclusive picture of the salmon on the salver. That alone will pay for our operational expenses to date.'

'He describes John Macnab as "a most ingenious, skilled and energetic opponent." Skilled and energetic – any truth in that, kid?'

Kirsty hid her face behind the paper.

Charlie barked out in the yard and Murray dived away from the table.

'Car!' he hissed.

'Into my room and under the bed, you two,' Kirsty said as she went to the window. Neil grabbed the two extra cups and plates and hurried into the kitchen.

'It's Jim MacIver,' she said. 'Remember you've every right to be here.'

Neil threw himself down on the settee and picked up the nearest paper as she went out into the yard.

'Skilled and energetic,' he muttered. 'Bastard.'

Kirsty came in with Jim MacIver. He wasn't in uniform and had an amiable grin on his face, but his eyes were as sharp as ever.

'Good day to you, Mr McGillivray. It'll be raining later, I'm thinking.'

'Neil, please. I take it you are off duty, Jim?'

'Aye. Aye . . . Just a wee social visit.'

'Coffee, Jim?'

'Thanks, Kirsty. I see you've been writing in the papers about the Macnab business. And Mr Aziz has been verra helpful. Good, good . . .' He stood in the middle of the room, glancing round. 'D'ye mind if I use your toilet?'

'Go ahead.'

Jim MacIver went to the bedroom and opened the door and stood there a moment.

'Sorry, wrong room,' he said. 'My memory's not so good these days.'

'Too much overtime, Jim.'

'This is what it is,' he said mildly and somehow managed to go to the bathroom via the kitchen and the bedroom.

'I was just wondering about yon black van out back,' Jim said when he returned. 'I suppose you hired it?'

Neil was about to agree when he became very aware of the notebook in MacIver's pocket.

'I borrowed it, to help Kirsty move some things. From a friend.'

'May I ask the name?'

Kirsty bustled noisily between them, picking up newspapers.

'Whoever Macnab is, he's put this place on the map,' she said. 'It's all over the radio and TV as well. Bet the Tourist Board are pleased.'

'Sutherland,' Neil said. 'Alasdair Sutherland.' He saw, because he was looking for it, the almost imperceptible nod. MacIver had checked out the registration. 'Would you like his address?'

'Och, I'll not be bothering you. Thanks for the coffee, Miss Kirsty.'

'You're welcome, Jim. I suppose this Macnab will have moved on by now if he's really going to do the Inchallian estate next. So you can catch up on your sleep.'

'Maist likely,' he said.

He paused at the door and looked back at them.

'Pity,' he said. 'I've an inclination to buy that man a dram. Before I put him in the cells, of course. Good day to ye.'

Kirsty slowly closed the door behind him.

'Good thinking, boy wonder,' she said. 'I hadn't considered the van registration. Doesn't miss a trick, does he?'

As she went past she squeezed his waist. Neil stared after her.

'Time we got out of here,' he said. 'Things are hotting up a bit fast for me.'

She reappeared from the kitchen and leaned against the door-frame.

'I thought that's what you wanted, a little bit of excitement.'

'Like you?'

They looked at each other. It was like when she'd fenced at her last school. The same alert wariness and pleasure, going with the moves while trying to control them.

She was standing that near, he could feel the warmth coming off her. He looked away. Not supposed to notice. Not supposed to be aware.

'All right, you two. You're under arrest!'

Murray and Alasdair crawled out from under the bed, covered in several months of fluff.

'It's a fair cop, guv.'

'That's the last time I go under a bed with you, matey. Five minutes is too long.'

'Oh, I don't know,' Kirsty said. 'The homoerotic possibilities in John Macnab are considerable.'

'Hey, is she talking dirty again?'

It must have been round this time that, some four hundred miles to the south, Ms Ellen Stobo received her instructions. They were unusually indefinite even by the standards of the Department. The Department was four rooms off an obscure corridor that linked or separated the two Ministries. The Commander's office was marginally the largest and least dull of the four. He was marginally less dull than most in his position, though what his position actually was resisted all definition. Ellen reckoned that it was because no one had yet succeeded in defining it, the Corridor hadn't yet been taken over or axed.

He turned away from the blinds and told her something had come up in Scotland, and he was asking her to postpone her leave.

'But it's been postponed twice already, sir,' she protested.

He nodded and bent tenderly over his cactus as though the explanation was there.

'I'm sorry, Ellen. I can't order you to, but . . .'

She nodded glumly.

'I know, no one's job's secure. And there's my pension.' She stopped and ran a hand through her short grey hair. 'I can't believe I'm talking about my pension!'

The Commander nodded, though he couldn't wait for his. Ellen shrugged and resigned herself as she had to many things. Resigned herself. Reluctantly. Not entirely.

'So what is it?'

He circled back behind his desk and poked the grey file towards her.

'It's a lot of nonsense about some poaching.' She stared back at him, and he did look embarrassed. 'There may be . . . implications. It's in the file.'

Shaking her head, she picked it up and began to flick it through. She inquired whether this obfuscated gem came from Security or MI. The Commander looked longingly at his cactus. He had fantasies about Arizona which he'd never make the mistake of trying to realize.

He made vague hand gestures and explained – magnificently avoided explaining, she realized later – that it was quasi-official. A request. Close to the Palace. Balmoral, actually. In a manner of speaking.

She turned another page, read the handwritten note and the signature at the bottom, raised an eyebrow. She turned the next page and sighed.

'VIP Protection Squad's in on this?'

Goodbye to freedom. So long the long-planned ride the length of the Pyrenees trail. Farewell to the Camargue.

Yes and no. She had a watching brief. Interdepartmental liaison but, ah, unofficial direct reports to himself.

'Is that officially unofficial, or unofficially unofficial? Sir.'

That raised the first smile of the week. The sad thing was he seemed genuinely sorry for her. Which made her a pretty sad case too. Only later did she realize he'd never answered her question.

He made an attempt to be hearty, almost put his arms round her shoulders, then wisely adapted it to opening the blinds a touch.

'You've been complaining about being desk-bound, Ellen. This is a chance to get back in the field.'

Sounds like a cow at the end of winter, she thought. She nodded gloomily.

'It'll probably come to nothing,' he assured her. 'It's just that we, well, I . . . assurances. A watching brief.' He released the blind and went back to the desk, opened a drawer. Almost a smile.

'You might require some extra reading on the way north. I suggest this.'

He placed a copy of *John Macnab* on the desk. She looked at it, at him.

'You cannot be serious.'

He cleared his throat.

'Thank you, Miss Stobo.'

The 'Miss' was purely to irritate her. He'd started it after her divorce and refused to get his tongue round 'Ms'. She took the book with the file and made to leave. He coughed again.

'Scotland, Ellen!' he said. 'Magnificent hills!'

'Drizzle and midgies,' she said firmly. 'If God had wanted me to go up hills, he'd have given me a helicopter.'

The Commander's mouth twitched. He hesitated and she had the sinking feeling he was about to make a joke.

'I'm afraid my budget doesn't stretch to a helicopter, Miss Stobo. But I'm told mountain bikes are very versatile . . .'

She stared at the cactus. Surely it hadn't changed or grown in the five years she'd been attached to the Corridor. She reached out and touched it, very lightly. It keeled over. She looked up at him.

'I'm afraid your cactus is dead, sir.'

She beat a hasty retreat.

As soon as it was dark, that night they shifted their Operational Headquarters out of the Spey Valley.

Pete's cottage was hot and inquiries had been made at Murray's B & B. Neil and Kirsty would stay where they were – moving so soon after the Mavor hit would be suspicious – but Alasdair and Murray needed a new Op. HQ. Any suggestions?

The Strathdon house was Kirsty's idea and no one had any better. So she phoned her friend Eddie who was doing his two weeks' off-shore catering on the rigs. No problem. The key was under the big stone to the left of the gate. Make yourself at home. No one would call – everyone in the village knew when he was on and off shore.

Alasdair gave them the drill. Kirsty drove some ten minutes ahead in the 'sterile car'. If there were any problems on the way, police checks or even a roadblock, she was to double back a few minutes later to warn them in the 'hot van'. That was how Special Forces did it, and the IRA in their time.

Neil drove the black van, wincing at every headlight that came up behind them. In the back were Murray and Alasdair, the retrieved motor bike, the tweeds and climbing gear, the wet suits and rod and guns.

'We put all our eggs in one omelette,' Alasdair had insisted. 'Just one run and we're in the clear.'

Kirsty was driving ahead in her Wolseley. She relaxed a little as she crested the road and drove through Tomintoul and out of Jim MacIver's patch. She glanced as always at the solid Victorian hotel, remembering. The freezing panelled lobby. The bedroom with the gigantic radiator gurgling, and heaps of hairy blankets on the bed, their comfortable weight, and Tom's weight and warmth, and him singing and clowning around in the bathroom as scalding brown water spat into the boat-like bath with the plunger plug.

It had all seemed possible then. The straight life and the wilder bit out on the margins. Her career, the band, the weekend life of high intensity clubbing and gigging. And her father's starched agony and her mother's lush despair were distant voices she could drown out for weeks on end.

Like the time itself, it had been a bright bubble quivering before it burst, leaving only soap in the eye and an aversion to techno-beat.

She stopped at the outskirts of Tomintoul, pressed her knuckles into her eyes till she saw white points of light, then relaxed and let them fade out in red.

She wound down the window and let the night blow in. She longed to stop and buy cigarettes at the hotel, to walk into that lobby one more time and see if it was still the same. That had been their last break before he lost it and she went too far.

No. No more addictions.

Who would believe it if they saw her now, near tears at the edge of Tomintoul? Perhaps Shonagh. Perhaps Neil. But what business was it of his? She didn't mind him looking at her breasts and trying so hard not to look. In fact she quite enjoyed the power though he made no moves at all, but she wished he wouldn't keep looking for the person behind them.

She pushed the Pretenders cassette into the player, stepped on the accelerator, and soon was singing harmony to her beloved Chrissie. Stop all your sobbing. Missie Chrissie Hynde wouldn't be found greiting on the outskirts of Tomintoul.

Soon she was moving the old car nicely into the curves. Couldn't Neil afford anything better than his crappy Escort? Surely there was money in advertising. Not his kind of advertising, he'd assured her. Brochures and flyers, reports and jingles at best. Maybe he should get a new job. Maybe he would, he'd replied. Always maybe.

She drove on, watching her lights skew across the darkness outside. The ploy was still afoot, as Al would say, the run was not yet raced. In the end she'd outpace them all.

'This is an ace Op. HQ,' Alasdair enthused as they shifted the gear from the van into the house. 'Phone, no visitors, see anyone coming up that lane. Three or four minutes' warning.'

Once they got the stove going, the Strathdon house was perfect. A bit damp and peeling, stuffed with electronic equipment and diving gear, but a big range in the kitchen, and three bedrooms up the stair.

Neil stood at the door waiting for Kirsty to return with carry-outs from the pub. He could see the occasional headlight moving along the road half a mile away, and off to the right the first few lights of Strathdon. Nice pub there, she'd said. Lively social scene, interesting mix of folk, some good musicians. Eddie's a pal.

It could be good to live in a place like this. Be part of something. Sell the flat, move here and do all his copywriting work by fax and e-mail. Finally find the time to write that sodding book, rake over the past and then be done with it.

He pushed his hands through his hair and went back inside. There was a lost air about this house, for all its clutter. The photographs of children and the children's drawings, together with the complete absence of children and any photos of a woman, told a familiar story, one that always depressed him.

He was still muttering to himself as Kirsty elbowed open the door and loped into the room with an armful of booze.

'You are my sunshine,' she sang and stacked the cans on the table. 'My only sunshine. Cheer up, Neil, it's already happened.'

He thought it happened only in books but the woman really did lope. As in great tawny cat, as in hungry, at ease, as in free.

'The Second Hit. Brace of grouse. The Inchallian estate.'

Alasdair spread the map on the table. 'Owned by a Dutch consortium – right, Kirsty?'

She yawned and nodded.

'The head's one Maurice Van Baalen, lives in The Hague but the whole party's due over for the Twelfth. I'm trying to get an interview with him like with Aziz.' She glared at them. 'And no sniggering in the back, please.'

Alasdair blushed, and went on to tick off the outstanding problems of the Inchallian hit.

First, it was primarily a deer forest and there weren't that many grouse on it.

'Forest?' Neil said. 'There's no bloody trees at all. That's the biggest problem – no cover.'

'That's just what it's called,' Alasdair said patiently. 'If there's a hillside with deer, it's called a deer forest. There would have been trees once but the deer ate 'em.'

'Even less grouse now,' Kirsty said. 'Word in the village is factor MacLeish has the ghillies driving them off.'

Alasdair nodded.

'Our second problem – MacLeish. The real snake in the ointment.'

'Isn't that spanner in the grass, Al?' Neil asked innocently.

'That too! My uncle Benny knew him – MacLeish is a hard, humourless bastard and good at his job. Third problem is this.'

He got up, pulled the shotgun out of a pack and put it on the table. Neil picked it up, turned it over in his hands, broke it open then checked the triggers in turn.

'Nice,' he said. 'Beautiful, in fact.'

It was a .410, the lightest you could get. It would be quieter, but he'd need to get close.

Kirsty watched him, picking her way over some conflicting feelings. She admired competence but had reservations about guns.

'So you're the shootist, huh?'

Neil didn't look up.

'Used to. Among other things.' He glanced at her. 'Long time ago. Targets and clays, not animals.' He sighted along the barrels. 'And the moment I pull the triggers the sky falls in – right, Al?'

Alasdair nodded and gestured them over to the map.

'I'm thinking of getting you in from the north by night. But come daylight the cover's next to nil, and MacLeish will have watchers on all the tops. When that gun goes off, Neil's a sitting dick.'

Kirsty nudged Murray and leaned earnestly towards Alasdair.

'My, you do have a way with words, Al.'

He modestly smoothed his moustache.

'I know, old girl – though some say they've a way with me.' He looked up at her earnestly. 'I don't function well below twenty thousand feet. Like yaks, you know . . .'

While the others struggled with this information, Murray frowned at the map, found the boundary with Mavor to the west, considered it then shook his head.

'The getaway's gonni be south, right? Down . . . Maiden Braes. To the road here. Kirsty picks up.'

Kirsty shook her head.

'The ground's not good – steep, broken. You couldn't move fast on it, and there's the deer fence at the bottom. Lachie says it's patrolled twenty-four hours.'

They considered the problem for a while. Every so often one of them would start a suggestion then break off, seeing the objection. Finally Alasdair stretched and said he'd thought of Neil dressing up Dutch and infiltrating the shooting party, plugging a couple of birds and slipping away. But it was, he admitted, a bit dodgy.

'It's completely AWOL,' Neil muttered. He considered the map again. 'What's the worst if we get caught, Al?'

'Most likely we'll get a beating, then they'll charge us. And the beak will make an example of us for sure. I'll lose my, ah, association with Special Forces, Kirsty might lose her job. You self-employed guys will be OK, but I think Murray's Party will drop him like a hot tamale.'

Murray and Kirsty looked at each other and shrugged. Neither of them seemed too put out at this prospect.

'We'd look right eejits,' Murray said. 'That's worse.'

'Anyway,' Alasdair continued, 'a wee spell inside never hurt anyone – eh, Murray?'

They looked at each other. A challenge maybe, or a recognition.

'Have you two been inside?' Kirsty said. 'What interesting company I keep.'

'Politics,' Murray said briefly. 'A couple of times. Miners' strike and poll tax. I'm no ashamed of it.'

'It didn't exactly bring in the Republic!' Alasdair said. 'And you think I live in fantasy-land, chum?'

Neil saw the fist tighten on the table and Murray's face go pale.

'Hey, guys – John Macnab, OK?'

'Aye, right,' Murray muttered, and pushed his sleeves back up his forearms. 'Just keep the squaddie off my back.'

'Behave yourselves, boys! So what were you in for, Alasdair?'

'Youthful indiscretions, young Kirsty. Nicked a few cars after doing a runner from Gordonstoun. Got pretty good at it, flogged a few. And as for that other business in Morocco – long time ago.'

'Neil?'

He looked up from his glass.

'I was young, I was drunk, it was very dark. What about you?'

She seemed disconcerted.

'Drove the wrong way up a one-way street once,' she muttered. 'Story of my life.'

They seemed to have ground to a standstill. Post-op. fatigue, Alasdair called it. Murray pushed up his sleeves and looked at them.

'I'll take the bike south the morn. I'll bring up Tricia and the kids as arranged. They'll be good cover for the recce and they're dying for the holiday.'

'Joys of family life,' Kirsty said. 'Must be nice.'

Alasdair grunted into his coffee, then summarized the GP.

They'd take a couple of days R & R. Murray would go south. Neil would include some discreet recce work in his hillwalking. Kirsty had her own work to do, and once the photo of Murray with the salmon came back from the printers, she'd claim it had been posted to her anonymously (as in a way it had), and use that as a basis for a colour-supplement piece to generate more fighting funds. She could try for an interview with MacLeish or Van Baalen.

Alasdair would go over to his uncle Benny's where he'd retired, in Lochinver. He hoped to find out more about the organization of Inchallian and where the grouse would be at this time.

Wasn't Jane back from Chamonix yet? Kirsty asked.

Alasdair nodded briefly. Apparently she'd had a great time, had some really big flights. Even launched herself off the Brevant, seven thousand feet down to the valley. She'd gone with this Jean-Pierre, who fancied himself as a rock climber, and they'd both parapented off the top of that. In tandem.

Kirsty kicked Murray under the table and cut off his chuckle. 'She must be good at this paragliding,' she said.

'She is. Very good.' He sounded proud. 'She's even better at ski-mountaineering. She's done the Haute Route between Cham and Zermatt in ten days, and that's class skiing and navigation.'

'Pity we weren't doing this in winter,' she said thoughtfully. 'Do you ski, Al?'

'Not in her league.'

'And does she climb? With you?'

'A bit. Not often. We're just into different things. Maybe that's the problem . . .'

Kirsty reached across and put her hand on his arm.

'But you asked her to come up, Al?'

He frowned at the table like it was a particularly thick client.

'Not really. No.'

'Why don't you? More the merrier.'

'If she wanted to, she'd have said.'

'Maybe she wanted you to ask.'

He shrugged.

'Maybe I wanted her to suggest it.'

She raised her eyebrows in despair.

'I can see you two have your communication sorted out.'

'It's no use, Kirsty,' Neil said. 'They're both stubborn as goats.'

'But—'

'Drop it, Kirsty.'

She looked round the table. The three men avoided her eye.

Kirsty looked straight ahead as they came up on to the plateau and through Tomintoul.

'Nice place for a romantic weekend,' Neil said, and nodded at the grand Victorian hotel. 'Had a lovely one there once.'

'Really.'

He glanced at her, thinking how different she looked when she ran out of steam. Displaced and vulnerable. The corner of her jaw looked unhappy, momentarily defeated.

Projection. You invent her distress (which is probably your own) and then think you're the one to solve it. Desire's such a liar it would be better to stop listening altogether.

She glanced over at him.

'You all right?'

'Just tired and a bit confused.'

'Me too.'

'I know.'

She drove on in silence most of the way back. Eventually he began to sing quietly 'Life is Just a Bowl of Cherries', and after a while longer the corner of her mouth tugged up, just a little, and she hummed along for a bit.

She dropped him off outside the Atholl.

'Goodnight, Macnab.'

'Goodnight, partner.' She leant across the front seat and kissed his cheek. 'And thanks, you cheery sod. Sleep well.'

She drove off down the street. He stood and watched till her lights rose up the hill, twitched sideways then disappeared.

Neil lay in bed with the bedside light on and looked at the ceiling. Nothing very interesting there, just a number of cracks that made no significant pattern.

He began to relax for sleep by visualizing himself expanding with each outbreath, bigger and bigger like cotton wool teased out, more and more loose and insubstantial. It was a routine he'd developed after Helen. Insubstantial, nothing solid, nothing permanent. A bowl of cherries, nothing more. Sweet. Pretty. Tasty. Perishable.

Visualize the body the size of the room now. Drifting out through the walls, the size of the hotel. How light that would be. Now the size of the town, hovering over it like a fine mist, the wind blowing through the pores as the body drifts without harm through the streetlamps and hilltops, expanded so much now it covers the whole Spey Valley, the whole Cairngorms, the whole beloved country, the body so huge and light and empty it's very nearly nothing but never quite nothing for there's a centre somewhere that holds you together, so nearly nothing but not quite.

11

Neil padded into the bar in stocking feet, greeted Shonagh and sat on what had become his bar stool.

'Good day?'

'Another couple of Munros in the bag. Not that I'm counting.'

'Of course not. So how many's that?'

'One hundred and thirty-seven. Pint of that so-called Special, please.'

He gently massaged his feet while he waited. A few abrasions apart, he felt much better after a couple of days by himself in the hills. Not alone, it never felt like that, and the hill silence was never silent. His own heartbeat in his ears, that was real too.

'Shonagh, did you work in the Clachaig in Glencoe?'

'For a couple of winters when I was ice-climbing.'

'I went sometimes with – with a friend.'

'So you knew Clackmannan and Slide, and the Red Rope crowd?'

He nodded.

'Did a couple of routes with Graeme McGlashan when him and Jimmy fell out.'

There was a short pause, as there often is when people who climb come to names from the past. The small silence as we jump over the dead. The jump gets longer as we get older.

'So,' she said and leaned forward across the bar to him, 'having established your credentials, you want to know more about our Kirsty.'

'Well . . .' He buried his nose in his pint. 'Not really. I mean . . .'

'You were just wondering, like?'

'Aye,' he said gratefully. 'Just . . . wondering. Like.'

'Like her, do you?'

She pulled out a Silk Cut, offered him one. He shook his head and bought some time as he rolled one of his own.

'Yes. She's very . . .'

'Lively?'

'Aye, lively. Sparky.'

'Bonnie, would you say?'

'She might come between some folk and a good night's sleep.'

He took a light from her and returned her wink. He was enjoying Shonagh.

'Jim MacIver was in here. He thought it was odd you spending money staying here and not up at her place.'

'Maybe I'm loaded and old-fashioned.'

She looked at him closely, pursed her lips.

'Maybe . . . but she's certainly not. Funny she didn't mention you before.'

He spread his hands on the bar like he was about to play it.

'Well, she can be quite secretive. As you know?'

He glanced up at her.

'She can that. It's like she'd no past at all, or she thinks it doesn't count.'

He played through the intro to 'As Time Goes By' on the bar top before he said quietly, 'I think she's wrong there.'

'So do I. She does very occasionally get letters sent to a friend or something of hers. Someone called . . . Tarbet, I think. I'm not supposed to know that.'

He opened his mouth to say something, but she was called away to the other end of the bar where someone had the nerve to want a drink. He tapped away on the bar, missing his keyboards, trying to think.

'So,' Shonagh said when she returned. 'We've established you know as little about her and like her as much as I do. And she's very vague about you.'

He put his hands palms up.

'I'm an open book, Shonagh. Ask me anything.'

'We could start with the wedding ring Annie who does the rooms says you had on your bedside table.'

He blinked at her, opened his mouth, closed it again.

'Hell's bells, another customer. That's the trouble with bar work, people want drinks.'

When she came back he was still looking down at the bar.

'I'm sorry,' she said. 'That was impertinent. It's your business and I'll keep it to myself. Just don't ask me to approve.'

'It's not—' he said. She thought he looked quite grey. 'I mean—'

She stubbed out her cigarette.

'Like I say, it's your business and whatever you and her are up to, she seems to be enjoying it.' She hesitated. 'If all you want is a wee Highland fling, she's good at that. But if you want more you'll find it hard work. And I'll thank you not to hurt her.'

He took the lighter from her hand and relit his neglected roll-up while he considered her.

'So tell me she's not your type,' he said.

She winked and leant towards him.

'She's not my type,' she whispered, then she straightened up. 'Hell, I'm sorry—'

She hurried through to Reception and came back with a note in her hand.

'I clean forgot to give you this. A fella phoned through while you were out. Said it was urgent.'

Summit meeting Strathdon. Tonight nineteen hundred hours. Caithness.

Caithness, Neil thought. Subtle as a flying polo mallet.

Ellen strapped up her case and took a last look round the flat. Three weeks in Scotland, all expenses, part of the job. Think of it as a freebie. The cats were taken care of. Leave the curtains open. Sod the plants. Let the seat covers fade. Let water mocassin die.

She dried the last mug. The drying towel slipped from the rail. She left it there. It would be in exactly the same place when she came back. That was living alone, correction, by yourself. Nothing changes place while you're away.

She checked the answerphone was on. She put off the gas, the electricity, left the fridge door open. It wasn't bad at all. It was better than being married. She'd come to terms with all that.

Trouble was, the terms were never quite hers. She'd got a neat haircut that she hoped looked like Judi Dench at that age, but her opinion about the looming fifty wasn't relevant. Take it or leave it, that was the only negotiation left.

She stood at the window looking out at the graveyard conveniently situated across the road. She was fit, she was trim, she had no aches and pains, she had two discreet lovers who knew better than to bring chocolates. But whoever said you were as old as you think you are had told a great lie. It was in the bones, she could feel it. Age was in the mind as a heaviness of experience. It was in the mouth as a preliminary acceptance that things would never be that different, and in the eyes as a hope it might be otherwise.

The entryphone buzzed. She picked up her suitcase, pushed the little handgun and authorization down beside *John Macnab* in her overnight bag, slung it over her shoulder and took the lift down to the street.

(Eve pasted up a scrapbook from the newspaper cuttings Murray took. And the notebooks survive, along with lists, a few photos, stills printed from the TV Battle of Maiden Braes, Alasdair's campaign plans and a diary. And moments when the mind clicked like a shutter. Between the stills is reconstruction. Reanimation. Linking things that must have been with what might have been.

A lawyer once told me the most convincing alibis are the incomplete, imperfect ones. They contain areas of uncertainty, even contradiction. That's what's convincing about them.

I made up the bit about the water mocassin.)

Kirsty turned away from the Inchallian map and found herself looking into the kind of cornflower-blue eyes she'd only seen in gardening catalogues. Tricia was as thin as Murray was solid, with no discernible hips at all under the Indian print skirt, but the same air of inner balance, and an additional easy merriment. Her hair was long and loose; she looked like someone who saw no good reason to change her style from early seventies hippie. Even as they shook hands, Kirsty liked her.

'Pleased to meet you, Tricia. I need some reinforcements around here.'

'I doubt that. Murray says you're completely raj.'

'Is that good?'

Tricia put down her pack and pushed her hands back through her hair.

'Depends how he says it.'

'So how does he say it?'

'Mostly good, I'd say. Neil!'

Tricia hugged Neil as he came through, grinning broadly. She kissed his cheek. They were old friends, easy and long-standing.

A young girl came in, carrying a backpack and a guitar.

'Eve, this is Kirsty. Kirsty – Eve.'

'Hello, Eve. Glad to meet you.'

Eve stared as she put down her things. Her yellow hair was

long and straight. Her movements, like her face, were graceful and serious and calm.

A small boy pushed in the door, tripped over his backpack and burst out laughing.

'This is Jamie.'

'Hiya, hiya!' Jamie said and ran up the stairs still giggling.

Eve had wrapped her arms round Neil and leant her head on his chest, saying nothing. He kissed the top of her head. He looked up and over at Kirsty and she thought there was some moisture in his eyes.

'God-daughter,' he said, almost apologetically. 'Eve, I think Kirsty's on our side.'

Eve studied her until Kirsty felt self-conscious and an intruder. She didn't know what these people had shared. Eve held out her hand quite formally.

'Hello,' she said. 'Dad says you're gallus.'

Kirsty smiled.

'Hmm. Is that good?'

'It means you're a bit crazy and you probably drink too much.'

'Evie!'

Kirsty glanced at Tricia and shook her head, then concentrated on Eve again. She had to get this right.

'Your dad's a good judge of character, Eve. I'd like you to be in my gang and keep us in line.'

Eve looked at her, glanced up at Neil. She picked up her guitar.

'Aye, OK. But easy on the booze.'

The front door banged open.

'All right, the game's up!'

'Don't tell me – you claim your exclusive?'

Alasdair did the round of greetings, then sat down grinning broadly. A couple of days away seemed to have done him good.

'So where were the patrols? I walked up the path in broad daylight and caught the lot of you at it.'

'This is an innocent family gathering,' Murray said as he poked his head through from the kitchen. 'Get some sauce down yer neck while I get the scran going.'

Tricia picked up her pack to go upstairs.

'I'm afraid Murray's no the world's greatest cook, like,' she said, and Kirsty placed the light Geordie accent.

'But we give him lots of encouragement,' Eve added.

* * *

'That was great, Murray,' Kirsty said, winking at Eve. 'I'm only in this for the booze and vino.'

'Have some more,' Tricia said and passed the nearest bottle.

'No, thanks. I'm driving back tonight.' Neil waved the bottle away too. 'So's Neil.'

'Why not have another drink and stay here?'

Kirsty looked a little uncomfortable.

'There's not really enough room or beds.'

'Isn't there? But—'

Tricia looked around. Murray grinned broadly, gave a very small shake of the head.

'Oops, sorry.'

'Things develop slowly in this neck of the woods,' Murray said.

'Away and nip yer heid, Murray.'

'Bile, Kirsty,' he said patiently. 'Awa an bile yer heid.'

Eventually they sorted it out. Neil would sleep on the couch, Kirsty went in with the kids – 'Yes!' Jamie shouted – Alasdair had the single room.

Neil got up from the table to fetch the whisky.

'Looks like I'll need a bottle of muscle relaxant,' he said. 'I'm out of practice at couches.'

'And some earplugs for me,' Kirsty muttered. Jamie seemed incapable of doing anything at normal volume.

Eventually Jamie was persuaded upstairs with a bribe of two stories from his dad and a double spiral of liquorice. Eve, who'd been silent through most of the meal, scarcely taking her eyes off Neil, didn't want to go.

'I know what you want to talk about. I'll not tell. I won't.'

'Can she keep a secret?'

'Eve's silent as the grave, Kirsty,' Neil said. 'Let her stay.'

'You won't blab then, kid? Not even under torture?'

'Uncle Alasdair, I won't even tell my husband.'

'I didn't know you were married, Eve.'

'Of course not,' she said scornfully. 'I'm going to marry Neil. Aunt Helen said she wouldn't mind. She said—'

There was a terrible pause and no one looked at anyone. Eve looked like she was going to be sick or burst into tears.

Neil put his arm round her shoulder.

'Don't worry, Eve,' he said gently. 'Ask me on a leap year. How long will that be?'

It took her only a moment.

'Three years,' she said.

'I think you'll have someone else by then. Now – Eve's staying, so can we get the maps out, please?'

As she cleared the table, Kirsty caught Eve's grateful look and Neil's returning smile. That was kind of him, she thought. I wish I knew all that's going on here.

Eve won't forget that evening, sitting quietly at the end of the table while the adults discussed their Big Secret. The smell of whisky, wood smoke and roll-ups will always quicken her eyes and bring back that sense of being on the edge of the grown-up world, like stepping into a new, unexplored estate. Even as an old woman in an unimaginably different century she'll return to that evening with magic and loss heavy in her chest.

There were her mum and dad, their heads nearly touching over the table. Uncle Alasdair with his thinning hair and silly moustache and funny ways as he pretended to be a soldier. And Uncle Neil with his sadness and gentleness and understanding towards her, all thin and dark and blue eyes glancing at her as she sat forgotten, the man she could never marry and the man she would always marry, whoever she married.

Alasdair spread the map, opened his notebook and summarized the CI ('Current Intel., chaps and chapesses.' His eyelid flickered in Kirsty's direction.)

'What Neil and Kirsty have learned ties in with what I've heard from Uncle Benny. There's not that many grouse on the estate and MacLeish has had the ghillies driving most of them off. He doesn't mind where they go, but his problem is he has to leave some for the Twelfth. We can discount the bare tops and most of the plateau – no feed, no grouse. The heather's in the long valley coming in from the north, all the way up to the bealach and some more down the far side.'

'But that's a huge area,' Tricia said. 'Surely they haven't enough men to cover all that.'

'They don't need to. Because there's no grouse there. That's mostly deep heather. They'll lie up there in bad weather but they prefer to feed among the short stuff coming through where it was burnt the year before. And that's where it gets interesting.'

He cracked open another can and waited as long as he thought he could get off with before continuing.

'My uncle Benny's checked with a mate of his from the old days, and this is the glen MacLeish has prepared.' With a pencil he sketched a ragged oval. 'Glen nan Eoin. He's left grouse there for sure. But with the shooters and beaters, and guards up on the tops here and there and *here,* I'd say Neil's chance of getting in among them, popping off a couple and getting away is virtually nil.'

There'd been a long silence then. Eve sat quietly and thought it was like they'd just had a treat cancelled.

'*However,*' Uncle Alasdair said, and his teeth flashed under his moustache, 'there is one possibility.' The heads bent towards him as he sat in the middle of the long table like he was conducting the Last Supper. 'According to Benny, if MacLeish has concentrated the remaining birds in Glen nan Eoin, there's a fair chance some will stray over the col and down into pockets near this burn here, the Inch burn. He said it often happened in his time. And MacLeish can't scare them off in case he scatters the main body. You see?'

Alasdair looked round them all, caught Eve's eye and winked. The adult heads bent again over the map.

'That's a fair stroll in from the north,' Neil said. 'About twenty miles.'

'Fifteen. Now, because Neil's a fit young squaddie, he could manage that. We might get past the guards at night – as you say, it's a huge area. He might even raise a few birds at first light. But as soon as he shoots, he's trapped. MacLeish is bound to know about these pockets, even if he doesn't know we know, and he'll have stationed people on the surrounding tops. Frankly, I don't see how Neil can make it back out.'

There was a long silence as they studied the map.

'The shooter needs a hiding place,' Kirsty said.

'And we gotta recce Maiden Braes.'

Neil shook his head.

'That'll not be easy. MacLeish has got the heavies there. They've already duffed up two lots of hillwalkers. Says it's Aggravated Trespass and he'll prosecute.'

'I'll give him Aggravated Trespass up his retentive—' Murray growled. 'Sorry, Trish.'

Kirsty reached for the bottle, ignoring Eve's look.

'I've some ideas on how to deal with factor MacLeish if things get heavy. I'll need Tricia and Eve if they're game.' She lifted her glass. 'Let's get physical!'

Eve looked at her and shook her head.

'Gallus,' she said sadly.

The whisky and wine went round as they considered the remaining problems of the getaway and the delivery. Every so often one would start to say something, then tail off with a shake of the head. Eve sat very still and quiet so they wouldn't notice her. She was always good at that.

Kirsty stretched her legs and leant back from the table.

'You know poaching's the only crime where you have to demonstrate your innocence? And the powers of a water bailiff exceed those of the police.'

'Shows who the laws are made for round here,' Murray grunted. 'Bastards.'

Alasdair spread his hands and appealed to them.

'If there weren't stupid laws there'd be no fun breaking them,' he said. 'That's the difference between me and Murray. I *like* stupid laws. We need a totally brilliant GP.'

'I've already got one,' Kirsty said. 'She tells me to keep taking the pills.'

'Game plan,' Alasdair said patiently, ignoring some little sniggers in the ranks. 'Though we may need a doctor if MacLeish gets hold of us.'

'He broke Lachie's brother's arm once,' Kirsty said. 'A disagreement over a couple of salmon.'

A small, uncomfortable silence hung over the table like a cloud of midgies.

'OK, team!' Alasdair clapped his hands together. 'We recce it for the next couple of days with the kids for cover. Kirsty and the maidens are responsible for the Braes. We check out everything and hope to hell someone has a bright idea.' He reached for another can of cheap lager. 'If you do your research before you order lunch, something always turns up on your plate.'

'Rommel?' Neil asked.

'Monty. He won and so will we! I'm not prepared to accept we're a nation of losers.'

'A-bloody-men to that,' said Murray.

And then they started arguing about which nation each of them meant, and why fun was the one thing politics left out, and it turned into adult talk and the next thing Eve knew she was being carried upstairs by Kirsty, who turned out to be nice after all and easy to curl up next to in the big bed in Strathdon.

Seventy years on, old Eve will shake her head as she remembers. They'll be dust then, the rest of these people, myself included, dust in the moonlight that floods in her window where she lives in the mountains. And the ploy was a foolish one, but it's still possible for her to smile as she listens to their footsteps and laughter fade down the whispering gallery of her memory.

12

Next morning Tricia drove with Kirsty and wee Jamie to the south-west corner of the Inchallian estate, just along from the boundary with Mavor.

Jamie ran round and round Tricia's Polo as the two women looked up the steep, unbroken hillside. No trees, no evident cover at all. Instead there was bracken and thick heather down at the bottom, then steep grass with rocks, then a series of small cliffs and loose boulders all the way up to the skyline. Maybe a thousand feet or more.

Kirsty checked the map.

'Thirteen hundred feet,' she said. 'Tough maidens in those days. I suppose they used to run up it before breakfast.'

'We still are, but I don't see Neil scarpering down this lot.'

'We'd better go and have a closer look. Remember, we're just going for a picnic.'

They walked along the road till they came to the high stile over the deer fence. Jamie went over first, shouting with delight. Then Tricia. Just as Kirsty was stepping over, a Land Rover pulled up.

'Hey, you! Get out of there! Yon's private land.'

A lean, grey-haired man strode towards them. A broader dark man with a shotgun followed him a couple of paces behind.

Kirsty stopped at the top of the stile and looked at the face of the first man. It was bleak and hard as the land he policed.

'Mr MacLeish, I presume?'

'The same. Get down from there. And you and the laddie.'

Jamie grabbed Tricia's hand and half hid beside her.

'I'm a journalist,' Kirsty said firmly. Her legs were shaking. 'And we've every right to go for a walk here.'

'Bloody journalists! The estate's crawling wi ye. This is a shooting estate no a damn picnic site, and I'm telling you to get out.'

He was standing at the bottom of the stile, the other man right behind him. Out of the corner of her eye Tricia noticed two more men had appeared from nowhere, on her side of the fence.

'It's four days till the Twelfth and you're not shooting now,' she said. 'And stop frightening my boy.'

MacLeish came up the ladder till he was standing one rung below Kirsty.

'I can throw ye aff for Aggravated Trespass,' he said. 'You're shifting the grouse and I can use reasonable force. Which is what I'm going to dae right now.' He nodded to his sidekick. 'Jimmy.'

Kirsty glanced at Jimmy.

'He doesn't look very reasonable to me. We're just going for a picnic up in the rocks, and there's no feeding grounds here.'

'Don't be clever, girlie. My orders are to clear everyone off and that's what I'm doing. Now – aff!'

His grip on her tightened and he jerked her forward. She looked into his eyes, not a spark of humour or forgiveness there. God help your wife, she thought, if you have one. She tried to pull her arm free.

'Kirsty!' She looked round. Tricia was looking up at her, with the two men beside her. They didn't look willing to argue fine points of law.

'There's no point, Kirsty. We'll just have to picnic somewhere else.'

She pulled her arm free.

'Get your hands off me. I'm coming down.'

She sat beside Tricia in the car.

'Shit!' She thumped the dashboard. 'Jesus! Sometimes I see what Murray means. I'll get that bastard.'

They sat waiting for the Land Rover to drive off. It didn't.

'Is he right, Kirsty? I mean, can he throw us off?'

Kirsty sighed.

'It's a . . . grey area. Very complicated. Basically, there hasn't been a criminal law of trespass as such in Scotland. There's a traditional right of access to the hills. Not so much a right as no law saying you can't. But civil law allows them to protect their game, and to prosecute if you frighten the game or interfere with the shooting, because that's damaging their legitimate business.'

'But we're not.'

'As I tried to point out to him. That's why he brought up Aggravated Trespass from the Criminal Justice. That *is* criminal law and basically means you can be prosecuted just for being there. More or less.' She frowned at the Land Rover in front of them. 'Though so far in Scotland they've had trouble making it stick, because that means establishing ownership, which is surprisingly hard.'

Tricia thought it over. She looked at Kirsty.

'You seem to know a lot about this.'

Kirsty shrugged.

'You live round here, you pick things up. In this case muscle is nine-tenths of the law.' She thumped the dashboard again. 'Bastard! I'll not be bullied like that.'

'I don't see what we can do about it. Come back with the lads?'

'No, drive back to town. I've a couple of phone calls to make.' She put her hand on Tricia's arm and grinned. 'You'll see MacLeish squirm yet. I promise.'

Even with Eve for cover, Alasdair and Neil had stuck mostly to the stalkers' paths. The Inchallian estate had accepted the Access Concordat, a recent compromise between the landowners and access groups that accepted the principle of 'responsible' freedom of access in exchange for the landowners being able to place 'reasonable' constraint on that access, in particular during the shooting season. This appeared sensible. It was also extremely vague, and being purely voluntary had no powers to bring more stroppy estate managers into line. The struggle wasn't over yet.

For a huge estate, there seemed to be few empty areas. There was always someone up on the summits or where the paths divided, or sitting in the corrie's throat, or bustling down the track towards them. They were not hillwalkers, they were too purposeful yet erratic for that. Every so often there were distant shots as more birds were driven off.

Round midday the recce party cut up from the track and slogged up on to a long curling ridge of short turf and sharp quartzite stones dumped by retreating glaciers. The ground was dry and flecks of mica flicked the sun back into their eyes. Within a minute of being on the skyline they were met by a fit-looking young man with a shotgun, binoculars and a radio. He asked where they were going; and was told for a picnic and a first Munro with their niece. Eve tried to look as niece-like as possible while the man checked them over, took in the absence of guns and binoculars, and Alasdair's lime-green baggy shorts and Neil's unsuitable trainers and the unspeakable nylon jackets they all wore.

He nodded and told them fairly pleasantly it was all right if they stuck to the summit ridges and went back out along the track. But they weren't to go down into the Glen nan Eoin or any of the lower slopes by the Inch burn, because it was closed for shooting.

Alasdair and Neil asked stupid questions and received some quite useful answers. Eve chipped in and asked if he worked all night, did he sleep on the hill, did he spend the whole day alone? While they were talking, a couple of calls came in on the radio, the second sending him off to help drive some stray birds out of the next corrie, and he hurried away.

A useful little meeting, they concluded as they lay in hot sun in the lee of the summit cairn and looked across the great roll of the estate to the north. An observer – and most of the time they were observed – would have seen a charming if ill-equipped family group, a girl sometimes holding the hand of one or other of the two men. Sometimes she'd get up and stand on the cairns and look out in all directions. Or the taller, thinner man in the vile green and pink ski jacket would wander off for a smoke. The other man seemed lazy or tired, he spent time lying down with his jacket over his shoulders or the little girl beside him. Either way, it was impossible to see if he was holding anything in his hands. And after all, why should he be?

After an hour, Alasdair put away the miniature binocs in the bottom of Eve's small pack and they set off down the shoulder to the col that led in the direction of Glen nan Eoin.

A journalist puffed up to them with stories of how he'd been virtually manhandled away from certain areas. He was doing some background research for a story about this crazy John Macnab. Oh really? The family party had read something about that, though they were anti blood sports themselves, particularly the little girl who got quite passionate on the subject.

Were there grouse around to be shot? They hadn't come across any.

The journalist had seen a few that morning, in a hollow above the stream over the next ridge. But if they wanted to avoid hassle, they'd best stay away from there.

They assured him they would. They waited till he'd gone then traversed below the skyline right round Glen nan Eoin, hurriedly cut over another col and there they were, looking down towards the Inch burn. They sat down for another flask of tea with the girl half-obscuring the man lying on the ground. There were two pockets of short heather down there before the bracken began in the softer ground. Shouts above them, a man in tweeds gesturing them away. The family group waved back cheerfully and drifted on to the south.

In late afternoon they descended another slope towards the same burn. They were now below the pockets of short heather, aiming for the stalkers' track that ran east out of the estate. They scarcely twitched as a small group of grouse rose from the lower pocket and whirred low over the col.

Eve by this time really was tired but, determined not to show it, set off to run down across the slope. She was perhaps eighty yards ahead when the two men came round a small outcrop. They stood there dumbfounded. Eve was nowhere. She wasn't on the track or by the burn. She'd vanished.

The two men looked all around, back up the slope in case she was playing games. Nowhere. And there was no cover, just scrappy peaty ground with some long grasses swaying in the breeze and a tongue of short bracken following up a tributary.

They went further down the slope and began to call her. No reply. A little pale and saying nothing now, they started to cross the peaty ground and the bracken. Had she got to the track and somehow sprinted along it and out of sight?

Then there was a small cry, just an additional note in the multi-voiced gurgling of the burn. They stopped. There it was again. But it wasn't coming from the burn. It seemed to come out of the earth itself.

Neil shouted, waited. He felt sick. Another feeble cry. He walked carefully in its direction.

He was standing above a narrow slit between two peat banks. He went down on his knees, parted the grass and was looking down on a pale face. She was standing upright and muddy in what was almost a cave, a deep gash left by an old burn that had hollowed out the peat before it closed up again.

'I'm sorry, Uncle Neil,' she said. 'I was running along and I just fell in.'

Neil and Alasdair reached down and helped her out. She was muddy and shaken but unharmed.

'I'm really sorry,' she said. 'I hope I haven't spoiled things.'

Neil looked down into the hole. It must be six foot deep or more. He glanced across at the track, then back up the short stretch of slope they'd descended. He looked at Alasdair.

Then he put his arm round her.

'Eve, I think you may have done something wonderful,' he said.

The Atholl lounge bar around five in the afternoon is seldom busy. Neil and Kirsty sat at the table by the window and compared notes. He told her about Eve's slot. A big, big grin. She seemed right back on form.

'Things are looking up for us too. I think I've a fight ahead.'

She filled him in on the Maiden Braes confrontation.

'Are you sure you and Tricia want to go without us tomorrow? MacLeish could turn nasty.'

She laughed, turning the glass in her hand.

'So can we. No, this one's down to the women and children. Trust me.'

'Why do I think you're preparing another theatrical event?'

'You'll hear all about it tomorrow night back at Strathdon.' She knocked back the whisky and picked up her half-pint and smiled to herself. 'You might even see it.'

Then she accounted for the rest of her day. An interesting chat with a disgruntled Lachie whose dislike of Macnab had been overshadowed by his loathing of MacLeish. There was no way he'd ever work for him. He was happy to tell Kirsty everything he knew or had heard from friends who'd been taken on as extra men to patrol the estate. Quite a number of them, having been beaten on their own ground, wanted to see Inchallian fall as well.

Interesting. What about security round the Lodge?

Desperate. According to Lachie, a rabbit couldn't cross that ground without getting its neck twisted.

'This Lachie – he's the one with the dog's teeth hanging from his lugs, who looks at me with sulphuric-acid eyes?'

Kirsty laughed.

'Foxes' teeth, actually. Yes, he might be misinformed about our relationship.'

'You two used to—'

'In a bouncy sort of way.'

'He's a good-looking bloke,' Neil said.

'I've had worse,' she agreed. She squinted at him through the glass. 'It was nothing very serious. I'm not into serious.'

Then she'd gone to the newspaper office to keep old Dorward sweet, knocked off Fiona's Diary for another week, filed another piece on Macnab and insisted on the holidays due to her.

Then she'd phoned the Inchallian Lodge and found Van Baalen had just arrived with his shooting party. She introduced herself and made a similar pitch as she had to Aziz: a local journalist, now covering the John Macnab wager for one of the nationals, who wanted to get his side of the story. Could she see him?

Of course. But today? Regretfully, he would be too busy with Mr MacLeish. Why did she not come to the drinks party to celebrate the first day's shooting? He would talk to her there. She would see these Dutchmen were not so strange. He would explain the economic reality of owning the estate and she could explain why people would make this peculiar bet.

Yes, she'd love to come to the drinks party. Round five o'clock on the Twelfth? Could she bring a partner? And a camera?

She'd thanked him and said she'd try to inform him about Scotland and poaching and why people made strange wagers.

Neil watched her as she talked. The way a small knot formed and disappeared in her cheek as she smiled. How her mouth turned when she spoke, making that slight slur on the r. She was unknown yet deeply familiar. A pal. Not exactly slim, graceful and boylike in the manner of Buchan's women who were always fast on the hill, terrific with a rod and hated jazz and anything modern and over-sensitive. Chaps, really. Chaps with small discreet breasts.

No – and he had to look away – Kirsty was a pal, a good companion on a ploy, but definitely not a chap.

Kirsty got up, went to the bar. She plonked down two whiskies and a bundle of fivers.

'Our winnings from the Macnab stakes. Shonagh says her uncle lost a packet on the book.'

'Her uncle?'

'Owns the place.' She birled her chair round and sat astride it like she was on a horse, propped her chin on her hand and stared at him. 'Shonagh's asking if we want to go any further.'

'Does she think we should?'

'As the bookie, yes.'

'And as a friend?'

She grinned but didn't take her eyes off him.

'So what are the odds?'

'Eight to one we blow it. So?'

He put down his cigarette and shook his head slowly. She was never going to be restful.

'You look like a cowgirl on that chair. Next you'll be up on the table singing "The Deadwood Stage".'

A spark went off in her eyes. Like an opal, there were tiny green lights set in the grey.

'A fiver and you're on, Mr Maybe!'

Neil silently picked the glasses and ashtray from the table. Without taking her eyes off him, she stepped on to the window-seat and he gripped the table as she paused to jump on to it.

'Hey! Guess who's got to polish that table after you!' Kirsty looked over to Shonagh. 'Not "The Deadwood Stage" again, Kirsty. You mind what happened last time.'

Kirsty hesitated, then laughed, shrugged and climbed down.

She would have done it. He believed her. Anyway, he wasn't a betting man, though he did have a weakness for musical Westerns. Good, so did she. And what happened last time? Don't ask. She lost? She won. What's so terrible about that? She hadn't told him what the bet was. Don't even think about it, pal.

He thought about it.

'I'll put another tenner on Macnab.'

'Good man.' She raised her glass. 'You cannot win if you do not play.'

'Every silver lining has its cloud,' he responded. '*Slainte.*'

'*Slainte, m'eudail.*'

He looked baffled, but drank anyway.

Mid-morning the next day, Kirsty, Tricia and Eve pulled up at the lay-by opposite Maiden Braes. They got out and walked up the road towards the high stile over the deer fence. Each was carrying a small picnic sack. As they approached the stile, a man in tweeds came running down the last of the Brae.

Tricia put one hand on the ladder and began climbing. The man – MacLeish's sidekick from the day before – spoke into his radio and then ran up the other side and grabbed Tricia's arm as she came over the top of the stile.

'You twa again! Ye've been tellt – noo get aff. Aff!'

'Let go my mam you big – bugger!'

'You've no right to stop us.'

'We'll see about that, lassie.'

He put Tricia's arm up her back and began to force her down the stile while she flailed away. He released her and pushed. She fell down the last rungs into Kirsty and Eve.

The two women ran at him. Kirsty was not small and a pacifist in principle only. As he fended off Tricia, she thumped him in the ribs, grabbed an arm and pulled. Eve kicked his shins at the same moment and the man toppled off the ladder and landed, winded, on the rough ground.

For a moment he lay gaping up at them, then Kirsty took out her whistle and blew.

Then a number of things happened. Another whistle blew. Another gamie ran down to the stile and started climbing over. The first man launched himself at Kirsty, grabbed her by the throat and pushed her back against the fence. She kicked out, Tricia tried to pull down his arm. A white car pulled up and three burly people in Helly Hansen jackets, two with beards and one probably female, jumped out and ran towards the scuffle.

The fence swayed and bulged, one of Kirsty's boots found its target and her assailant turned white, hissed and doubled over. She started climbing the ladder but ran into the other gamie. With the Right To Roam three behind her swinging their placards, they might have gained entry, but a familiar Land Rover revved round the bend and slid to a halt. Three big men wide as their foreheads were low rolled out from the back, while bleak MacLeish strode over the ditch to the stile.

There was little discussion, no legal debate, no exchanging of precedents. This was physical quid pro quo. It was hands clutching, punches thrown, kicks and gurgles and the odd yelp. The scrum tottered back and forward between the fence and the ditch, part up the stile then back down again. Tricia clutched her head as the battle passed over her. Wiping mud from her face, she glanced up the road.

The cavalry had arrived.

A blue minibus pulled up and a number of assorted Right To Roamers and Ramblers' Associations jumped out and ran to join in. And they might have turned the tide, even with the committed pacifists standing on the fringes suggesting there must be another way of resolving their differences, until one party or another bumped them into the ditch. But then another Land Rover full of even lower scowling brows piled in and soon the scene looked like Murrayfield on a bad day.

The woman leaning against the side of the minibus with the TV camera resisted the urge to pile in and concentrated on doing her job, while the soundman fiddled desperately with volume levels. Close-ups and long shots, cutaways to new arrivals – she'd always wanted to film a live battle, and they'd show this one till the tapes fell apart. She was capturing in a small scuffle that revealing moment when Might vs Right disintegrates to Might vs Might.

She did a lovely pan to yet another car arriving, caught a red-faced man with thinning curly fair hair stepping out and with a grin lifting a megaphone.

'Gentlemen! Ladies! Your attention please!'

The scrummage wheeled and slowed. Fists paused, hesitated. Collars were released, hair pushed back out of the eyes.

Jim MacIver lowered the megaphone and ambled over.

'Thank you,' he said mildly. He looked over them all. 'I've seen a better fight at a shinty match. Mr Salmond, will you please let go that beard. Thank you. Young lady, would you put down that stick.'

MacIver went up to MacLeish and Kirsty as they still pushed and shoved each other at the foot of the stile.

'Sergeant, will you arrest these . . . people?'

'And why would I be doing that, Mr MacLeish?'

MacLeish panted and stared at him.

'They are trespassing on the estate.'

'Indeed they are not. The question seems to be – will you allow them on to the estate?'

'We only came for a picnic,' Kirsty said. 'Me and her and the girl.'

'Haivers!' said MacLeish. 'I warned them yesterday. They have come to disrupt the shooting.'

'There's no shooting till the Twelfth,' Tricia said scornfully.

'And there's no grouse on this side of the hill,' Kirsty added. There were shouts of 'Freedom to roam! Rights of access!'

'It's Malicious and Aggravated Trespass! And this is called reasonable force!'

MacLeish grabbed Kirsty as she tried to shin up the ladder.

'Get off me, you Presbyterian shite.'

'*Stop that!*' MacIver thundered. 'I'll have no language here. And I'll remind you, Miss Kirsty, I'm an elder of the Free Kirk.'

'Sorry, Jim.'

Kirsty struggled to climb the ladder, MacLeish clung on to her.

'Sergeant, I'm insisting you stop this stramash.'

'Indeed I will. Unhand her, Mr MacLeish. You'll no be breaking anyone's arm here.'

'But these people cannot—'

Jim MacIver put his large hand on the factor's shoulder.

'Mr MacLeish,' he said, almost sympathetically (for they were both elders of the same true Kirk), 'I do not think you nor your employer would want to embarrass yourselves any further . . .'

He waved a large paw towards the film crew by the mini-van. The camerawoman waved cheerfully back.

'Smile, please, you're on national television!'

The factor looked at the camera, the policeman, then at the red-haired Jezebel. He looked at the evenly balanced forces of ghillies and protestors.

He jammed his cap down over his eyes and scowled.

'I'll be revenged upon the whole pack of you,' he muttered (for he was a man who lived by classic texts, and knew himself wronged). Then with a nod towards his men to follow, he strode towards his Land Rover.

With victory cries, the protestors swarmed over the stile and spread out up Maiden Braes.

'Keep away frae the grouse!' MacIver bawled after them.

He took Kirsty by the arm as she went to climb the stile.

'A neat morning's work, Miss Kirsty. I'm thinking you and Mr John Macnab have a lot in common.'

She looked him in the eye.

'Just doing my job, Jim. I'm only here to have a picnic and observe.'

'Observe, by God! And what happens when you take part?'

'You'll never know, Jim.'

'I hope I do not.'

'Now we're off for our picnic. Want to come?'

He shook his head, which suddenly struck her as resembling a sunburnt turnip.

'I've enough wi preventing further shenanigans on Inchallian.'

'See you in the Atholl for the dance on Saturday?'

'Aye, verra likely.'

He turned and ambled back to his car, shaking his head. Behind him the victors of the battle of Maiden Braes climbed over the stile with glad cries.

From the top of the stile Eve looked down at her mum and Kirsty and shook her head.

'Honestly,' she said. 'Bampots.'

13

Food for the troops went down well that evening. Days on the hill had sharpened their senses and appetites for food, for exercise, for sleep. The world of their daily work and worry was distant and unreal. They were now well into the middle of the affair, so far in that they were losing a sense of its limits.

(For myself, I work day in, day out here, doing what has to be done and waiting for the moment when I can take some time for myself and surreptitiously slip the disc marked M into the word processor to set the record straight about that summer.

I'm neglecting my duties, I know that. And my partner suspects it. Things aren't very grand between us. And if the day comes when you can read this, perhaps you're neglecting your work too. I do hope so.

Do what you will. Nothing holds back the river nor returns the bird to flight. Some say that's the beauty of it.)

At the end of the meal Alasdair rapped on the table. He congratulated the squaddesses on their victory. Brilliantly conceived and executed.

As Kirsty nodded in agreement she wondered if her father the Major would see the Battle on the TV news. She wondered too if he would see it as another example of her delinquency, or approve the way she'd handled the forces at her disposal. She turned to Eve with a laugh and shrugged the past away as Alasdair called the meeting to order.

'We must crack on and get serious, mateys, because time's running out.'

And Neil glimpsed the hourglass again. Time running out. He pictured it as his granny's egg timer. She was long gone now, and the timer had also disappeared somewhere along the way. And every day he had more past and less future, and lately he wanted to cry out as he felt himself being squeezed at the narrow waist between the two as the minutes ran through him.

What a depressingly Scottish image. Its negativity was another thing that was true about his country. It went along with tholing, bearing, putting up with, and taking a certain satisfaction in the expected bad news when it came. He sensed it was a wrong picture. He was groping for another, still true but more affirmative. Perhaps somewhere in the hills it would come to him.

Once Jamie had finally been carried off, they pulled together all the information they'd gathered. They had some things going for them but not enough. They had a way in. They'd located the pockets where the stray grouse might be. Eve had found a bolt-hole for Neil. The actual getaway remained a serious problem.

And the delivery, Kirsty pointed out, was even more iffy. The Lodge was already closely watched. It had no cover around it. And as soon as MacLeish had news of the poaching, he could concentrate all his forces there.

'So here's an idea,' Alasdair said. 'We build a giant catapult, right? Wouldn't take much, just two trees and some really thick elastic and a pouch in the middle.'

'Like the Romans, Al?'

'Exactly!'

Neil put his finger to his temple and made a circular gesture. Tricia looked at the ceiling and softly sang 'A-roamin in the Gloamin.'

'Seriously, troops! We hide in the trees across the park from the house, put the grouse in the pouch, pull back and – whang! Two grouse on the doorstep. No problem.'

He was whacked over the head with a rolled-up copy of Kirsty's new colour-supplement piece. Smack across the front cover was the photo Al had taken of Murray at Mid Pool with the salmon in one hand and the other across his face, proof to silence the doubters who'd suggested the fish had been caught elsewhere. And a nice little earner for our Kirsty, plus operational expenses for further ploys.

'Just the same,' Neil said, 'though the man's a lunatic he might have something. I mean, from the air . . .'

But he could push the thought no further. It was just a feeling, an inkling.

Kirsty was driving, turning the big pale wheel of the Wolseley as they went west into the sunset. Neither of them had said much for a while, they just watched as the great glaciated plateau became two-dimensional against the last light. A blue-grey haze was settling into the glens but above the sky was saffron, scarlet, salmon-pink.

'I hate to say it,' Kirsty murmured, 'but it's . . . bonnie.'

Neil nodded and settled into an American voice-over.

'And so the sun sets on Scotland Heritage UK plc, a fully-owned subsidiary of Disneyworld.' Without taking his eyes off the scene outside, he began to roll a cigarette. 'Yes, it's an economic, social and environmental disaster, but it's bonnie.'

The sunset got wilder as it got darker.

'This getaway . . .'

'And the delivery.'

They turned to each other at the same time.

'You first,' she said.

'We need help and lateral thinking. Something totally unexpected.'

She nodded emphatically.

'So we need Jane.'

'Yes! And Aziz.'

'Aziz! But – but, I mean, but—'

She put one hand on his arm.

'Control yourself,' she said. 'I'll explain later. He can help us.'

'No. Definitely not. Anyway, why should he? Like, why?'

Kirsty didn't reply as she put her hand back on the wheel. The old car was heavy on the steering.

'You sound like a jealous man, Mr Lindores.'

'Not at all. You can sleep with the Sheik of Araby and his five thousand white stallions, I don't give a flying burrito. I just feel you should be a bittie . . .'

'Careful? I will be.' She drove on, knowing she should let it drop. 'Anyway, he's just a second cousin of Hassan II and he's got two wives back in Morocco and only half a dozen horses. He prefers flying to riding.'

'Fine. But suppose he wants to add to his stable?'

The road swung down into the darkness where a river gleamed. She took her foot off the accelerator but the heavy body drove the car on.

She laughed.

'You do fancy me, don't you?'

She hadn't meant to say that, she really hadn't. It just came out as part of the momentum. Neil shifted back in his seat. He seemed quite calm now she'd said it, but in her chest a fist was thumping like a bailiff at a barred door.

'Yes. Yes I do. But I don't toss and turn all night about it. It's a common side-effect of proximity.'

'Oh,' she said. 'Very passionate.'

'Come on, Kirsty, you can't be a pal and a *femme fatale*. You can't flirt and then play dumb if someone comes on to you.'

'Not that you are.'

'Exactly.'

The car thumped over the bridge, a brief flash of silver, and they were climbing again. Her head dipped for a moment.

'Sorry,' she said. 'My mouth runs faster than my brain sometimes. I just say things and I'm not used to someone calling me on it.'

He laughed and stretched, an unlit roll-up in his long fingers.

'Don't think twice,' he said, 'it's all right. It needn't be a problem – unless you fancy me too.'

The car scarcely swerved at all. He began to roll another one on the dashboard.

'You're fishing, my love,' she said quietly.

'Who cast the first line? So?'

She drove on. She had asked for this. Silly old tart, when will you grow up? She was furious at them both. She wound down the window to cool off.

He held out the cigarette to her. She hesitated.

'Would you light it?'

'Shall I take that as a yes?'

'Oh, just light it, damn you. Yes. Of course. Sort of. Maybe.'

'Fine,' he said, lit up and passed it over. 'No problem there.' He glanced out the window as she fumed. 'Think we've seen the best of it.' He lit his own roll-up. 'Just one of those things we have to learn to live with. So who's going to phone Jane and give her the good news?'

They got back to the Atholl just after the Battle of Maiden Braes item was on the TV news, and found themselves local heroes. Even Lachie looked half pleased, and those who were temporarily working for MacLeish clapped them on the back. Sergeant Jim MacIver stuck his head in the door to see what was going on.

He received such a round of applause and whooping and laughter that he went red as a beet.

'Naw, naw, lads, I'll no be drinking. But I'll mind your kind offers on Saturday night.'

'You're a star, Big Jim!'

'Just upholding the law, Stevie. And you'll be taking a taxi hame the night.'

With a wave, he hastily left.

'You or me?' she said quietly.

'Better from you, Kirsty. Al might suspect my motives. Here's the number.'

'You and Jane, there's nothing in it?'

'Give me a break! We went out for a bit years ago, that's all. Before she ever met Al. I mean, they're married, for Christ's sake. You don't mess around with other people's marriages. They're mined! They blow up!'

'Remain calm,' she said. 'Just thought I'd better check before we do our marriage guidance act.'

Neil sat and sipped in the corner while she was gone. He was very aware of Lachie standing near by, and concentrated on Shonagh till Kirsty slipped back in, smiling broadly.

'She's coming.' Her breath warm in his ear. 'She thinks it may be possible, but she'll need to see the terrain.'

'About Aziz?'

'Yes?'

'Perhaps you could explain what you had in mind.'

She bent her head to his and explained while Shonagh watched and Lachie glowered.

'It's crazy! It's the best idea since God left Govan. I love it. But can he do it? And why should he?'

'Three reasons. First, he'll save some face if Inchallian gets done over as well. Second, he thinks MacLeish is a racist bastard. Seems they had a bit of a run-in last year and he wants to get even. And . . .'

'Thirdly?'

'I may have changed my mind about the thirdly.'

'Ah. Do you think he'll do it?'

'Yes,' she whispered. 'I know he'll play. Because I've just asked him. In fact, he's tickled pink.'

'With you tickling, I'm not surprised. OK, OK. It's nothing to do with me.'

'And God's still in Govan.'

Her face was inches away. He could feel the warmth, her youth, her energy. It was like spring come to the frozen plateau.

'Some say so, Kirst.'

She squeezed his arm.

'That's the spirit. I'd better off home. I've another article to do, Charlie to feed, and Abdulatif to see in the morning.'

'Meet you here lunchtime and we'll pick up Jane.'

'How do you think Alasdair will take it?'

'He's stubborn as a pig. They both are. As he'd say, you can lead a mule to water but you can't make him piss.'

She kissed him, for the benefit of the others at the table.

'Have fun,' she said. 'They're a good crowd.'

She slipped away.

Neil picked up his pint, someone bumped into him and the beer slopped over the counter. Lachie. Swaying slightly.

'I want a word with you, mister.'

'Any time.'

Lachie put his face right up to him.

'Some of us think it's time you went back south.'

Neil looked around. Only Shonagh hovering just out of range seemed interested.

'Some of us . . . Any reason?'

'Aye. I dinnae like your face.'

Neil put his pint down to free his hands.

'I like your teeth,' he said. 'Yours, are they?'

Lachie's hand clamped Neil's right arm to the bar.

'Right – outside.'

'On you go. Mind and shut the door behind you.'

Lachie's other hand came up. Neil grabbed and held it. He sighed as they stared each other out. He hadn't had to go through this routine for years. He was also getting seriously pissed off and that pissed him off all the more.

'You leave her alone,' Lachie hissed.

'You're a gamekeeper, not hers.'

Not too brilliant, but it would have to do. They struggled silently.

'Lachlan Morrison!' Shonagh pushed between them. 'Behave or you're out!'

Lachie looked down at her.

'This is nuthin to do wi you, Shonagh.'

She thumped the palm of her hand hard against his chest. He staggered back. She was solidly built and seemed to have no fear at all. Lachie looked at Neil over her head.

'Right then – outside!'

Neil freed his right hand.

'Like I said – any time.'

Shonagh turned on him.

'You too, Neil! Daft laddies!'

She pushed them apart. Lachie gave a short laugh.

'Whit would you ken about men anyhow?'

She turned and seized him by the lapels and propelled him back against the bar.

'I know you need a good skelp! And if you've a problem with my love life, cousin Lachlan, I want to hear it.'

'Aw, Shonagh, I wis just sayin . . .'

'Don't!' She stood her ground and glared at them both. 'You two have a choice. You can have a whisky on the house and both – both of ye, mind – drink a toast to our Kirsty. Or you can have your stushie here or outside – and you'll be banned from this bar. And I know you're already banned from the Lochrin, Lachie, so it'll be Braemar for your drinking.' She put her hands on her hips. 'So what's it going to be?'

The two men muttered and glowered as Annie behind the bar silently set up three whiskies.

'All right, then? Peace, you big donnert gowks?'

Lachie looked at the floor, then at the whisky.

'Aye, all right,' he muttered. 'Braemar's ower far.'

'Sure,' Neil said. 'I've nothing against you.' He glanced around, the place was heaving. No one seemed to have noticed the incident at all. Shonagh handed them their glasses and picked up her own.

'To Kirsty and the women. And – hold it – the defeat of Factor MacLeish and all hard-hearted bastards everywhere. And peace in my bar.'

'John Macnab,' Neil said.

'Kirsty,' Lachie replied.

'Peace.'

They drank and turned to watch the TV news rerun the Battle of Maiden Braes.

When Neil and Kirsty walked into the Strathdon kitchen with Jane next evening, Alasdair looked at them blankly. Then just for a moment simple pleasure travelled across those roughened features. And dragging along behind it like a broken-down car behind a shiny AA van, came caution. Then suspicion.

'Oh, hi,' he said.

'Hi.'

'What are you doing here?'

'I was told you need me.'

'I've managed so far.'

'I mean—'

'I asked her, Al,' Kirsty broke in. These two needed their heads banged together. 'Me and Neil have a plan for his getaway and it involves Jane.'

Alasdair kept staring.

'Great!' Tricia said. 'Come on in, Jane. Great to see you. How was Chamonix?'

Nobody missed the hesitation.

'Fine,' she said. 'The usual. I had some grand flights. Grand . . . You lot have been busy.'

She put down her pack and hugged and kissed her way round the room. Alasdair got a quick peck on the cheek.

She sat down in the seat Murray had just vacated beside Al. She was a solidly built woman. Strong shoulders, weathered face like her husband's, short curly hair. A touch of Irish still lingered in her accent. Her round face was usually cheerful, quick to laugh, quick to rubbish Al when he was out of line. They had bickered and laughed and drunk their way through ten years together, equally matched. But now . . . Neil had never seen her like this. Edgy. Almost embarrassed. This reunion wasn't going as he and Kirsty had imagined. Perhaps it would be better when they were left alone.

'Welcome to the wunnerful world of John Macnab,' Murray said. 'Now tell us this amazing plan.'

Between the three of them they got it out. At first they were faced with disbelieving laughter. OK, so they were a bit thin on details.

'Thin?' Murray said. 'Man, it's anorexic.'

'Jane thinks it can work,' Kirsty said. 'She'll need a good scout around first.'

Alasdair sat nodding and frowning, his left knee jumping.

'This plan is as hot as a llama's testicles,' he said.

'Is that good?'

'Have you ever *felt* a llama's testicles, old girl?'

Neil put his head in his hands.

'Is that one l or two?' he inquired.

'D'you think I'm some kind of pervert?'

No one seemed in a hurry to answer that one.

'And I've an idea for the delivery,' Kirsty said eventually. 'Not so far removed from your catapult. Let me tell you.'

She told them. Murray let out a low whistle.

'Aziz? Have you lost yer toolies, kid? Marbles to you,' Murray added.

'He says he'll do it. In fact he's really chuffed to be asked.'

'He's no stringing you along?'

'That's a chance we have to take. No, I don't think he'll shop us.'

Alasdair looked down at his hands.

'I climbed with some Moroccan Army people in the Atlas. Face is very important to them, just as it is to me.' Jane nodded but couldn't look at him. 'And so is revenge when they've been wronged or insulted.'

The kitchen was silent. Alasdair coughed.

'So I think Kirsty's assessment is correct. We go with him and hope for the best.'

That night when they were finally alone in their room, Jane stashed the big black pack and unpacked her few things. Alasdair was already lying on his back in the single bed, looking at the ceiling.

She looked at him. She knew him so well and for the first time she didn't know what to say to him.

She unrolled her sleeping bag on the other single bed.

'Jane, I've got to ask you something.'

'I know.'

Kirsty and Jane were sitting among the rocks near the top of Maiden Braes. They'd spent the afternoon exploring it in some detail. A couple of gamies had wandered near, scowled and left when they recognized Kirsty. They were clearly under new orders. And anyway, with two other men sitting on the bald hilltop above them, with a clear view of anyone coming up from undulating pockets hidden on the north-facing slope, there was no threat to security.

Jane cupped her chin in her big roughened hands and gazed back down to the road.

'I know,' she repeated. 'And the answer is, yes.'

'Oh.'

They looked at the road for a while but that wasn't where things were happening.

'It's over and it won't happen again. I don't know why it happened – maybe my age, or because we've no kids. Can't.'

'Ah.' For once Kirsty felt out of her depth. 'Are you going to tell Alasdair?'

'Of course not. He guesses anyway.'
'And what if he asks you?'
'He won't.'
'Why not?'
Jane looked at her like she was simple.
'You don't understand, do you?'
'No, I don't. Not at all. But it sounds like you still want him.'
'He's pig-headed and strong-willed and he likes to be doing things – and I'm the same. Of course I do.'
'So why not—?'
'Al and me aren't like you or Neil. We're not . . . sophisticated. We, ah . . .' She spread her hands. 'We just do things. We don't think about them all the time. With us it's all or nothing and that's it.'
'But what if he – I mean, went with someone else?'
'I'd kill him.' After a pause, they both laughed. 'OK, so that's silly. But he wouldn't. He looks, you know that. He notices women. But he just wouldn't. That's the way we are. Or were.'
Kirsty sat feeling a little sick. She didn't feel sophisticated at all. She thought about her own life and felt stupid. Not a free spirit at all, just a shallow one.
'So you won't tell him and he won't ask you but you both know, so things aren't right.'
'Yup. You see . . .' Way down below, a couple of picnickers climbed over the stile. Well, Kirsty thought, at least we achieved something.
'The trust's gone.' Jane stuck her hands under her armpits and hunched over. 'It's like when you're doing a route together you each have to trust your partner will always be there if you peel off. That they'll never leave you on the hill.'
'I see,' Kirsty said. 'Trust. Yes, of course.'
Jane shook her head, quickly flicked her knuckle into her eyes as she stood up.
'I've seen enough,' she said. 'Let's get back.'
'But can you do it?'
Jane took a last look back at the crest of the hill, then down and across towards Aziz's estate.
'Icksy-picksy. I'll give it a go.'
As they worked their way back down through the rocks, Kirsty suddenly stopped.
'I'm not sophisticated,' she said. 'And I know trust matters. It's just that if I was with a man the rules would be different. Not

so hard and fast. Maybe that's me, or the kind of men I go for. But it would still be trust.'

Now she was feeling tearful. Jane put her arm round her shoulder.

'I know,' she said. 'I wasn't getting at you. Alasdair and me aren't so good at the words, but we feel just the same way you do. Race you to the bottom – last one to the stile is a sissy.'

'But I am a sissy,' Kirsty protested. But Jane was already running, so she set off after her.

About the same time, Abdulatif Aziz was standing hands on hips outside his stables. A large horsebox had arrived ten minutes earlier after driving north through the night. The driver reversed into the largest shed, jumped down then opened the rear doors.

Whatever was inside, it wasn't horses.

Abdulatif waved for him to stop. He glanced round but no one was there. He'd sent them all away.

He entered the shed and pulled the sliding doors shut.

14

The conspirators gathered again in the Strathdon kitchen and agreed the date of the second hit. The Twelfth was in two days, and that seemed the right time to take the mickey out of the annual slaughterfest. And the presence of extra photographers, journalists, anti-blood sports and access groups (still euphoric from their high-profile Maiden Braes success) could help muddle things further. And at least some of the gamies would have to be involved in the main shooting party. And Kirsty and Aziz had their invites to the late afternoon garden party that day.

So it was agreed: they hit Inchallian in two days' time. Even Alasdair almost smiled as he sat silently at the end of the table.

Jane went over her calculations and measured again on the map the distance from Maiden Braes to the boundary with Mavor.

'How heavy are you, Neil? In kilos.'

'No, Jane,' Kirsty interrupted. 'It'll be Alasdair.'

'But—'

A sharp kick under the table silenced Neil.

'Neil and Murray and me have rethought the plan. This is better.'

Neil and Murray exchanged baffled glances, then looked at Kirsty. She nodded imperceptibly then explained the new plan.

She had to go over it twice, and then draw it for Alasdair. There was a silence while it sank in. Alasdair fiddled with his moustache and ran his broad, battered fingers across the paper.

'But why don't I just go back out north before Neil starts shooting?'

She looked at Alasdair pityingly.

'By daylight? Another twenty miles? Anyway, the point is you're a faster runner than Neil, and the whole thing turns on speed.'

'Sure,' Neil said, nursing his bruised shin. 'I can't run for toffee apples.'

'So what happens to Neil after the hit?'

She explained and watched the grins expand round the table. Two men dressed in tweeds are interchangeable as Tweedledum and Tweedledee. They liked it.

'I don't know, sport,' Al said. 'It sounds like over-egging the omelette.'

'I agree with Kirsty,' Neil said. 'Some puddings need a lot of eggs.'

'Aye, right enough,' Murray agreed, wincing from the kick he'd received in turn. 'I mean, the richer the better, eh?'

Jane and Alasdair still were dubious, but in the end the others persuaded them. So Jane redid her calculations.

'It'll be close-run,' she said. 'We might deck out.'

'No more bread and butter pudding for you, Alasdair,' Tricia said, and passed it on to Kirsty who saw no reason to stint herself.

They stood beside their cars as the light faded.

'What are you up to, Kirsty?'

'Trust,' she said. 'When it's broken only the heat of the moment can weld it.'

'You're starting to talk like Al.'

'Trust me, Neil. You do trust me?'

He hesitated with his car keys in his hand.

'Put it this way: I might trust a wall to be a wall, but that doesn't mean it won't fall on me.'

'I suppose Confucius said that?'

'No, I did. Meaning I trust you to be you but I don't quite know who that is yet.'

She laughed. 'That's not surprising. I've very little idea myself.' She got into the Wolseley and wound down the window. 'See you at the dance tonight, sugar.'

'Is my presence required?'

'It would look strange if you weren't there. Cover.' She leered at him. 'Sure you can handle the proximity?'

She drove off before he could reply. He nodded as if something had been confirmed, then followed on in his car.

Tricia thought of Helen as she stood watching the two cars bump down the track into the dusk. As their lights faded she sighed and went back inside. Two cars, two drivers, one drive – such a waste of energy.

* * *

Neil and Shonagh had their heads together over the bar when Kirsty walked in. She noted he'd dressed up a bit but not overmuch. Black trousers, white shirt buttoned without a tie, a soft black jacket, clean dark hair combed back with a stray lock hanging over his forehead as he nodded and asked Shonagh something.

Kirsty exchanged greetings with the friends and acquaintances she saw every day as she worked her way towards the bar. No doubt about it, he looked good and that still wasn't a reason for anything except pleasant proximity. One adventure at a time.

Shonagh was smiling and laughing, cupped her hand and whispered something into his ear. Kirsty felt a slight stab, like someone had slipped a skean-dhu between her third and fourth ribs.

They saw her and separated. Neil smiled, a big pleased smile just to see her, and the skean-dhu was removed, leaving only the slightest scar. He likes me, she thought. He doesn't just fancy me. He really likes . . . me. So far as he knows me.

She ran her hand up the back of his neck while Shonagh watched her thoughtfully.

'Well hi, Mr Cool. Let's get some muscle relaxant in before the dance.'

'You look all right yourself, thirsty Kirsty. A Grouse?'

She winked at him.

'Two Grouse, please. And a half-pint. I've some catching up to do.'

'Och, and so have I.' It was Jim MacIver, out of uniform and in his best pullover. 'Am I thinking someone here owes me a dram?'

Dance Night went along its immemorial way, warming up as drinks went down and voices got louder and arms waved more freely. The talk was of the usual – midgies and touries, the coming shooting season and John Macnab, new babies, old stories, the future of the Forestry Commission and the bypass. The unmarried lads clustered round the tables by the dartboard pulling on pints and cigarettes, talking football and shinty and cars with outrageously big engines, and glancing at the knot of lassies laughing and knocking back vodka and Coke at the tables by the fire, and they in turn glanced at the laddies, while keeping each other up on the summer-season talent.

And the time came, unsignalled but understood by all, when

Dance Night rose to its collective feet, stuck some half-bottles in its pockets and handbags, then ambled, swaying slightly, round the corner to the village hall where the band had been playing heavy metal country and western to an empty room for the last hour.

A solvent of alcohol and accordions and mid-seventies guitar solos gradually dissolved all but the most blate and backward until they mingled sweat, perfume, whisky and aftershave into the heady brew of Highland Saturday night. Then Time took a breather and sat it out for a while as couples located each other in the slow dances, then reels and eightsomes wove the people together into the rough, warm communal material of the sort that has no name except 'Where we live'.

And the snogging in the corner, and the scuffles round the back, and the tears and fights in the girls' toilets, and Mad Pat's ravings, were part of that. And Neil, part inside and part outside, as he spun and caught another hefty lassie and locked elbows with Kirsty and spun off again in a Strip the Willow, felt himself part of something for the first time in a very long time. And as Kirsty caught the swaying Lachie and expertly pivoted and flung him back to the Deeside girl, she wondered why only three weeks ago she had thought this place had nothing more to offer. And as she and Neil crossed arms at the bottom of the line and swung round each other like binary suns, she remembered how soon this would be over.

Then Time dozed off again, its bony fingers still tapping out the beat, and she forgot it in the dance.

In the early hours, the remnants of Dance Night reconvened in the back bar of the Atholl and locked the doors. Billy May the fiddler was too drunk to talk but still able to de-tune and bind the wounds of the survivors with 'The Flowers of the Forest'. Then Kirsty got up and with Andy the guitarist sang 'Blue Moon' to a ragged but deeply sincere chorus of ruined voices. Billy replied with 'Moon on the Water' which left the bar so hushed the night would have ended there but suddenly Jim MacIver stood up and sang in a surprising clear tenor 'I Loved A Lass'.

Kirsty was called again from her bar stool beside Neil (who was trying to count the freckles below her hairline on the back of her neck but kept getting lost in big numbers) back on to the small stage. She looked round them all, and decided on something different.

'Some enchanted evening . . .' she began. Whistles and catcalls. She started again.

'Ah canna play yon shite,' Andy said. 'Gie us "Stairway to Heaven".'

He lurched over his guitar and fell asleep cradling it. Kirsty looked around, uncertain for a moment.

Shonagh nudged Neil.

'Go and help the lassie,' she hissed. 'Or do you only play on the bar?'

So Neil went up, aware he was still on trial here. He switched on the keyboard, sat down and looked at Kirsty.

Kirsty looked at him. His shirt was unbuttoned and his hair sweat-shiny. She hoped he wasn't going to make a fool of himself. Or her.

'Can you play honky-tonk, boy? Or have you just come to polish the keys?'

He flipped his hair back out of his eyes.

'Babe, ah can honk all night long!'

And he slammed into left-hand pumping 'It's All Over Now', so quick she missed the opening but caught up and they bawled it out, and second time round alternated lines and picked up the bar-room chorus and impromptu rhythm section of spoons, beer cans, handclaps, plus Shonagh and Pat on crisp box.

Whistles and cheers, and Jim MacIver punched the air in a way he must have seen once on television. Kirsty winked at Neil and leant over the keyboard.

'Guess you'll do,' she said.

She turned back to the audience, spread her arms out wide. She was flying now. She didn't know where she was going next.

'Honky-Tonk Laddoes!' she announced. 'Don't you just love them?'

And he was right in behind her, flicked the cheesy Rock Guitar 2 button, and the women of the room yelled out a home-brewed version of the old classic, made stranger still by Billy May's fiddle. Shonagh and Pat jumped on stage and offered competing Jagger-Richards impersonations. Neil cut the song after the second chorus, hit a different chord and modulated it with Rock Organ 1.

'You don't have to say you love me,' he began in falsetto, batting huge black non-existent Dusty Springfield eyelashes. It was only the second time she'd seen him let go and she felt vitality stream off him, an inventiveness that could go anywhere, like they'd just pushed off downriver on a white-water raft, and she clambered on board and they swept with full girlie chorus and hand signals through that song, then over the rapids of 'Baby Love', on over the appalling drops of 'Build Me Up, Buttercup', emerging on the calmer but vast waters of 'Dedicated to the One I Love' and round the bend to 'River Deep, Mountain High'.

The girlie chorus staggered off the stage clutching their drinks and ruined throats. Kirsty leant on the keyboard gasping for breath and helpless with laughter. Neil half stood up and bowed.

'Thank you very much on behalf of the group and myself, and I hope we passed the audition.'

It was an old quote, one Helen used to use after the rare occasions when she'd done a number. He grimaced and was about to leave but Kirsty pressed him firmly back on to his seat. Lachie deposited two whiskies on the keyboard.

'Braw, man,' he said. 'Bit retro, but braw. Don't suppose you ken any songs by Garbage?'

He grinned and staggered off stage. Neil put his hand on Kirsty's.

'One more, Kirst, then I'm for my kip. What d'you fancy?'

'How's about "One Night with You"?'

'Na, something quieter.'

He ran his hands over the keys, considered the options as she watched him. No doubt, she'd grown accustomed to his face.

He looked up.

'Let's try "Ain't Misbehavin'"? Like as a torch song.'

'OK,' she said. 'Though misbehaving might be more like it.' He looked down at his hands and she wondered what she'd said wrong. 'OK, OK. "Ain't Misbehavin'" it is.'

He waited till the room was quiet, then played the intro slow and almost brooding. She reached in for her breathy *chanteuse* voice, the hopeful, vulnerable one she let out just once in a while.

At the end of the verse with her left ambivalently happy on the shelf, he came in on a lower harmony, oddly serious. Saving himself, apparently. The room was quiet now, the kind of silence that passes beyond pleasurably controlling an audience and into communing.

In the second verse, when she suggested she was through with flirting, her voice quavered through a giggle. Not bloody likely. Then with him on a tight harmony below her, they crossed the bridge and swung into the middle eight, and in the end affirmed, twice, that they really really weren't misbehaving, and it is doubtful if anyone in the room believed them.

* * *

The night was mild, but he put his jacket on as the sweat cooled. Kirsty sat beside him on the low wall and they checked out the sky. Patches of mist, a few stars, moon spilling over the clouds like milk on a drunk man's floor.

'You should act on impulse more often.'

'You think so?'

They looked at each other. She moistened her lips.

'Yes.'

'Is that a challenge, Kirsty?'

She thought of Alasdair. You can lead a mule to water but you can't make him swim.

'A suggestion.'

'A recommendation?'

'All right, dammit. An invitation.'

And still the mule sat there. Then very slowly he moved his head towards hers and opened his lips and closed his eyes as she closed hers, and they both went into it blind.

She'd forgotten how kissing someone new is meeting a whole history of other kissers and other lovers. And once in a while it's also brand-new, and you're an absolute beginner, habit-free and capable of anything, even feeling.

The part of him that was still observing was astounded at how gentle her kisses were. Tender, at first almost hesitant. Then nothing held back at all, just hunger and giving.

He came up for air and looked at her. She opened her eyes. No wisecracks, no jousting. No flirting or teasing. She looked at him, wordless and direct.

He put his hand to her cheek and felt her hand on the back of his neck pulling him gently in. He thought: it's not a different mood, it's a different her. The one behind the moods.

His hand on the muscle of her arm, his wrist brushing warm on her breast like a kiss. Her hand on his shirt, fingers slipping between the buttons. Warm chest, fine hairs, heart beating, that old ache against his soft wrist. The way lips meet and part, the way you part inside.

They were adults, they'd both been around this territory long enough, they knew perfectly well how it lay and where it went.

He put his hands on her shoulders and gently eased her away.

'I'd best off to my bed, Kirst. Are you fit to drive?'

Her eyes widened. She stared back at him, a finger hooked round a button.

'Yes. I, ah . . . suppose so. If that's what you want.'

'It's lovely. You're lovely. And it's well past pumpkin hour for me.' He stood up. 'Shooting clays tomorrow, clear head required. The general danced till dawn and that . . .' He bent and kissed her gently on the cheek.

Twenty feet away, he stopped and turned round.

'Good suggestion though, Kirsty.' And then he was gone like he'd bailed out of a burning plane.

She sat on the wall feeling a complete idiot. What was that all about? She swore and kicked the rubbish bin. She got to make the smart exit lines, not him.

Shonagh was just locking up the hotel with Pat beside her.

'Shonagh, can you spare a cigarette? And some matches?'

'Neil run out? Sorry, didn't mean it like that. Look, take two. This is Pat.'

'Hi, Pat. No thanks. This is a one-cigarette problem and I don't even smoke. Catch you both later.'

She turned away and walked almost steadily down towards the river. Shonagh and Pat raised eyebrows, then linked arms and walked off down the street through the silent town.

The sky was getting paler and still she sat on the river-bank watching the white water and the brown. She felt the pre-dawn breeze on her cheek. Her bum was getting damp. The water was too loud to think.

She brushed her fingers across her lips. A kiss is just a kiss. Remember that.

She took a last drag then flipped the butt into the river. A brief sparking arc, then gone. She rested her forehead on her arms on her knees.

Damn. Damn. Damn.

She got stiffly to her feet and scrambled up the bank. On the street the lamps were starting to look stupid and pointless.

She got into the car and drove slowly back up the hill to Charlie.

Not enough hours later, Kirsty and Alasdair and Eve went reconnoitring Inchallian for the last time. None of them spoke much. Eve was normally silent anyway unless she had something to say. Kirsty had a mild hangover and wasn't feeling communicative. Alasdair had a brain-crunching hangover after a night in the Strathdon pub with Murray, Tricia and Jane, where he hadn't behaved well. Annoyed with himself and the world, he punished his body as he tried to whip himself back into shape.

No one carrying a fifty-pound rucksack full of rocks up and down a rough hillside is likely to be in a pleasant mood, so Kirsty gave him a wide berth.

They spent some time tracking through the deep heather to meet the long valley coming in from the north, then followed along its upper rim. Kirsty needed a break and sat on a rock a little below the skyline beside Eve with a question hesitating in her throat like an unresolved burp, but it wouldn't come out.

Alasdair sweated up towards them.

'Crime and punishment, Al?'

'Not very chipper today, old girl,' and he went on up without stopping. Kirsty felt his hostility extended to her, probably Neil too. He may have sensed they were trying to corral him in some way.

At last they reached the plateau, took out the picnic stuff and casually looked around. They picked out the watcher on the bare top to the east, and another to the west, but most activity seemed to be south. Half a mile away two men looked well set with flask, radio and binoculars as they regularly checked the slopes below them and off to the right in the direction of the burn.

So after a while the picnickers packed up and the charming family group wandered along the crest of the hill. The little girl waved cheerfully to the nice man with the binoculars. The nice man did not wave back.

They came to the main stalkers' path that ran alongside the burn. Some way up the slope on the far side another man was sitting. They waved to him and followed the track further up the glen where the heather was at the peak of its annual purple haze routine, though that was the last thing Alasdair needed in his thumping head. The track and the burn jinked to the left and the slopes turned to bracken and long grasses and short turf above.

'Here,' Eve said. 'It was here!'

'I know. Just keep walking and don't look round.'

A hundred yards further on, they sat down as if they'd had enough. Then they walked slowly back the way they'd come. Alasdair kept looking straight ahead and let his eyes do the wandering. About four minutes over the slope on his right would be the short heather pockets where there might or might not be the odd grouse.

For that hundred-yard stretch of track they were out of sight of all three watchers.

Alasdair sent Eve off to have a pee in the heather while the two adults waited nonchalantly. When she found the slot in the ground she turned and put her arm up. Alasdair took a quick bearing then signed for her to pace her way back. Ten yards away from him and Kirsty was a large quartz boulder like a lump of frozen milk fallen from the sky.

'Forty-seven steps, Uncle Alasdair.'

'Say thirty-nine for an adult. Even if it's still half dark he can't miss that boulder. Return to base.'

He put his head down and slogged along ahead of them with the heavy pack. With Eve lagging behind a little, Kirsty hurried to catch up with him.

'Al?'

'Mmph?'

And then the burp finally surfaced.

'Al, who's Helen?'

He didn't even look up.

'His wife, of course.'

When Eve came up to Kirsty, she was standing looking at her feet. She was white as the quartz boulder.

'I said you shouldn't drink so much. Or have you hurt yourself?'

Kirsty shook her head. And though Eve didn't normally touch people until she knew them very well, she took her hand for a while as they followed on.

15

There's a restless, hungry feeling when the light starts to ebb from the day but it's not yet night, leaving us stranded between one phase and another. Neil prowled and fidgeted in his hotel room. He was hungry though he'd eaten. He was unprepared though he'd gone over his maps and equipment a dozen times. He'd done everything but something was left undone.

He went over to the window. Curtains of mist opened and swished closed across the hills as they had all day. That would be uncomfortable but a help in going through the Inchallian estate. And the mist would deaden the sound of the shots.

Could he do it? That day he'd had two practice sessions with clay pigeons on Aziz's estate, under the supervision of a man whose light conversation was restricted to Mmph (Yes, or perhaps Good) and Gmmph (No, or No Bloody Good). There'd been no sign of Aziz. At the dance Kirsty had said he was busy with his own preparations and anyway, she felt this wasn't the time for them to meet.

He made a face and pulled on his tweeds. He looked at himself in the mirror and tried to think himself back into the time of John Macnab. A time when men were either single or married. A time when good girls were chaps with (presumably small) breasts. Janet Raden had been described as 'like an adorable boy', the same way the adventurer Sandy Arbuthnot was always said to have the eyes and grace of a girl. Presumably at the time no one had sniggered.

He shook his head. He felt weary though all he'd done since the dance was shoot some clays, catch up on sleep, read and spend the rest of the time lying on the bed looking at the ceiling. There'd been no answers there.

It's an adventure to be lived, Neil, not a problem to be solved. What would Helen say to that now?

He looked into the mirror and for a moment saw her extraordinary nicotine-coloured eyes looking back at him. But in the end it wasn't the colour of eyes that mattered but what was in them. Not the curve of the lips but the things they said. Not the body but the way it lived and breathed and loved.

She'd still say the same. Life was the creed she'd lived by, even as he'd held her while she fought for each breath, as her neck arched and eyes squeezed tight around the stunning pain behind them. As she finally unclenched and her bewilderment faded and he was left looking at merely empty eyes, it hadn't taken two panicking stewardesses to tell him she was gone.

No last words, no goodbyes. Just struggling for the next breath till there aren't any more and all the gifts are given back.

> And you must learn there are words
> with no meaning, words like *consolation*,
> words like *goodbye*.

It's not supposed to happen like that. Healthy young people aren't supposed to die. Not on an ordinary transatlantic flight, just a few hours from hospital. Not from what starts as a headache.

Leaning on the dressing table, he emptied his lungs and breathed deep and slow for a time that isn't measured. No point wondering whether if they'd taken insurance she wouldn't have got on that plane. No point at all.

He didn't greit much now, except on anniversaries, Christmases, birthdays and the like. Now it was more a passing nausea, a dry heave. He couldn't even summon up her face consciously these days. She was vivid only in dreams or brief, uncalled-for moments.

He opened his eyes and went to the bedside table, opened the drawer and took out the ring.

He eased it on. He turned it a few times and still felt rotten but more complete, like a retired gunfighter strapping on his guns again and going out for the showdown.

He smiled ruefully at his rhetoric. It had been worth trying to move on, but taking off a ring wasn't the way to do it.

He flexed the fingers of his left hand. An adventure, then.

He shouldered his burden and went out on to the street.

The car came round the corner right on time. Trish was driving with Alasdair and Eve in the back. He slung his bags in the boot

and got in beside Tricia as the car started to move.
'So where's Kirsty?'
'She changed her mind, Neil. She said she wanted to go with Jane and Murray instead, so we swopped places.
'Ah.'
Tricia glanced at him. He offered nothing further. They drove through the wet dusk up into the hills and after a while he twisted round in his seat and went through the final run-down of the GP with Alasdair.

In the empty lodge at the corner of Aziz's estate, Jane and Kirsty were sitting impatiently while Murray finished their make-up.
Back of the ears and neck, throat, hands. Eyelids. He stood back and looked at them and tried to keep a straight face. Jane in full tweeds, as befitted active service, was particularly fetching.
'My, but you're dead butch, Jane. Alasdair will fancy you rotten.'
Her teeth shone in her black face.
'You shut your gob and finish the artwork.'
He grinned back at her and took out the silver and yellow sticks. No response from Kirsty, but then she'd said little all evening as they'd packed the gear.
'Just a few finishing touches.'
He tried to follow Alasdair's instructions, unlikely though they seemed.
'Done. Now girls – nae perfume, deodorants, cigarettes or aftershave? Got your black gloves?'
The two women looked at each other.
'Shall we dismember him now or later?'
'Save our energy for better things. Christ, she looks like Aladdin Sane or something. You call that camouflage?'
Murray gave the Alasdair explanation. The best way to hide something was not by hiding it but by making it not what the eye was looking for. Then it doesn't register. So he hadn't completely blacked out their faces, which would leave a black face-shaped hole in a near-black night. Instead with these diagonals he'd broken up the symmetry of the face into an apparently random series of patches. That was the theory anyway.
'Looks like a Picasso on an off day,' Kirsty grumbled. 'I'm sick of deception and disguises.'
Jane and Murray looked at each other.
'Alasdair's usually right about these things,' Jane said.
Murray checked his watch.

'Let's go, ladies of the night!'

Tricia pulled into the lay-by on top of the moorland road and cut the engine and lights. While they waited for their night vision to come on, the men blacked up. Eve added some artistic touches in silver, yellow and green. Neil checked the shotgun and cartridges one more time, wrapped them carefully in cloth and slid them into his pack. Alasdair went through his mental check-list: map, compass, flask, scran, the harness, the palm-sized Satnav. On impulse he decided to add a short climbing rope.

'A-OK, old chap?'

'As I'll ever be.'

They sat on for a minute. The mist looked damp and solid and the car was warm and dry.

'Aren't you going to put on waterproofs?' Eve asked.

'Too noisy when you move, young 'un.'

Neil drummed his fingers on the dashboard, wishing it was a piano in a warm bar. He realized Tricia was staring at him.

'What's this? I thought you promised to make a new start.'

He turned the gold band gently on his finger.

'I did try, but there's no such thing as new starts. There's only continuing.'

There was silence in the car except for a whispering of rain. Alasdair shifted uneasily in the back seat. Eve sat twisting her fingers together.

'But there's continuing differently, Neil. That's not disloyal. I'd never ask that of Murray if I—'

Neil tugged the handle and got out of the car.

After a pause, Alasdair followed and went round to the boot to add the rope to his pack.

Tricia got out.

'I'm sorry Neil, it's just—'

He put his hand on her arm, quite gently.

'No, I'm sorry. It's not about loyalty to Helen. You know I've had a few flings since, and that didn't bother me but they didn't help much either, and I hurt somebody.'

The wet was starting to run off his hair and down his face. It felt good, cool.

'Who are you afraid for, Neil? Kirsty's a big girl. Or yourself?'

'Ouch,' he said. 'You punch well for your weight, Trish.' He settled his pack on to his shoulder. Alasdair was waiting and there was a long slog ahead.

'Good luck, Uncle Neil.'

Eve was leaning out of the back window. He kissed her forehead.

'Thanks, darlin.'

'Ready, youth?'

'Aye, sure.' He smiled to Tricia. 'Right now I'm most feart of meeting Mr MacLeish on a dark hill.'

Alasdair checked his bearing and the two men set off into the mist and vanished.

Tricia sighed and got back in.

'Will they be all right, Mum?'

'I hope so, Evie.' She turned and looked at her daughter. 'The thing to remember in this life is that nothing's the end of the world except the end of the world. Now – do you want to sit beside me while we drive back?'

In the thin belt of trees at the very south-east corner of Aziz's estate, three damp people crouched behind the boundary fence and waited as the mist came and went and came again. Murray passed over the night vision glasses Alasdair had mysteriously acquired.

'There's still only one gamie, sheltering behind that big rock halfway up. I think there's another lying on the skyline but it's too far to be sure.'

Jane nodded and looked through the glasses. Things were roughly as bright as an average winter's day in Fort William. She could pick out half a dozen hinds sheltered in the upper corrie.

She checked along the fence again. Nobody. Well, even MacLeish hadn't expected anyone to come in from Aziz's estate. The southern approach, by Maiden Braes, was another matter.

'Lachie's told me they've taken on another fifty men for the week,' Kirsty said. 'But most of them are just lads signing on at the DSS. If nothing else, we've provided a little extra seasonal employment.'

'Aye, but what do they pay 'em?'

'Three pounds an hour, if they're lucky. But there's a bonus if nothing gets poached, and fifteen hundred quid for whoever catches us.'

Murray whistled quietly.

'Our price has gone up.'

'Yeah, I've always wanted to be a wanted woman.'

'I'd hae thought you were.'

'Only by the wrong people.'

The mist came down again. Jane pushed up the glasses.

'Let's go, Kirsty. You've got to get back here before daylight.'

Kirsty got stiffly to her feet.

'Right,' she said. 'Let's go get the sods.'

Murray cut the bottom strands of the fence and rolled them back.

'I declare this estate open.'

The two women crawled through the hole, dragging Jane's bulky black pack and Kirsty's smaller but heavier one. They waved once, Jane grinning and Kirsty looking grim, then they were gone.

Murray twisted the cut ends together, pulled the poncho over his head and settled back against a tree to wait.

It was a long dreich bastern night and the drizzle was of the wet variety. By the time Neil and Alasdair had slogged up fifteen hundred feet and into the hanging valley, they were as damp inside as out.

Al knelt to take another bearing.

'Couldn't be better,' he said.

'Compared to what – an at-home with Noel Edmonds?'

'In these conditions, no one will see or hear us unless we stand on them. Which would be bloody bad luck, but we'll still keep off the paths.' He checked his watch. 'Better crack on.'

He shot off at top speed. He'd been doing this all over the world for twenty years. Plus serious TAB with Special Forces (yomping, as he'd explained to Neil, was the marines' word for it, and therefore low-life). He felt his muscles begin to warm and burn as they hit the uphill again. He put his head down and grinned to himself. This was the business. This at least he understood.

She'd better bloody be there.

Fortunately for Neil the ground was mostly good – short turf, a few peat hags and the odd boulder-strewn corrie. After he'd gone sprawling a few times, he stopped checking the ground and learned to let his knees be loose and flow along.

As always on a long hike, he went through different stages. Excitement and adrenalin at first. Then sweating and heaving for breath. Then settling to the rhythm, with time for thoughts, welcome or otherwise. And somewhere in the second hour as they left behind slopes and bogs, heather and scree slopes, thinking too got left behind and all that was left was movement. Every so often he came to himself in the middle of this mist-wrapped dream and found he was terribly happy. On a long downhill slope he felt they were skimming over the surface of the earth. At other times he seemed to be very angry and arguing with someone or other. Then he went back into the dream of movement and forgot everything.

He thumped into Alasdair's back and fell on the ground.

'What the—'

'Wheesht!'

Al was lying beside him. Neil peered through the mist and rain and saw a glimmer of white up ahead. Fifty yards? Ten? It seemed to waver and move. It disappeared. Then reappeared.

Alasdair got slowly to his feet and walked forward.

He leaned on the sign. WALKERS ARE PROHIBITED FROM THE HIGH GROUND DURING THE SHOOTING SEASON MID-SEPTEMBER TO MID-FEBRUARY. THIS IS NECESSARY. IGNORING THIS SIGN COULD BE DANGEROUS.

'Well, we stand warned.'

Neil shook his head.

'This is pathetic. These are our hills and they're asking us to keep off them for five months of the year so a few bored bastards can blatter a lot of wee beasties.'

'Not everyone looks at it like that, mate. Especially our Mr MacLeish. I reckon this is one of his notices, because this is meant to be a liberal estate. But what's reasonable depends on your point of view, don't it? Relative, like.'

Neil wiped the rain and hair off his face. This was not the time or place.

'Are you on their side?'

'No. But I can understand their reasoning, so I enjoy beating them.'

'Al, you're a Tory-anarchist bampot.'

Alasdair leant against the sign and grinned.

'Yes, but answer me this – did beer ever taste as good once you were old enough to drink legally?'

Neil slid to the ground against the pole.

'Is this a rest stop or a philosophical interlude?'

Alasdair checked his watch.

'Three hours. Good going for a copywriter. We'll take five here and get some scran in.'

* * *

Kirsty tilted the plastic flask top to chapped lips and drank.

'How are we doing?'

Jane squeezed in tighter behind the boulder.

'Not badly. If we contour now we should come in about three-quarters' way up the Braes. Well above the fellas down by the fence and the lower slopes. I'm more worried about the two at the top.'

'What two?'

'You didn't see them when the mist lifted?'

'I've just been following on trust. Here.'

Jane took a swig and wiped her hand across her mouth.

'Glad somebody still trusts me.'

'Things are still the same?'

'Pretty much. No action on the bed front. You?'

'Me? No. No.' She gulped down the last of it. 'Matter of fact, I'm keeping my head below the parapet from now on.'

'Sure, till next time.' Jane made short work of a Mars bar. 'Great thing about this lark is you can eat as much as you want because you just burn it off.' She laid her head against the rock and looked up at the tattered sky. 'This is fun, isn't it?'

'Fun? Fun?'

'Well, it's stopped raining and we could be asleep with nothing happening and instead we're having an adventure.'

Kirsty looked up. A few stars. Smell of the night wind. Sodden breeks. Thirst and hot tea. No men.

'You're right. It is fun. Sorry I've been such a ratbag.'

Jane chuckled and pushed the flask into Kirsty's pack.

'Now we go softly-softly. With the sky clearing, this could be the exciting bit.'

Alasdair and Neil had TAB'd another hour or more, contouring along just below the skyline because they were getting deep into enemy territory. Neil was trying to return to his earlier trance state but only found burning legs and a sick feeling. The side-slope steepened and suddenly they were clinging and scrambling on broken rock and wet turf. The sky was clearing and way down below Neil saw a faint glitter.

'Is this right?'

'I'm not sure.'

'What d'you mean, you're not sure?'

'We've been going at such a lick I've not been counting paces, and with the mist and the contouring and everything . . .'

'You mean we're lost?'

'Not exactly . . . lost. Just not quite found. We may be in one of two places.'

'And what if we're not?'

A pale grin through the darkness.

'Then we're somewhere else. Time for the navigator's friend.'

He unzipped a pouch and took out something that looked like a small mobile phone. He pressed a button, a green light came on and a dial lit up.

'Beam me up, Scottie?'

'Nearly but not quite. This is a Satnav I liberated from the stores.'

'Come again?'

'Satellite navigation device. It plots your position from three satellites. Mostly used at sea, but if you key it into the OS before you start, it gives your position to within ten metres.'

'That could save a few lives on these hills.'

'Then again, most interesting things have happened to me when I've got lost . . . Right! Thought so.'

He took the map and stuffed it back inside his jacket, then zipped away the Satnav.

'You weren't really lost, were you, Al? You just wanted to show off that gizmo.'

'You'll never know. But I'll tell you this, chum' – he poked him in the chest – 'no one's ever as lost as they think they are when they think they're lost.'

'Run that by me again?'

'Just something I picked up in Tibet.'

They retraced their steps till the slope lessened, then cut up sharp left. Neil followed on, shaking his head. Sutherland, Sutherland. It could even be true if it made sense.

They re-emerged on to the plateau and the moon tore away from the cloud.

'Down!'

Neil was already face down. He'd seen the men too. Three of them, maybe a hundred yards off. Two sitting on a rock, one pacing back and forth. The plateau had narrowed drastically. On the right was a dark lochan. On the left, where they'd been, the ground sloped steeply then fell a thousand feet or so to a long narrow loch that glittered with bits of broken moon.

'Clever,' Alasdair muttered. 'MacLeish isn't daft. He's cut off the corrie where his grouse are, and our pockets. I'd forgotten all about this bit. But get past them and we're in.'

Neil took a good look. There was no cloud in the blue-black sky, nothing to come to their rescue, and the men weren't going anywhere.

'I'm not turning back after that bloody slog. How about going into the loch and trying to wade past them that way?'

'You are determined, aren't you?' He considered it. 'No. Even with the breeze they might hear us. And against the water we'd be too visible. No, there's a better way but you're not going to like it.'

Alasdair explained. They could down-climb part of the slope to the left – not much gear and Neil would just have to tie the rope round himself old-style and falling would be a bad idea. Not very far, just about three hundred feet, though it got damned steep. But then there was a ledge of sorts that ran along to the far end. Not a very wide ledge, admittedly, and not exactly level and there wasn't time to put in protection. At the far end the corrie laid back and they could scramble up and emerge at the far side of the sentries. Not a very big problem.

'You're not saying no problem.'

'I'm afraid not.'

'No problem with you is bad enough. Shit!'

Neil lay and thought about it. He'd never liked unprotected climbing, especially on rock. Snow and ice was different, somehow. He didn't really like exposure, and even less in the dark. He liked mountains, that was different.

'Look, I could take the shotgun and go on myself and see if I can ping a couple.'

'No! Thanks, but no,' Neil continued more quietly. 'This is my hit and my problem. Anyway, I've seen you and you're a rotten shot.' He lay for a moment with his face on his fist on the sodden grass. Nobody's ever as scared as they think they are when they think they're scared. Something like that.

'OK. Let's get it over with.'

A quick clap on the shoulder.

'First we crawl off this plateau. After that, do exactly what I say and be damn careful. It's my neck too.'

'I'll keep it in mind.'

Trust, Neil thought as they slithered off the plateau. Even though you could be wrong. He wanted to see Helen again, but not that quickly. There were still a few ploys to play out first.

* * *

The stars were already hidden and the moon was beginning to hide, but still the head and shoulders of the man looking down from the crest of the hill were evident enough. Kirsty pressed her face against wet rock where she lay after she'd fallen. Not a very big fall, but enough to send a few stones rattling down the hill and bring the sentry back on to the skyline.

She lay cursing her clumsiness. This was not her world, not really. Maybe it was time to go back to her natural habitat and start again in a city where no one knew her.

Torchlight swept over the rocks and heather, fell on her black gloves. It lingered on the painted side of her face. With her eyes screwed tight she still felt the light.

The man swept the beam away then on impulse brought it back again. He saw uneven pools of shadow, the glimmer of heather, short grass and angular rocks, some of which sparked as the torch fell on mica and quartz.

He heard an owl hoot further down the valley, and then again. It could have been a rabbit, a weasel, a fox, even a ptarmigan that had set off the stones.

Or perhaps not.

He switched off the torch though his night vision was already ruined. The rain came on again, sweeping in from the west.

He pulled up his hood and walked away from the crest of the hill, back towards the small knoll with the cairn where he'd been sheltering. If there was anyone down there, they'd be spotted as soon as they came over the crest and on to the bare top. And even if they got in past the other ghillies, they had no chance of getting back out in daylight.

Despite the hood, rain was dripping down under his collar again. He cursed and hoped Macnab came his way so he could thump the bugger a couple of times before hauling him off to collect a grand from MacLeish. A grand! He could get smashed for a year on that.

Jane's hand on her sleeve, tugging. Kirsty nodded and began to follow her, this time keeping a very sharp eye on the dim ground beneath her feet. It was beginning to feel natural. She hadn't noticed it yet but something had changed. She felt like an animal, a red fox maybe, eyes and ears alert, moving at home across the hill in light rain on a summer night.

'I said you wouldn't like it.'

Neil waved away the proffered hand, made a little bridging move and hauled himself up over the top of the chimney, sat down then fell over on his back and lay looking up at the black sky as the rain came on.

He tested his scraped knuckles. Three were bleeding from hand-jam abrasions. He hoped he could still shoot straight after this.

He sucked the blood away, tasted the wedding ring, smooth and metallic on the side of his mouth.

'Let's crack on,' he said. 'Gotta get there before first light.'

Alasdair passed him the chocolate and chuckled.

'You really didn't like it, did you?'

'Some day I'll remember what we just did and I'll wake up screaming. It was horrible and you know it.'

'The ledge was a bit narrow,' Al conceded.

'What ledge?'

Alasdair got up, looked back. They must be well past the men at the narrow neck. Ahead lay the broad shallow corrie where MacLeish had corralled the remaining grouse for the day's shoot. That would be stiff with sentries. But all Macnab had to do was skirt round that, keeping under the rim of the bowl, then down over the little bealach to the pocket where a covey of stray grouse might or might not put in an appearance.

Neil stood beside him, finishing the last of his chocolate.

'Thanks for staying tied on to me,' he said. 'I thought that was pretty trusting in the circumstances.'

Alasdair Sutherland settled his deerstalker more firmly on his head.

'It's called motivation through responsibility,' he said. 'I reckoned that if you knew you were risking my life as well as yours, you might concentrate a bittie harder.'

'You're . . .'

'Officer material? Absolutely, old chap.'

'Several cartridges short of the full clip, I was going to say.'

'I told you – officer material. You know what the life expectancy of a junior subaltern was in the First War? From about now till the weekend.'

'You're a mine of disused information, Sutherland. Now I've failed to kill you, perhaps we should get on.'

'A-OK.' He started to move on, then stopped a moment. 'And by the way, well done. I think I must have confused that ledge with another one somewhere . . .'

* * *

'You'd best get on back, Kirsty. It'll start getting light in an hour.'

'You'll be all right here?'

Jane settled against the big black pack. They were under a small overhang about thirty feet from the crest of the Brae, the spot she'd chosen during their picnic recce. Unless the watchers left their knolls, wandered some four hundred yards and peered over the edge, she should have a quiet hour to herself to rehearse her next move.

'Right as rain.' She pulled off her black woollen hat and ran her hand through her wet hair. 'Though I sometimes wonder what's right about it.'

'I'll be off, then. I don't know how you managed that pack.'

Jane eased her shoulders.

'I've been humping it around Chamonix the last three weeks.'

Kirsty giggled quietly.

'Not the only thing you've been . . . Sorry.' She nudged Jane. 'Inside me there's a sensitive person trying hard not to get out.'

Jane grunted, didn't seem very convinced.

'Thanks for the company anyway,' she said. 'And the extra gear.' She craned her head and looked up behind them. 'Odd to think that the lads should be only half a mile away.'

'If they're there.'

Jane yawned and settled back.

'Oh, I should think so. As a rule they're to be trusted.'

Kirsty made a sound like a Pekinese with nasal congestion, picked up the compass and stole away the way they'd come.

Jane made herself comfortable. All she could do now was wait for a whistle or shots or both. He'd better be there. He would be.

She stuck her hands under her armpits and waited.

'This is it,' Al whispered.

They were lying at the edge of a small pocket of short heather surrounded by shallow grassy banks.

'You really think there's grouse here?'

'Not yet. If they come at all, it'll be at first light. They start moving at dawn to where they want to feed. They'll come over the bealach in short glides. They're lazy and don't really like flying. Let them come and keep your head down. Remember with the .410 you need to get close. You act as your own beater – just lob a stone or shout. They'll almost certainly fly directly away from you, and they keep low.'

'I've been practising that one with the clays. It's the easiest shot.'

Alasdair nodded.

'You'll probably only get two shots, then they'll be off. Make them count, old sport.'

'Do my best.'

'I'll be waiting. Soon as I hear the shots.'

'See you in a while.'

'Cheers, Neil.' He hesitated before moving off. 'Look, I might have said something to Kirsty—'

'Save it, Al. Later.'

He was already drawing the shotgun from his pack. When he glanced round, Alasdair had gone.

He took out four cartridges, loaded two. He propped the other two on the tussock in front of him. Then he rested his chin on his hands and waited for dawn, as he'd done many times in the months after Helen.

Prepared, empty, he lay waiting for the curtain to rise.

16

Alasdair hunkered down in the peat slot, looking up at a narrow patch of dim sky. The rain had brought a small burn flowing down between his feet. He'd wedged his boots on either side but they kept slipping down the wet earth and he'd come to with a start to find cold water running into his boots.

He turned sideways, wedged both feet against one bank and his back against the other and let the top of his head emerge from the slot. The rain had stopped. Just as well: in heavy rain the grouse would find a lee slope and not come out.

He began to nod off again. Jane. They'd argued, sulked, bickered many times in ten years, but always there'd been an escape route. Now it was like they were stuck halfway up a route on separate ledges, both unable to down-climb or top out. And the longer they waited there, the more impossible movement became. They could just die up there, waiting for a sign, a line let down from above.

He opened his eyes and saw a very strange thing. He was looking up at a salmon the size of a Zeppelin.

He blinked but it was still there. The dawn sky was breaking up, and there was the silver and reddish underside, the big grey dorsal fin, the tail flexing. The huge curved mouth opened and closed.

He should never have taken those drugs back in the seventies.

The wind shifted, the tail detached, the mouth gaped and dissolved, then all that remained was patches of drifting cloud in the dawn. The salmon in the sky . . .

He lay gaping upwards like a gaffed fish. Then he heard the distant shots. One. Two.

He levered himself out of the slot. Then more shots. Three, four. So Neil had failed. Then a whole volley of shots, but very faint, even for a .410.

The shoot had begun.
'Er . . . hello.'
Still on his knees, he turned round. Three very surprised people were looking down at him. They were almost as muddy as himself, and carrying placards.
STOP THE SLAUGHTER!
GROUSE HAVE RIGHTS TOO!
'Ah, hello,' he said. 'I'm campaigning for access rights, myself.'

It was full light but not one grouse had showed. Not a solitary flying sausage. As the damp tweeds clung to him, Neil was shivering with cold. He felt desperately exposed on the short heather. Sooner or later someone would come by and he'd have to run for it.

It had always been a gamble anyway. They'd known that from the start. He thought he'd accepted that.

Then he heard the shots. One or two, then a whole barrage. The shoot must have begun. It sounded close, just over the bealach behind him. He could even hear voices carried on the wind. If the beaters got to the bealach, that was it. A minute, maybe two. The shots were getting closer. He began to flex his legs, ready to run.

And then they came, skittering over the col. Not many, a dozen maybe, in short whirring flights, crying *Go back! Go back!*, driven by the guns.

They're going to fly past. One dropping down at the edge of the pocket. The rest follow, craning their necks, very skittery and nervous.

The guns are silent. They must be reloading. Or perhaps the wind's shifted and blown the sound away.

In little glides and darts, the grouse are moving to the centre of the arena. Heads go down, up, down again.

He gropes for the gun, slowly, slowly. His fingers are so stiff he doesn't know if he can pull the trigger. They're so beautiful, these birds, all those browns, and the red patch round the eyes of the two males.

The stock against his shoulder. Damp against his cheek. Barrel smooth and chill in his left hand. White finger through the guard, crooking stiffly round the first trigger.

Yi-yah!

The birds are up, flying directly away. Barrel up. The male on the right. Bang! The grouse wavers, drops. But already he's swinging to the second. And misses as it turns.

Fumble in another cartridge. But they're disappearing over the slope. No second chances in this life.

A solitary grouse, greedy or slow or plain confused, rattling by right to left. Aim ahead.

Bang.

It drops like its cord has been cut.

On his feet and running. Pick up the second grouse. Poor dead beautiful thing. Warm. Blood on his hands. Where's the first one? Bottom of the slope. Dead too, thankfully.

Shotgun into pack. Hurry, hurry! They must have heard those shots. Sling it on. Birds by the legs, tucked under the arm like a rugby ball.

Then he's pounding up the slope, over the top and haring for the try line.

Round the corner, past the white boulder. Thank Christ, there's Al. And three people he's never seen before. He looks at them. They look at him. Al mouths something at him.

'Anti-blood sports!' Neil gasps. The three look at him. Camouflage streaked across his face, the blood smeared over his hands. 'Saboteur. I pinched them from the shoot. Unfortunately I think they may be dead.'

The three gape at him. For a moment even Alasdair is at a loss.

'I'd better get 'em to hospital then, old chap.'

He grabs the grouse, stuffs them under his jacket and legs it. He disappears over the hill, heading south.

The three protestors turn their attention back to Neil. They look faintly puzzled and not very happy with the situation.

Neil spreads his arms wide.

'OK, so I know our methods are unorthodox.'

He hears the shouts. He lowers himself into the slot. Looking up, he puts his fingers to his lips and winks, then crouches down.

He hears the ghillie running down. No, two of them.

'Got you bastards!'

One look and the ghillies know they're mistaken. No gun, no grouse, the placards. Down in the slot, Neil hunches round his pack and waits. It's out of his hands now. He has to hope and trust as he listens to the muttered debate.

'Let's throw these wallies off.' London accent.

'Aye, but there's the money, Hugo.'

Hugo? Neil wondered. Since when are ghillies called Hugo?

'So which way did he go?'

A pause. Neil twists his ring like it could do magic which it can't.

'That way,' he hears the woman say.

The feet thud off.

'You can come out, pal.'

Neil raises his head cautiously. The two ghillies are heading east, across the river.

'Thanks. I appreciate it.'

The bearded man shrugs.

'I don't know whose side you're on, chum, but it's definitely not theirs.'

The distant shooting starts up again. The three pick up their placards, take out their whistles.

'Are you coming with us?' the woman asks.

'Think I'll just rest here for a while. But you go on. Disrupt like crazy.'

'We will.'

They set off up the slope in the direction of the guns.

'And don't get shot!' Neil calls after them.

They wave, but don't look round. 'We won't,' drifts back on the wind.

Neil settles into the slot, hugging the pack and still feeling the shock of the warm birds in his hands. But he's done it and now it's up to Al and Jane.

At that distance Jane didn't hear the shoot starting up. Crouched among the boulders, she could clearly see a line of men by the deer fence at the bottom of the Brae. And two – no, three – others stationed about halfway up. Then there'd be the men up on the bare knolls over the skyline. And the ones patrolling the western slopes, up from Aziz's.

She looked at her watch. A watery sun began to edge into her hiding place. For the first time she began to doubt her husband. And she wasn't happy about the wind direction.

Then, very faintly, a shot. A second. A pause, then a third.

She was on her feet, scrambling round the overhang with the black pack over one shoulder. She came over the top, lay belly down and looked around. She didn't think the people by the fence had seen her yet. She could see a man on the knoll to the west, maybe four hundred yards. And one to the east. They'd heard the shots too. They were waving and pointing across the distance.

Come on, come on. Where are you?

Faint whistles. She spotted two more men come on to the skyline further to her left. Then three tiny figures running separately down the bare slope to the north – a good distance off but coming her way. The net was closing but Al wasn't even in it. Where was that man?

Stumbling over the hill to the north-east. Leaping then rolling down a steep heather bank. Coming to his feet with one arm still clutched round his chest. Absurd. Ridiculous. Himself.

She knelt and pulled the pack open. Working feverishly, she spread the canopy and strapped herself in. Straightened out the rigging lines. Clipped in.

She looked round. The men on the knolls had seen her now of course. One was racing her way. The other was cutting across to intercept Al. The others were closing in behind him.

Alasdair was not really a runner. He never had been a runner, and two knee operations for moraine-ruined cartilages hadn't made him any quicker. He glanced behind. The long, lean lad was gaining. They got younger every year. The others looked knackered. It was a long run over deep heather.

He hugged the grouse tight under his jacket, jumped the burn, hit the down slope with his shoulder and rolled to the bottom. On his feet again. Men closing from the right. Where was she? Be there. Just be there.

Hell's javelins, another squaddie coming in from the left. And there she was, standing a hundred metres off, top of the bare stony hill. She bent over, clipping herself in. Go, Jane!

The last uphill stretch. This guy's going to cut him off for sure. Jane whazzes the black canopy up into the air, the tubes fill and the wing pulls tight above her. She turns into the wind and fights to hold it steady.

OK, Alasdair, here comes the laddo looking for his thousand quid. Remember the old rugger team.

They close on each other. Alasdair checks, gives the keeper the old hand off, then sticks out a leg. You learn some useful things in public school, like how to play dirty. The lad trips and goes flying, crunches into the side-slope.

And there's Jane, waiting, nodding, shouting him on. You can trust Jane. Solid as a rock, old sport.

The breath in his chest is harsh, metallic. This hurts. His legs are moving but he isn't going anywhere. The lad behind is getting up. The fella on the right a hundred metres away and closing.

Jane is shouting something. Yes, yes! He opens his jacket, holds the grouse in one hand and fumbles for his harness with the other. Falls on his knees at the top of the slope. Staggers into her. She clips him into the D-ring. Then the other. The canopy is nearly out of control, the wind's too strong.

'What's that Al? What is it?'

He retches on to the ground. The two men come over the top.

'Hate . . . flying. Ha . . . y . . . y . . .!'

She runs forward, dragging him behind. Her feet leave the ground, she's off the top and then the paraglider lurches as Al's weight comes on. She flicks the left lines, the wing recovers and they're off, skimming away from the baffled group gathering on the stony top, way over the heads of the men on Maiden Braes, flying down into the sunlight.

They're losing height too fast. Find an up current. She turns back in towards the slope. The wind that's bouncing up it lifts them like an invisible crane.

'What you say, Al?' she shouts over her shoulder as they go up.

'Brilliant!' he yells. 'Totally magic ace wild gobsmack brilliant! You teach me!'

She nods and nods, struggling with the awkward eddies. She doesn't want to tell Al, but if they have a front tuck here, they're dead. Drop like twin stones five hundred feet. Very romantic but no thanks.

She regains control and straightens out the wing.

'Stop bloody wriggling!' she shouts, then turns the pont for the long descent towards Aziz's woodland strip.

'Here they come,' Murray said. 'But have they got the birdies?'

The black canopy, like a batwing, overflew another group of stumbling keepers.

'It's getting low,' Kirsty said. 'I don't know if they'll clear the fence.'

The two of them crouched in the undergrowth. Kirsty's grip was starting to cut off the blood supply to Murray's arm.

'Come on, come on! Up!'

The paraglider wasn't going to make it. Then one of Jane's arm's twitched and the inflated wing veered right. It passed over a patch of burnt heather and suddenly it wasn't coming down but rising slightly in an up draught.

'They're going to make it! He's waving at us!'

She was jumping up and down.

'He's not waving, he's showing us something! Camera!'

As the canopy glided over the deer fence and into the trees a hundred yards along from them, with a faint wheesh and thrumming noise, Alasdair was waving the grouse in one hand and pointing at them with the other. The camera clicked, the paraglider hit the treetops. There was a pause, then shouts, a crackling and crunching, then silence.

'Did it! We fuckin flamin did it!'

Murray and Kirsty embraced. She drummed her fists against the nearest tree. Murray was doubled over laughing. It was something to do with Sutherland's airy gesture, his supreme confidence as he sailed majestically into the crash.

'We'd best find them and gie them a hand.'

'Oh, I could kiss that man! Did you see how she flew that?'

They slipped back into the trees as the Inchallian squad stopped on their side of the fence. Relations between the estates were not good, and they had no authorization to cross.

Kirsty and Murray pushed through the trees and undergrowth in the direction of the crash-landed canopy. Murray stopped.

'Wait!'

'What is it?'

Kirsty and Murray stood listening. Through some now ruined birch saplings they saw a huge rhododendron bush. Spread on it were the remains of a paraglider. And from inside the bush came giggling and laugher and low, unmistakable sounds.

Murray looked at Kirsty.

'Fuckin time too.'

She looked back at him.

'In this case, I think you're right.'

They tiptoed away.

17

Neil was half-starved. Perhaps he had been for a long time before he'd noticed it. His feet were numb and the guns had been silent for ages. Maybe the shoot was over for the day. Maybe they broke for whisky and smoked salmon sandwiches and came back later in the afternoon.

Enough maybes. Down in the slot he cleaned off his make-up, folded the tweed jacket round the shotgun, then levered himself back up into the fresh air.

Clouds, wind, patches of sunshine sweeping the hills. A couple of larks somewhere up in the blue lift. A drone drifted by with a bee attached, three ptarmigan scuttled away over stones. The world was big and open after hours in the slot.

The sun was hot on his legs as he changed out of the damp tweed breeks and pulled on an old pair of black 501s. For a while he just sat looking down the slope at the burn flashing and the khaki-coloured hills beyond.

There was nothing virtual about this reality. This was as real as a warm dead bird in his hands. This belonged to itself, not to Maurice Van Baalen. On this ploy for once they were creators, not consumers, and that made all the difference. That's where the healing lay.

Eventually he stretched, slung the pack on his shoulders and ambled down to the burn to drink while it was still free. He crouched over the water, scooping it from palm to mouth, seeing what he lost shine as it fell back into the pool.

He crossed the burn, gained the path and set off towards the road. He whistled as he went, looking round casually from time to time.

'If you've to do something furtive,' Alasdair had instructed, 'for God's sake don't furt about.'

So he was a rambler wandering home after a fine morning

asserting his rights of access. The shotgun in the pack was unfortunate. But the beaters and ghillies had no cause to look for him. If they'd seen anything after the shots, it was one man in tweeds running away, disappearing, then reappearing heading in a different direction. And if Al and Jane had got their act right – and he'd spent some time envisaging all the ways it could go wrong – MacLeish would already be concentrating his forces round the Lodge.

He heard voices. A group of beaters, students by the look of them, were catching up on him. With one hand on the strap of his pack, ready to jettison it and run, he waited for them.

How had the shoot gone? Not bad. Early start to get the first grouse down to London for the posh restaurants. Bit of a clarty job, wasn't it? Rotten pay but as much as you could eat, and the wind had kept the midgies off. Fat Freddie had caught some buckshot in his ear when one of the clients got overexcited.

Neil walked down the track with them a way, enjoying their youth and light-heartedness. Nothing very bad had happened to them yet. They told him there'd been some sort of chase, oh and that poacher fella, looks like he'd got away with some grouse. Just took off like the bird-man of Alcatraz. The gaffer had completely done his nut. Then there'd been some shoot saboteurs who drove off half the birds with whistles and got in front of the guns. So they'd all had a good laugh and a rest while that was sorted out. Then there'd been more beating and some good shooting and now they were finished for the day, heading for the pub.

They hurried on and Neil let them go, in no hurry now he knew the result. He'd done – they'd done it. It didn't make everything all right, but it helped.

The burn flashed and gurgled, the kestrel hung against the sun, Helen was in the ground knowing nothing.

It helped. And there was the road in the valley below, and friends at the end of it.

Tricia and Eve picked Neil up at the phone box. He put the pack in the boot and got in the car. Eve passed him sandwiches and a flask. He kept his hand out, and with a sigh she handed over his tobacco and papers.

Kids these days, the new Puritans. As if not smoking guaranteed virtue, or a long life.

In the Strathdon headquarters he hugged Murray. This was a

first – they were Scottish, after all. Jamie ran around the room going Bam! Bam! and jumping off the chairs with his arms out then dying noisily on the couch.

'Where's Al and Jane?'

Murray gave a broad grin and pointed upstairs.

'Getting reacquainted.'

'Kirsty's gone back to get changed for the garden party,' Tricia said. She sounded apologetic. 'But she said to say congratulations.'

Kirsty knelt and said goodbye to Charlie. She'd been rather short with him the last couple of days. He couldn't help being male. She put him on the long tether and left him woofing and whining as she got into the Wolseley.

She drove slowly down the road and checked herself in the car mirror. This wasn't a dinner party for two with Abdulatif but a garden party for the Glorious Twelfth with sensible Dutchmen. So it was the tweed hacking jacket, white blouse, green choker, green pleated tartan skirt. Hair back in a band, light make-up. Wholesome. The ideal daughter.

She winked at herself in the mirror and wondered how Abdulatif was doing.

There were two men at the big gates. She had no written invitation and her press card did not go down well. She persuaded them to get on their walkie-talkie and while she waited she glanced round. There seemed to be men every fifty yards all along the railings.

She was let through. As she drove up there were more men ringing the Lodge. It was more like an Arab-Israeli summit than a Highland garden party. She left her car alongside the BMWs and Citroëns and went in.

She was shown through the hall, along a panelled corridor, then out through the far side, through the French windows and on to the lawn where a marquee had been erected. Along its ropes were twined Union Jacks and the Dutch flag and even the occasional saltire. There were some fifty guests, some still in shooting gear, one or two formally dressed, a few in kilts, standing in small groups balancing plates and glasses.

She spotted Shonagh behind the makeshift bar and made towards her.

'Miss Fowler? It is my pleasure you are here.'

Van Baalen was not wearing a kilt but casual slacks and a sports jacket. For that she liked him. They shook hands. He was somewhere in his fifties, balding and tanned. He reminded her of the uncle, earnest but kindly, that she'd never had.

'Where is Mr Aziz? He is not with you?'

'He asked me to apologize. Something has come up but he'll try to drop by later.'

He got her a drink and steered her away from the others. He leant towards her and exchanged pleasantries as though she was the only person there he wanted to talk to. She saw MacLeish, in full dress kilt as was expected of him, standing awkwardly among his employer's friends and clients. She was sure he felt a right fool and felt a brief sympathy for him. Shonagh said his people had once farmed here. Now, for all the authority he wielded in his master's absence, he was essentially a hired hand.

He saw her, scowled and looked away.

'I do not think my factor likes you much. He told me about the trouble he had with you and your friends. I have to say the publicity has not been good for us.'

'I'm sorry, Mr Van Baalen.'

'Maurice, please.'

'Trouble wasn't our intention, Maurice. We only wanted to walk on that hillside as people have here for hundreds of years.'

'Mm.' He looked down into his drink, then at her. 'I am told there is no legal right to roam on the estate.'

'There is nothing to say we have a legal right to breathe or go for a swim. Equally, there is nothing to say it is illegal. The basic tenet of British law is still – just – that whatever is not illegal must, *ipso facto*, be legal.'

'You argue like a lawyer, Kirsty.'

She grimaced and looked away for a moment.

'Well, perhaps. But you take my point. It's a very grey area. A lot was never resolved when the old clan territories began being bought and sold like factories or shirts. And that's leaving the Clearances out of it. The old clan chiefs didn't *own* the land in a modern sense. They represented it. Held it in trust, or something – a lot of people round here still think of it like that.'

'This is not the way Mr MacLeish talks about it. Interesting. He says you are invading the estate and damaging the shooting, which I would not like to see.'

He peered at her through pale brown eyes, waiting for her response.

She smiled at him; usually it helped.

'We did not intend to damage anything on Maiden Braes, and

we didn't. There's nothing to damage! There are no grouse there, as you must know. And I understand the importance of shooting in the economy of an estate. But to seal it off from mid-August to the end of February is quite unnecessary when you only shoot in one small area at any one time. It's bad PR and it's not even good management.'

He nodded, not agreeing or disagreeing.

'The Criminal Justice Act—'

'May be legal but it's not honest. And you'll find you're chasing your tail if you want to make Aggravated Trespass stick. Take my advice, Maurice – avoid confrontation.' She had the grace to grin at this. 'You'll just pull the sky down on your head.'

'I will think about this. We must talk more. I have a big meeting soon with the Landowners' Association, and we will be talking to these Ramblers' Associations.'

'You said the publicity has not helped the estate. There's a way to make that good. Instead of fighting it and making yourself unpopular, you give me an interview and say that for the time being, without prejudice, you are prepared to accede access to the estate anywhere that does not directly interfere with the shooting. This will cost you nothing and make you a friend of many people.'

'Mm. You are persuasive. I will consider this and talk with my lawyers.'

She put her hand on his arm.

'Never talk to lawyers, Maurice. Listen to yourself and then decide. It's a great deal cheaper, and more honest.'

He began to steer her back towards the drinks table.

'I must talk to my guests. But thank you for this conversation, Kirsty. Tell me, what do you think about this John Macnab?'

'I must talk to my lawyer before I answer that.'

He put his head back and laughed loud and natural.

'If you want a job someday, please contact me. I have a small PR company for my business. You are not only clever and, if I may say, very striking, you are also funny. That is good. Sometimes I am so deep in business I forget about fun. We are, as you know, a serious people.'

'Thank you. I may need a job soon.' She accepted another glass of champagne. Shonagh winked at her, seemed to be trying to attract her attention. 'So I hear John Macnab has got his grouse.'

'Yes, but I do not think he will deliver them back to me.'

'If that scallywag sets foot here, I'll break his damn neck.'

MacLeish at her elbow, radio in hand.

'Mr MacLeish takes his work very seriously,' Van Baalen said apologetically. 'In this we are alike. He is good at his work.'

'I'm sure he is. You certainly seem to have the house surrounded.'

'A mouse couldnae get past my men without being caught. We'll have him if he—'

MacLeish broke off. One or two of the guests near them seemed distracted. People were looking round, listening to a sound that was growing louder. Something that sounded like a power saw. Or a scooter.

Someone pointed up. A hundred feet up, something was flying over the trees. It looked like a metal dragonfly. It buzzed closer. Someone sat on it, dressed all in red, with red gloves and a red helmet with the smoked visor down.

The engine drowned out the conversation. Glasses halted midway to mouths. It had rotors but it wasn't a helicopter. It was small, like a motor bike, with a propeller at the back and blades above.

Kirsty had never seen an autogiro before. She glanced at MacLeish. The man was gaping as if John Calvin himself was doing a fly-past. The figure leant over the side, dangling something from its hand. And then, right overhead, let it go.

A little white parachute opened up. The forward momentum carried it over their heads as it fluttered and skewed across the lawn then burst through the greenhouse roof in a shower of glass and feathers.

The pilot waved once and the machine dwindled to the west.

Maurice and MacLeish were already running towards the greenhouse. Kirsty let them go. She knew what they would see, though the parachute was an unexpected touch. She reached for another glass of champagne and raised it briefly to the distant dot in the sky.

Shonagh reached forward and picked something from the back of Kirsty's jacket.

'Congratulations! *Seadh,* I think you'd best put these in your pocket, *ma ghoil*. And I want to hear the whole story later.'

With the merest blush, Kirsty took the two grouse feathers and pushed them into her breast pocket. Then she picked up her camera and strolled over towards the greenhouse and another exclusive.

18

The long black limousine emerged through the trees and came to a halt in Kirsty's yard as Charlie snapped furiously at the wheels.

'Friend of yours?' Neil whispered as he crouched behind the curtains.

'Somehow I doubt it,' Kirsty said.

They could make out nothing behind the smoked-glass windscreen. Charlie circled the car, then lifted his leg and left his ID.

'Special Branch, or I'm an old fart,' Alasdair muttered.

The kids were already under the bed with Murray. Tricia and Jane were hiding behind the bathroom door. Seldom had a celebration broken up so fast, as if someone had announced an evening of performance poetry would commence in thirty seconds.

The passenger door opened. A figure in black uniform stepped out with a peaked cap pulled down over a pair of very dark sunglasses. Whoever it was stared straight at the cottage window. A gloved hand went into the jacket and came out holding something flat and silvery. Neil felt Kirsty shiver beside him.

'I do like a good entrance,' she whispered.

The driver's door opened and an identically dressed figure stepped out, holding a large white box.

Neil gripped Kirsty's arm. It was the first thing she'd said directly to him since the night of the dance. She seemed to have taken the huff, but he didn't know whether it was because he'd kissed her or because he'd stopped kissing her. He didn't know what to say to her or how to explain why he'd panicked, and she didn't seem to want to hear it anyway.

'I fancy a good exit,' he said.

The leading figure in the yard took a cigarette from the silver case, put it to his lips and pushed the peaked cap up on a brown forehead. Kirsty ran out of the door, across the yard, and flung her arms round the shoulders of the man with the cigarette. She led him by the arm into the cottage.

'This is Abdulatif Aziz, gang,' she announced. 'He's brought an invitation we can't refuse.'

'Want to bet?' Neil muttered.

Abdulatif took off his hat and shades and looked round the little room.

'I apologize for this intrusion. Perhaps I watch too many American movies.'

The chauffeur opened up the white box and began to produce champagne from the cooler.

'This is John Macnab,' Kirsty said. Alasdair stepped forward and shook his hand firmly. Abdulatif recovered his hand, wincing only slightly.

'You are the army man, I think. Congratulations on your campaign.'

'Nothing to it, old chap.'

'And this is John Macnab.'

Neil held out his hand. Yes, this could be Kirsty's type – poised, alert, cultivated, and just a little dangerous. And serious wealth is seldom a handicap.

'You did well with the autogiro, mister.'

A flash of white teeth.

'And you with the shotgun, *mon ami*.'

'And this too is John Macnab.'

Murray hesitated, then shook his hand.

'How's it going, pal?'

'And you must be the communist fisherman who took my salmon.'

'I'm a socialist and it was naebody's fish. Aye, it was me.'

'Then I salute a fine piece of fishing.' Jane, Tricia and the kids trailed in. 'Are these John Macnab also?'

'We're aa John Macnab here,' Murray said. 'Like Jock Tamson's bairns.'

'Excuse me?'

'Quaint Scottish expression meaning we're aa equal, whether loaded or skint, punter or laird.'

'I see.' Abdulatif looked round at them all. 'We Muslims say something similar, though in this world it is not true. Does this mean you will accept me in your company when Mr MacLeish does not?'

'You got it, pal.'

The champagne was opened and poured into assorted mugs and glasses. Abdulatif kissed Eve's hand and gave Jamie his cap and shades.

'I propose a toast,' he said. 'To all John Macnab's, ah, bairns.'

'John Macnab's bairns!'

Abdulatif rapped on a bottle with his cigarette case.

'*Mes amis*, I have to make a short speech. In the past I have complained that life here is dull. Never again will I say this. You won your wager against me by fair means. Unfortunately for our socialist friend, as an alien I cannot vote in your general election.' Murray made a face. He'd been so carried away by the idea he'd never stopped to consider this. The same of course would apply to Van Baalen – and, for different reasons, to Balmoral. 'And today I have had great fun and settled a small score with certain people.' He paused. 'I am honoured to have been part of John Macnab, and I would be honoured further if you would accompany me for dinner tonight at my house.'

Only Murray and Neil hesitated. But it was pointed out that refusing this offer would be an unforgivable slur as well as a loss to their stomachs, and they relented, and they all bundled into the limo and set off for the big house.

'If only life was like this,' Alasdair sighed as he sat in the back in his best fatigues, squeezed in next to Jane. 'Another glass of champagne, dear heart?'

They ate Moroccan-style, round a big table with all the food in the centre, each reaching in with their fingers for whatever they fancied – salmon, trout, grouse, venison – dunking bread into sauces. For the rest of her life the smell of fresh-cut coriander will take Eve back there, to that wood-panelled room of clattering glasses, laughter that grew louder as the candles burned higher, the carry-on of slightly drunken adults feeling young and easy for a while.

She licked her fingers and glanced at Mr Aziz at the head of the table. He caught her eye and raised his glass and blew a kiss. She refused to blush and caught the kiss and bounced it back.

'Normally I hate rich bastards,' she heard her dad say. 'But for you I'll make an exception.'

Kirsty said something, and Aziz laughed.

'My friend,' he said, 'I will make you an offer. If you teach me this Spey cast, I will open the way to the waterfalls.'

Murray pushed back his chair.
'You're on. Got any rods here?'
'Several.'
They swayed out through the French windows into the garden. In the gloaming Eve could see them casting on the lawn, laughing as they tried to land the cast on a dinner plate by the rhododendron bushes. Alasdair was deep in conversation with Aziz's brother who'd just arrived that morning, talking climbing and army. Jane and the chauffeur, who was really Hugh from Birmingham, went to the stables to look over the autogiro. Uncle Neil was teaching Jamie to tap-dance.
Then more food appeared – mountains of profiteroles, sorbets, fruit, cheese. New glasses, sweet wines, the smell of coffee and cardamom. The company drifted round the table, waving their arms as they re-enacted the day's events – the long hike in by night, the shots, the pursuit, the flight from the hilltop, Aziz's fly-past.
Neil had left the table and was sitting by himself in a window-frame, looking out at the darkening hills. Eve saw Kirsty hesitate beside him. He offered her a cigarette, she shook her head and moved on. Neil lit the cigarette for himself and just sat there looking out.
When the music started, Eve soon slipped away to the study, switched on a lamp, found a big book with pictures about the High Atlas mountains and settled down in an armchair by the open window.
'Did I mention I saw a giant salmon in the sky today?'
She glanced out the window. Alasdair and Jane were swaying past down the gravel, arms crooked together.
'No.'
'Thank goodness for that, old girl . . .'
Eve closed the window and went back to studying pictures of Mount Toubkal in spring. She would go there some day. She would travel and watch and write about what she saw. She would never allow herself to be unhappy.
She faintly heard footsteps on the gravel. Kirsty and Neil were standing by the limousine, caught in the floodlights around the house. Neil had his hands in his pockets as he stared at the ground, Kirsty held a glass across her chest and wasn't looking at him. Neil started waving his arms and seemed to be asking her something. Kirsty put her head back and drained the glass. Neil sat on the bonnet of the car and held out a hand. Kirsty came

closer. She put her head on his shoulder like it was too heavy for her. Then she stood back, her free arm waving, and kicked the car tyre twice. Neil leaned forward and held out his hand again.

For a moment they were still. Then Kirsty raised her right arm, smashed the glass on the gravel and walked quickly back into the house.

Neil sat on the car bonnet. Eve saw his face tilt back and look up at the sky. She really shouldn't be watching this. It isn't nice to watch someone who thinks they're alone. But it's really interesting.

Neil slid off the car, put his hands in his pockets and walked slowly into the house.

Eve poured a pale yellow drink into a glass and sipped it. It had a twisted taste. Perhaps she'd get used to it. Why did people let a good day go wrong?

She went back to the big dining room. The table was cleared, the chairs had been pushed back and there was dancing. Jamie was asleep on the window-seat wearing the dark glasses. Even Dad was dancing. Kirsty was with Mr Aziz and she was laughing loudly. Uncle Neil was talking with Hugh from Birmingham, so she asked them to do the Dashing White Sergeant with her and everything was fine for a while. Then she saw Kirsty and Mr Aziz disappearing into the garden with Kirsty still laughing and one arm round her, the other holding a bottle.

'Mum, what's the name of Kirsty's friend at the hotel?'

'Um . . . Shonagh. Why?'

'It's for my diary. Thanks.'

She went out into the hall and found the phone.

She was nearly asleep in her armchair in the study when she heard the car come up the drive. Then the front doorbell rang. She watched from the door into the hall as Shonagh and her friend in the black jacket were let in by Mr Aziz's brother. He then went to find Mr Aziz.

Shonagh winked at Eve as they went past and into the sitting room where Neil was now at the piano singing that life was just a bowl of cherries and too mysterious to take serious. Mr Aziz came in from the garden and shook hands, and then Kirsty came in by another door with her hair all crooked and a look in her eyes like she wasn't quite a real person. Then Shonagh and her friend led Kirsty out into the garden, one on either side of her. Eve went back to the study because she'd done everything she could.

She woke in the morning, still in the armchair. Someone had put a travelling rug over her. On the table beside her was the Morocco book and an ashtray with the remains of a roll-up cigarette.

19

MACNAB NABS ANOTHER!
STRIKE TWO!!
GOTCHA GROUSE!!!

When John Macnab struck for a second time, it became the story of the silly season.

Television, radio and all the papers covered it. (Eve's cuttings from this episode alone fill two scrapbooks: they gather dust beneath her bed.) Kirsty's photo of the grouse lying on a bed of glass and geraniums on the greenhouse floor was syndicated alongside her interview with Van Baalen and brought more rainy-day money for her and the Sandy Arbuthnot Development Fund.

The stories of a Cabinet Minister's half-brother's highly original sex life and a TV presenter's miscarriage were relegated to the second page. The Secretary of State for Scotland condemned this latest outrage in the strongest possible terms by phone from the Canaries. The Leader of the Opposition had nothing to add to his previous statements on the subject. The SNP spokesman hailed it as the greatest victory over foreign intervention since Bannockburn – but of course could not approve of breaking the law. The sales of John Buchan books and membership of the Ramblers' Association went up. Class-war posters appeared in the cities that August: *Open Season – Smash the Landowners.*

But this time the Macnabs did not meet up again for an orgy of newspaper-reading and self-congratulation. By unspoken agreement – or perhaps it was just down to several raging hangovers – they went their own ways for the following couple of days.

Alasdair frowned as he lay in bed next to Jane, flicking through the papers. Neither the Palace nor Security had made any public comment; in fact they were being particularly tight-lipped about the whole affair. Only a small 'sources close to the Prince of Wales' comment suggested HRH was coming North personally to supervise the defence of the Balmoral and Lochnagar estate, and when Alasdair phoned a couple of Special Forces mates there was a definite buzz on. Worrying.

'Rise and shine, Ally,' Jane murmured.

'I don't want to get dressed yet,' Alasdair groaned. 'I'm trying to think.'

'Don't try too hard, sweetheart. I'm just asking you to rise one more time.'

Alasdair forgot about his worries for a while.

Murray and Tricia took a last walk along the forestry track above Strathdon. Tomorrow she and the kids had to go South for school and her job at the framing shop.

'So, fancy anither of these rugrats, Trish?'

Tricia blinked and watched Eve up ahead lose patience and wallop the ball into Jamie's back.

'It won't hold back the river,' she said at last. 'I think we should stop while we're ahead.' He just nodded and that was that, as they carried on in silence along the red-blaze track. 'Maybe you should too,' she added.

'Macnab?' Murray looked on the way their children were heading. 'It's *worked*.'

'But don't push it.'

'I'm hearing you.'

As they walked, Murray went on to admit Maiden Braes had been an eye-opener. The stushie round it and John Macnab had raised issues of land use, land access and land ownership in Scotland in a way years of doorstepping couldn't. Maybe that was the way to go.

'If you get caught you'll not make a selection list again.'

He shrugged. He hadn't realized how hacked-off with party politics he'd become, nor how much that loss of faith had left him sour and empty. Somewhere in the last two weeks he'd found a new direction. He'd never approved of single-issue politics or political theatre but they sometimes worked.

'And it'll make me look a right arse.'

'That wouldn't do you any harm.'

She laughed, then he did too. Up ahead Eve and Jamie broke into a run. They went running away down the track getting smaller and smaller, shouting to each other as they ran through a patch of sunshine and vanished into the forest.

Tricia and Murray looked at each other, then followed on while they still could.

The morning after Aziz's party, Neil went south for a couple of days. On the long descent from Drumochter towards Perth he realized the world of the Macnabs had been so total he'd forgotten anything else existed. Now the green shock of this rich farming land, so many trees. And being on his own again felt odd.

Then flickering flat out across the Forth, he glanced in the rear-view mirror back at the Lomonds, Ben Vorlich and the rest of the Highland Line. So much emptiness out there to fill.

Into the city, the city where there was more to desire than anyone could possibly ever possess, so that even the rich suspected they were missing something and the poor were bloody sure they were. The city he'd lived in for ten years now.

He walked across Marchmont, expecting to recognize most of the faces he passed, but this wasn't a small Highland town. His flat, their flat, the flat he hadn't got round to leaving after Helen, was exactly as he'd left it – the pen on the floor, the squint photo, the shirt across the bed, the cassettes still left out of their boxes. Nothing had moved an inch – well of course it hadn't.

He sat on the kitchen table and felt he'd moved a mile.

Next morning he went to the Asian flower shop at the corner and bought blue cornflowers for her birthday as he did every year, then drove to Stirling and on to Blairlogie. He looked up at the Ochil hills for a while, then went through the kirkyard gate which still needed oiling, crunched along the gravel until he crouched yet again by her stone and carefully fitted the long stalks into the little vase. He stood and looked down.

HELEN MAY ARMSTRONG
Sept 23 1960–Aug 16 1991
Missed always

For four years this had been the most real moment of his life, and now it wasn't. It was just a bunch of short-lived wild flowers, a slab of granite, and a man who'd lingered too long.

Once she'd got over her Aziz hangover, Kirsty kept her head down and worked, mostly in the office because she felt safer there. She did her pieces for the *Deeside Courier*, then a couple for the nationals. She went out and did the interviews, then was interviewed herself for TV and the radio. People seemed to think she had a hot line to John Macnab, though she insisted he'd just posted her the photos.

She kept away from the Atholl. She didn't want to see Neil, nor have a heart-to-heart with Shonagh, not after the Aziz episode. She winced at what she could remember and had hot flushes at what she couldn't. The champagne hadn't been a problem, but the whisky and a stiff joint in the bushes with Abdulatif certainly had been. Her father's pride and her mother's self-indulgence – she'd combined the worst of both of them.

So she worked the phone and the fax and the word processor, kept her distance, made useful contacts and delivered work on time. And at night she drove home with a thumping head and a fish supper. Locked the door and lit the lamp and drew the curtains. She ate, made coffee and lay out on the settee, made notes and talked to Charlie. He agreed, whatever she said. That was because he didn't understand anything except food, sex and affection.

Then again, what else was there to understand?

She brushed her hand over Charlie's adoring head. Food, sex, and affection: they're not that hard to find if you don't ask for more.

She kicked off her shoes but couldn't get comfortable. She lay picking hairs from Charlie's brush. Smashing that glass on the gravel had been childish, not theatrical. She'd got no satisfaction from the look on Neil's face. Neither from his shock nor his puzzlement nor his concern. Particularly not his concern.

She swung off the settee and checked through all the drawers, under the bed, behind the cooker, on top of the books, but she couldn't find one of Lachie's cigarettes. By now she wanted one very much indeed. Then between *Oklahoma* and the Cocteau Twins' *Heaven or Las Vegas* she found a squashed packet of Golden Virgina. No papers, but she could improvise something.

She knelt and unfolded Neil's packet. Half a dozen dried-up strands and a little dust shook on to the carpet.

She could still drive down to the Atholl. Tobacco, friends, sex and affection were available there. Love, real passion, commitment? Sorry, right out of that.

She got off her knees and sat on the edge of the settee. She was even thinking about Tom urgently, for the first time in ages. Had he got himself together? Was he inside? Had he tried to find her? Did he think of her?

She was tearing off her little fingernail with her teeth. The break ran down into the quick at the side of the nail. She pulled it out and sucked the sting and the blood. Bad time of the month, that must be it.

Just because someone's married doesn't mean they're still together. They could be separated. Getting a divorce. Helen could be going out with someone else. Anything. It happened all the time. All she had to do was ask. And make herself look jealous and stupid and needy.

Ah, sod it. She picked up her jacket, nodded to Charlie, and they went outside and tromped up the faint path through the trees till they came out at the top of the hill. They stood there a long time, looking down at the lights of the small town.

At last she gently pulled Charlie's ear and set off back down to the cottage. She'd been poaching it for years, but tomorrow was always fair game.

It was after midnight when the bog-standard blue Escort turned into the hotel car park. Neil got out of the car, picked up his bag and stood smelling the soft and different air.

He went in, picked up his key. No messages. He reached up and checked in Mr MacPherson's mouth. Nothing there either, just a stilled tongue. He patted the moth-eaten muzzle and went quietly up the stairs, thinking this felt like home.

He unlocked his door and went in. On the dressing table was a vase of yellow lilies and a note. He unfolded it. *Welcome back, Mr McGillivray – Shonagh.*

As he leaned over the basin to wash his face it came to him: sell the flat. Clear as a voice in his head. Sell the flat.

He slowly dried his face and stood at the window with the towel in his hands looking down on the lamplit street. Something had changed. He didn't know when it had happened – perhaps during the sunlit walk out of Inchallian after emerging from the slot, or while driving South over Drumochter, or while crouching down to fit the cornflowers into the little vase. But it had happened.

He began to shave, trying to get used to the new feeling.

Alasdair spread out the large-scale maps of the Lochnagar estate on the table.

'So – Balmoral. The Lochnagar estate. The stag.' He paused and fiddled with the fronds of his moustache as he looked round them all. 'Fact is, team, this one could get very heavy-duty.'

Neil looked at Kirsty, got no response.

'I don't see why,' he said.

Alasdair leaned forward and patiently explained.

'Look at it from Security's point of view. John Macnab has threatened to sneak around the Lochnagar estate with a high-powered rifle while HRH is in residence to take up our challenge. The rumour is they're extremely twitchy. They don't believe John Macnab is necessarily what he claims.'

Murray shook his head.

'Paranoia for beginners,' he muttered.

Alasdair folded his arms and looked at him.

'You haven't joined one of those flaky republican or class-war groups, matey? Not planning on using Macnab for a much bigger hit?'

Murray pulled out a thin cigar, pushed up his sleeves and stared out the window.

'Only in ma dreams.'

'Neil? You're pretty set on this independence lark.'

'Sure I've joined.' Neil stuck the cigarette into the corner of his mouth and reached into his inside pocket. 'Though I meant to keep my SRA membership secret.'

He flipped a card on to the table. Alasdair picked it up and squinted at it.

'Hm. This appears to entitle you to take home videos from the Majestic Video Club. Says nothing about political assassination.'

'I was misinformed,' Neil drawled, tugged his ear and got the ghost of a smile from Kirsty.

'Aren't you going to cross-examine me, then?' she asked.

'No. Sorry.'

'This is blatant discrimination, Mr Sutherland. I demand to be interrogated. I want the bright lights and thumbscrews.'

'We could take you out for a night in Aviemore,' Jane offered.

'No, no – I confess!'

In the case of Balmoral, Alasdair continued, unless HRH changed his mind and went somewhere else for his morning constitutional and water-colour painting, they could be up against the pros. Special Branch, Special Forces, VIP Protection Squad – take your pick. Plus overhead surveillance, infrared imaging, the lot.

'So you suggest we call it off?'

'I'm suggesting we reconsider the advisability of this deployment. We've opened a right can of beans here.'

Neil picked up a flicker of a smile from Kirsty.

'We should jack it in,' Murray said. 'We've had fun, made our point, got the debate goin. Now it's back to reality. We've got a living to earn.'

Kirsty made a face.

'I'm a purely recreational reality-user myself.'

'Exactly,' Neil said. 'I can't believe I'm hearing this.'

Alasdair glanced at Jane, but there was no guidance there.

'For once I agree with the red dwarf. I don't think you two understand what we're up against here.'

Neil offered Kirsty a roll-up. She shook her head and kept staring at Murray and Al. Neil leant back and lit up.

'So tell me,' he said.

'We could be talking STK.'

'Come again?' Kirsty asked.

'Shoot To Kill,' Jane muttered.

'Bit embarrassing to kill a poacher, surely.'

Alasdair shrugged.

'They can disappear the body. Or fake an accident.'

'Can they do that?'

Alasdair and Murray looked at each other.

'Yes,' they said.

A long silence.

Neil leaned forward on his elbows and stared at Murray, then Alasdair. He looked at Kirsty across the table but she seemed engrossed in picking some old chewing gum from the seam of her denim jacket.

'You two have got what you wanted out of this. And I've had a great time too.' He paused, looking for the right words. 'I've been chased, sent up, got fit, got drunk at someone else's expense, been to dances and sung songs and . . . lots of fine stuff.' Kirsty was still refusing to catch his eye. 'We've led half the country a right dance and got off with it. And I know sooner or later we all have to go back to the daily bread that should taste so much better but doesn't. But the fact is,' he leaned back and exhaled slowly as he looked round them all, 'I'm not ready to finish yet, and I want to go on.'

There was a silence round the table. Kirsty tried to work the chewing gum out from under her thumbnail. No easy way of getting rid of these sticky messes, she thought. We just transfer them from one place to another.

'What are we in this for?' Neil tried again. 'Is life a damage-limitation exercise or what?' Even Kirsty looked up, hearing something thicken in his voice. 'We can be canny and play safe and not make waves and not smoke, and keep our heads below the parapet our whole lives – and what difference does it make? Life-insurance brokers keel over in squash courts, a healthy young person gets on a plane and is carried off dead at the other end. You don't get a second shot for good behaviour, and I want one big adventure before I accept adventure's over.'

This is new, Kirsty thought as she studied Neil looking flushed across the table. So this is what makes him run.

She transferred the gum from thumbnail to index finger.

'Surely Security will all be concentrated round the Castle and HRH, right?' Alasdair nodded. 'They haven't sealed off the whole Lochnagar estate, have they?'

'Doubt they will,' Alasdair said. 'First, it's too big. Second, it's had PR the royals could well do without right now.'

'So if we stay well away from the Castle, we're really only dealing with the gamies.' She paused, gave it time to sink in as she looked round them all. 'Another thing – I think the anti-blood sports people are right. It's tacky to kill a stag for a bet.' She was slightly surprised to get nods all round. 'So we should issue a press statement like that. It might reassure Security and help keep public opinion on our side.' She laughed quietly. 'It might make all the difference between a fine and jail sentence if we're caught.'

'When we're caught,' Murray muttered.

'I'm an optimist,' she retorted. 'The fact remains that Security will concentrate round the Castle because it's the VIP they're protecting. They're not really trying to stop a poacher.' Neil nodded gratefully. 'If we stay well clear of the Castle, we could still pull it off.'

A long pause in the Strathdon kitchen. Murray pushed up his sleeves again but said nothing. Kirsty persuaded the gum to stick on the underside of the table. Finally Alasdair nodded.

'You could be right. If I was Royal Protection Squad I'd concentrate on blanket surveillance for a mile radius round the Castle, the Lodge and any other buildings that could be a propaganda coup. I'd liaise with the ghillies, but I wouldn't worry too much about one stag or another.'

'It's just the man with the gun they're bothered about,' Jane said quietly.

'Right.' Alasdair glanced at her.

'Time to put it to the vote,' Neil said. 'I propose we run this to the end.'

Kirsty put up her hand.

'Seconded.'

'Murray?'

Murray kept looking at the table. Alasdair sat back frowning, arms folded across his chest.

'How does the third hit go in the original book?' Jane asked.

'They get the stag but they get caught because one of them's dead noble,' Kirsty said. 'Oh, and the twit Archie Roylance marries slim, boyish Janet Raden, who's a jolly sporting chap.'

'I'm all for happy endings,' Alasdair said. 'I vote we go for it.'

'Murray?'

Murray opened his eyes and his children ran off into their future.

'You're sentimental fantasists and I'm no,' he said slowly. 'But I stick wi ma freens. So we do it.'

'You've all read the reports, and it's bleeding obvious we could be up against pros. This so-called John Macnab claims to be some kind of bet, but our analysis suggests there's been military-style planning behind it. So we have to take them seriously. Now, if we look at the first incident . . .'

The discreet conference room, hastily relabelled *Development Control: Private*, was airless and overheated. It was stuck somewhere in the back of the Aviemore Centre, and from where she sat Ellen Stobo could glimpse only a small rectangle of hill and blue sky through the only window set high on the wall. With an ache it reminded her of summer with her father in the Rockies, the year her parents had separated. Anger, tears, the silences worst of all, thickets of tangled emotion she couldn't push through. And finally taking a horse along through the woods and emerging at last above the tree line, a cool morning right before the fall. Scratched, sweating and breathing hard, but out into the open again.

In the middle of life, in the middle of a dark wood, she thought. I have to do it all over again but I can't remember how.

She put her hand over her mouth to cover a yawn as Colonel Mitchell ran the meeting. Never trust a man with no neck and no accent. She wearily stuck up her hand.

'What kind of an assassin tells the entire country what he's going to do and when? It makes no sense at all. What grounds do we have for thinking this John Macnab really is a threat?'

Mitchell leaned forward on his desk and jabbed a finger at the blackboard.

'Intel. rates these people as semi-pro. They say they're planning an operation on Balmoral. I don't know what you do in the Corridor, but in this Squad we're simple-minded. We put two and two together and get four. Right?'

Or twenty-two, she said to herself as the Home Office man put in his Minister's concerns. Not everything is a plot. Some things are just bad luck, like me being here instead of the Pyrenees.

She flipped back through the brief reports on Inchallian and Mavor. She was bored, as she often was since she'd messed up and transferred to the Corridor to keep the scandal quiet. She'd become a pen-pusher, an attender at the edge of departmental meetings, a drafter of reports chasing funding not criminals. She envied John Macnab. For the first time in years she thought of some wild things she'd done that summer in Alberta, like a little amateur rustling on a neighbour's ranch just to see if it could be done. She'd got a helluva kick out of that till she'd been caught.

The meeting went on. Fairly standard procedures. She didn't contribute. After all, she was only here as an observer. She had no formal powers whatsoever. She'd even had to push to be allowed to keep the gun and shoulder-holster, like it was a big deal or something.

Only when the Anti-Terrorist chief said they were pressing for unofficial STK on John Macnab did she raise her eyebrows. And she thought the Home Office representative looked a bit uneasy too. He'd be thinking of the political fallout if they screwed up.

Ellen looked out at her patch of hill and sky as she listened to the arguments. Yes, they were rattled. They liked things simple and that made sense. And she had to admit John Macnab made no sense at all. Maybe that was the point. It could be just what it claimed to be – a joke, a way of raising an issue, a cure for boredom.

It was called having fun. Goofing off. A challenge for the sake of it. What had all her dedicated career years left her with? A failed marriage, no children, many colleagues, few friends, the odd obliging lover, an inflation-proof pension. And sitting in yet another airless room with fifty not so far off, still dreaming of horses and hills in summer above the tree line.

She took out her pen and underlined two names that kept recurring in the Macnab reports. This journalist woman with her photos and talent for being in the right places at the right time. And the local cop. She'd read his reports. They were lucid and comprehensive. So why did she get the feeling he was holding something back?

When the meeting finally broke up, she approached Mitchell on his own. She flattered him discreetly, then said she had a proposition. She pointed out that his VIP still seemed set on winning the poaching challenge. There was a chance it was genuine, and if through a little freelance detection work she could prevent it, well there'd be Brownie points for his Squad – and for himself, of course. And if it didn't work, there was nothing lost and he wouldn't have wasted any of his own time.

She watched Mitchell think it over, looking for hidden angles. He was not a stupid man. He knew that if she'd been fully authorized she wouldn't be asking his go-ahead. So the Corridor was playing silly buggers again. She could see he didn't like it.

He went away, had a word with the Chief Constable, came back and nodded. She could check out the poaching angle on John Macnab, and the letter of authority would arrive that afternoon. It would at least get her out of his hair.

She thanked him, picked up her files and left the building with a little hop and skip as she emerged into the open air. Time for a little goofing off.

'OK,' Alasdair said. 'But forget the paint gun. We tranquillize it.'

'We sidle up to a stag and say, Hey, big boy, fancy some lithium?'

'A tranquillizer gun, idiot. Can you get hold of one, Al?'

'Uh-huh. But there a problem comes with it,' Alasdair said. 'The range of one of those guns is about forty metres. Which would mean one of the better stalks of all time.'

'Then there's the dead-weight of a stag,' Neil added. 'We're not exactly going to run off the hill and up to the front door of Balmoral with it.'

Jane looked up.

'You promised you weren't going near Balmoral.'

Alasdair looked shifty.

'Not if we can help it, old girl.' He tugged his moustache for a while but it remained in place. 'We need something so far-out amateur whacko that neither the ghillies nor Security would consider it. Any ideas?'

'Only sensible ones,' Neil said. It didn't seem likely he'd get any nearer to a stag than he would to Kirsty.

Kirsty laughed and got to her feet.

'If all else fails, we fall back on outrageous coincidence.'

'Where's that whisky?' Alasdair inquired.

'Gone to bed,' Jane replied firmly. 'Would you two like to eat here and stay over?'

'No thanks,' Kirsty said. 'Got to get home and see a dog about his tea.'

'Me too,' Neil said. 'I've got to phone a man about a copywriting agency we once ran.'

They left, as they'd arrived, in separate cars.

20

Next morning Neil daundered down the main street of the Highland town that felt like home. He was humming 'Lily, Rosemary and the Jack of Hearts', thinking about his sister whom he very rarely saw these days. They'd been very close for a while after Helen died. He was thinking about deerstalking, he was thinking about the law.

Most of all, he was thinking about a change of heart.

He'd dragged Helen's death behind him for years like a ball and chain. Now somewhere along the line he'd let it go. Today his footsteps didn't drag on the pavement.

He decided to celebrate by getting a haircut. Change of style, change of season. The bell pinged as he went in. Old leather chairs, smell of Brylcreem, yellowed cuttings of shinty heroes on the wall. He smiled, feeling his childhood all around him for a moment. Just because things don't last doesn't mean you can't love them. My, but his head was in a chatty mood this morning.

As he waited, he flicked through damp copies of the *Beezer* and the *Beano*, old *Victor* annuals. He reached over for a *Scots Magazine* and leafed through it. There was an article about royal water-colourists. He turned another page and he was looking at a not bad painting of a stag with a group of hinds at the edge of a lochan. *Deer Drinking at Dusk near Balmoral.*

He checked the date of the painting. Just a few years back. Even the lochan looked vaguely familiar.

'Johnny, could I take this magazine away for a whilie?'

'Surely, Mr McGillivray. So how d'you want it?'

Neil settled back into the cracked red leather. The face in the mirror looked almost like a regular citizen of the Republic of Scotland, a state mythical and real as John Macnab himself.

'I feel like a change. Give me a Number four all over.'

He sat still as the warm clippers massaged his scalp, and

fervently hoped royal water-colourists were of the literal school.

Ellen Stobo walked briskly past an old-fashioned barber-shop, turned left at the end of the street past the police station and found Sergeant Jim MacIver in his council-house garden, stroking his roses.

'Washing off the greenfly,' he explained after she'd introduced herself.

She knew nothing about roses apart from the fact some people thought they were romantic and she hadn't been given any in a long time. She watched patiently while he finished. He wasn't on duty and she had no particular right to bother him. Besides, she didn't think it would help to rush this man, and she took the time to study him. He looked like a farmer, hefty, but unlike Mitchell, he had a neck and possibly a sense of irony lurking in those apparently guileless blue eyes.

He straightened with a sigh and offered her some lemonade. She sat on the garden bench as he went inside. She'd scanned his file this morning. He was fifty-two, his wife Joanna had left him for an Australian and emigrated, he was good at his job in a low-key way, and appeared to have no ambition whatsoever.

They sat in the garden looking at the hills and drinking remarkably good home-made lemonade. They talked about gardens, about Denver where his sister had once lived. They talked horses, about which he was surprisingly knowledgeable. He admitted as a laddie he'd wanted to be a cowboy. She noticed him notice the slight bulge of her shoulder-holster under her jacket. And finally he emptied his glass and looked at her with a small smile.

'And what can I be doing for you, Miss Stobo?'

She showed him the letter of authorization from the Chief Constable. He read it carefully then handed it back, apparently unmoved.

'The Chief Constable is awfa vague about who you represent,' he said.

'Sometimes I wonder myself!'

She waited for him to press the point. He waited for her to go further. Eventually he took a drink and looked at the hills opposite.

'I'm thinking someone like yourself must have better things to do than chase a few poachers, Miss Stobo.'

'Ellen, please.'

'Miss Ellen,' he responded calmly.

She leaned towards him and loosened her jacket. It was surprisingly warm out in the garden.

'Sergeant MacIver – may I call you Jim?'

'They tell me that's the London way.' He considered. 'And here's me spending my weekend writing reports on the poaching for your Security people.' He glanced at her. 'I left nothing out.'

'They're not my people,' she said. 'I'm only on attachment as an observer.'

'Ah, well now. You'll be enjoying Scotland?'

She didn't buy this country bobby act.

'I've read your reports,' she said carefully. 'And I don't think you left out anything you were sure of.'

'Sure of,' he echoed. He flicked old greenly from his gardening trousers. 'That would be right.'

'I'm more interested in the things you're not sure of. Any guesses, hunches, ideas you might have.'

He looked away from her, up at the hills.

'I'm thinking nobody should be arrested because of a guess of mine, Miss Stobo.'

'Jim, it's not arrests I'm interested in. I don't care what John Macnab's done so far. In fact I rather like it. It's the future I'm concerned about.'

Now she was beginning to get his attention.

'I seldom give it a thought, myself,' he said calmly, 'Ellen.'

She almost smiled as she went on to tell him about the conference she'd attended. That so far as Security were concerned, John Macnab could be a cover. There could even be an STK policy on the estate.

Jim MacIver kept looking at the hills as she spoke, and his hands were relaxed on the deckchair, but she didn't miss his absolute stillness. He was more than concerned. He was worried.

'I just want to stop some innocent – or nearly innocent – pranksters getting shot,' she concluded. 'Nor do we – the people I represent – want them arrested and sentenced. I think you can understand why.' He nodded slowly, though she was sure his thoughts weren't slow. 'But if they get away with it, well . . . So I'm meant to defuse the situation before it gets to that. And I think you'd want that too.'

He turned his big farmer's head and looked at her. His look was so intent she felt herself reddening.

'And what is it you're wanting to know?' he said at last.

'You're the local man. Anything. Anything at all.'

'Anything. That's a grand big subject.' He considered the hills again.

'You could start with a Kirsty Fowler.'

He blinked once. There was a long silence. Then he got to his feet.

'You'd best be coming inside.'

Neil reached the little gallery and museum just as the curator was closing for lunch. Would she mind if he looked at just one picture for a couple of minutes? Perhaps she knew something about it?

The curator was a born-and-bred local with time on her hands, and he seemed an amiable and interested young man. She told him everything she knew. In fact she told him about every other exhibit in the museum as well before he could get away. He finally emerged into the street an hour later with a feeling in his stomach that wasn't just hunger.

As Jim MacIver cleared away lunch, Ellen sat back and frowned at her notebook. Maybe Kirsty Fowler was just a good local journalist who'd got lucky with some invitations and photos. She had a boyfriend who'd first appeared a few days before the first poaching episode. They'd been sitting in a black van without lights near the Mavor estate the night before the salmon was taken. Courting. It wasn't a crime. And he'd freely admitted the van wasn't his, and gave the owner's name which Jim had already checked out.

She was almost disappointed. She'd been starting to enjoy herself. There were no other leads here. Still, just to be thorough, she'd check a last couple of details through the computer before she left.

She asked if by any miracle he still had the licence number of the black van. No, but he could mind it fine. She made a note of it, quite impressed. And Miss Fowler's car? A green Wolseley, everyone knew it. Licence plate? He frowned, trying to picture it. Last week, parked outside the Post Office on a yellow line. Got it.

She wrote that down. And this Neil, whatsisname, McGillivray. Did he have a car? A blue Escort, but no memory of the registration. Staying at the Atholl Hotel. And Kirsty Fowler could often be found there around lunchtime. Or at the *Courier* office.

She thanked him for his time and lunch. She got up and shook his hand. She'd drop in at this Atholl Hotel. And perhaps he could phone ahead to the station and get her access clearance for the computer?

He waved goodbye again at the corner of his garden, checking the canes on his giant sunflowers, grown here against all the odds. He whistled as he pottered about, but the faint frown wouldn't go away, nor a persistent sense of unease.

At the Atholl Hotel, Ellen talked to the receptionist and asked to see the register. No car registration or passport number. Seemed like they didn't always bother with things like that round here. She went into the car park round the back and found the blue Ford Escort.

When she came back in, the receptionist had gone through to the bar. Ellen glanced round, ignored the disapproving gaze of the stuffed stag's head, found the pass key under the counter and nipped upstairs.

She came down five minutes later, looking puzzled. Odd. Interesting.

She went to the police station, logged on to the computer. After twenty minutes and a few high-level access clearance codes, she began to get some of the items she needed.

When Ellen Stobo emerged from the police station around five o'clock, there was a new spring in her step. She had two pieces of paper in her pocket that could mean nothing at all. Then again, this could be Denver and she could be a blushing Eskimo bride.

Next stop, the office of the local paper.

Kirsty left the office and went out on to the street. She'd just knocked off six hundred words of pure conjecture for *Scotland on Sunday* about John Macnab's next move. Rainy-day money. The odds were she'd need that soon enough.

To celebrate, she decided to call in at the coffee shop for a quick *pain au chocolat* before going to the hotel. She sat munching happily, glancing out at the street. A woman in a rather smart blue jacket went by, her determined face younger than her short grey hair. A bit like Judi Dench, Kirsty thought. I hope I look like that when I get old.

On the edge of the Lochnagar plateau, Alasdair lowered his binoculars. He'd been watching Murray since he'd come into view, descending a ridge above the glens at the far side of the river, about a mile from Balmoral. Tastefully dressed in rave shorts,

Union Jack T-shirt, gym shoes and baseball cap on backwards, this youth had to get Pillock of the Year award. No gamie in his right mind would glance at him twice, except to curl his lip.

'Home, Corporal,' Jane said. 'Enough recce for one day. I'm dying for me pint.'

But Alasdair swung the binoculars and picked up an old Transit van coming slowly down an estate track leading out of the estate. He watched the van halt at a closed gate where two gamies were waiting. On the other side of the road was a soldier, automatic rifle across his back. A number of kids were inside the van, sticking their heads out to get some fresh air.

Interesting. He focused on the logo on the side of the van. Some kind of youth conservation project. The driver jumped down from the van and stood chatting with the gamies while the young squaddie leaned against the side of the van and talked with the kids inside.

Alasdair whistled quietly, adjusted the focus and zeroed in again on the driver. Very tall, thin bloke, long beaky nose, fair hair thinning on top. Even from this distance he could practically hear the sardonic Leeds vowels.

'It's Fang!' Al said and lowered the binoculars.

'Who?'

'Fang Farrell. One of my first clients. He was training as a dentist till I had him on a week's course on the Ben. Turned into a bit of a star. You met him once.'

The gamies opened the gate. The driver hopped back in, drove through and turned towards Braemar.

Jane looked at Alasdair, he looked at her.

'Outrageous coincidence, what?'

He was grinning in that alarming way. She'd known him long enough.

'No, Ally,' she said firmly.

Kirsty was reaching up to check in Mr MacPherson's mouth as Shonagh hurried through from the bar.

'Afternoon, stranger. You just missed Neil.'

Kirsty lowered her hand and shrugged.

'So?'

'Ah.'

'Ah yourself.'

'Also you missed some kind of plain-clothes policewoman who was asking about you and Neil. Said she'd come back.'

She stared at Shonagh.
'Did she say what it was about?'
'What do you think?'
Kirsty's pulse started to make up for the beats it had missed.
'Soon as you see Neil, tell him to get over to Strathdon.' She hugged Shonagh. 'Sorry I've been a sulky cow. Catch you later – I need to go somewhere.'
She hurried through the lobby and pushed open the back door. The woman in the blue jacket stood there blocking her way.
'Miss Kirsty Fowler?'
'Sorry, I'm in a hurry.'
'I'm afraid I can insist.'
Kirsty took her time reading the letter and checking out Miss Ellen Stobo's credentials. She handed back the letter.
'I'm afraid you can't.'
Kirsty was damn sure she wasn't going to be the first to drop her gaze.
'I'm afraid you're right. But it could be for your own good.'
'And I'm the Big Friendly Giant.'
'You may be tall, but you're not very friendly.'
Kirsty looked down to hide a smile. In another situation she could like this woman.
'Nothing personal. It's just that I'm very busy and I really don't think I can help you. Anything I know about John Macnab is in the papers, and I've already gone through it with Jim MacIver. Now, I've got to go back to the office.'
Kirsty turned and walked quietly across the car park. Without appearing to hurry, the Stobo woman was alongside her.
'Mind if I go with you?' Kirsty shrugged. Odd accent, she thought. London with a tint of Midwest in the vowels. They turned out on to the main street. 'It's your boyfriend Neil McGillivray I want to ask you about.'
Kirsty stopped. In the past Ellen had debriefed and cross-examined many women and knew a flush is hard to fake. What it means is another question.
'He's not my boyfriend.'
They started walking again.
'Sergeant MacIver says he is. Your friend at the hotel says so too. I gather he's said so. Maybe you have communication problems.'
That flush again, and a tightening round the mouth.

'OK, so we were. Sort of. Now we're not. I don't want to talk about it.'

'Mm. I have that impression.'

They'd reached the door of the office. Kirsty took out her key.

'Sorry I can't help you.'

'Why does he call himself McGillivray when his name's Lindores?'

Kirsty stopped with the key in the lock. She turned round.

'Because he's married. OK?'

Then she went in and banged the door behind her. Ellen stood looking at it for a few moments before she turned away. There are some other emotions that are hard to fake, and she'd just seen two of them.

Outside the Braemar Hotel, Alasdair and Jane waved goodbye to Fang Farrell and got into the car.

'You mustn't get him into trouble, Ally.'

'Totally deniable, old girl. If it comes to it, he'll say I spun him a yarn and he doesn't know me from Adam.' He rubbed his hands and sat for a moment with his knee jumping. 'It's time we got into some conservation work, don't you think?'

'And she knew Neil's real name!' Kirsty said.

An emergency meeting in Strathdon, not quite panicking but shaken. Kirsty had just told them about her encounter, leaving out only the last exchange.

Alasdair nodded. Now both knees were jumping as he sat at the table.

'From his car reg. Which means they can access all his records. And they'll run the same on you, young 'un.'

Kirsty looked away, biting her nail. At the window, Jane kept watch on the track up to the house.

'Can they do that?' Neil asked.

'From the letter this woman showed Kirsty, she must be Home Office at least. Maybe Special Branch. Or MI. Yes, they can do it.' He considered for a moment. 'But if she is, and they're serious, you wouldn't be sitting here, believe me. I don't get it.'

There were many things in this world that Alasdair Sutherland didn't understand, but only a few bothered him. This one bothered him.

They ran through what Ellen Stobo could know or guess. It wasn't very much. Only that Neil had arrived shortly before the first Mavor hit. That he'd signed in under another name – but with no sign of intent to mislead, or defraud, that wasn't a crime.

The hotel staff might say Neil had missed a few breakfasts, but then he could have been staying up at Kirsty's. It was striking that Kirsty had possession of the Macnab hit photos, but it made sense that he'd send them to a sympathetic local journalist. She'd happened to have been there when both deliveries were made, but on each occasion she'd been invited.

The woman had talked to Jim MacIver, but what more could he tell her? That he'd seen them necking in the black van the night before the salmon was taken. Big deal – what does a bit of snogging mean?

'Not very much, I guess,' Neil said.

Kirsty hastily went on to point out that there was nothing to connect herself and Neil to the others. Ellen Stobo was clutching at straws.

'The van,' Neil said quietly.

'Aye, but Trish has got it stashed.'

Kirsty shook her head.

'Jim MacIver had checked it through and he might still have a note of the reg. He's very sharp.'

'Hell in a Lada! That changes everything.'

Alasdair jumped up and paced around. He stood next to Jane and looked down the track. She nudged him and shook her head fractionally.

Alasdair nodded, then gave his instructions. Kirsty should check through her cottage and get rid of anything even vaguely connected with John Macnab. Remember to erase her answer-phone messages. Murray should move out. Take the tent and pick a big camp-site – the most anonymous places on earth. Murray sighed but agreed. For the time being, Jane and Alasdair would stay on at Strathdon, subject to review, and use the Polo. If the police traced the Fort William address they'd find an empty house.

'Shouldn't Kirsty and me leave?' suggested Neil. 'Go to a hotel or B & B somewhere with each other for cover?'

Kirsty made a face. Not on your nellie, she thought.

'No. If you both suddenly disappear it looks damn suspicious. Neil can move out tomorrow if he wants. Kirsty had better stay, but low-profile.'

They went over the arrangements one more time. If they were

very careful, they should be in the clear. The Stobo woman would probably move on tomorrow.

'Think careful, think tight,' Alasdair concluded. 'Be very, very normal but paranoid at all times. Remember – someone's out to get you.'

Time then to make fresh coffee and catch up on progress to date. Murray went first. An exclusion zone had been marked out round Balmoral with stakes and pink flags and tape. Inside was patrolled by soldiers with flak jackets and automatic rifles, some dogs, a chopper. Anyone who went near was handed a map with the exclusion zone shaded in, and politely but firmly told to go away. Murray handed them his copy of the map. A Territorial Army training exercise, it said.

'TA my teenage fan club,' Alasdair said. 'At least some of those laddoes were regulars, and I clocked a couple who had to be Special Forces.'

'But outside the exclusion zone?' Jane asked.

'Just gamies. A lot of them.'

'A-OK!' Alasdair crowed. 'Neil?'

Neil produced the old copy of the *Scots Magazine*.

'Picked this up at the barber's this morning.'

'I'm glad you got something besides yon hellish haircut,' Murray said. 'You look like a Buddhist monk.'

'Nothing wrong with Buddhist monks,' Kirsty said. Neil looked pleased. 'They don't get married or have affairs.'

Jane coughed and put down the magazine.

'I don't see the relevance of this,' she said.

'This painting is only four years old, and apparently done on site by HRH. It was painted in late August. Around now. *Deer Drinking at Dusk near Balmoral*. And this' – Neil put the end of his teaspoon on the OS map – 'this is the lochan where it was done. Lochan nan Ciste.'

They craned their heads and looked at it. Neil lit up and sat back.

'What I'm suggesting is Zen and the art of deerstalking. We don't stalk the stag. It comes to us.'

'Sounds iffy to me,' Kirsty said. 'And how do you propose to get there with a bloody great tranquillizer gun?'

Neil looked at Kirsty's bright hair hanging over the map. Regret is like a midgie, irritating and near impossible to locate and squash.

'Got any better ideas?'

Alasdair looked at the map again. The lochan was less than a mile from where Fang's mob were repairing footpaths. And just far enough outside the EZ.

'The farce is with us,' he said. 'I take it we're all for unpaid conservation work?'

Then he filled them in on Fang Farrell and the conservation kids. The result was gratifying. The adrenalin was building, they were beginning to be a team again.

Neil sat back from the table.

'I like it,' he said. 'But how the hell do we make off with and then deliver an unconscious stag?'

Alasdair swigged more coffee and hunched over the map again. He studied the lochan, the burn that fed it and the burn that ran out of it. He looked at the River Dee as it wound its way through the glen, past the Castle then on towards the sea. He looked very closely at the contour lines between the lochan and the river. Then he began that slow terrible smile.

Yes, Alasdair Sutherland had had an Idea.

'Gather round, lads and lassies – this one's so far ahead, it's beautiful.'

21

Ellen Stobo sat in her hotel breakfast room by the big window and watched the hills play peek-a-boo with clouds. Now you see me, now you don't. Her head too was full of little clouds that lingered round more solid things, like a hillside track with no one on it, a big man bending gently over roses, the slow fire of whisky in a bar where people sang and knew each other.

She stared out of the window. She was getting soft. She'd have no children now. She was tired of cleaning up other people's messes. She was struggling in the middle of life and lately her moods swung like a budgie, chattering in the cage at its own reflection.

She settled up, left the hotel and walked slowly across the square where the first beech trees were turning from tired green to brown. She called in at the police station to say goodbye to Jim MacIver and thank him for last night's guided tour through Speyside malts.

He was sitting reading with his feet up on the desk as she came in and put down her overnight bag. She accepted coffee and told him how she'd phoned Aziz. He'd been smooth and charming but when she'd pushed him a little, feeling something was still left unsaid in his account, he'd politely suggested she spoke to his cousin the Ambassador. And the Lindores-Fowler lead just petered out. He was married all right, and using another name, but it wasn't a crime. Nothing to connect them to a third member.

'I'm disappointed in our Kirsty,' Jim said. 'She's a bittie wild, but she should know better.'

'In my book, he's a rat.' She said this with some feeling and he raised his eyebrows inquiringly. 'I've been on the receiving end.'

'Ah.'

'You too, I gather. Sorry – I had to look in your file.'

He grimaced into his coffee.

'Aa by wi now,' he said quietly. He nodded towards her case. 'So you're away then?'

'With nothing new here, it's time I reported in. Then I expect they'll want me to be on hand at Balmoral. Pity. I've really enjoyed this . . .'

As she bent for her bag, Jim held out the papers he'd been reading.

'I'm thinking you might like to see these first.'

She flicked through the first print-out. It confirmed that one Kirsty Fowler owned the green Wolseley. Her insurance was about to run out, and she had an outstanding traffic offence in Inverness. A faint footnote referred her to a different form number that she couldn't quite make out.

'What's this smudge next to her name?'

Jim shook his head.

'Nae idea. A midge in the printer? I'm looking into it – but try the next one.'

As he sat back grinning she picked up the second print-out. It was a report on the owner of the black van Kirsty and Neil had been seen in. Mr Alasdair Sutherland had a police record – a few adolescent car thefts. A dodgy credit status. Nothing so special about that.

Attached to Special Forces training, as climber and survivalist guide. Details and profile to follow.

She blinked at the pages that followed. The little clouds in her head cleared away. *Experienced mountaineer and survivalist. Full training. Psychological profile: impulsive, erratic, operates well under stress, easily bored. Challenge-dependent. Works well alone or with a team. Highly motivated. Public school (Gordonstoun – expelled). Security clearance to appropriate level. Married. No children. No particular religious or political affiliation (Conservative). Forty-two.*

She held the faxed photograph in front of her. Close-cropped hair and moustache, weathered face. Trying to look serious and responsible but not quite succeeding.

'Mr John Macnab, I presume,' she murmured.

'Or I'm a Hottentot. Kirsty, Lindores and Sutherland, the three of them just like in the book.' He hesitated, the triumph went from his voice. 'You'll be after telling Security about this?'

For a man with no experience of her world, he understood its outline very well. Decision-time. She looked out of the window at the plantations of Sitka spruce spreading up the hill. Cloud shadows moved into the upper corries, a stalkers' path turned over a ridge and out of sight. It must be so fine up there above the tree line.

She drained her coffee and turned away from the hills.

'We'll keep it to ourselves till I've asked a few pointed questions of our lovebirds, starting with Miss Fowler.' She nodded at her overnight bag. 'Can I leave this here?'

He turned back to the computer with a big grin.

'Long as you like, Ellen.'

She sat in the car, tightened her shoulder-holster and adjusted her jacket. She knew Jim didn't approve. She didn't either but she'd been wrong before and people had been hurt. Sutherland just might be holed up at the cottage. He was probably a joker, but then again . . .

She sat on, turning her car keys round her fingers. All of her training said she should already have phoned the Corridor or Mitchell and one or the other would take it out of her hands. That's what her hands were for, to have things taken out of them. That was the definition of a good pair of hands.

She'd been caught by Sheriff Coulter trying to return the few head she'd rustled all those years back when she still spent summer vacation with her dad. He'd leant out the window of his big old Ford and looked her over as she stood there with her knees knocking. At the very least she'd get a walloping from her dad.

'Godammit, Miss Ellen, get 'em strays back home!'

She'd nodded, unable to speak. He winked, put his shades back on, spat once in the dust, then drove away.

Perhaps it was time to repay that debt. She started up, put on her shades, didn't spit, and drove up the back road to Kirsty's cottage.

Murray stood at the end of the Strathdon road with his pack on his back. It was good to be on the move and stepping over the line again. Committed. A few days more and he'd be back with Trish and the weans, or else in the jail.

He held out his thumb to a white van and grinned broadly. The van hesitated, then slowed. He ran after it and jumped in.

Neil took one last look round his hotel room. Partly to check he'd left nothing behind, no incriminating sketches, lists or phone numbers in the waste bin. And partly because he'd become a habitual looker-behind, someone who had to drain the last drop of regret.

Well, no more. He had Kirsty to thank for that at least. Time to put some distance between them.

He went downstairs to find Shonagh and settle the bill, rehearsing what Alasdair had told him to say. He pinged the bell at Reception and waited. He studied the blue-finned guppies in the fish tank kissing clear glass walls, and wondered if they could sense there was an ocean somewhere.

He pinged the bell again.

Still a little hung-over from the night before, Kirsty left Shonagh's flat and set off to walk home. On impulse, instead of walking up the road, she took the short cut up through the trees.

As she came to the brow of the hill she heard a frenzy of barking from Charlie. Then a sudden silence. So she dropped to her knees and crawled through the high bracken that was just starting to turn the colour of toast. She parted it gently and peered through.

By the back of the cottage beside her Wolseley there was a car she hadn't seen before. She saw a shadow move inside her bedroom and then disappear. She inched closer till she was staring through the fronds into her front room.

The woman with the grey hair was flicking through her books. She saw her pat an adoring Charlie, then lift the copy of *John Macnab* from the table.

Kirsty claimed later that her first impulse was to bang on the window and demand what the hell she was doing poking round her house. And perhaps she could have faced it out. She hesitated and watched the Stobo woman leaf through the telephone pad and open the drawer in her desk where she kept her few personal papers.

Even then Kirsty could have intervened, but as the woman leant forward over the desk her jacket swung open and Kirsty glimpsed something she had seen only in films.

The shoulder-holster and dark butt clinched it. Kirsty squirmed back through the bracken. She could have owned up. She could have explained.

Instead she did what she'd done once before. She got to her feet and bolted.

* * *

'Don't be the stranger, Neil,' Shonagh said and hugged him goodbye.

'I'll send you a card from Skye.'

'Sure you will.'

He bent to pick up his case.

The back door banged open. Kirsty lunged in and bent heaving over the Reception counter. Her hair was sweat-stuck over her face and she seemed to have a lot of twigs and bracken stuck to her clothes.

'Hey, please leave Birnam Wood out the back.'

Kirsty tried to straighten up. Her finger pointed in the general direction of Archie MacPherson.

'Late for your cue, *ma ghoil*?'

Kirsty looked at Neil and kept pointing up the stairs.

'Five minutes,' she gasped. 'Please.'

When they came back down the stairs ten minutes later, Kirsty had her arm through Neil's. Shonagh looked at them. Kirsty seemed more composed and Neil less so, as though one overfull glass had decanted some of itself into an empty one.

'There's been a slight change of plan,' Neil said.

'We're both going to Skye,' Kirsty added.

'What about you-know-who?'

'We've decided two out of three is good enough. So we've packed in Macnab, and me and Neil are going to elope or something.'

'Hmm.' Shonagh looked them over. They certainly were radiating something. 'Is this true, Neil?'

'Absolutely. And we're leaving right now before the urge wears off.'

'If anyone asks I'll be back in two weeks, Shonagh. Good luck with Pat.' She hugged her hard then bent and kissed her cheek. 'Coming, lover?'

'Right ho, hot babe!' He winked at Shonagh. 'We're just mad impulsive fools.'

Kirsty took Neil's pack and waltzed with it towards the door as Neil picked up his case.

'They tell me I'm a cock-eyed optimist,' she sang. 'Byee!'

And they were gone.

'Well bugger me,' Shonagh said to the glassy-eyed stag. She stood in the lobby, fingers on her cheek. 'No accounting for taste, but "hot babe"?'

'*Och, dearie me,*' said Mr MacPherson.

* * *

At the first village, Kirsty jumped out of the car and phoned Alasdair. He was in slow mode till she told him first about the gun, then that she had a horrible feeling she might have left something about Strathdon on her phone pad or somewhere.

She got back into the car.

'Well?'

She pulled her hair back off her face. She felt sweaty and grubby and in a mess. She had nothing with her, no spare knickers, no comb, not even a toothbrush. Just her wallet and not much in that.

'Drive like the West wind, babe.'

He thumped the wheel.

'Yeah!' As he drove flat out for Strathdon, he glanced at her. 'Journeys made in haste,' he said. 'Don't you just love them?'

'Sometimes,' she said. 'Not all the time.' She looked down at her hands. 'I also like being somewhat in control.'

He took her hand and squeezed the tight muscle round her thumb till she had to look at him. He seemed truly delighted. All his hesitation, the slight dark delay in him, had disappeared, like the night they'd jammed together on the wee Atholl stage.

'My, you're the reckless boy,' she said.

'Kirsty, we can do this. We really can.'

Full eye contact.

'Both hands on the wheel, please,' she said quietly. But she laughed a little before settling back to view the options that opened up as the trees whizzed by.

Ellen prowled round inside Kirsty's cottage with a strong sensation that something important was slipping away from her. She went back to the copy of *John Macnab* and noted the sections where someone, probably Kirsty, had underlined or made notes in the margin. At a glance these were restricted to *Crap!* or *Oh my God!*. The word *Strathdon?* was scrawled in the inside flap. On the back flap, perhaps drunkenly, *Oh the married men . . .*

She put the book down and went out into the yard and sat on the wood pile. The Fowler car was still there. Surely she wouldn't have done a runner without it. Anyway, the passport was still in the drawer.

She knew what she ought to do, had known it since she'd skimmed the file on Alasdair Sutherland. To do anything else would be a gross dereliction of duty or, worse, pure arrogance.

She went inside and picked up the phone.

'Jim. I need your advice. Can you check for our game at the hotel, then come and meet me at Kirsty's?'

Alasdair and Jane were waiting at the door in Strathdon as Neil and Kirsty bumped up the track. The bags were packed, all evidence removed, papers burned, the answerphone tape scrubbed. Alasdair went to the green Polo and took out something wrapped in sacking and handed it to Neil.

'Spare plates,' he said. 'Your Escort will be hot. Better put them on while I adjust my thinking skates.'

Neil and Kirsty changed the licence plates while Jane loaded up the Polo and Alasdair tried to discipline his thoughts. This was the crux: now each move had to be precise and right.

'OK, troops, let's get our rabbits in a row here. First, are you absolutely sure there's nothing to connect Murray with us? No notes, no receipts, no registers? He paid everything in cash, right? In that case, the Polo isn't hot and Murray's dinky-do at the campsite. We must assume they've put out an alert, and they'll have photos, so it would help to change our appearance. I'd better take off the moustache for a start.'

'Some good's come out of this, then,' Jane said as she passed carrying luggage for the Polo.

'They think you two have eloped to Skye. We've got to reinforce that. Kirsty, give your cashcard to Jane. She'll take the train from Inverness to Kyle and use your card there. That should convince them.'

'Can they really find out that kind of stuff? I mean, bank transactions are private.'

Alasdair shook his head sorrowfully.

'It's a wicked world,' he said. 'So Jane goes on by train to Sheffield and uses my card there and spreads the word we've gone off to the Lakes. You two had better stick together and the Escort should be cool, so long as you stay well away from round here.'

'Huntly,' Jane said. 'There's a nice wee hotel there. The Huntly Arms.'

'Separate rooms, different names,' Alasdair said. 'It's not the kind of place that asks for ID. Pay in cash, right? Don't unpack your bags and be ready to leave at five minutes' notice. I'll phone you tonight.'

He got into the Polo and started up as Jane strapped herself in.

He wound down the window and stuck his head out.

'We stay at large for three days,' he said. 'That's all we need. At this time of year there's thousands of people moving through the Highlands. We're like a straw in a haystack. They'd need a miracle to find us.'

'What are you going to do?'

Al shook his head.

'I'm operating on a need-to-know basis.'

'That means he doesn't know,' Jane said.

'Now that's what I call security,' Neil said. 'Great.'

Alasdair turned the car and leant out of the window again.

'What name shall I ask for when I phone?'

'Montrose,' Neil said. 'Mr Montrose.'

Alasdair grinned.

'Nice one. "He either fears his fate too much, or his deserts are small" . . . Three days! See ya.'

The car lurched off down the track. Neil and Kirsty looked at each other.

'"Who dares not put it to the touch. And win or lose it all",' she murmured. 'And I thought I was so reckless.' She locked up and put the key under the white stone by the door. 'By the way, what happened to Montrose?'

'Sticky end.'

'Thought as much.'

They got into the car and bumped down the track for the last time. They turned on to the main road and drove east with the sun in their eyes and a long day ahead, and neither said very much along the way as their pulses drummed and they let the road carry them on like a bright and winding river.

22

'Worse than bloody midgies,' Jim said. He eased himself into Kirsty's armchair and took the mug of tea Ellen held out. 'You reach out and think you've got one . . .'

'You believe Shonagh – they've run off to Skye?'

He hesitated.

'I believe the lassie believes what she says. It could be you've scared them awa, if they've a grain of sense atween the two of them.'

'And do they?'

'Och, they're no daft. Kirsty's maybe a bittie wild.'

'Wild enough to go further than poaching? Capable of being talked into it by Neil?'

He plonked his big hand on the armrest and looked at her.

'Nivver.'

'That's just a feeling?'

'Just a feeling, Ellen, aye.'

She nodded. Feelings were to be listened to though not necessarily trusted.

'They can't exactly have eloped.'

'Aye, well . . . This came through at the station.'

He handed her the note from Records. She skimmed through it. Neil Lindores's spouse, Helen May Armstrong . . . had died some four years back, age thirty. On a transatlantic flight. Copy of death certificate. Cause of death: streptococcal meningitis.

'Pair lass,' Jim said quietly.

She nodded, thinking he looked as much relieved as puzzled.

'I've heard people pretend their spouses are dead where they're not, but never the other way round. Does it make any sense to you, Jim?'

'It does not. But it's not a crime. So what's this advice you're asking?'

'You know perfectly well, you big chookter.'

He put his mug aside and sighed.

'I'm no really a tea-drinking man,' he said. 'And it's *cheuchter*. The sound is soft, as in loch. And please don't be throwing that mug at me.'

She got to her feet and went through to the kitchen.

'I should have passed this up the line already. Officially I'm not even here.'

She switched on the kettle again, found Charlie a couple of biscuits. Jim was beside her, measuring out the Mountain Java.

'So they tell me, Miss Ellen.'

She levelled the teaspoon at him.

'Ms,' she said. 'The sound is mizz. As in show biz. So what do I do?'

'You're asking me as a policeman?'

'As a policeman. As a friend. As someone who maybe understands whatever the hell is going on here. Please.'

Jim stood beside her looking across the yard at the trees and the hills beyond. A large and very comfortable man, she thought.

'These Security people are maistly English,' he said eventually. 'No Highland men, anyway. Because it's not about money they canna understand it, pair things.'

'And you do?'

He eased himself back against the counter and looked out through the side window down to the village.

'Oh aye. I'm no saying it's right, mind, and a lot's changed between that old book and now. And I've no time for commercial poaching – a hillside of slaughtered hinds is not a pretty sight. But if you take this to your English Mr Mitchell, he'll see Sutherland at least as a potential security threat and you ken better than me what that means.'

The kettle boiled. She poured a little on the grounds, let it seep through, then poured in the rest and listened to it drip, drip, drip like blood in the quiet kitchen. When it had dried up she raised her head.

'OK,' she said. 'We keep it to ourselves a while longer and try to get to these Macnabs before Security do. That's still roughly my brief.'

'We?'

'It just takes a phone call to the Big White Chief. All I can offer you is blood, sweat and overtime, but I need your help.'

He poured her a mug, then his own.

'Nae blood, please. But for the rest, I'm your man.'

'That'll be an education for us both,' she said. 'Cheers.'

They drank down the coffee. Ellen picked up the *John Macnab*.

'So what's Strathdon?' she asked.

'It's a bittie place no far off. I've a cousin in the force there.'

'Best get on the phone to him. Go over there if necessary, but keep it low-profile for now. I'll go to the station and start on the computer.'

She washed out the mugs and glanced at the *Scots Magazine* on the counter. It was four years old and she hadn't seen any others about the place. She picked it up along with the Macnab file as they left.

A busy day for Alasdair, hands drumming on the wheel as he drove to Inverness, went over the last details with Jane then waved her off on the train to Kyle. Left knee bouncing as he thrashed the Polo to Murray's camp-site and found the youth sunning himself while alternating between *The Acid House* and *Advanced Angling*. Popping Nicorette in his mouth as he filled him in on the change of plan. The Balmoral hit had been brought forward. A few items to pick up in Aberdeen, then tomorrow morning do a dry run together for the hit. Appropriate dress. O eight hundred hours. A1, OK, see you, matey.

Then a call to Aberdeen to arrange a safe house and another to pick up an advance order with a vet friend for an unusual rifle. A chemist in Nairn for a new razor, some brushless shaving cream and a pair of blue shades. He shaved with one hand as he belted for Aberdeen, head bobbing as he turned 'Only Happy When It Rains' up to the max while giving Elgin the bodyswerve, flickering through Keith in the time it took to tie on a bandana.

He made Aberdeen just in time to hit a big ship's chandlers and make some bulky purchases and write a large cheque. By the time it registered in his account, Macnab would have won or be in jail.

Time to call on friends, old friends from Creag Dhu climbing days. Now mathematicians, teachers, and carpenters' wives, that sort of thing, but still a bunch of renegades at heart. A safe house, a shower, then maybe eat. Round up some suitable kids. Look out the maps for tomorrow. Phone Huntly, go over the Game Plan. Score some amphetamines (for military purposes only). Keep moving. A fugitive at large. Win or lose it all.

Alasdair Sutherland in full Go mode. Not a pretty sight, perhaps not entirely sane, very hard to stop.

The first he knew of her was warm breath at his right ear.

'We must stop meeting like this, Montrose.'

'Jesus! Don't sneak up on me like that, Kirsty.'

'The name's Fife. Fay Fife. Kirsty met with an unfortunate accident.'

She pulled out a chair and sat opposite him in the bar-restaurant on Huntly High Street.

'How did your shopping go?'

'Got my very own toothbrush.'

'You like the hotel?'

'Got a partial view of the river, if I hang out of the window by my heels. Romantic, if you like that sort of thing.'

She kept looking and grinning at him, her hand half over her mouth, like one of them had done something very silly and he hadn't realized it yet. Then he saw exactly why her face, her head, her eyes had changed.

He leaned across the table and gently took off her new tweed cap.

'You didn't say you had this unfortunate accident in a hairdresser's.'

What was left of her hair was short, slicked down on her forehead, cut tight in round her ears and neck. It made her neck longer, her head smaller, her face paler and younger, and focused everything on the eyes that were looking back across the table at him.

'Alasdair said they'd have photos out on us all, and I don't have a moustache, so . . .' She tailed off as a group of noisy yahs took over the other end of the room. 'I haven't had my hair short since, well, a long, long time ago. Don't you like it?'

He thought she looked totally fucking adorable.

'You look totally adorable,' he said.

She grinned and put the cap back on her head.

'I know, but you don't have to use language,' she said. She flinched as a bray of laughter erupted across the room. She hunched her shoulders away from it and leaned closer. 'Do we have to eat here?'

'I'll just finish my drinks.'

She reached over and drank down half his pint then handed it back. As he drank and watched her she knocked back the whisky. He'd wanted that.

'For Christ's sake, can't you settle down a bit, Kirsty?'
She rattled the empty glass and stared at him.
'No one settles me,' she said. 'I'm a free spirit, don't ya know.'
He put down his pint.
'I can see you're free. And I know you'll do near anything for an encore. But can't you be for real once in a while?'
She sat back and gave a hammy pout.
'Oh, pooh! Why be real when you can be giddy on whisky and unreality?'
Exasperated, he leaned across the table and kissed her.
'Christine!' One of the yahs was standing beside her. She flinched and looked away. 'Christine Tarbet! It's Donnie.'
'Hi, Donnie,' she muttered.
'So this is where you've been hiding out. And is this a new friend, or a client? But you don't have clients now, do you?'
Kirsty clamped her hand on Neil's arm.
'This is Neil. Neil – Donnie. Now bugger off, Donnie.'
'Excellent! Excellent! Same old Christine, hanging round with the low life. Keeping out of trouble, we trust?'
Neil's other arm shot across the table and grabbed Donnie by the throat.
'Want to be charged with assault, old chap? Need a good lawyer? There's plenty here – and Christine, of course.'
Kirsty pulled Neil down.
'Leave this slimebag alone, Neil. Believe me, he's not worth the hassle.'
'Excellent!' Donnie straightened his tie. 'The courts have been quiet since you left town, Chrissie. Haven't had a good laugh for ages. By the way, chum, she isn't worth the hassle. Bye.'
He staggered slightly and went through to the toilets.
Kirsty stood up. Her hands were trembling and she was very pale.
'Can you just let this go?' she said, mostly to the table.
She pulled her cap down over her eyes and ran out.

Ellen and Jim sat round the remains of a carry-out in Jim's sitting room. These Macnabs were becoming irritating. By the time Jim and his cousin had identified the house in Strathdon it was empty. But they'd been there all right. They'd used cash in the shop, pub and petrol station, but Jim had positive IDs from the photos. The Sutherlands' house was empty too. Cashline withdrawals in Kyle of Lochalsh and Sheffield. No sightings in Skye of the young

lovers. Perhaps they really had called it off.
'Do you believe that?'
Ellen picked at a few cooling beansprouts.
'It's . . . possible. But they've been persistent so far.'
They went out into the garden and sat while the light faded. They talked it over, with long thoughtful silences as darkness settled like silt into the valleys.
'Does it no make you feel a bit grubby, Ellen, poking around in folk's lives?'
She put her hand on his arm and left it there.
'Often,' she said. 'But I like to know the truth about things.'
They sipped their whiskies. Jim started like he'd been bitten by a cleg.
'Oh my sweet Lord!'
'What's up, Jim?'
'There's a fourth Macnab! Mind yon photo they took of the mannie with the salmon? Sutherland did the climbing. Kirsty's no fisher, even if she pulled the stunt with the motor bike, which I doubt.'
'Neil, then.'
'You've seen him. He's a lang streak. If he's the man holding the salmon, I'm an Episcopalian. There's another one.'
She looked at him, then at the darkening hills. They'd been obsessed with three because there were three Macnabs in the original book. She could see it now. There had been three, then Kirsty had joined them.
A fourth Macnab. An unknown. A wild card. Someone who'd taken the others along for a ride? Someone who might be for real.
'More coffee, Jim?'
And when he came out with it she picked a couple of midges from her eyebrows and said, as much to herself as him, 'If we don't crack this soon, I'm going to have to go to Mitchell.'

Neil put down two whiskies on the small table at the corner of the little residents' lounge. She just nodded and didn't look up. She looked pale and very tired as she sat turning her new cap round and round in her hands.
'So,' he said. 'Christine Tarbet.'
Her head moved, just a fraction.
'So?' she said. 'So what?'
'It's maybe not my business.'
'It isn't. I said you wouldn't like real me.'

'You could take a chance on that.'

Slowly, her head came up. Her eyes were puffy. She picked up her glass.

'Sorry about my friends,' she said. 'Though they never were that, even then.'

She drank the whisky back then flipped the glass over her shoulder, caught it. He wrapped his hand round hers.

'Come on, Ms Macnab,' he said. 'Too many secrets.'

With her other hand she prised two of his fingers away and bent them back sharply.

'Damn right. Like this.'

'Like what?'

'*This*.'

She was squeezing his wedding ring up against the knuckle and it hurt.

'Helen. Your wife. Wherever she is.'

He retrieved his fingers and massaged some life back into them.

'Oh boy,' he said. '"Wherever she is." You sure can turn a phrase.'

He drained his glass in turn.

'You don't even know where she is?'

'Kirsty, or Fay or Christine, Helen's in a hole in the ground and we're alive and wasting our precious time. That's all I know about anything right now.'

She stared at him. She went white, then red to the tips of her ears. She opened her mouth and nothing came out.

He pushed back his chair.

'Neil—'

He went to the bar, had a few words, then came back to the table with a half-bottle in his hand. He stood looking down at her bowed head.

'I'm going down to the river with this truth elixir. I'd appreciate it if you came too.'

She reached out and picked up her cap.

'Yes,' she said. 'Jesus. Of course.'

Alasdair Sutherland lay propped up on his side in a sleeping bag in a boxroom somewhere in Aberdeen. He was poring over a large map, calculating weights, contours, distances and hours of darkness. Eventually he switched off the light and lay on his back till sleep came, running through everything he remembered from years of climbing and walking round Lochnagar and Loch Muick.

His mind gradually filled with rock and turf and heather, midges, sun and rain, till finally by a process of displacement the last thoughts of the day were driven from his head.

Murray slipped out of his tent. The camp-site was silent now the last pub revellers had finally turned in. Usually he liked moonlit nights but this one didn't suit his purposes or his frame of mind.

He lit his meths stove and put on the billy. The grass was damp under his bare feet as he hunkered down. He watched the yellow flames and felt the night breeze caress his neck as he thought about his next move, and as he thought and waited for the billy, his head sank lower and lower till his chin finally rested on the dark hairs of his chest.

Ellen Stobo wasn't sleeping. She lay on her bed in the little hotel room, chasing Macnabs in her head. Every time she'd pinned down three of them, there'd be a fourth moving away. And when she went after that one, the others would be off again. It was like rounding up sheep.

Trouble was, the fourth one could be a wolf.

It was as dark now as it was going to get, what with the moon up. Neil glanced at the faint glimmer of the side of Kirsty's face. Everything that needed to be said had been said and for the past however long they'd been sitting listening to the night breeze through the long grass. At least, he had. He had no notion what, if anything, she listened to now.

He hefted the empty bottle in his hand, clambered softly down to the river's edge and let the air gloop out as the water glugged in. Displacement.

He knelt and let what little he knew now of Christine Tarbet displace what he thought he'd known of Kirsty Fowler. Former solicitor by day; vocalist, lover, occasional band member, good-time enthusiast by night. Deacon Brodie in drag. And then she went too far. Lucky to get off with a suspended sentence, by the sound of it.

He drank from the bottle and filled it up again. She must have needed something from whatsisname – Tom – very badly to go that far over the line. Her voice had been hoarse. Humiliated. He'd put his arm round her then and it had been nothing to do with desire. He'd felt many things about her, but this was new.

Neil drank more water. His knees were damp. He didn't think he'd ever get off them. He could understand now why she'd cut off from the past, from family and friends, so drastically. And he'd been preaching owning up to the past, when really he'd lugged it around like his personal tombstone. Face it – an excuse in the end.

An excuse for not going back up the slope with an open heart to whoever waited there.

He got off his knees. He wasn't drunk now, just very, very tired. He scrambled up the bank, carrying water for her. She was speaking mostly to herself.

'He was in pain all the time and he needed me so I couldn't leave. Maybe I needed . . .' She shook her head. 'I'll never get caught that way again.'

He hunkered down beside her and offered the bottle.

'I do think you need this.'

He drove carefully back to the hotel. Carefully because he was well over the limit. Carefully because her head lay on his shoulder and the few things she said along the way left the night so full that the least jolt, the least careless move, could spill something precious.

At Reception he opened the telephone message for Mr Montrose. *Stay put, will phone tomorrow night. Enjoy – Caithness.*

At the door to his room she suddenly held and kissed him. Then she stood back and looked. Her lips parted slightly but nothing came out. No quips, no laughter, no acting. Just Kirsty, looking at him.

Old doors squeaked open, rusty screens swung wide, some ancient portcullis creaked up. She backed away, then reached out and touched his arm in an almost kindly way as though he was slightly ill and she was slightly concerned. He didn't know quite what had happened in those few seconds in that hotel corridor, only that something had opened and she had come in.

'Guess I'll off to the Green Room.'

'Night, Kirsty. Is it Kirsty?'

'For you it is.'

She kissed his cheek, went along the corridor and into her room and closed the door.

He finished washing his face in the basin and when he reached for a towel she was standing there.

'Your room's got a much better view than mine,' she said thoughtfully.

'Not at night.'

'But it would be nicer to wake up in, don't you think? If you've no objections.'

He put the towel down carefully. Folded it over the rail. There, that's better.

'But there's no sex in John Macnab.'

'That was then – this is now.'

'Are you sure of that?'

'Are you?'

She went over to the window and drew back the curtains. It was beginning to get light. She crossed her arms and peeled her sweater off over her head and tossed it in the corner, theatrical to the last. She stood with her back to him, arms around herself. He could count the freckles on her pale shoulders as her head turned to look back at him.

'I think it's time we put it to the touch, Mr Montrose.'

23

He opened his eyes into blue sky above the curtains. Loose white clouds revolved slowly, joining and parting in the current. A morning breeze brought the river through the open window. There was nowhere else he wanted to be.

She lay turned away on her side. Matted red-brown hair, pale neck almost white, tanned and freckled upper arm. He matched his hand and arm alongside hers.

Her other hand came sleepily round her shoulder. Long fingers moved down his upper arm, squeezed the elbow, slid down the muscles of his forearm, then loosened.

'Were you really a lawyer? Was all that true?'

She opened her eyes and looked at the far wall.

'Everything I have told you is true.' A small crease at the corner of her mouth. 'You must decide whether to believe that or not.'

They lay like that for some time. White clouds kept drifting and rearranging themselves across the blue, never sticking in one place long.

The green Polo bounced across the camp-site blaring the Levellers from the cassette just as Murray dropped the cap on his meths stove.

'Ready for the off, old sport?'

Al in blue wraparound shades, purple bandana, tie-dye shirt and breeks-of-many-colours from the cheaper end of the market in Namche Bazaar. New Reebok trainers, ski pole propped on the seat beside him. A couple of gold-plated chains, one made of entwined snakes, hung round the neck of a man who seldom knew when to stop.

Murray squeezed into the front seat alongside two giggling teenage girls.

'Like the surfer shorts, old chap. Truly tacky. Nice. And the pink furry baseball cap – neat. Totally excellent.'

'I feel totally naff,' Murray grunted as a teenage bottom wedged itself into his groin. 'Hey!'

'They'll see us a mile off, take one look and pass on by. By the way, meet the gang.' He waved towards the back seat where another four teenagers squashed together as they fought over one set of Walkman earphones.

'Aye, aye, gang.'

'Hi, Murray!' they chorused.

Murray groaned as the girl on top of him bounced while they went over ruts. He must be getting too old for this when teenage girls only reminded him of his daughter.

'Where did you get this lot?'

'Borrowed from friends for a couple of days. Don't be fooled, they can walk.'

'What d'ya say when they stop us at the checkpoint – excuse us, we've just escaped from California?'

Alasdair looked at him, deadpan.

'Not at all. I'm training them for their Duke of Edinburgh Award.'

He slewed on to the main road and put his foot down for Ballater.

The way an ordinary window in a country cottage when you walk alone by the river can suddenly catch fire and be hanging sheets of gold. A couple more steps and every window in the house is blazing and it seems there's nothing solid there, and for a moment there's no boundary beyond which you cannot pass. You stop and stand and stare until there is no more *out there*, and feel the eyes of the house burning and yourself shimmering golden, on fire from head to foot. Then a few steps more and there's just simple windows and low, bright early sun and your usual solid self, and all the boundaries are back in place but you can never quite look at any of them the same way again.

She stuck her hands in the pockets of her jeans and walked back to the hotel for breakfast.

Ellen pulled the fax from the machine. The squashed midgie asterisk by Kirsty Fowler's name had finally buzzed into life. She banged the sheet down in front of Jim MacIver and stared out of the window at the blue and green and the purple beginning to fade on the hills. For God's sake, did nobody use their real name around here?

She looked down at Jim as he sat, head bowed over the fax. His precious Kirsty Fowler had changed her name by deed poll some three years back. Before that she was Christine Andrea Tarbet. The former solicitor specializing in criminal law hadn't actually done time. Suspended sentence and probation, thanks to mitigating circumstances and Major Daddy's expensive lawyer. But possession and supplying Diconal and MST even for a musician boyfriend with chronic back pain isn't exactly nothing.

Jim shook his big head wearily as he pushed the fax away.

'I canna believe . . . Och, it's so stupid.'

'Forging prescriptions on stolen pads bought from one of her ratty little clients – yes, she's a stupid girl.'

Jim grimaced. He seemed more like a worried parent than a policeman.

'She must have been awfa desperate.'

Ellen folded her arms and leaned back against the wall.

'So. Debarred, end of career, big scandal. Falls out with Major Daddy, does a runner, changes her name. Moves to rural paradise but can't resist another walk on the wild side.'

He looked past her out of the window.

'There are no simple swear-words in Gaelic.'

She squeezed his arm on her way to the door.

'I'm going to go lean on that woman at the hotel. Catch you later.'

He sighed and reached for the fax as she left. That 'Catch you later' was pure Kirsty. And the Sutherlands, Kirsty, Neil Lindores, the fourth Macnab, all seemed to have disappeared in a very small country.

Neil pushed away the bones of his kippers, reached for the toast and glanced across the dining room at Kirsty. She sat with her back to the window, the light behind her as she drank tea and wrote whatever in her notebook. How could he know what this meant to her? Perhaps last night she'd told him with her hands and her eyes, and he'd missed or misunderstood it.

This morning she'd insisted they keep up this farce of being single and separate. As though the least observant waitress couldn't see the golden strings strung across the room and make Kirsty's smallest movement tug in him as though it was his own.

She glanced across at him as if she'd never seen him before but was mildly curious. Then she winked, held up five fingers then pointed upstairs. Then back to her notebook.

He poured himself another coffee and rolled the first cigarette of the day. He lit up and looked across at her again. She was still there. Amazing.

The Transit van was very full that morning as it turned on to the dirt estate road and halted at the gate. Fang Farrell wound down the window and exchanged the morning with the two ghillies, waving his hand at the extra teenagers and the two garish adults. Extra work party. Duke of Edinburgh Award. Finish the job quicker, more time in the pub.

The soldier detached himself from the gatepost and wandered round the van. Two of the girls blew kisses at him. He blushed to his neck because he really was a very young squaddie. He bent down and looked under the van. No hidden marksmen there. He put his hand through the window and accepted a cigarette from the crazed hippie with the bandana. He should probably have gone into the van and checked among the heaps of rucksacks, spades, saws, wood and hammers but the giggling teenagers and their comments were more than he could face.

He nodded to the ghillies, the gate was opened and the van lurched through. The girls pressed their lips to the rear window. The soldier tried to scowl. A van full of sex-crazed teenagers, most of them probably on drugs. Some people have all the luck.

He took a quick look round then lit the cigarette.

Very occasionally there comes a day off in the world. A day like a large present is handed to you and inside it there is another present and you open that and inside there's yet another. And you don't hurry because presents are everywhere and there seems no end to them, and your eyes and hands and heart are full. The sun agrees to shine even in the Central Highlands, the wind agrees to drift just right, and when you go down to the river the water will slow and dazzle as it should.

As you step from the shower after breakfast your lover, the most mysterious and powerful present of them all, is there. And you find yourselves touching again, and presently your bodies find they have things left unsaid from the night before, and they are ready to say them now, and you go along because some days your body has it all worked out.

As you slip and loosen and lie in parallel again, the first unease touches you because you know this can't last. Maybe it even shouldn't last, because the two of you are distinct beings and there are many things to do in the world and few days off. And there has to be an end to the opening of presents.

You both know that because you're not children any more and this isn't your first time round.

'So which bit did you like best?'

He looked her up and down as she lay sprawled and easy. Her fox-brown pubic tuft alone could break a heart.

'Every part. Utterly beyond criticism.'

'Of Macnab, idiot.'

He lay back and thought about it.

'Beginnings, when it's all still ahead. Your "Room service" entrance. Going into Inchallian through the night with Al. You?'

'When Jane and Al flew away over those ghillies. Driving away with Murray and the salmon in the boot. I do like a clean getaway.'

'You're forgetting the delivery. The return of what's owed.'

'That's the most dangerous part.'

They looked at each other, then away. He kissed her quickly, sat up and swung his legs off the bed.

'There's a big world out there – let's go play.'

'You're in a bouncy mood today.'

'I do seem to have mislaid my ball and chain.' He pulled on a sock, wondering how long it would take before this seemed normal, to dress beside her and not feel awkward. 'Personally I think it was the haircut that did it.'

'You could be charged as an accessory for withholding information.'

'Accessory to what?'

'You tell me.'

Shonagh stared back at Ellen. There was a silence in the little office. Ellen shrugged. The direct approach hadn't worked. Shonagh had just repeated what she'd said before: so far as she knew, Kirsty and Neil were still in Skye. No, they hadn't been in touch.

On the whole, Ellen believed that part. She'd probed about John Macnab. Shonagh pointed out that with working at the hotel, there was no way she could have been actively involved. Ellen had nodded, but that unnecessary 'actively' was still buzzing quietly in the air.

She looked at the young woman who sat revolving in the

managerial chair by the desk. A change of tack, then.

She said she didn't give a toss about a bit of poaching. Shonagh raised her eyebrows. Ellen repeated it then leaned forward and said she cared a lot about protecting one or two lives. Perhaps Kirsty's. Perhaps Neil's.

Shonagh stopped revolving.

Ellen gave her the rest, with some exaggeration for effect. She explained Security's attitude to John Macnab – the exclusion zone, armed soldiers and Special Branch, and with HRH now in Balmoral, the likelihood of a Shoot To Kill policy. If Kirsty or Neil or their friends the Sutherlands – she didn't miss there, saw Shonagh stiffen – were still going ahead with the third hit, they would be in real danger. She had to find them, warn them, stop them. And very soon, otherwise she'd have to tell the Security forces everything she'd found out or guessed, and they wouldn't be understanding in the least.

Shonagh had to tell her everything she knew. Now. The poaching affair wouldn't go beyond these walls. But she had to know about John Macnab. Especially about the fourth one, the one who'd caught the salmon.

Shonagh reached out to the desk to steady herself. When she took her hand away, Ellen saw the handprint in sweat.

'Murray. His name's Murray.'

Got him.

'Murray who, Shonagh?'

'I don't know. God's truth. No one ever said.'

'Where is he now? Where's Alasdair Sutherland?'

'I don't know. I don't know where any of them are.'

Lost him.

Ellen took a deep breath, then suggested some coffee.

For the next hour, she went through everything Shonagh told her. That there'd been three Macnabs. Then Kirsty had joined them. Then the Mavor and Inchallian hits. Van Baalen's party where Aziz had delivered the grouse and Shonagh had picked the grouse feathers from Kirsty's jacket and guessed the rest.

That was all Shonagh knew. Murray had a wife and two kids, they'd been involved in the Battle of Maiden Braes. Kirsty had been too busy and caught up with Neil since to go into more details.

'Is this affair with Neil real, or just cover?'

Shonagh bit her lip and started revolving again.

'I don't know. I don't know if Kirsty knows.'

'Did you know Neil Lindores – McGillivray – was married?' Shonagh nodded. 'And that his wife's dead?'

'No. I'm glad. I mean, shit that's terrible. I'm sorry. I just want the best for Kirsty.'

'So do I. Believe me. So we've got to stop this.' Ellen got to her feet. 'We've twenty-four hours at most. If I can't find this Murray and call the others off, this passes out of my control.'

Shonagh looked at her hands and nodded. Ellen felt uncomfortable. There was fear and awkward love in the little room, and she'd stirred it up.

She picked up her bag and tape-recorder. She wrote down some phone numbers in case Shonagh remembered anything more. Anything about Murray. Anything at all.

She squeezed Shonagh's shoulder gently and left. She glanced at the river as she hurried back to the station and although the clouds in the west hadn't joined up yet, it seemed the current was already moving faster.

'Wave, you buggers! Wave!'

'Mister, is that the polis?'

Murray looked up at the army chopper thundering overhead.

'No exactly, Sharon.'

It was the second time that morning they'd been overflown. As he waved with barmy enthusiasm, Alasdair was noting the downward-pointing lenses and the bulky camera cradled by the man in fatigues who sat at the open door of the helicopter.

The chopper circled once then drifted back towards the exclusion zone and out of sight over the hill. Fang nodded to Alasdair and the Macnabs downed tools, picked up a couple of mallets and bundles of short stakes and twine, and with a couple of kids for cover moved higher up the heavily eroded path the team was rebuilding.

They worked slowly. Plenty of time to look around as they demarcated the next area for repair. Time to get the feel of the organization of the ghillie patrols from the valley of the Dee up to the Lochnagar plateau. Time too to take in the level of activity inside the exclusion zone a little over half a mile away.

'TA my Hieland granny,' Alasdair muttered. 'These are regulars plus some Special Forces. I trained with the chap who passed us in the Land Rover.'

Murray nodded and examined the map. Then he looked at the sketch of the exclusion zone, then at the terrain to the east. He grimaced, because Lochan nan Ciste was awfully near to the line.

'Don't worry,' Alasdair said. 'I promised Trish to keep you out of trouble. The EZ is definitely the very last resort.'

Murray folded the map away.

'Like Dunoon, eh?'

Alasdair grinned and nudged him. The two Macnabs were studiously hammering stakes into the soft ground near the path as the ghillie patrol went by.

Neil leaned over the bridge and looked down at a pool as calm and full as he felt. The surface was absolutely smooth. He wondered what was moving beneath it.

He looked over at Kirsty. She was sprawled on her side in the long grass by the bank, seemingly asleep. Not a goddess nor a nymph nor a muse, just human flesh and blood. Just? When the body is glowing, swarming, humming like a golden hive?

There was a quick *gloop!* in the water below. He looked and saw ripples spreading out, ring after ring, and he finally saw why sand running through an hourglass was the wrong image of time. Being alive was more like being wrapped in expanding circles, like rings in a pool or in the trunk of a tree. That's how it grows, idiot.

He glanced down at his left hand. It wasn't about taking off one ring and replacing it with another. Nothing is truly left behind, not even the dead, and one love doesn't chase the next into oblivion. Instead there are expanding and including rings, spreading wider as the years go on. They would reach their fullest expansion at the moment of his death. He could only get bigger and bigger, if he allowed it to be so.

He stared down into the water, feeling everything being rearranged.

She was propped up staring at the sun on the water. Then she gestured, a wave, a beckoning, and he left the bridge and went down to the water to join her.

In the afternoon Alasdair and Murray took a small working party through the shimmering heather to within a hundred yards of the little Lochan nan Ciste. Alasdair noted with satisfaction the overhung peat banks and a few deer turds by the track. As a bonus, the EZ was out of sight over the shoulder of the hill. Surrounded by a group of kids happily swopping cigarettes and cassette tapes, like a pair of Pied Pipers the Macnabs went on to follow the stalkers' paths above Loch Callater. It was fine and peaceful up there, the distant chopper droned a dizzy bee, the air was heavy with pollen that sent Sharon off into a sneezing fit.

They'd seen the two Land Rovers a mile off, bumping along towards Loch Muick. But when the vehicles stopped and a cluster of figures got out, Alasdair nudged Murray and the whole party took another picnic stop.

The focus of the Land Rover group moved up the slopes to the south, while the remainder spread out wide.

'Well, well. Looks like himself's come to direct operations.'

Alasdair handed Murray the binocs. In the centre of the group was a thin tallish figure in a muted kilt, gesturing with a long stick.

'He's no feartie, I'll gie him that. If I'd a high-powered rifle and sights I could take him from here for all his bodyguards.'

'If you'd a rifle, matey, you wouldn't have got past the first checkpoint today. Looks like he's enjoying himself, poor bloke. Now let's have a chat with these charming ghillie-wallahs heading towards us, then get back to the van.'

Murray fancied himself as quite fit, but was beginning to droop by the time the band of gypsies wobbled down the track with their gear towards the main work party. He was amazed the kids were still on their feet. In fact, the wee bastards were beginning to sing 'Hey Jude' over and over.

He fell in behind Alasdair, who finally folded away his wrap-around shades and sauntered along with his hands in the pockets of his Nepali trousers.

'Thought there was meant tae be a deer population explosion.'

'There is. Big problem. But Balmoral's got the resources to keep it under control. Not like some of the others. Too many deer, not enough hind-culling, so no natural reforestation. Deer starve in winter, bothies and lodges fall apart, fewer and fewer keepers. Pretty depressing, old sport.'

'So where are the deer?'

'Upper corries on the lee slopes. The hinds set the pattern and the stags follow. They're there all right. And there's been some at our lochan recently.'

'So have the gamies. Place is hoochin wi the buggers.'

Alasdair grinned.

'It is. The Royal Protection Squad are having kittens and Charlie's taking on our wager, no doubt about that. Amazing how indiscreet some of these extra gamies have been to the kids.'

Down below, the main work party were loading gear into the van. A long time had passed since the last rain had fallen and dust and pollen clung to their boots turning them grey-white as Murray and Alasdair followed the interminable *Na-na Na Na* chorus down the last of the track.

'There's a cure for the deer population in the Highlands,' Murray said. 'Shoot the landowners and leave the deer alone. Don't these kids have any songs of their ain?'

The Transit van shoogled down the dirt track towards the gate. In the back the Na-na Na Na was going strong. At the gate the morning's routine was repeated, the soldier bummed another cigarette and then they were through.

'Your plan's daft as pan-loaf,' Murray said quietly, 'but it's not entirely half-baked. Of course the delivery won't work.'

'Trust the river road,' Alasdair replied. 'It always sees you home in the end.'

Shonagh and Pat sat in the little office behind Reception. Their relationship was at that tricky stage when a series of weekends might or might not be called a relationship. When the present tense begins to need a future. When neither lover knows if the other wants that, nor what unfinished business remains from the past, and neither can ask if this is more than a series of one-off good times.

Pat was silently lacing her fingers between Shonagh's as they both sat looking out of the window because it seemed the neutral place to look. Shonagh watched the streetlight blinking on and off as it had for days now. She really must get the Council to come and fix that.

Then she tightened her grip. The Council. Something Kirsty had said in passing about Murray, something that had seemed unlikely at the time . . .

Got it. She kissed Pat's lovely sullen mouth, then reached for the phone.

The phone rang in the police station. Ellen sat still with her feet on the *Scots Magazine* on the desk and her hand hiding her eyes.

'Aye. Himself.'

Jim blinked, then put his hand over the mouthpiece.

'It's Shonagh. She's phoning from a call-box. She thinks the hotel line may be bugged.'

Ellen's feet came down smartish.

'She thinks right.' She glanced and checked the tape was running. 'What's up?'

'Aye. Aye. Murray. What? You're sure, lass? Aye, of course. I'll tell her. We'll do our best . . . I'll be getting you a dram or a medal. Goodbye.'

He put down the phone. Jim and Ellen looked at each other in the silence after the tape-recorder clicked.

'Kirsty said Murray had been a councillor.'

She flattened her hand on the desk.

'That's all?'

'By God, it's enough! It could be a District or Regional Councillor, and she was pretty sure he'd resigned. How many Glasgow councillors can there be of that age, called Murray somebody, married with two kids, wife probably called Tricia, resigned from the Council, say in the last ten years? We've got him!'

She thought about it, then reached out and switched on the computer.

'This could take a while.'

He grinned and shook his head.

'I have a nephew who's a political journalist for the *Glasgow Herald*. Young lad, but with a memory like his uncle's, though say it I who shouldn't.'

'Jim, is there anyone in Scotland to whom you're *not* related?'

'In the West and Highlands, guy few.' Another grin. 'And they're maistly deid.'

He opened the desk drawer and took out an address book. 'I hope young Alec is no out on the town again. Oh, and apparently young Kirsty made a joke about Sutherland doing some special shopping in Aberdeen. I'll work on that the morn.'

Her fingers drummed on the desk as she waited and watched the late evening turn to drizzle and mist, grey as the empty screen before her.

Neil knocked on Kirsty's door and went in. She was sitting in a small armchair with her long legs up on the window-sill, looking out at nothing in particular.

'All right, Kirst?'

She didn't look round.

'I've been thinking about Tom. Not something I do very often.' She tapped one foot against the glass. 'When it was good it was love and drugs and rock 'n' roll, the whole bit. Felt I had everything.'

Neil nodded. He remembered that.

'Young . . .' he said.

She tapped her forehead like she was trying to push something inside her skull into place.

'Three years . . . Then things weren't so good, but then he had his accident and I couldn't leave, not then. You understand?'

He nodded and perched on the window-sill and waited. He didn't know what to do for her, even if she'd let him.

'And?'

She finally looked up.

'I'd have to tell you lots of boring stuff about my mother and father, before and after they split. She drank and, you know, men. Runs in the family! She couldn't cope very well, she needed me. And as for Dad, he needed me to be, I don't know . . . Whatever it is I can't quite be.' She looked away then, out of the window into the rain. 'I'm a sucker for other people's need. I *don't* want to be trapped like that again.'

He reached out and took her hand but it felt dead.

'Kirsty, like you said – that was then. It's a new world.'

'It seems a very old and tired one to me.'

'How about a quick chorus of "Life is Just a Bowl of Cherries"?'

'How about you leave me alone?' She shook her head. 'I'm sorry. Rain depresses me and I'm a silly old tart.'

'Don't be daft – you're not that old.'

He almost got a grin and a response from her, then there was a knocking further down the corridor.

'Mr Montrose! Phone call for you.'

He pulled a face and headed for the door.

'Neil?'

'Yes?'

She looked across at him. 'Serious, then – am I like Helen?'

'No. Not in any way. You've both made me feel incredibly happy to be alive, that's all you have in common.'

'Good,' she said. 'Thank you.'

She turned back to the window as he left.

Jim MacIver peered at his notes. Either his writing was getting worse or he was needing spectacles.

'Murray Fitzgerald Hamilton. District Councillor. Resigned over the poll tax. Charged twice for obstructing the police, resisting arrest, assaulting a police officer. Maist likely trying to eat truncheons. So he'll be on our files.' He peered closer. 'Oh, and young Eck thinks there was a wee carry-on during the miners' strike, and he was inside for a bit. Here's his address. Is that enough for your computator?'

But she was already typing it in.

For once none of the computer systems were down, all the different networks were talking to each other, the pass codes were accepted. Even so, it took nearly an hour as Jim paced and muttered and looked anxiously out of the window.

The computer screen filled, the printer chattered. She got the faxed picture. Next to it Jim placed the newspaper photo of the Macnab holding the salmon with his hand over his face.

'No doubt?'

'Nane whatsoever.'

As he leaned across her chair, she looked over what they had already. CP member, then Trotskyite, then member of some splinter group who probably met in a phone box. Finally joined Labour Party in 1983. Probable Militant Tendency. Catholic mother, father Protestant. Atheist. John Maclean Society. Prominent in 'Brits Out' campaigns (a couple of murky, snatched photos from marches). Visits to N. Ireland and Irish Republic (dates to follow). Assault on police officers during miners' strike. District Councillor, resigned over poll tax.

Even allowing for MI5 paranoia, it was enough.

She looked up at Jim.

'Much too Identikit. I don't buy him as a security threat.'

Jim nodded slowly.

'Aye, this one believes in politics, not guns. But your friend Mr Mitchell will like it fine.'

'He's not my friend. But still . . .'

'Aye. Aye, I know.'

His light blue eyes were oddly sympathetic as he passed her the phone. What a very unusual policeman, she thought. What a very unusual man.

'Damn right I don't like it! So I dump the inflatable then sit on my arse till it's all over while you men do the derring-do on the hill. Wowee!'

'It's just operational logistics. We need a driver.'

'Logistics my sweet arse. Al's just trying to protect me. So are you, and I don't need it!' She paused, flushed, her back to the darkness outside. 'You lot never let me in, not really.'

'Are you letting me in, really?'

She turned away and drew the curtains. Her voice was muffled.

'So what does Al want you to get twenty feet of chicken wire for?'

'He says we're going to play chicken.'

'That man is a track short of the full CD.' She turned round and made herself busy as she produced a half-bottle and two glasses. Her face eased as she filled and passed his glass.

'To tomorrow, whatever.'

'To tomorrow.'

She drank hers down in one, and looked up at him.

'So,' she said. 'Bed.'

'Your room or mine?'

'Yours – I'm better playing away. Give me ten minutes.'

At the door she kissed him, and for a moment held him very tight.

'Lovely day,' she said. 'Whatever happens next, I want you to know it's been lovely.'

'Pick you up at eleven hundred hours. Keep a low profile and don't contact anyone under any circumstances. No knowing who they've got tagged.'

Murray nodded as Alasdair ran through the GP one more time, then rang off. Murray stood for a moment at the camp-site pay phone, then started feeling in his pockets for change.

Ellen Stobo walked alone through the empty drizzling streets. It was after midnight now, but more than coffee kept her awake. She'd finally been able to talk to the Commander but his instructions had been so vague and subtle and contradictory they hadn't been instructions at all. Basically she had to do everything and nothing. She had to defuse the Macnabs but endanger no one. She had to play Mitchell by ear but withhold the score. He would relay her report back to the Palace but she remained officially unofficial. He'd smooth her way but couldn't intervene.

And so on, padded as a man dancing in felt slippers. She felt herself pushing through thickets again, struggling in herself, struggling in her job. She wanted some clear instructions but all she had to guide her was a picture in her head of emerging intact above the tree line those cool mornings in the fall, and the way that felt.

She found herself at the river and watched it roll for a while. Then she came by Jim MacIver's and saw a light still on in his kitchen, and she hesitated outside his door for a long time with her head bowed and the fine rain shaking on the cuffs of her Drizabone.

24

When he woke she was propped up on an elbow looking down at him. In the morning light at close range her eyes had green and hazel glints, and she was trailing her fingers very lightly as though trying to determine the nap of his skin.

'Hi.'

'Hi yourself, mister man.'

She went back to grazing and soon under her touch he began to feel like a lush meadow being given the once-over by an exceptionally gifted herbivore. He began to giggle as she sat up.

'That's your lot. Better save your strength for the Boy's Own Adventure.'

'It's your adventure too.'

She shrugged and her exceptionally perfect breasts turned away from each other as though they'd had a falling-out, then swung slowly back as though they couldn't bear to be apart. If this happened every time she sulked and shrugged, he thought he could roll with it.

'I once thought so, but it's pretty clear you don't need me on this one.'

'You said you don't like being needed.'

'That was relationships,' she said firmly. 'This is pleasure. And stop goggling at my tits when I'm talking.'

'And you get the exclusive of the century.'

Her hand kept drifting over him of its own accord.

'Yeah, written from the comfort of my prison cell.'

He laid his index finger lightly along her cheek. She turned towards it as he stroked, and began to nuzzle. The neonate reflex, he thought. It never leaves us.

'I'm right gone on you, Kirsty.'

'Sure you are,' she muttered through his finger.

'Far gone. Right now I don't give a toss about Macnab.'

'Wow, that *is* serious.'

She leant down and quickly kissed his forehead, the way you would a departing friend.

'Kipper-time. Better have two for the big day, then go and buy your chicken wire.'

'You can't leave me like this!'

She grinned, and curled her fingers lightly around his morning erection.

'You've a fine cock, Mr Montrose, but I'll just leave you like this, with something to remember me by.'

She rolled out of bed, pulled on a T-shirt. She paused, long-legged in front of the mirror, ran a comb through her hair and stuck out her tongue. Then she was out of the door and along to her own room, leaving him growling at the ceiling.

In the Portakabin that served as a temporary HQ, Mitchell looked very big. He seemed to inflate further with each Macnab file Ellen laid in front of him. But she had to admit he was professional. He waited till she'd finished before bawling her out.

'You know bloody well you should have brought these to me pronto. And don't talk to me about your flaming Corridor! Jesus! *Johnston!*'

Jesus Johnston opened the door as though he'd been outside listening, which she reckoned he had, the little thug. He smirked at her as Mitchell handed him the files and gave his orders.

He wanted these people found – now. Prioritize Sutherland and Hamilton. All known addresses, associates checked, general on the car registrations. Circulate the photos. Approach with caution and, ah, appropriate force. Get on to Hamilton's wife and the woman at the Atholl Hotel.

She tried to protest. Shonagh had nothing to do with it. In fact, she was fairly sure most of the Macnabs were just jokers.

'Most? Fairly sure? Look, Missie, one man with a rifle is all it takes.' He pointed out of the window at the Castle behind them. 'I can't even get HRH to stay in one place. These people could be Left, Right, across the water – either side – or the Scottish Goldfish Liberation Front! So far as I'm concerned, anyone within a mile of him or the Castle is fair game.'

'You mean Shoot To Kill.'

He picked up the red telephone.

'One warning. One chance to surrender, then shoot.'

'Surrender? Like in Gibraltar? Like in—'

'Shut it,' he said. 'It's out of your hands now.'

The chicken wire and pliers took some finding. In the end Neil had to drive to Keith. After that he bought emergency rations – some fatigued-looking sandwiches plus chocolate – for the troops as instructed. He was still ahead of schedule so he had coffee in a café off the High Street, trying to calm his stomach and get into operational mode. It wasn't easy. His eyes and ears and skin were still full of Kirsty.

He drove back to Huntly, needing to see her again. She was essential as the cigarettes, though possibly as bad for him.

He corrected himself. A false analogy. This was good for him. An old numbness had been blown away. Whatever happened next, he was all there again. He had hoped this would happen one day, he'd just never thought it would.

'I thought you might want to know what Mr Sutherland's been buying in Aberdeen.'

Ellen stood outside the Portakabin with the mobile pressed hard to her ear.

'Tell me.'

'Och, let's see now. He paid in cash and he was wearing some outlandish clothes, but the man in the shop was sure it was him. He bought himself twa of yon space-blankets. And in a fisherman's supplies shoppie he bought a large net. And you'll not guess what he got in the chandler's by the harbour.'

'No, but if you don't tell me in the next ten seconds I might explode and then you'll be sorry.'

She heard the chuckle above the static.

'I would that. An inflatable. A black rubber inflatable. He insisted it had to be black.'

The cord through her gut was so tight now she felt her heart dislodge.

'Jim, get back as fast as you can. And keep this to yourself.'

'You mean you're not telling Mr Mitchell?'

'Burn rubber, you big choochter.'

'And you avoid answering a simple question like a Hielander. Are you sure you've no true blood in you?'

She switched off the phone and stood for a while by the river, then went back into the hut and ignored and was ignored by Mitchell as she examined the Balmoral and Lochnagar maps on the wall. This was either very professional or inspired amateurism.

If they went into the exclusion zone they were crazy or a serious threat, in which case it wasn't her problem and she didn't have to protect them. If they just came to poach then they were not a threat and they were her problem. But where the hell were they?

Think about the inflatable. She left the Portakabin and went down to the river to use her mobile. It took a while but she finally got on to the factor and quietly arranged for extra ghillies to be put as soon as possible on the river approaches to the estate.

She paced up and down the bank in the light drizzle and mist. The Macnabs surely didn't think they could just paddle their way in. Who did they think they were, the SAS?

Neil whistled 'Annie Laurie' as he walked into the Huntly Hotel. He tried to look leisurely but his heart was hammering. Half an hour before the rendezvous for the last hit. His room key was no longer hanging on the board beside Reception. Maybe Kirsty had picked it up, maybe she was waiting in his room with some last-minute theatrical stunt. He ran up the stairs, still whistling.

His door was open but there was no one inside, just his copy of *John Macnab* open on the bed at the second-last chapter.

He hurried along the corridor and tried her door. Locked. Knocked. No answer. Knocked again.

He went slowly down the stairs, counting them. He asked for her at Reception. Miss Fife had paid and left an hour ago.

She had left a message. Here it was.

He opened the folded note.

You really don't *need me. Keep it that way and good luck always. Thanks for the gig – Janet R.*

'Thanks,' he said. 'Thanks.'

He went very slowly up the stairs. Maybe he'd always known.

He stood by his car outside of Ballater with the small pack over his shoulder. The Polo swung round the corner, braked. He squashed the chicken wire into the boot beside the inflatable and got in the back. Murray driving, Al on the floor.

'Where's Kirsty, man?'

'Gone.'

'What you mean, gone?'

'Departed. Bailed out. Fucked off. Done a runner. Wede awa. Destination unknown. OK?'

'Fuckin hell.'

'Jeez. I'm sorry, man.'

'Uh-huh.'

Silence, only the engine idling.

'I'll hae to do the inflatable,' Murray said. 'You two hump the gear and shift the stag yourselves. Better pick a wee yin.'

Murray put the car in gear and drove for the rendezvous with Fang as Alasdair pulled Neil down behind the seat.

'Where's your tweeds?'

'She took them. A souvenir, I guess. Or maybe a trophy. Something to hang on the wall, right?'

'Take it easy, old chap. You can use Murray's tweeds now he's not on active service.'

Murray dangled a carrier bag back over the seat.

'All yours, pal. Mibbe a bit on the short side.'

Neil lay on the floor and felt the car swing round another bend. He felt slightly sick. He'd never know what it had meant for Kirsty. She'd never said. He'd just thought she had.

The car pulled up beside the Transit van. He saw the small knot by the side of her mouth. *Everything I have told you is true. You must decide whether to believe that.* Then he was out, carrying the chicken wire and the rifle inside it into the van, greeting all the new faces there as Murray drove away.

The Portakabin was empty as Mitchell and his associates walked up and down the river in urgent consultation. The trouble was, Ellen envied them. At least they knew what they were supposed to do.

She turned away from the window and flicked open the MI report lying on Mitchell's table. Scottish Republican Army thought to be inactive or extinct. Rumours of activity among splinter groups within Republican and Loyalist, but then there always were rumours. That's what informants get paid for. Assessments of Greenpeace, access groups . . .

She shook her head. This made no sense. At the bottom was a small handwritten comment.

Possibility of extreme Right and/or Protestant group (inside Security Forces?) targeting HRH for destabilizing Monarchy and intent to disestablish Protestant Church cannot be ruled out. *M. M.*

She looked at it for a long time. She'd been wrong about Mitchell. He did have imagination. Too much.

Yet he could be right. Sutherland working with a rogue unit inside MI? It had happened before. Thinking of it that way, his profile could fit. Together with this mysterious Murray. And Kirsty and Neil taken along for the ride? Kirsty suspects and cuts out. Or they suspect she suspects and they . . .

She shook her head. Paranoia was an occupational hazard. And sometimes justified.

She made another coffee. Nothing could be ruled out. Somewhere out there in the mist people were moving, and she could only wait helpless as they closed in on their target.

At first the checkpoint replayed as the day before. The two gamies exchanged the morning with Fang, the soldier glanced inside and put away for later the cigarette Alasdair offered. He asked about the chicken wire and was told it was for building a hide for bird-watching. Sharon and her weekend romance were pawing each other in the back. The soldier looked away and went back to his gatepost; it really wasn't fair.

'Who's the new fella?'

Fang explained this was a social work trainee. The wee fella was catching up on paperwork. Neil greeted the inquisitive gamie from inside the van and tried to explain the value of the Duke of Edinburgh for deprived kids.

'Dinni look very deprived to me.'

Looking at their flushed faces and the general air of raised hormones, Neil was inclined to agree. He said their deprivation was emotional. Antisocial behavioural patterns, drug problems, promiscuity – manifestations of galloping insecurity and incipient psychosis. A week of fresh air, hard work and magnificent scenery would give them some self-reliance and a glimpse of another way of living . . .

The ghillie's eyes had already begun to glaze over by the time Neil went on to say that he was taking a group of them camping overnight on the hill so they wouldn't be in the van on the way out this evening.

The ghillies opened the gate and waved them through.

'Here, mister, who're you calling a nutter and a slag?' Sharon complained.

'You!' the rest of the group shouted, and the van shoogled on up the track.

Murray was patient and methodical, he only did what he believed in and he was lucky. He didn't believe in luck. He would never buy a ticket for the Lottery but he had Trish, and they had always been a solid item so he was lucky.

He shook away Neil's face from earlier as he slowed where the trees were thicker on the left, keeping an eye on his rear-view mirror. Gutted was the word for it: that morning his pal had looked like a trout caved in with its insides gone and the colour fading.

He chose the small picnic-area car park on the right among the pines and beech. Even with false plates he'd have to be quick. He hopped out of the car and stood by the boot and looked and listened. As a car came down the road, he eyed the trees opposite. There was little underbrush, which was good for moving quickly but poor for cover.

The car went by and silence flowed back gradually till he could hear the river again. He shivered slightly in the morning mist, feeling the damp collect in his beard as he thought about Kirsty and where and why she'd gone, and what would happen with him and Trish once Eve and Jamie were old enough to run off into the future and not come back much.

He pushed up his sleeves, hoiked the inflatable out of the boot and staggered across the road and into the trees. Ten yards in he hit the ground as a car went by much too slowly. He lay with his face in the first damp autumn leaves but what he smelled mostly was the inflatable beside him and it smelled like a giant condom. The truth was he and Trish were a good team with the kids, his political work, her picture-framing business fitting nicely to his joinery. An item, a good team.

The car faded slowly, he got up and half-dragged, half-carried the inflatable deeper into the trees, ducking under beech, the rowan berries glowing darker as the chill came on. They'd been that busy being a team for that long he wasn't quite sure who they were other than a team, only that somewhere down the line there was a change coming on.

He crawled the last bit and lay on his chest under the bushes and long grass near the river's edge. The river was quite wide at this point and not too deep, grey and white and bubbling a bit where the shallows ran. On the far side he saw the upper part of the grey signal rock agreed on the day before. There was no one visible on the opposite bank; he could go for it now.

He waited because he was that kind of person. He waited because his father had taught him to wait in fishing and in politics, and because he didn't believe in luck. Sure enough, a few minutes later a tall man in old tweeds stirred out of the trees across the river and stood on the bank looking all ways. He looked and waved to someone further down the river, just a shape in the poor light under the trees who then disappeared, then tweedie picked a way carefully up the bank and round the bend.

With the inflatable in his arms and over his chest like a huge floppy baby, Murray jumped into the river. The cold of the water took a few seconds to hit, and he staggered with it up to his knees, not looking at anything now except the far bank as he thrashed on.

He clawed up the bank and dragged squelching into the trees, crackling through bushes and branches to the base of the rock. The cave was under its lean, screened by rhododendrons. He bent over gasping, then pulled the inflation canister from his jacket and scraped and swiped leaves and twigs over the lot.

He crouched at the entrance and waited for the ghillie patrol to show. His wet jeans clung cold to his legs. He'd never fancied anyone else, being so focused on his work and politics and family, but that didn't mean Trish was the same. When they'd had that wee talk and he'd asked if she wanted any more kids, there'd been a flicker of surprise and that wasn't because of the question itself but just because he'd asked her something personal about where she was at in her life. It must have been too long. Not good. Not good at all.

A few yards away the tall ghillie went by, silent and alert as a heron. He remembered Helen who should have been here for this ploy, and Kirsty who had been. He'd liked and rated them both, and knew Trish still missed her confidante. How easily a fish or a man is hooked and knifed and gutted.

He hit the river again and its chill was almost welcome. He'd anaesthetized so much of his life in political activity. He splashed up the far bank and hurried through the trees. The car was still there and no one around. He was luckier than he deserved.

He jumped in and drove away fast. It wasn't too late yet.

Tricia was going through *Where's Spot?* for the fourth time with Jamie when the knocking began. What's wrong with the bell? Why is being a parent sometimes so incredibly boring? Where the hell is Spot?

'Eve, will you get that please!'

Downstairs, Eve put down her guitar with a sigh and went to open the door as the banging started up again.

It took some shouting on her part, but in the end Mitchell allowed Ellen to talk to Tricia Hamilton on the phone. The woman wasn't cooperating and he was getting desperate.

'Tricia, my name is Ellen Stobo. I'm a friend of Kirsty and Shonagh and I've met Neil and I know about Alasdair. No, I don't want them hurt either. Right now they're all in danger, including your husband. I'm really sorry about what they've done to your house and Eve and, uh, Jamie. Yes, they frighten me too. Now listen. The problem is, some people here have a crazy idea that . . .'

When she put the phone down, she handed Mitchell the pad she'd scribbled on.

'He phoned her from this camp-site last night and told her they were going in today.'

'I'll bet they are.'

'She swears she doesn't know their plan. I believe her. She's desperately worried and I think she'd tell us if she knew more.'

Mitchell handed the pad to a subordinate.

'Probably too late, but check it. Leave two men there. Approach with care. Usual procedure. And I want that car found.' He turned back to Ellen. 'Well done with the Hamilton wife.'

'Sometimes putting a woman in an armlock and frightening her kids doesn't work too well.'

He shrugged.

'You still believe in this John Macnab nonsense?'

'She does, I'm sure of it.'

'They're on the estate, they're armed.' He pointed through the Portakabin door at the upper windows behind them. 'And I've a royal who won't do what he's told. You expect me to follow the rules?'

Neil checked the rifle was secure in the roll of netting and set off with it on his shoulder after Alasdair and the kids as they humped gear and backpacks up the burn track. The carrier bag with Murray's tweeds was in his free hand. Even let down, they'd be ridiculous on him.

He swallowed hard and lurched on. He might as well play this till the end though it no longer mattered, like hanging on at a party after the person you wanted to meet has left.

In mid-afternoon, through light mist and drizzle, they came over the brow of the hill and there was Lochan nan Ciste. Small water lapped on the shore, a heron dragged itself off on slow wings. They followed the bank round to the lee shore of the light breeze.

'This'll do, troops.'

Fortunately HRH was of the realist school and painted what he saw. Heather, a steep bank, then some mud, then the water.

'Perfect,' Al muttered. 'Chicken wire, Neil. Pliers. Space-blankets, Siobhan. Sharon and Terry, start cutting heather, not all from one place.'

The Sutherland Infrared Stag-shooting Hide would make a fine exhibit in a Museum of Highland Infamy. First the chicken-wire cage, bent and secured into the bank, leaving a gap behind. Then the space-blankets to muffle heat emissions from its occupants so that overhead surveillance wouldn't pick them up. Then a second wire cage. As Alasdair secured the structure and pulled the gear inside, Neil and the kids applied the designer heather, threading the roots in through the mesh.

They all stood for a moment and looked at their handiwork. Up close the hide looked obvious. Twenty feet back it was an odd piece of bank. From forty feet, you couldn't pick it out at all.

Alasdair slipped the kids their travelling expenses plus twenty quid extra each, then shook hands with each of them. If all went according to plan, they'd meet up again at the hostel the next night. Sharon ran back and kissed him, on a dare, then the gaggle of youngsters disappeared into the mist.

He watched them go for a moment. Kids. Children. Fun, but it wasn't to be. Probably best borrowed, anyway. He and Jane would make other ploys: with enough imagination there need be no end to ploys.

'Inside!' Neil hissed as he changed into Murray's tweeds.

Alasdair checked over the camouflage one more time. Not bad. Convincing enough from a distance and from the air. With hessian sacking he swept over the footprints in the mud and followed Neil inside.

'Cosy, eh?'

Neil grunted, rearranged his pack beneath him, stored the rifle upright in its case to his left. They sat cross-legged, slightly hunched, contemplating their navels like a pair of heretical tweedy Buddhas. Grey light was filtering in around the edges of the hide. They had a few hours to wait.

'Care for some tea, old chap?'

It tasted incredibly good. He longed for a cigarette but wasn't allowed. It was time he learned again to break with these addictions.

'She's water under the brigantine, surely,' Alasdair murmured.

Neil didn't move. To wait for longing to blow away like mist, to let it pass, terribly slowly, hours of nothing.

Ellen walked up and down by the Dee in front of the Portakabin in front of the Castle with her mobile and Mitchell's disgusting pork pie. No new reports, no sightings, no developments. But she had a vibrating cord stretched tight across her stomach, through her abdominal wall and tugging at the bottom of her ribcage.

She had once enjoyed stake-outs in a funny kind of way. The buzz, the banter, the long silent waiting, the not knowing. All very Zen, her brother used to say. Zen with guns.

Then someone had got shot who wasn't supposed to, and there'd been an inquiry and she'd allowed herself to be persuaded to move into the Corridor. Management and paperwork, meetings and conferences. It was called promotion.

She looked at the river and saw the next ten years flow away, then retirement.

Damn it, she wasn't that old. She wanted something more. She wanted something *else*.

She closed her jacket against the mist and crouched hugging her mobile and envied Jim his peace of mind, and waited some more.

Alasdair took his head in his hands and tried to twist it back into place. He was getting too old for this lark. He wondered if he was also getting piles.

'I reckon Murray's in the pub having a pint. Or in Aviemore chatting up the local talent.'

'Can you see it?'

'Talent in Aviemore? Not quite, old chap.'

A silence while they recovered from this exchange. They were learning to spin out the waiting. A little speech, a lot of silence.

'He's been in a funny mood this last while. He's not been around to be around, even when he's around. If you see what I mean.'

'Just another mid-life crisis.'

A long silence. They both shifted and wriggled, looking for a less uncomfortable position, though it had been established for a while that none existed in the cramped hide.

'In an hour we can have another sandwich.'

'Gee whiz.'

Neil poked his finger in the chicken wire and enlarged a peephole. Nothing much happening out there. Mist, water, a solitary dead tree on the far side.

'Ever seen *Waiting for Godot*, Al?'

In the police station, Jim MacIver swivelled restlessly. He told himself he wanted this to be done with so he could get back to the quiet life, so he wouldn't have lively, troubled, bright-eyed women turning up on his doorstep after midnight, and being company and warmth in his kitchen and stirring memories and desires that were best left forgotten.

The screen was empty, the evening outside was empty, and restless was a young feeling he should have left behind. He reached over and picked up the *Scots Magazine* Ellen had left. It smelled faintly of her, a whiff of pine trees, something evergreen at least.

He couldn't know where Kirsty was.

She was loping down a street of old tenements in the early morning rain. She was turning without hesitation down a narrow close that opened on to a courtyard with stairs. She was at the foot of one of the flights, then going up two at a time. She checked the name on the door and knocked lightly. Then she knocked loud, and the door opened and she was standing in the hallway where she never thought she'd be again.

'Chrissie.'

She put down her small case.

'Hello, Tom.'

It may have been like that.

Shonagh left the bar to Annie and sat in Reception. She leaned on the counter and had words with Mr MacPherson. She told him exactly what she thought of the two men who'd called earlier, their endless questions and the sense they gave off, like a brutal aftershave, of unstated but unlimited power. At one point she'd asked to call her lawyer, though of course she didn't have one. They'd brushed that aside like magic. They didn't have to play those rules.

Archie MacPherson offered no comment. Pity they hadn't tried to interrogate him.

She went back into the office and closed the door.

She still felt a bit weak at the knees, and she didn't like the look of the man who sat patiently in the lobby, idly flicking through old editions of the *Scots Magazine*.

She swivelled in her chair and looked out of the window and thought about Kirsty and thought about Pat, wondering if one would come back and the other would stay.

Even in the hide, the sound of the chopper was deafening. It must be right overhead. It didn't move away. The roar got closer, louder. The heather shifted in the downdraught and Neil shook himself from his sorry dwam to cling to the few stalks he could reach.

He glanced at Alasdair, who sat examining his fingernails, apparently relaxed.

Ah, stuff them, Neil thought. He didn't really care. Speculation is a waste of time.

The chopper moved away, slowly working along the shore of the lochan.

'In forty-three minutes we can have another sandwich and half a mug of tea.'

It sounded like half-time in some game.

And how has the season gone so far, Mr Lindores? Played three, won two. Lost one, the one that mattered. He didn't care that much what happened in the last leg. A draw. An honourable draw, he'd settle for that, though with the rifle beside him it seemed unlikely. This one was win or lose.

Alasdair stretched out his leg.

'Another hour. Let's get some decent spyholes made. There'll be a few young stags on their own. Or . . .'

'Or?'

'Or there won't be. But if something turns up, I'll take you as close as possible, then it's up to you. One shot is all we'll get.'

Neil leant forward and started poking a hole at his side of the cage.

'This should have been Kirsty's hit,' he muttered. 'I think she took the huff about that.'

'She never shot a gun in her life. I asked her at the beginning.' Neil didn't reply, so Alasdair began making a hole on his side. 'Don't wish to be personal, old sport, but surely it was worth it? I mean, better to have loved and lust and all that.'

Neil put his eye to the spyhole. A misty stretch of bleak shoreline, nothing animal or human there. He sat back, looked at the false wall in front of him.

'Al, there's no accountancy system in existence that can do the Profit and Loss on that one.'

He reached for the rifle and began peeling off its rubber casing.

In the back of Smiffy's in Aviemore, Murray ordered another coffee and took out the pad he'd bought. He'd done what he could do, now it was time to do more. He had a notion to write to Helen and tell her how he still missed her, how her absence left a small silence in his marriage – some sentimental crap like that. Or fire off a card to Kirsty, wherever she was, telling her to get her act together and come back to see it through.

Dear Tricia, he wrote. It felt odd, it looked odd. Must have been ten years since he'd written to her, and it took him right back to the beginning when he bombarded her with cards from climbing trips with Neil and Al, desperately trying to interest her, make her laugh, keep himself on her mind. He remembered the fear, the excitement, the uncertainty. He felt the touch of it again now.

It's been long enough since I wrote to you. That's the trouble wi living thegither, we've no reason to write. When this started, Al and Neil needed a change and me, I just thought it was politics and a bit of daftness. Now they've got their change and it's me – us, Trish – that needs to wake up and look around . . .

He paused, checked his watch, took out a thin cigar. He pushed up his sleeves and bent over the pad again. He had a lot of time, which was as well because he had a lot to say and didn't know yet what it was. That was the thing with real letters. Like a real adventure, they could take you anywhere and there was no knowing where it would end till you got there.

I've been anaesthetized wi politics and forgot . . .

The light was failing now. In half an hour it would be dark and then it would be too late. Alasdair and Neil lay belly-down in the heather, peering up over the bank of the lochan. Still nothing happening. Alasdair pointed off to their left, near the exit burn, then signalled for Neil to follow. Stooping low, they worked their way along the shore.

The burn was quite loud now through the mist. Just a gurgling and the faint hiss of the breeze over wet heather. This is nowhere, Neil thought. Absolute nowhere, connected to nothing.

Alasdair was turning his head this way and that, like a disorientated pointer dog. He licked his finger and held it up, frowned and sniffed again. He pointed into the grey and nodded.

Clutching the rifle, Neil slowly put his head over the bank. Then he smelt it – like cattle but thinner, sharper.

And then there was an eddy and the mist parted. Not hinds, but three – no, four – young stags, moving slowly, delicately down to the burn. With their fledgling antlers and oddly tubular bodies, they looked like russet bagpipes on legs. Maybe forty yards.

Neil brought the bulky rifle to his shoulder, half standing, half lying against the bank, an awkward angle. Back of left hand scraping wet heather, right fingers round the cold trigger-guard. Very gently, he flipped up the sights.

Scarcely breathing, he picked out the one on the left because it was closest. He settled the ring sight at the base of its neck. His finger began to squeeze.

The stag's neck dipped as it drank. He followed it down. Now. He must do it now. He looked through the ring sight and for a moment was back on a bridge, looking down at rings expanding on a sunlit river and Kirsty lying on the bank. Maybe that was when she'd decided. So much for visions. It wasn't going to be that way.

He became aware of Alasdair, frowning and nodding urgently. Do it. Do it.

Things weren't any way but this. As the stag's head came up, he fired.

25

Despite the mist and the silencer, the gun sounded deafening. The stag did a vertical take-off, came back to earth, spun round to the west and headed off. The others simply disappeared.

'You missed!'

But as it vanished into the dimness, they saw the hindquarters wobble. Alasdair grabbed the netting and they launched themselves after it into the gathering dark.

Nearly a mile away, Sandy and Simon on overtime heard the shot. Very faint, oddly muffled, but unmistakable. They looked at each other. Their instructions had been clear, and they had a two-way radio. Then again, there was two thousand quid for whoever first laid hands on John Macnab.

They set off across the rough moorland towards where they thought the shot had come from. They were experienced, they knew the ground. They used no lights and moved quiet and fast.

The stag lay sprawled on its side. Alasdair risked the pencil torch, removed the tranquillizer dart, checked the animal was still breathing. Neil finished binding up its legs, then Alasdair took out the netting from under his jacket.

Just getting the stag into the net was a sweat. Neil was astonished how heavy it was. Even between the two of them it would be a struggle to lift it. Neil felt for the animal, caught in a net as it slept.

'Do you know where we are?'

'Not exactly. Wish I'd brought the Satnav.'

'We could try to find the lochan and get our bearings. There's still our clothes to pick up.'

Alasdair glanced at his watch.

'Scrub that. We're behind schedule and this beauty weighs a ton. Did you have to pick the heaviest one?'

Neil chuckled.

'Sorry about that. Biggest target.'

Alasdair crouched over the map and compass.

'We'll just have to take a bearing off. That way we'll hit the burn sooner or later, though it'll add on more time.'

Neil hitched the rifle over his shoulder and they each picked up a corner of the net. With the stag slung between them, they began to walk along the approximate line of the compass bearing. After thirty yards they had to stop and massage their fingers. They bent towards each other in the darkness.

'This will take hours.'

'Got to make the river by dawn or we're shafted.'

'We could just leave it here.'

'You are kidding.'

They took up their burden again.

It was late as Murray returned from Aviemore humming 'Freedom Come All Ye' and turned the car into the camp-site. In the headlights he saw the two men walking away from his tent, saw the flak jackets and the automatic rifles and a torchbeam turning his way.

He did a skid turn and roared back out through the gateway, knowing he no longer felt lucky.

Ellen was sitting in the corner of the Portakabin, hoping that if she kept quiet enough they'd forget about her. She was only an observer, after all. That was her only responsibility.

She leant forward and began to nibble her thumbnails, one in each corner of her mouth. She glanced at the men huddled round the transmitter, still hoping against hope that she was right and they were wrong.

She had to tell them about the inflatable. No word from the factor on that score. But the river was well guarded in the immediate vicinity of the Castle. Infrared nightsights and beams, marksmen, searchlights ready for use. No way through there, no way. The Macnabs must know that. They wouldn't choose that way. They'd surely do their poaching in the far corners of the estate . . .

She noticed where her thumbs were and hastily removed them before anyone noticed. A dumb kid's habit. She folded her hands together, almost in prayer, another leftover from childhood when things had been bad.

Grow up, woman. She had to tell Mitchell and hope that the Macnabs had the sense to put their hands up straight away when they were caught by the river, as they would be. She began to get to her feet.

Then the call came in. The suspect car had entered the campsite and driven off again at full speed, heading east. One driver, no visible passengers: from the description it was Murray Hamilton.

As Mitchell ordered the roadblocks into place and authorized the use of appropriate force, she sat back down again. She folded her hands again, and this time she found she really was praying.

Jim MacIver sat alone in the police station. He scanned the faxes that had come through in Ellen's absence. None of them were important enough to warrant getting on the phone. He'd occasionally been tempted to try to access his own files, just to see what they said about his life. In the end, he'd always not bothered. Whatever was in the damned files, it bore as much resemblance to his life as Death Valley did to his garden.

He swivelled restlessly in the seat. The drizzle hissed on the window. In a few hours it would be getting light again. He should be in his bed like a sensible God-fearing divorced man in late middle age.

He picked up the *Scots Magazine* again and began to flick through some more pages.

Murray came fast round the corner and the roadblock swung in front of his headlights. He spun the wheel to the left, shaved the oil drums as he went up the banking, glimpsed the startled faces at the barrier. He thumped back on to the road, then the two parked cars facing him switched on their headlights, he called them for everything and swung off to the left again. This time the ditch was deeper. One wheel dropped in, then the other, and the Polo slammed sideways into the trees.

He was lying on his side. The windscreen was blown out and full of light. He reached up for the driver's door and slowly climbed out. He staggered back against the car, half-blinded by headlights. He saw the men silhouetted, the flak jackets and the automatic rifles, and he knew this was nothing to do with John Macnab.

He took a deep breath and straightened up. He put up his hands and waited for the bullets.

The mist blew away from the stalkers' path, the moon cleared for a moment, and the two soldiers were five yards from the two ghillies. For a second no one moved.

'Haud there, Mr Macnab! We've caught ye!'

The soldier swung his automatic rifle up and round.

'They're ghillies, you fool!' the other soldier shouted, and knocked his arm as it came up with the weapon.

Three shots stuttered into the air, then silence. The ghillies looked at each other.

'Si, this isna worth two grand.'

Jim MacIver turned another page of the *Scots Magazine* and found himself looking at a small reproduction of a water-colour painting of a lochan and some deer, like a hundred others he'd seen. But this one had been bordered by a blue biro, and someone had put a large question mark in the margin and underneath that was scrawled something. He looked more closely. *Lochan nan Ciste.*

He read the caption. *Deer Drinking at Dusk near Balmoral.*

The chair went spinning. He stood before the large-scale map, and using language only his Maker and some forty thousand other native Gaelic speakers would understand, he searched wildly for the lochan. He found it. He looked at the lochan, traced a broad finger down the exit burn to the River Dee, then east to Balmoral.

He saw it all as if it were already daylight outside. He saw them waiting at the lochan, however they'd managed to get there. He heard them grunt and sweat as they dragged the stag up the bit brae then down towards the river. And he knew exactly what they were going to do when they got there.

Neil knelt by the burn and scooped water into his face. His hands stung, rubbed raw by the netting. He reached into his jacket for his last rations and glanced across where one dark shape bent over another.

'Come and hold the torch. This young fella needs another jab.'

The stag was beginning to stir. Its legs rotated inside the net, huge eyes stared into the torchlight. Neil grimaced and shifted the beam.

'Hurry up, Al, the poor thing's frightened half to death.'

Alasdair took out the small plastic case and flipped it open. He eased out the syringe, selected an ampoule.

'He'll be fine in a few hours. My vet mate promised me. Bring the torch closer.'

He ran his hand lightly over the neck, looking for the vein. Neil was struck by the calm gentleness of his movements.

'You should have been a doctor.'

'I often wanted to be.' He shrugged. 'Just didn't quite work out. Not clever enough, you see. Too busy climbing. Ah!'

He parted the coarse hairs with his thumb while Neil watched, and thought how strange and touching it was when someone you thought you knew showed another side. He wanted to hug Al, or some such un-Scottish display. Instead he just knelt closer with the pencil torch as Alasdair exposed the vein.

'You learned the paramedic stuff with Special Forces?'

'One of the reasons I got involved, old chap.' Alasdair flicked the needle in as though it was a dart. 'The A & E was as gripping as climbing. Had to do everything right under pressure.' His thumb took the plunger to the bottom. 'That suited me. Might even have done some good in the world. Strange thought, eh?' He plucked the needle out, and with the syringe loose in his hand glanced up at Neil. 'One of the things I love about Jane is that she's a good nurse.'

Already the stag's legs were slowing. Neil stroked the side of its head as the eyes began to close, and thought again how dumb he was. How he thought he understood his friends, Kirsty, himself, and every so often glimpsed that he didn't have a clue. He'd felt so close to Kirsty, it seemed she was completely revealed to him, eyes inches away, her laugh and whisper in his ear. So candid, so completely offered.

He shook his head, looked down to where the river must be and flexed his raw fingers. The sky had cleared of rain, it would soon be first light.

'Ready, old sport?'

Mitchell stood in the Portakabin doorway looking triumphant.

'We've got the bastard. It's Hamilton all right.'

'Is he injured?'

'Not much. Yet. We'll soon get the others out of him.'

'Was he unarmed?' she asked quietly.

Mitchell was almost disconcerted.

'Looks like it.'

'Nothing in the car? No explosives, mortars, intercontinental ballistic missiles?'

'Eh, not that we've found yet.' He looked at a loss for a moment, then his face cleared. 'I'd put my money on Sutherland. He's got the gear and Hamilton was just the runner. Or a decoy. Or something.'

'Or something,' she muttered. 'Jesus. Did you find the stag?'

He stared at her.

'There was no bloody stag! Now we're in for a result.'

As he hurried out, Ellen's mobile phone burbled.

'Ellen? I know where these scallywags are.'

Even as her heart began to yo-yo, she had to smile at that 'scallywags'. She walked up and down along the bank as he told her. She'd begun to get a feel for John Macnab, and this fitted. She'd been right.

She looked to the east where the sky was growing pale over the hills. They'd have to move fast to cut off the remaining Macnabs before Security got them. She checked the map and gave Jim her instructions, grabbed her car keys and left on the run.

As she ricocheted along the estate road, she took another slip of paper from her pocket and jabbed out the number written there. She got an equerry or something. She insisted on speaking to the man himself. It's very, very important. Tell him it's about catching John Macnab.

She nibbled her thumbnail, trying to remember the correct form of address. The mobile phone crackled.

'Sir? I'm sorry to wake you.'

'I haven't been asleep. Too many things . . . Who are you?'

'You don't know me, sir, but I think we're about to catch John Macnab.'

She couldn't keep it to herself any longer. In any case, she needed to cover her back for when the inquest started along the Corridor. A minute's conversation and it was done. She switched off the phone and sped on to where Jim and the two ghillies were waiting for her.

She slewed to a stop beside them. A glance at the map, then they started to run along the stalkers' path towards where the Lochan nan Ciste entered the Dee.

Down by the river it was still half dark as Alasdair tugged open the inflatable. He attached the cylinder, twisted the valve and compressed air began to hiss in.

Neil looked up. He could hear the chopper but couldn't see it, somewhere up in the hill behind. He looked along the banks, astonished to find themselves still alone. This is when they could have done with their naff gear so they could then separate and just stroll off the estate, but it was still in the hide by the lochan.

The black inflatable was ready. He and Alasdair bundled the stag in, grabbed the handles and dragged it into the water. One push and it was on its way, turning slowly in the current.

'*Bon voyage*, old chap.'

For a moment they stood and watched it go. Alasdair nudged Neil's arm as he stashed the rifle in the cave. He turned, saw the hand held out.

'See you in Ballater.'

Then the first shouts. Two ghillies running along the path, two other figures stumbling behind.

The remains of John Macnab ducked back into the trees. The two ghillies looked at each other.

'Si, these boys havenae got guns?'

'That's what the woman said, Sandy.'

'Two thousand quid.'

They looked at each other.

'Fifty-fifty, mate.'

They ran into the wood after the fugitives.

'Jim! Wait!'

Jim MacIver stopped thankfully. He was in no condition to go running through trees or scampering over the heather. It was fully light now, and above the woods they could see the open slope that rose towards the lochan. They looked down the river towards Balmoral. Nothing there.

'What now?'

'You check out where the stream runs into the river. They may have left the stag there. I'll wait here with the radio in case they give the keepers the slip in the trees and try to break out across the hill. They mustn't run into Mitchell's boys.'

Alasdair waited till he could hear the ghillies coming into the wood. Crouched beside Neil, he considered the options. Not back down to the river where the other two would be waiting. He could try to lose the ghillies in the trees, but they were professionals in their way, and Neil wasn't used to moving quietly.

The hill, then. Back into the gully of the burn, use it as cover.

The burn ran awfully near to the EZ but if they made it back up to the hide, they could lie low there till night. It wasn't over yet.
He signed to Neil and they set off, ducking low through the dense trees, aiming for the far side of the wood.

Ellen wasn't happy with where she was. She couldn't see enough of the open hillside because of trees in front of her. She turned and ran back the way she'd come, gained the stalkers' track and followed it back up the hill, wishing she'd spent a bit less time behind a desk.
She'd wanted something different, and now she'd got it.
Panting, she scrambled up a small outcrop that rose above the dark wood till she could see over the trees to the open hillside. She took out her radio and binoculars and waited.

The last of the Macnabs made it to the far side of the trees. The burn was maybe a hundred yards away to their right. The hillside was more broken and undulating than it had looked before. Some cover there.
'Ready, youth?'
Neil dragged bits of forest out of his hair.
'What are we going to do when we're too old for this?'
'Something exciting, maybe.'
They took a deep breath and began to run.

Ellen lowered her binoculars. She'd last seen one of those figures across a crowded bar. The other had to be Sutherland. They just didn't give up.
She switched on her radio. Luckily one of the ghillies – Sandy, she thought – was still tuned in. Head them off before the stream, she instructed. Don't let them get to the skyline. For God's sake keep them out of the exclusion zone.
She frowned down the binoculars again and picked up the two running figures as they went down into a dip and disappeared. She trained her glasses on the other side, waiting for them to reappear.

Neil looked back and saw the two ghillies emerge from the wood. They'd spotted him all right, and they looked young and fit. Alasdair veered away from the direction of the burn, making for another fold in the hillside. Neil sighed but ran on. He really didn't think they could shake off the ghillies there.

And they wouldn't have, but for an utterly unexpected intervention.

Through the binoculars, Ellen saw a lone figure in tweeds haring off downhill towards the burn. She was sure she couldn't have missed Neil and Sutherland emerging from the dip. How many Macnabs were there? They seemed to breed like rabbits.

She saw the ghillies falter and hesitate, then both made off to intercept the single runner. In vain she tried to alert them on the radio but they'd switched off, not feeling like sharing the reward money.

Neil and Alasdair crawled through some loose boulders to the top of the dip. They looked down and saw the two ghillies running off below them, and the lone figure they were pursuing. It seemed to have come out of nowhere.

'Who the hell is *that*?'

Neil felt very strange.

'Don't quote me, but I think we're looking at the ghost of John Macnab.'

The tall figure was clad in tweeds. Jacket, deerstalker, plus-fours and long socks, old-style. Stumbling a bit, but making good time downhill towards the gully, drawing away the pursuers.

'I think he's going to make it.'

'Is this for real?'

Alasdair's hand squeezed Neil's arm.

'I don't know, but this is our chance. Up the gully on the far side of the burn.'

Neil looked at him.

'You mean into the exclusion zone.'

'It's that or get caught. Your call.'

Neil hesitated, looking at the little pink flags and tape blowing in the early light. It seemed like that line had been waiting for him since Helen died.

'I think we can make it,' he said, and started running.

I really think they might have made it, though some still argue that the situation was now too far gone for even Alasdair Sutherland to retrieve. Alasdair's response to that contains explicit language.

But two Special Forces men used their initiative and drifted to the very edge of the zone and over the brow of the hill. They looked down the gully and saw two figures crouch-running across the rocks and heather.

They knew what to do. One signed to the other – thumb down for *Enemy*, hand gesture for pincer movement, then thumb up for *Give them the good news*. They unslung their rifles and set off down.

Ellen saw them from her outpost and knew what it meant. She looked across the line of the forest, but the two ghillies and their quarry had disappeared.

She cursed, then scrambled down the outcrop and into the trees. It was thick in there: branches scraped and tore as she stumbled and thrashed towards the higher ground as though someone's life depended on it.

Neil tripped on a heather root and the first bullet cracked off the rock above his head. He looked up and saw the two men in flak jackets, one above, the other coming in from the side, guns at the ready. He looked to Al for the next move.

'Sorry, old sport. Face down, hands out, and don't move a fucking muscle.'

They lay there. Neil heard the boots clacking over the rocks. He tried not to think of Gibraltar. Shoot To Kill. He smelled the heather thick and musty up his nose and tried very hard not to sneeze. And this morning he'd thought he didn't care if he lived or died. Bollocks. Right now he cared very much.

He felt the shadow fall over him, heard a metallic click.

Then the boot went into his kidneys. And again. He heard a thud and Al groan. Hands passing expertly over his clothes.

'Turn over, you Fenian bastard. Very slowly.'

Very slowly and still wondering about the Fenian, he did as he was told. A heel went into his gut and he was looking into a small black hole that had no bottom.

'That's enough, sonny. These aren't terrorists.'

A woman's voice, panting. He twisted his head and saw short grey hair and a face he'd seen a lifetime ago.

'Mr John Macnab, I presume.'

'What's left of him,' Neil croaked.

Jim MacIver was bending over the discarded rifle and inflation canister when he heard shouts above him. He saw the two ghillies first, then a man in tweeds dashing past on the other side of the rock. He stuck out his foot and the figure went sprawling.

'All right, lad. It's been a braw game but it's over.'

The man in tweeds groaned, sat up and slowly pulled off his deerstalker.

'You got me bang to rights, guv,' Kirsty said.

26

It's common convention to conclude a drama by assembling all its principal characters in one place at one time. The return of John Macnab began with life taking cues from fiction, and it ends the same way.

So picture a large sitting room in the Castle. There are two doors – there must always be two doors for this kind of scene – and high French windows that look down the lawn to the River Dee. On the lawn, two men in plain clothes clutching mobile phones are walking up and down. It's a cool mid-morning for the season has tilted into autumn, and inside a wood fire is burning in the grate.

Murray, Neil and Alasdair are already there, in a group by the windows, wondering what's going to happen to them. They have cleaned up a bit; two are still in tweeds. All of them have bruised ribs and various pains which make it difficult to laugh, which they do, in a nervous way. It's like waiting in the headmaster's study. They huddle together, wondering how much this is going to hurt. No one has told them anything. They assume they're under arrest but no one has told them that either.

Murray fingers his bruised jaw and says not being under arrest would be more worrying – he knows fine what the State is capable of.

Unusually, Alasdair agrees with him. Right now he'd say this is not happening. He says this, then brushes his non-existent moustache. Privately he's astonished the Special Forces men hadn't take them out. Unlike the others, he knows the true meaning of Let's give them the good news.

Neil is just glad to be alive. For the moment he's not prepared to think past that.

They look round as a door opens. It's a thin and elegant man in a light summer suit that only just shows a bulge above where his heart should be. He stares at them, nods, then takes up position beside the door, feet slightly apart, hands clasped behind his back, saying nothing. They will never learn his name or function.

The door opens again. Indoors, Colonel Mitchell looks very big. He takes two steps towards Murray and glares at him. Murray stares back, memorizing the face. If Tricia or the kids have been harmed by this man, he will kill him if he possibly can.

Murray is also worried about the green Polo. Trish will give him a right bollocking for losing their no-claims discount. He wonders if, under the circumstances, an insurance claim is possible.

Ellen Stobo walks between him and Mitchell, gives the three Macnabs a quick smile, then takes Mitchell by the arm and leads him to the far corner of the room. They have a lot to sort out.

And Neil is pale, for behind Ellen Stobo he has just seen a ghost, the ghost of Joys Past. Kirsty is wearing his tweeds with long wool socks and the trousers turned up as though plus-fours. She doesn't run and embrace him as the script demands. After a muttered Hi, she doesn't look at him or the others. She sits down in an armchair. She doesn't seem to know what to do with her hands. Perhaps she feels that if she speaks her voice will not sound like her own, like Gerry Adams's used to on TV.

The other door, the one that gives on to a small and very private study, opens and the illustrious personage comes in. He is wearing a kilt and a light sweater whose cuffs he seems unhappy with. His eyes and hands never settle in one place long, his head jerks as though seeking an exit that isn't there.

Ellen comes over and does the introductions. Kirsty gives a sort of bob, half-remembered from childhood. Alasdair virtually stands to attention as he shakes hands firmly and calls HRH 'Sir'. Neil goes through the motions; he has other things on his mind.

The illustrious personage stops in front of Murray.

'Ah, the republican.' His eyes swivel away, then back again. 'The man with the salmon, eh?' He grimaces as though he's found a loose filling with his tongue. 'I suppose one cannot expect to be called Sir?'

'Nuthin personal. It's political, like.'

'Political. Yes, yes. Of course. Too much politics in this world, in my opinion. Only my opinion, of course.' His eyes make a quick dash round the room, a very brief smile slips by on its way out the door. 'In that case, one may call one Frank.'

'Frank?'

Much fiddling with the sweater cuffs.

'One has always wanted to be called Frank.'

For once Murray is lost for a reply.

'Uh, OK – Frank.'

'Good. Good. A fine piece of fishing too, by all accounts. Ah . . .'

HRH goes over to the fireplace and frowns at it for a while. He beckons to Colonel Mitchell and Ellen and they begin to speak together quietly. The four Macnabs stand and look at each other, all except Kirsty. Neil has not seen her embarrassed or ashamed before, and he takes no pleasure in it.

The conference breaks up. Colonel Mitchell leaves the room, followed by Ellen Stobo. As she goes through the door she gives them a small encouraging wave. A minute later, she and Mitchell will reappear on the terrace outside and wait there, not talking to each other.

HRH turns away from the fire. He coughs apologetically. Perhaps he's about to make a royal quip.

'I suppose I am expected to say one is not amused.' He coughs again. 'As it happens, I am. Jolly few chances to be amused.' A brief frown. 'I read *John Macnab* when I was boy here and thought it marvellous. I thought, I used to imagine . . . If one were a free man . . .'

For the only time in this scene, the elegant man in the summer suit stirs. He goes into the study and comes out a moment later with a silver tray. On it are five glasses and a bottle of twenty-year-old malt. Alasdair glances at Neil, who sort of smiles. Yes, he remembers fine. If the echo means anything to Kirsty, she doesn't show it as she stares down at the carpet.

'Unfortunately, one is not a free man,' says HRH. 'Cheers.'

'Cheers, Sir.'

'Cheers, Frank.'

A short pause for the appreciation of a very fine whisky. Then the royal face resumes its agonized expression.

'Please, do sit down, Miss, ah, Tarbet. And the rest of you. Please.' They sit down. 'No, ah, this is not a game, d'you see? One simply cannot have people threatening to poach stags on the estate. Lots of them, of course, but Security don't like it. Colonel Mitchell is not amused, though I cannot imagine what *would* amuse him. But rifles and suchlike . . . No.'

'You were never in danger from us, Sir.'

'Yes, yes, Mr Sutherland. You did jolly well too, I thought.' Another devastated frown. 'One sometimes thinks, ah, cameras do just as much damage as rifles. Don't you think? Yes. But the press, don't you see? They have to be told something. Otherwise, you know, they make things up. Yes.'

He sips his drink, and puts it on the mantelpiece. His hands try to escape along the ledge. He clasps them behind his back.

'So what are we to do with you, eh? If you go before a court, they will punish you in the way they think fit. A jail sentence, perhaps. Colonel Mitchell has his own ideas . . .' His hands escape and claw at his elbow. 'But one must not create martyrs. Not a good idea.' The Macnabs nod enthusiastically. 'On the other hand, one cannot simply let you off. You have gone much, much too far, and the law would insist . . . No. So what are we to do with you? What are we to do?'

A car draws up on the gravel drive outside. It's the bog-standard blue Ford Escort this account began with. (I can't help it, these things do happen.) Sergeant Jim MacIver winds down the window as Ellen leans to talk with him, hand on his arm.

'I have taken advice from . . . advisors . . . and we want to propose a deal. A deal, yes.'

Standing at the mantelpiece, with as much hand-wringing as Lady Macbeth on one of her bad days, in fits and starts HRH proposes the deal. The entire John Macnab affair was a hoax. It never happened. It was concocted by a group of people, with the cooperation of two landowners, for their own amusement and to raise publicity about land access rights.

'Land ownership and all,' Murray mutters, then winces as Alasdair sticks an elbow in his ribs.

HRH continues. Miss Tarbet will write this story for the newspapers. It will be her exclusive, and John Macnab can even keep the money she makes from it. Various people have to be squared, talked to, silenced if you like. With the end of the summer silly season, the whole affair will be forgotten very quickly.

'A lot of people might believe it,' Kirsty says, 'but there's some won't. What if they start asking questions?'

Ah well. Yes. To keep the conspiracy theorists happy, a rumour could be started that in fact the security services were behind it all. That they'd set it all up as a training exercise. Or maybe even to ensnare a renegade terrorist cell which has now been rendered inoperative. And if anyone investigated further, the Home Secretary was prepared to use D-notices.

'And whit happens tae us?'

A fleeting smile.

'You won't be named, for reasons of security. You say nothing to anyone, and go back to your normal lives as though nothing has happened. I mean to say, not much has happened, has it?'

'Or too much,' Neil mutters.

'Well, that's the, ah, deal. I'm afraid you'll have to sign some pieces of paper that will be fairly, er, binding. What d'you say?'

The man in the summer suit stirs but says nothing. HRH fidgets with the fire tongs. The Macnabs go into a huddle by the French windows. Outside they can see, sitting in their cars and strolling on the lawn, the forces of Law and Order.

Do they have a choice? Alasdair grins – they're getting off with it. Kirsty nods. Neil shrugs. Murray swears under his breath, but he can't be a good father when he's in jail, nor can he give time to whatever comes next for himself and Tricia.

They agree to the deal. The whole thing was a fiction. In a way, it fits. It's what Neil had suggested at the very beginning, in the chalet that rainy week when they were all restless and bored and needing something new. With his friends' input he'd wanted to write a contemporary retake on *John Macnab* till Alasdair persuaded them it would be much more interesting to do it for real.

('Yes, blame me,' Alasdair says. 'Everyone else does.')

The glasses are filled again and smoked salmon sandwiches are produced. The Macnabs polish them off. They're very hungry and suddenly rather knackered. Time to ring down the curtain and go home. Time to sign the papers, close the book and get some sleep.

'A fairly honourable draw,' HRH says reflectively. For a moment he seems at peace, standing with his back to the windows and a dram in his hand. 'Delivering the stag was always going to be too hard, eh?'

'Um, Frank . . .'

'Yes?'

'Something seems to be happening on your lawn.'

Two security men are bending over a black shape at the river's edge. They jump back as something assembles itself on the bank, a wobble of legs and netting. A stag begins to veer across the lawn, shadowed by two men who appear in some doubt about what to do. Ellen is laughing openly, Jim MacIver grins broadly as he steps from the car. Colonel Mitchell reaches into his jacket, then hesitates. He has little experience of four-legged security threats.

The stag looks at its audience. It is still a bit drowsy, and the whole situation is too complicated, and like the Macnabs it hasn't eaten for hours.

It puts its head down and starts to graze.

It's time for the characters to leave the stage. HRH stands at the top of the steps on to the lawn and shakes hands with the Macnabs.

'Jolly well done,' he says. He looks at the hills. His wrists are crossed over each other as though he were handcuffed. 'There's so much more I'd like to hear. Perhaps one day . . . No, perhaps not. No.'

He turns to go back inside. Half in and half out of the windows, he hesitates.

'One did enjoy being Frank.'

A flutter of the hand and he's gone. It's over.

'One last thing,' Kirsty says.

She hands her camera to the man in the lightweight suit. He takes the photo of the four Macnabs at the top of the steps. Neil and Alasdair are standing in tweeds with their arms crossed like characters from an Edwardian football team. Murray is in the act of pushing up his right sleeve. Kirsty's crouched at the front, grinning at the camera. She could be the captain or the mascot, it's hard to say which.

The man in the summer suit begins to lead Kirsty towards the police car where Jim and Ellen are waiting. She's to go with them to be briefed by the press secretary on what she's to write. She doesn't protest. It's then that Neil finally understands she is leaving and he will not see her again. He must learn to accept this.

He runs over and stops her. Summer suit turns away slightly and inspects his impeccable shoes.

She meets his eyes at last. She puts her hand on his arm and leans towards him like she has something important to say. But for once nothing comes out.

'Don't give up on this,' Neil says. 'Please, you daft bat.'

He feels her hand tighten on his arm.

'Some presents you can't take home with you, Neil.'

'Why? Why not?'

'I was carried away. I was . . .'

She turns her head and looks away. He'll never know whatever it is she was.

'Kirsty, once this is over . . .'

'When I've done the story, I'm going to spend some of John Macnab's money on a long holiday. I don't know where I'll go when I come back, but it won't be here.' When her head comes round, she is smiling like it was easy. 'We were just in it for the fun, we both know that. Hey,' she whispers, 'this isn't a tearful scene. You've got to learn to grin and walk away.'

His hand comes up. He brushes strands of her cropped beech-leaf hair back behind her ear.

'Maybe you've got to learn not to.'

Something stirs in her eyes, then is gone. She steps back. Summer suit has finished inspecting his shoes.

'I'll send you the tweeds when I've had them cleaned. Thanks for the loan. Thanks for everything.' She steps forward and lightly kisses him. 'Now I'm giving you it all back. Enjoy it.'

She almost runs to the car. Summer suit opens the door. She turns round and looks back at the remaining three Macnabs.

'Bye, guys. Great doing the gig with you.'

Her fingers touch her lips, touch her heart, then extend towards them, open-palmed.

Neil is the only who doesn't wave as the car moves off. He watches the back of Kirsty's head intently as she sits very upright next to Ellen. Just as the car turns the corner, her head dips down and Ellen's arm comes round her.

'The kid aye made good exits,' Murray says, and puts an arm through Neil's.

'Damn good entrance too, old sport,' Alasdair adds, and firmly takes Neil's other arm. 'Wouldn't have missed it for the square world.'

The two of them escort Neil to his car. The key's in the ignition so he turns it, and they leave without looking back, with a police car in front and another behind, on their way to a lengthy debriefing before finally putting their names to some more official lies, the ones you read in the papers if you remember that Macnab summer at all.

One distant toot on the horn. The stag looks up, then resumes grazing the aristocratic lawn.

27

Everything I have told you is true. You must decide whether to believe that or not. In the cluttered corner where the work gets done, I enter Save File, and the return of John Macnab is done.

Four incomplete people came together and for a while made a nearly unstoppable whole. That was the fish seen in the sky, that was the stag shot but not wounded, that was the bird that was winged but flew on, this was the story that cannot be told.

That was then, this is now. Outside the sleet is melting as quickly as it falls, it weeps down the window – a pathetic fallacy, but there it is. I can't help it if I'm lucky.

For weeks now the sky has been lowered like a pan lid over the city. In time spring will come. However late and however briefly, it always comes. And then another summer, though there'll not be another like those three weeks in August. Writing this has been my autumn and winter work, done in time stolen from my real work, the kind you do for money.

My dad used to say there's things you can't buy, and then there's the things you have to pay for. I begin to see what he meant. Macnab gave me a lot, and I'm still paying for it.

Since we disbanded that day at Balmoral, I've had some time on my hands. And it got to weigh a little heavy, so over the last months I've written this account for my own amusement and to set the record straight, though it will be a long time before it's publishable, even if the names and places were changed around. It's based on what I know, what the others told me at the time or later – even Jim MacIver and Ellen Stobo were helpful up to a point – and, all right, so I invented and dramatized a little at times. No doubt we all did, that summer.

Murray signed the papers, withdrew his name from the candidacy short list, and went back to joinery and decorating. He and Trish never got the insurance money to replace the wrecked

Polo – the company weaseled out over some clause about Acts of Terrorism. He shrugged and submitted the wreck for a contemporary sculpture exhibition under the title 'Political Theatre Lesson One: Keep Left, Watch for the Trees'. It wasn't accepted. Now it's out on his back green, quietly turning the colour of the Forth rail bridge.

He's increasingly involved in stunts and ploys for Greenpeace and access rights. Jamie has moved on from biting and growling to throwing small balls very fast, and Eve's guitar playing is getting good. She has a fondness for corny old songs from the fifties that I sometimes find painful, and I try to persuade her to listen to the music of her own generation, but she'll have none of it.

Some weekends I drive over there. The house is less settled, Murray and Tricia are edgy and alert to each other as though they've only recently met. This is not necessarily a bad thing. We laugh a lot, we have a good time, stay off only two subjects. Though I couldn't resist asking about the gleaming armbands that now hold up his sweater sleeves. From Tricia? He just grins and shrugs. 'Someone's telling me tae get a grip,' is all he says.

And the Sutherlands? Alasdair phoned the other week on his way back from guiding on Creag Meagaidh. 'Happy as clover in shit, old chap. Time we thought up another ploy – I'll see what I can do.' He's also now got a nice sideline giving lectures to Special Forces on the strategy, tactics, planning and execution of John Macnab, and the lessons to be learned from it. He's also become fanatical about paragliding, though Jane says it's only a matter of time before he leaves a dent in a mountain because he's not actually very good at it. 'Pigs might fly, old sport. So why shouldn't I?'

Round Christmas we all got together and had a fine evening with nearly everyone there. A lot of whisky and laughter, retelling and wild exaggeration and slagging-off. Old friends, good friends. I warm my hands at their fires.

Kirsty did a good job on that last John Macnab story. With photos, interviews with Aziz and Van Baalen confessing their part in the hoax, and a few hints that it had served some wider Security purpose, it was very convincing. It was her last and biggest exclusive, and it was a fine and stylish lie.

The parcel came a week later by special delivery. Inside were tweeds and deerstalker, and another little parcel. I unwrapped it and found a bottle of shampoo and a note.

Use frequently till all irritants are gone. Be happy. Kirsty.

Her last act, and then she bowed out. When I went back to see, the cottage was cleaned out. Shonagh had inherited Charlie. No forwarding address, Shonagh said. She seemed puzzled, disappointed, angry, something like that. Kirsty had come by to say goodbye, and there'd been no word of her since. She didn't do anything by halves. If she's still working as a journalist somewhere, it's under another name.

As I waited in the dim lobby while Shonagh closed up the bar, I remembered something. A very outside possibility. I reached up and felt inside Archie's open mouth, the drop-off place we'd used once or twice before. In under the tongue, I felt something soft, slightly damp.

I unfolded it. A ten-pound note. And a slip of paper, her writing. *For 'The Deadwood Stage', pardner – K.*

Shonagh and I had a private session that night. Some of it must remain private, including the pains and pleasures of her on-off life with Pat ('Let's just say there's three cigarettes in the ashtray at the moment'), but we spent a lot of time, laughter, and a little moisture about the eyes, going over all the things that did and didn't happen that summer. She hugged me hard before I stumbled upstairs to my old room in the hotel.

'I'd thought better of her,' she said. 'You know, it wasn't *your* need she was scared of.'

And I say: that was then, this is now. The flat's for sale, and my partner George and I know that I'm leaving the business – for what, I don't know yet. I've gradually put away most of the photos of Helen that used to fill this house with emotional booby traps. In this room there's just a small one of her taken around the time we first met. She's laughing and pointing away to her left at something I can't see. She laughed a lot, and she was right to. And above this desk there's another photo, the last one taken of the four Macnabs in front of Balmoral.

George has just been in with another bundle of job outlines.

'So how's the Highland Views brochure?'

'Sick. Tacky. Unfinished.'

He puts down the files and sighs, sits on the edge of my desk.

'How's the copywriter?'

'Sick. Tacky. Unfinished,' I reply.

He starts to wave his arms around a bit.

'I know this account is crap, but it pays. That's what people have to do – crap for money. The real world, Neil.'

'Seems pretty virtual to me.' As he sighs I say, 'I'll get it done, George. Promise.'

He nods because in the end I do still deliver. He stands with his hands in his pockets, looking at the photo.

'Who are those people?'

'Just some folk I met on my holidays.'

He looked closer at the terrace, the front of the Castle, the shadowy kilted figure looking out from behind the French windows.

'But isn't that –?'

'No,' I said. 'Definitely not.'

He shrugs and leaves me to it, with a plea that I finish the copy for the brochure today.

I think about her a lot, and what I think is between me and the photo. Sometimes my head still turns when I glimpse a certain colour of hair in the street, or see a certain jaunty, loping walk, or hear particular songs. There are many interesting women in this world and none of them are her.

I should be grateful. We obscure one loss by superimposing another on top of it, like the Highland Views transparencies in front of me.

But tell the truth. I'm still pissed off as hell with her. She said things during our brief time together, she said most of them without words so I can't be sure what she was really saying, but she seemed to mean it. It felt like a whole, real Kirsty, the one I could have sworn I knew. Loved, if you must. But I think now she was already backing away.

The last real thing she told me was how she went down to the river and saw plain glass windows become burning sheets of gold and for a few seconds she saw everything differently and anything seemed possible . . . till she moved on and they became ordinary windows again, and I guess she changed her mind.

I look out of the window. The sleet is beginning to settle along the edges of buildings. I roll another cigarette and prepare to write some guff about the Highlands.

'This came in earlier. I'm not sure who it's for.'

George hands me a typed fax.

Further adventures of John Macnab? Romanno Bridge seventeen hundred hours. Public transport only. Bring passport, cash, change of clothes. Be there or be nowhere. Regards – Ross & Cromarty.

I stepped down from the bus with my overnight bag. Down here in the Borders the snow was lying but the sky had cleared. It was already beginning to get dark as I walked towards Romanno Bridge.

Ross & Cromarty, my arse. I'd phoned Jane and she'd just laughed, said she'd no idea what her man was up to. He loved a good wind-up – maybe it was his way of saying I needed a new ploy of my own, which was true enough. I had a long walk in upper Nepal in mind, not a freezing stroll in the Scottish Borders. Then I'd phoned Murray and Tricia to see if they were part of this, but all I got was a recording of Eve singing 'Life is Just a Bowl of Cherries'.

There was no one on the bridge. The Lyne Water was grey with melted snow. I walked across and looked down. No expanding rings there, no visions, no friends bearing ploys. What else did you expect?

When my feet lost feeling I hoisted the overnight bag over my shoulder and walked back over the bridge towards the phone box to give someone a good talking-to.

There was an old-fashioned car in the lay-by before the phone box, silhouetted against the fading light. Someone in tweeds was sitting on the bonnet, hands in pockets, back turned, looking out across the river.

I decided to keep on walking.

'Neil?'

I stopped. I shook my head, at what I don't know. Perhaps our eternal foolishness, our absurd hopes. Then I walked over to the car.

'Hi,' she said.

'Hi yourself.'

We stared at what we could make out of each other.

'You're still mad at me.' I nodded. 'I can't blame you. But it was too much too soon. I got . . .' There was a struggle, but nothing came out. I thought of what Shonagh had said to me.

'Scared,' Kirsty said. It came out thick and difficult as phlegm. 'I got scared, so I ran.'

She put her hands on my shoulders and whispered something in my ear.

'Oh really?'

'Really really,' she said. 'I needed to think about it. You?'

'Let's say I washed my hair. A whole lot.'

'Oh,' she said. 'And did it work?'

'Pretty good, thanks.' I stepped back and blew on my hands. I was chilled through and saw no reason for making this easy for her. 'So what's this further adventure?'

'You're looking at it,' she replied and her eyes were wide and candid as can be, and all kinds of ancient shut-down mechanisms started creaking open in my chest.

'Ah.' I put my hands in my pockets where the cold wouldn't make them shake. 'Really.'

She pushed me back so I was half sitting on the bonnet of the car and our eyes were on a level.

'Something tells me you're up to it, big boy.'

'Is this another act? Another joke?'

Slowly and seriously and not taking her grey eyes off me, she shook her head. Then she laughed, stepped back and flung her arms out wide.

'No – but it could be A Very Big Adventure!' She dropped the pose. 'There's no guarantee it works out, but I'll give it my best shot and I'll aim to deliver and I'll try not to run out.'

I looked at her and said nothing. Her hair had grown again; it was slipping out from under her deerstalker. I think I preferred it that way.

'Our best shot, Neil? I'll jolly you up a bit and you can insist I be for real. No one's ever wanted that of me. So?'

I shrugged like it was not a very big deal.

'Are you asking?'

Even in the dimness her eyes flashed and I knew she wanted to kick something, probably me. Let her sweat a little. It wasn't just bruised ego on my part, though there was that too. We might as well start this on equal terms.

'I won't beg, if that's what you want,' she said at last. 'How many times do I have to say I'm sorry?'

'You could try once.'

She looked away. She couldn't say it, of course she couldn't. I was certain her father never said it and her mother did all the time.

Her chin came up.

'I'm asking,' she said.

She wouldn't take her eyes off me. They were grey and deep as the river itself. I didn't know where they would carry us, but somewhere irreversible and different, that was for sure.

I bent down and picked up my bag.

'Your place, or mine?'

'Is that a yes?'

'Of course it's a bloody yes.'

'First things first, then.'

Her lips were as frozen as mine but inside there was warmth. Perhaps between us even warmth enough for a cold night in a cold world. Eventually she stepped back and glanced at her watch.

'We'd better get a move on or we'll be late. That scene took longer than I'd allowed for, touching though it was.'

'Late for what, Kirsty?'

She looked at me, all wide-eyed innocence. As if.

'Didn't I tell you?'

'You did not.'

She got into the car and revved it up.

'There really *is* a further adventure. I'll tell you about it on the way to the overnight ferry. My advice is: get in, or be nowhere.'

I slung my bag in the back and got in.

She put the car into gear, made a wildly illegal turn across the road and headed for Peebles. I took one last keek in the rear-view mirror at the buried, wintering country, then the bridge faded and night flowed in over the snow and all was refreshed, recast, far and near.

She drove on, stabbing our headlights into the mirk. And after we'd begun to say what needed to be said, I struggled for a long time in the warm leather interior to stay awake and alert to everything that happened as it was happening. Whatever was up ahead it would, for sure, contain nothing so clean-cut as an ending.